BREACH CANDY

Luke Jennings trained as a dancer at the Rambert School
of Ballet and spent a decade with classical and contem-
porary companies in Britain and overseas. Retiring from
the dance world at 30, he studied Indian Languages at
the Sorbonne before producing and directing the award-
winning *The Last House in Bombay* for Channel Four
Television, a documentary project requiring him to live
for seven months in a Bombay slum. In 1989 he turned
to print journalism, and since that date has written for
*The Times, Sunday Times, Guardian, Independent,
London Review of Books, Vanity Fair* and *The New
Yorker. Breach Candy* is his first novel.

FOR NICOLA AND BASIL

Luke Jennings

BREACH CANDY

V

VINTAGE

Published by Vintage 1994

2 4 6 8 10 9 7 5 3 1

First published in Great Britain by Hutchinson, 1993

Vintage
Random House, 20 Vauxhall Bridge Road,
London SW1V 2SA

Random House Australia (Pty) Limited
20 Alfred Street, Milsons Point, Sydney
New South Wales 2061, Australia

Random House New Zealand Limited
18 Poland Road, Glenfield, Auckland 10,
New Zealand

Random House South Africa (Pty) Limited
PO Box 337, Bergvlei, South Africa

Random House UK Limited Reg. No. 954009

A CIP catalogue record for this book
is available from the British Library

ISBN 0 09 930851 7

Printed and bound in Great Britain by
Cox & Wyman, Reading, Berkshire

I

~~~~~~

'June, what are you doing?'

'I'm just taking some swimming things.' I shouted through to her room. 'I thought I might to go Naaz Cafe for lunch, take a book, maybe go on to the Nepean . . . whatever it's called.'

Silence from Beth. I rubbed some cream into my nose. There were pink patches where it was beginning to peel.

'Can I get you anything while I'm out?'

'I thought you were going to Chor Bazaar with Alma Benson and Kimmie Kitzinger.' There was a tiny accusing note in her voice. I put a dab of cream on to my lips.

'We hadn't arranged anything,' I said, tasting the Nivea on my tongue.

'I spoke to them on the phone. They said they were going about eleven.'

'Beth, please. I just want to spend some time, you know . . .'
Pause.

'Well, could you at least ring them and say you're not going?'

'Look,' I banged the Nivea down on to the glass bathroom shelf, rattling the tooth-glass, 'I never said I WAS going.'
Silence.

The celebrated Beth Webster injured silence. I raised my eyebrows into the mirror. The skin of my forehead felt tight, still slightly sunburnt. I reached for the blue and white box again.

'Beth, please. I'm sorry, I'm an ungrateful cow. A bad sister. I abase myself.'

The silence continued as I smoothed on the Nivea. There were the beginnings of darker roots at my hairline. I should have had them done in London.

'I'll ring Alma and Kimmie. You go on.' Her voice trailed to near inaudibility. 'Have a good time.'

Death of La Dame aux Camélias. And I thought *I* was the artiste around here.

If I'd learnt one thing in Bombay, it was that every outing, like it or not, was a full-slap performance. Even if you were feeling, as Grace would have said, like the wreck of the *Hesperus*, you couldn't just schlep, anonymous. Your presentation had to be considered. A brave face. Best foot forward and so on.

When I first arrived this had driven me crackers.

'June,' Beth had said on my first morning (in an exaggerated Southern drawl intended to deflect attention from any sting her words might carry), 'you just cannot go outside the hotel like that.'

'You're kidding!' I'd had some idea of letting the sun loose at my pale December shoulders.

'I'm serious, June, really. I mean this in the nicest possible way, but dressed like that in the street you'll be taken for some kind of hooker. You'll have guys staring, and . . . please, June, believe me, I've been here long enough to know what I'm talking about.'

My initial reaction was to assume that this was some kind of vicious sisterly ploy to send me out looking like a cheese, but then I'd caught a look in her eye. Serious, no-bullshit, concerned, even. I'd fallen into line with a print dress, very Sandra Dee, and of course the moment I stepped into the hotel lobby (the cynosure, as they say, of all eyes) I'd seen just how right she'd been.

The first venture Beth had devised for me had been a taxi ride to the Taj Mahal Hotel, a sandwich and a Coke (or a Thums-Up as it turned out) in the Sea Lounge, a quick sashay round the block to check out the bric-à-brac ('Buy NOTHING, June, I MEAN it') and a taxi back to the hotel.

Once I've gotten to trust the teacher I've always been a fast learner, certainly of choreography. There was all sorts of stuff that Beth made me remember for this initial trip, taxi negotiations and so on, without which I have to admit I would have been lost. The directions, of course, were easy. I've always had an exceptional sense of direction; on stage, for example, I could always tell where everyone else was at any given moment, even if I couldn't actually see them. It was something you had to learn as a *corps de ballet* dancer, of course, but I think that it was something I had always had, a very particular sense of myself in space.

A very masculine characteristic, Grace had always very sweetly insisted. Whichever, I wasn't one to get lost in a hurry.

Poor Beth, it must have been dreadful for her. The one thing that she had really been looking forward to was introducing me to her world, explaining the ground rules, showing me the shops and the sights, and generally displaying familiarity with an environment which she knew I would find threatening and strange.

She saw all this as something to be undertaken responsibly, not only as my older sister, but also as some kind of ambassador for gracious American womanhood overseas. This is where we go; this is what we pay; these are the clubs we join. The oil business, of course, wasn't quite the Foreign Service, but I could see from day one that she had learnt to think of herself as ... representative.

And, poor babe, she hadn't even been able to collect me from the airport.

Her driver had come, explaining that Beth Memsahib had been sick; it wasn't until the next morning that I'd seen, in the hazy hotel daylight, just how bad she was. Her skin and the whites of her eyes were the colour of old mustard, and although I hadn't seen her in eighteen months, I could tell that she had lost weight.

She had jaundice. To her fury, of course, her elaborate food precautions having slipped up at some point.

The hotel doctor, apparently, had been quite good. He'd spoken to the kitchen staff and devised some kind of rotating diet for her. Lots of fruit, boiled vegetables, carrot juice, that sort of thing. No alcohol. No kissy-kissy. Special cutlery.

Beth, seething, but desperate to resume normal expatriate social life, had acceded to all this with an adequate if tight-lipped grace; my instructions on my first morning in Bombay had been to return from the Taj Bookshop with a selection of paperback bestsellers.

Without looking at the covers, I'd bought the ten thickest in the shop. Beth had been well pleased, both with the books and with the success of her instructions which had enabled me to return, un-raped, from my first foray into India.

As I got into the taxi, making sure, as I'd been told, that the driver switched the meter on, I felt for the first time that I was getting some sort of handle on the place.

The night drive from the airport, although I hadn't admitted it to Beth, had been one of the creepiest experiences of my life. Something about the swampy stink and the endless huts and the hopeless moonlit tenements had really spooked me. The men and women sleeping at the roadside looked like corpses laid out after a plague. Even the things which at first glance looked familiar, the schools and the cricket-pitches and the old-fashioned seasidey buildings, had seemed sinister; bad-dream versions of forgotten childhood places.

I suppose the truth was that I had not wondered for five minutes what India was going to be like. I had simply climbed on to the plane at Heathrow with a bag full of holiday clothes and no idea as to what lay at the other end.

Well, now I had some idea.

The traffic on the road from Cuffe Parade to Marine Drive was bad. I had to wind up the window against the exhaust. At the side of the road was a slum settlement occupied by fishermen and their families. They looked tough but undernourished; what the exhaust was doing to their lungs I didn't like to think. The huts were made of sacking, plastic sheeting, old iron, rotten boat-planking, anything. Each morning the women put shrimps and fishing nets out to dry on the pavement. This was the same place that, later on in the day, their children liked to take a crap, so there was a fly-blown twenty-yard stretch where even through the windows of the taxi the stench was vividly awful.

Beyond the huts lay the ocean, the Arabian Sea. It was a dead, brown colour ('the shit-line', Kimmie Kitzinger had explained at the Willingdon Club one night, 'it goes out approximately a mile . . .'). On the opposite side of the bay, on a reclaimed headland, stood a high-rise building site. This area, a desirable part of town, apparently, despite the shit-line and the cheesy smell, was dominated by the large, rather ugly hotel in which Beth and her husband lived. Or to be more accurate, where Beth lived, and where her husband slept when he wasn't on the rig or overseas, and where I, until such time as Beth and I had a fight from which there was no recovery, was staying.

We accelerated up Marine Drive. It was a hot day, although if you'd seen a film of the scene there would have been nothing to show that it was hot. There was no brightness. Not that you couldn't burn your skin in these conditions, you could, and I had.

I watched the pavement from the taxi window.

One of the things that I had learnt, in the time that I had been here, was to watch people covertly. If you stared, caught people's eyes, they always took it wrong. They either thought you were coming on to them or offering money or wanting to listen to their hard-luck story. Even from a taxi you had to be careful. Catch the wrong person's eye and you could find them barrelling through the traffic, palms outstretched. You had to sneak glances. Constantly not looking at people, I found, was a pressure. I had taken to wearing dark glasses.

Beth, needless to say, had an official and definite line on beggars. Never give to the able-bodied, there are plenty of vacancies for servants. Never give to women with children, the children are not their own, but kidnapped from middle-class homes in Delhi and drugged. Never give to cripples, their limbs are broken at birth by unscrupulous parents and you are encouraging the practice. Never give to children, it only encourages them, they should be at school, and besides, their parents only use the money to buy alcohol made out of battery acid. Never give to beggars in South Bombay, there are Fagin-like beggarmasters who drop them off at their pitches in the morning and pick them up in the evening in minibuses. Never give to priests, they are all drug dealers who own import-export agencies. Never give to those who beg outside the smart hotels, they earn more than all the rest of us put together. And so on. I suppose it made a sort of sense but, to begin with at least, I had found it hard to keep my hands in my pockets or my window wound up. Standing at an unshaded main road intersection for eight or nine hours carrying a baby, drugged or otherwise, looked like pretty hard work to me. I evolved a system of giving if there was only one of them but not if there were more. There would only have been a stampede.

We ground our way slowly up Malabar Hill. I was beginning to be thirsty. My nose was still sore. I checked in my bag. Block-out cream, sun-cream, pre-insect-bite cream, after-insect-bite cream and, just in case, heavy schlock paperback. If I got fed up with trolling through my past in search of clues as to what I should do with my future, I could always lose myself in the four hundred breathless pages of *The Lotus and the Flame*. Love and Destiny, the cover promised, under Perfumed Oriental Skies. My kind of thing absolutely. Or one part of me's thing absolutely. Theatrical digs and pink socks and gas fires. Kitsch opening-night-of-the-season presents. Long pissy train journeys on tour. Screechy behaviour in provincial restaurants. That part.

One Christmas I had covered the Arabian Dance in *Nutcracker* in one of our killer seasons at the Festival Hall. Grace had said that I was a dead ringer for the film-heroine of *The Thief of Baghdad*. I could never remember her name although it was the sort of fact that Grace always had at his fingertips. For once, I had liked the comparison.

Which reminded me once again, because that had been the Christmas of my Blonde Decision, that I was going to have to do something about my hair. I could put the whole thing, I supposed, into the hands of Beth. She'd certainly know where to go, who to see. It would give her a brief authority, a tiny reason to go on living.

Why, hush my mouth, did I say that?

I did. I said it and I'm glad, as Grace would have said.

Enough about Grace. He was part of a world I no longer occu-pied by right and outside which, as he had often said himself, he couldn't survive. It was a banal enough truth, I supposed, that you remembered the details of friendship long after you'd forgotten those of love. Watching through the taxi window as middle-aged women, straight-backed as any Covent Garden cygnet, head-loaded pans of cement on a building site on Ridge Road, I won-dered if I myself could survive for any length of time outside that world. I had a brief but desperate stab of longing to be standing, jittering, pointe-shoe ribbons tight at my ankles, false eyelashes stiff as I blinked, on the stage of an opera house. There was a very particular moment as the orchestra finished tuning their instru-ments, as the entire ensemble held a single long note and you heard the call for first positions and felt your heart thump and the tiredness fade as the adrenaline kicked in . . .

6

At thirty-one, I felt old. In the end, it was a bitter enough addiction that we'd all shared, despite its baby sweetness, its apparent innocence.

Life was not a rehearsal. Ask a ballet dancer.

We stopped at the lights outside the Hanging Gardens and there was the inevitable tap on the window. A woman was pulling down a baby's lower lip to display the sores in its mouth. She went through the whole routine but I wasn't in the mood. Eventually the lights changed.

I liked Naaz Cafe. You could sit over a cold drink or a cup of their horrible coffee for just as long as you liked. The rather grave, elderly waiters left you completely alone except for flicking a duster over your table from time to time and it was classy enough, or at least expensive enough, that, as a girl alone, you didn't get hassled. It also had the most wonderful view in Bombay, over the whole sweeping curve of Chowpatty Beach, Marine Drive and the Back Bay. You could see (beyond the shit-line, of course) the brown of the sea turn to blue.

I took a corner table in the shade and ordered a Thums-Up. I didn't particularly like the taste, but I couldn't think of anything else. They were clever, these Indian soft drinks. They quenched your thirst for a minute or two but then the sugar brought it raging back. On the other hand, for the sake of my head if not of my reputation, I wasn't about to start drinking pints of Indian lager in the middle of the day. The answer, Beth had explained, was to order club soda. It seemed a rather austere solution. I couldn't sort my life out to the taste of club soda.

The café was half full. At the next table to mine were a couple, he in a turban, she fatly pretty in a long shirty thing over baggy trousers. They weren't speaking to each other, just sitting there in the sort of amiable, glazed silence that I had seen in elderly Britons in pubs. Beyond them a large and passive family was paying far too much attention to a gross child who was badly in need of a good smacking, and in the far corner, smoking, sat an aristocratic and definitely good-looking Indian in a blazer. The blazer man kept darting rather obvious ironic-type looks in my direction, for which, with typical June Webster illogic, I thought the less of him.

*

We are in Bradford, for a week, at the Alhambra. It is raining, and the night of Pauline Faull's first *Bayadère*.

Back at the digs (a word I hate) I am in bed with Charlie de la Tour. All things considered, there are many worse and colder places to be. Charlie and I are nowhere near in love, but we are good friends and it has been a long tour. By and large, I have discovered, the straight men in the company can be divided into those who are promiscuous because they love women and those who are promiscuous because they hate them. Charlie adores women, and even if he is no great brain (he has chosen his stage name, after all, off a wine label in a Sydney nightclub) his amiable drawl and country-boy good looks, not to mention his bravura technique, ensure him a patient following of corps-de-ballet babes.

Charlie has been Pauline's partner this evening. She is lucky, he is strong and confident-handed.

Like I usually have Grace, or Graham Finucane, as he was actually christened, Pauline usually has Charlie.

Except that Charlie is straight.

'What was it like tonight,' I ask him, sitting up suddenly, 'with Pauline?'

'What do you mean, what was it like?'

'I mean partnering her, handling her, all that. Was she sweaty? What was her breath like?'

'Junie, give us a break.'

'No, really, I want to know. What does Pauline Faull smell like when she's really frightened? Because she was, you know, really frightened tonight.'

'Come on June, she did damn well. As you saw.'

'What was it like? Tell me.'

'I won't tell you, Junie, because . . . You know what it's like with a partner, that physical-trust thing?'

'Tell, Charlie, tell.'

'No.'

'Why not.'

'There's nothing to tell.'

'How did she smell when you lifted her, when you had your face pressed into her, tell me.'

'She didn't.'

8

'Didn't what?'

'Didn't smell.'

'Not at all? Not even of deodorant?'

'Not at all.'

'So her, what, INTIMATE HYGIENE was to your satisfaction?'

'June, drop it. I mean it.'

He rolls out of bed and pads, naked, to his rehearsal bag, where he finds a can of lager.

'Maybe you'd say,' I lean after him, 'that the confidentiality between ballet partners is a bit like that between two ... sexual partners?'

'Yeah, I would.' There is a hiss as he opens the can. 'That's exactly what I'd say.'

'So in that case you'd say that your experience with Pauline on stage this evening was in some ways comparable to your experience in this bed with me twenty minutes ago? Would you say that?'

'Junie, sweetheart,' he answers tiredly, sitting down on the bed with his back to me, 'you know, you KNOW the answer to that is no. Tonight Pauline danced her first *Bayadère*. Of course she was scared; so would you be. But she got through it, all things considered, bloody well. If you can't be happy for her, well, fine, just don't make it into a THING ...'

He looks around for somewhere to put the can. The marks from the elastic straps of his tights still show on his shoulders. I can stop this, I think, right now. I'm being very stupid. I can easily be nice, be the old me.

'Which would you rather do again?' I find myself saying.

'For fuck's sake, Junie, just drop it.' There is real anger in his voice. I suddenly feel cold; pull the sheets up over my breasts. I am terrified he'll go, although where, in Bradford, at two in the morning ...

'OK, I'll drop it, Charlie. I'm sorry. I'm a vicious premenstrual bitch and you're a sweet man and you and Pauline looked great tonight. I mean it.'

I have some idea of making him laugh, as he does, easily and often, but find instead that I am crying.

Of the clubs that Beth had recommended to me, I liked the

Nepean Sea Bathing Club the most. It wasn't the smartest, in fact the place had a definitely run-down feel to it, but it was quiet and undemanding. I was left in peace.

The club's only facilities, as far as I'd been able to tell, were a huge salt-water swimming pool, a barracks of a changing block, a clubhouse which served terrible food, and a bar. There was also a room with trophies on the shelves and names on the walls where you could play ping-pong.

The best thing, though, was the space and the quiet. There were sprinkler-fed lawns surrounding the pool on three sides and around the outside of the grounds were a number of tall, large-leafed shade trees. In one corner a volleyball net had been suspended between two of these, and most afternoons a bunch of young guys would turn up and punch a ball around. The place I liked to go, though, was in the opposite corner; not to avoid the boys, they looked sweet enough in a slightly hustly, look-at-me sort of way, but to avoid the expatriate Americans and Brits, who tended to corner new people rather avidly.

Being as far as it could be from the clubhouse, mine was an awkward, unfashionable spot. Waiters had to carry my tea-trays the best part of a hundred yards in each direction. I didn't feel particularly good about this, especially as a couple of the older ones limped rather badly. On my first visit I'd offered to carry my own tray, but the headwaiter, smiling, had made it quite clear that this was out of the question and Alma Benson, who had taken me, had been quite cross and embarrassed.

It had occurred to me since, of course, that if we all suddenly insisted on carrying our own trays, a dozen or so well-tipped jobs would be lost by people who probably couldn't afford to lose them. At the time, though, I'd just been conscious of the waiter's shoes. They'd been old and cracked and slit at the side. He must have had bunions. I could have helped him with those; I knew all about bunions.

'Don't worry about these guys,' Alma had said. 'Compared to the rest of them, OUT THERE,' she gestured vaguely towards the entrance, 'they do just fine.'

Alma, who always carried a little candy-striped freeze-box containing ice-cubes made from mineral water, was an organised sort of girl.

*

Truth or Dare.

Dare was go for a swim, take some exercise for the first time in two months, which I sorely felt like not doing. The water was too warm to be refreshing, and afterwards I'd only have to take a shower afterwards and wash the salt out of my visibly dark-rooted hair. In short, a performance.

Truth was resisting the temptation to open *The Lotus and the Flame* at page one, and instead, putting in some constructive thought as to my situation. The advantage to thinking rather than reading was that I could lie on my back with my eyes closed. You couldn't read a heavy book lying on your back. On the other hand this would mean putting block-out on my already pink nose. Would this mean that my nose tanned at a different rate to the rest of my face? Might this be unsightly?

Choices. Mercy me.

Truth?

Truth, then.

So, where to start?

June Webster, 31.
Nationality: US citizen.
Academic qualifications: none.
Garment size: 10.
Hair: blonde, naturally darker, needs attention.
Lumbar spine: evidence of persistent trauma.
Mental condition: see Lumbar spine.

Ha.

Should I wear sunglasses or just close my eyes?

Could the southern-hemisphere sun penetrate my eyelids, burn my retinas? Retini? Retinae?

On the other hand, if I wore sunglasses, might I not end up with panda eyes to go with my nose? Did pandas have white eyepatches on a basically black face, or was it the other way round? It was going to be a problem, my non-education, I could see that now. Where, for example, was Calcutta? In Bengal. Where was Bengal? I had no idea. East somewhere. People said, though, that parts of Bombay were worse. I could well imagine it.

Above me, in the sky, there were crows. It was hazy, the sort of light condition in which you could get burnt.

Skin type: combination, tendency to freckles, tans eventually.
Breasts: could be bigger, frankly.
Legs: longer than average for spinal length; swayback type, hyper-extended; right knee scarred subsequent to surgery.
Shoe size: European size 37 broad; hyperextended arches, evidence of surgery (ingrowing toenails) and visible bunions both feet.

Ballet mistress?
I couldn't. I just couldn't. Swanning around in stretchy slacks and Spanish shawls, banging out the counts on the top of the re-hearsal piano, a quick cup of tea after class, isn't she marvellous and so on, eyes like a hawk, never misses a performance? Uh-uh. Pur-lease.

Choreographer?
Was there such a career? For a handful, I supposed. Twenty in the world or something. But you had to, really, have started laying the foundations in those deadly choreographic workshops the com-pany was always trying to get off the ground. If I'd been serious I'd have done all that, all those plotless little flesh-coloured all-in-one pieces expressing the alienation of the individual and so on. I couldn't go back now, though, begging odd hours of studio time and dancers with nothing better to do. ('Pauline? Well, she's very tied up at the moment, dear, she's got *Coppélia*, and the new Kylian piece to learn . . .')
No. You leave, you leave. I had left.
Curtain and curtsey.

It's raining. It is always raining in Girdle Ness, it gets dark right after lunch and we all still hate it. Dad's away on oil-work, Mom's changing upstairs to go out, 'Doctor Who' is on the TV and we are to cook our own dinner of hamburgers and chocolate sundaes. Steph is on the sofa, wearing make-up and pretending to read an article in a magazine. Doctor Kildare. Steph's read the article already but isn't about to speak or look up because she's mad with me and Beth for fighting and getting all three of us bawled out by Mom. The whole thing, in fact, is my fault for giving Beth a Chinese burn in return for her saying that I was the one who broke Mom's scent sprayer, which of course I was, but it wasn't for Beth to sneak on me or to kick me quite so hard when she knows that bruises always show on my legs and I've got the tap competition coming up.

Beth is vile. Steph treats me like a baby who can't be told anything. I hate this house and I hate Scotland and I wish we could all go back to Mineola and everything be all right again. I just don't understand why Mom has to go out tonight. The only slightest bit good thing is that Steph and Beth aren't quite sure either, so none of us are feeling great. The hamburgers and stuff in front of the TV are supposed to be a big deal, but I think we'd all rather she stayed in and we just had stew or something horrible like that. She's been out already this week and came back so late that there was a horror film on the TV and I was so scared I'd wet the couch.

Mom comes down. What looks strangest is that she's dressed sort of like she dresses US except with blue eye-shadow and she's done her hair with a fringe like Dorothy in *The Wizard of Oz*. I almost want to tell her she looks creepy but it's really raining hard outside in the dark, and although she's got her big-treat smile on I can't kiss her goodbye because I know that if I do, that'll be it. I'll cry.

So I turn my face away. Which is when I notice that she's carrying something in her hand which I haven't seen before, a round box thing. She notices that she's holding it and pushes it into her handbag. She tells us to be good, now.

Beth knows what it was. So does Steph, but she won't say and won't let Beth say. I pretend to forget it, and then ask Beth again when Steph is in the kitchen.

'Pinch, punch and side-splits,' says Beth.

'OK,' I say.

She pinches me on the bottom, really hard, using nails, and then gives me the hardest dead arm she can. I shake the arm a bit and then quickly slide down into side-splits.

'Yee-uckerama,' says Beth, looking close, 'that's disgusting.'

But she tells me, and when Steph comes out of the kitchen I start singing and go into a sort of Scottish sword dance in the middle of the lounge.

> 'Die-a-fram, die-a-fram, di di die-a-fram,
> die-a-fram, dia-a-fram, di di di-a-fram . . .'

Steph slaps Beth in the face this time, harder than I've ever seen her do it before, but this time, for some reason, it's her that's crying.

'What's it mean?' I ask, coming to a stop. 'What's a dia-fram?' But they don't hear me.

I ordered a plate of sandwiches. By the time they arrived I had finished the first chapter of *The Lotus and the Flame*. It was pretty good stuff. An English boy, son of a general, was growing up in the India of the Raj. His childhood sweetheart was the almond-eyed Anjali. And we all knew where almond eyes led.

There was a breeze which came off the sea at the end of the afternoon. Its arrival seemed to serve as a signal for people to stand up from deckchairs, think about a drink, maybe, or get ready for the evening.

Beth, I thought ruefully, alone in the hotel room with the curtains drawn and the air-conditioner rattling. I should get back.

When I did get back of course, feeling terrible for not having picked up the phone all day, she was having the time of her life. Enthroned in pillows, fragile, wan, she was holding court for half a dozen of her friends. There was evidence of extensive room-service. She looked up with a brave smile as I let myself in.

'June, sweetie, hi. You've really caught the sun, was it blissful? Come and meet the gang.'

II

〜〜〜〜〜

'I'm a life member,' I explained, 'name of Collinson. Stanley Collinson.'

'One moment, Sir, I will consult.'

The man in the heavy glasses disappeared from the window and returned with a large, damp-swollen book. He frowned as his finger tracked down the long alphabetical list of names.

'Collinson, Stanley?' he demanded, sternly.

I held my passport to the window. He nodded and, slowly, smiled.

'Welcome back to Nepean Sea Bathing Club, Sir. Since how many years you are not coming?'

'Four or five, I suppose, now.'

'Very nice. I remember your Daddy, a very nice man. And your Mummy also very nice.'

'I'm afraid I've forgotten your name,' I said.

'Chatterjee, Sir.'

'Good to see you again, Chatterjee.'

'Thank you, Sir. Any problem, you ask for Chatterjee, *thik hai*?'

'*Thik hai*, Chatterjee, thank you.'

'Enjoy your swim, Sir.'

I didn't get changed straight away, but carrying my bag, walked towards the clubhouse. A peon in brown shorts and jacket, seeing me coming, opened a deckchair and arranged a shade above it. I lowered my bag. With the exception of three waiters, two gardeners, five peons and two elderly Parsee women in elaborate bathing costumes, the place was deserted.

I sat there for an hour, my legs outstretched in front of me, my eyes closed against the morning brightness of the sky. I felt restless, overstrung from the long flight of the day before. Maybe, I thought, I should stretch my legs. Come back in the afternoon for a swim.

15

*

I walked up one of the steeper side-roads of Malabar Hill, past cracked concrete walls and ochre-painted political slogans. Neglected villas and bungalows stood beyond padlocked gates, and dead palm branches hung over dusty areas that had once been gardens. High-rise blocks stood blank against an even sky; there were no shadows. The blocks were new, I hadn't seen them before, but they were already tired, stained, half a century old.

It was midday. Little Gibbs Road became Ridge Road. The smell of frangipani hung in the air, overlaid by succeeding waves of urine and exhaust. Sweat prickled my scalp, and the soles of my shoes slapped against my heels as I picked my way over the guy-ropes of the stalls and lean-tos, past the smoking stoves and blackened vessels. Eyes looked up briefly as I passed, watched narrowly, and returned to a closer focus. There had been a time when I had known by name some of the people who lived here amongst the cigarette stalls, the tiny shrines, and the hopeful pyramids of fly-blown sweets. But I recognised none of the faces.

Outside the Kamla Nehru Gardens I followed the pavement past the bus-stop and into a sudden staring confusion of shouts and backs and turning heads. At its centre, two women were writhing and tearing at each other. The younger of the two, a Koli fish-seller, had a fist clenched tightly in the roots of the other's hair and was trying to drag her opponent's face within range of a short scale-covered cleaver. The older heavier woman, face quivering with pain and effort, was forcing the cleaver away from her eyes with one hand, and desperately tearing at the Koli's tight cotton blouse with the other. Fish and parts of fish skidded and smeared beneath them.

The watchers, men, stood in tight uneasy silence, clutching themselves, eyes flickering, pretending casual amusement.

Gasps and grunts, straining, from the ground.

There was a hand at my back and oiled black hair moved in front of me; I stepped back into an outraged scream, something rolled underfoot, and I turned to see that I had trodden on the paw of a chained monkey. Its owner was fat, with a hot, tight smell, and teeth as dark as his animal's. He jerked at the monkey's chain, and pressed forward heavily against me, urgent for a better view. To my left a neatly barbered man in a blazer stood slightly and proprietorially apart from the group, smoking. He turned to me, interrogative, as I looked away.

The Koli fisher-girl screamed and dropped the cleaver as the other's teeth ground into the muscle of her thumb. With the blade's fall, the hard brown fingers of the older woman hooked into the top of the Koli's turquoise blouse and wrenched down and across, tearing at the darkened fish-slimed cotton, nails furrowing into the small black-pointed breasts beneath.

There was a slight frowning shift of weight in the crowd, and the monkey-owner's hand went to his groin. Otherwise no one moved as the Koli, wounded hand pressed to her mouth, the other still clutching her opponent's hair, was forced on to her back.

Standing around her we stared, frowning. We stared at her lips, drawn back from her teeth, and at the torn halves of the choli falling away from the small shuddering blood-beaded breasts and the narrow, heaving chest.

The eyes of the Koli, furious, wide with pain, ignored us, and • never left those of the other woman.

Several things happened simultaneously. A fat, hard-looking man in a dirty white kurta forced his way through the circle of watchers, grabbed the older woman by the upper arm, wrenched her clear of the small crowd and, with two open-handed blows delivered at full strength, sent her staggering heavily into one of the stalls. Its proprietor turned to see his elaborate display of varnished sea-shells and customised marine artifacts swept to the pavement. He was already screaming abuse and moving to intercept the husband as the dazed woman, with much splintering and crunching of dried puffer-fish, pulled herself heavily to her feet.

The onlookers separated the two men.

The Koli girl, lifting herself up from the pavement, carefully and painfully knotted the choli, and watched as the other woman was led away. Slowly, she bent to pick her cleaver and empty fish-basket out of the gutter.

There was the rattle of a tiny drum. I turned away from the seamed smile and brown teeth of its owner as, wearily, the monkey started to dance.

*

'She's a Waghre. They came from Gujarat originally; round here they mostly sell vegetables on the street. Probably some argument with the Koli girl about a pitch. Those Waghre women have always been . . . people talked about the FIGHTING Waghre women. The men are pretty useless, in the usual way, but the women . . .'

Leaning back in his chair he looked over the city with deep, if slightly absent, amusement. The expression appeared to have been cut into the spare, clean-shaven features; the barbered hair and gold-buttoned blazer gave him a look of a figure from an old photograph album; suggested cricket, women in white-framed sunglasses, deckchairs.

'But maybe you know about the Waghres . . .' He yawned, and apologising, uncrossed his legs. He looked at me more directly; smiled more.

'Tell me about yourself. Am I right in saying that you've been here before?'

I hesitated as the waiter arrived with a tray. My companion ignored him and leaning back, reached into the blazer for a silver cigarette case which sprung open as he offered it to me. Inside was an inscription which, upside-down, I couldn't read. He handed me a heavy silver lighter, and watched as I lit one of his American cigarettes.

Smiling, he had appeared alongside me as I was leaving the disintegrating scene of the fight, and suggested that I join him for a beer at Naaz Cafe, fifty yards up the road. I had been thirsty, but I had also meant to go to the café alone. I'd wanted time to consider the widening eyes, the slimily rending cloth and the blood jumping to the nail-tracks, time to fix events accurately in my mind.

He had seemed to register all this before choosing to ignore it. He had introduced himself as Victor Das, at my service. We had shaken hands in front of a *bhel*-puri stall, like ambassadors.

The waiter placed the refrigerated beer bottles on the table, along with four glasses, two of them filled with water. Without comment Das clamped a thumb over the mouth of one of the bottles and upended the neck into a glass of water. He removed his thumb, and a viscous, sugary liquid began to stream into the water from the beer.

'Glycerine,' he explained in his newsreader voice, 'used to pre-
serve the beer. Gives you a cracking headache if you drink too
much. You're not a doctor, are you?'

'I'm afraid not.'

'What do you do? No, don't tell me, let me guess. Pharmaceut-
icals, no . . . garment industry? Import-export?'

'No.' I pulled a shirt tail from my trousers and started to polish
my glasses. 'Nothing like that. I work in television.'

'Oh, really? BBC?'

'No, a small independent production company.'

'I see.' We smoked in silence, and I polished the second lens
with the white tail of my shirt.

This Victor Das. What exactly, I wondered, was the pitch going to
be. He had definitely forced his company on to me; on the other
hand, he didn't really look the type who needed anything, and I
was pretty sure that I didn't look as if I had much to offer. Physically I didn't feel on top of things. The armpits and back of my
shirt were wet; the front of my trousers grubby where I had wiped
my hands. Mosquitoes, I was reminded by the clawed bumps that
were already at my ankles and neck, always go for the newly
arrived, the newly returned. In the same way as the mosquitoes,
the city could still smell my long absence; I was pale as the sky,
there were blisters at my heels, and I felt hopelessly visible. As a
result the streets were, for the moment, indecipherable. Only with
the widening of the Koli girl's eyes had I, for a moment, seen an
opening, become invisible myself. Now my conversation with this
slightly ludicrous figure was closing that opening before I'd
secured it.

Which of us, I wondered, was going to make the first move to
pay for the beer?

'You're here to make a programme?'

'We might be doing a documentary,' I said, 'on the actress
Lakshmi Khandekar.'

Das nodded, amused.

'Do you know her?' I asked.

'Bombay is a very small town, really. In fact India is a very small country. There are only fifteen hundred or so people in India, actually, and they all know each other. As I'm sure you know. I'm right, aren't I, in saying that you've been here before, that you know . . . how things work?'

For the first time he looked at me directly. The dilettante smile had dropped from his face as if it had never been; the amused eyes were unamused, hard.

'I think so,' I said slowly, 'I grew up here.'

Twenty-three years ago I had been at this same table, staring out over Marine Drive and the bay, my stomach churning like wet gravel, a strawberry *fallooda* untouched in front of me. It was a typical late-May Bombay day; the monsoon had broken the week before, and between downpours the city stood wet and dark against a loaded sky.

I was to go ahead, to prep school, and my parents were to shut down the house, and follow me to England. We would be staying with relatives on the south coast, in Worthing.

Up to the week before my departure I had simply put the whole thing out of my mind. Now that the day was here, and to be faced, it seemed to be dragging itself past with deliberate and leaden slowness. Over-organisation had left none of us anything to do. I had spooned the *fallooda* untasted down a tight throat, unable to look at my parents, terrified of catching a sympathetic eye, even that of the old waiter. I remember my father in his blue suit, uncomfortable on the metal chair, alternately glancing at his watch and, worriedly, up at the sky.

And my mother, polka-dotted, frowning tightly into an enamelled powder compact; as miserable to be leaving, and probably as near crying, as I was.

I looked up. Das, smiling ironically again, was holding out a card. I replaced my beer glass carefully on its soggy mat.

> Victor Das B.A.,
> C.I.D. (Bombay)

He was watching for my reaction.

'Do you play cricket?' I asked.

'Not really,' answered Das. 'TT's my game.'

'TT?'

'Table tennis.'

My first impression of Das as a regimental type, as a useful seam bowler and a dangerous man in the slips, dissolved, immediately ludicrous.

An official of rank. That certainly put a different spin on the smile.

'Do you play?'

'Only badly,' I answered.

In the end it was Das who paid for the beer. I found a cigarette stall, picked up a couple of packets of Indian Chesterfield, and took a taxi back to the club.

I'm standing with my back to the white paintings amazed, frankly, that I'm getting this sort of attention. This complete attention, no moderating frown or polite smile, no flickering check of the faces beyond my shoulder, no level sweep through exhaled smoke of the suits and the eyes beyond, nothing. Just all of her attention.

What's more, I haven't (more than routinely) given the impression that there's more to me than there is, or that I can order events more than I can. She's taking me at face value and giving me her full attention.

What I shouldn't question, at this moment, is where I am finding this fluency, this articulacy. I'm talking about myself and my work, and, as I said, not more than routinely pointing it up, and even to me it all sounds good. I don't know where I'm finding the fluency. I must stop soon, in fact, because I haven't said anything stupid yet, or not that I've noticed, and I think I could look at her more easily if I was listening rather than talking.

We're at this launch thing, party, in some Mayfair art gallery (I saw it from the pavement and just walked in. It's not the first time I've done this, I've always found a certain pale excitement in the irrelevance, the randomness of these occasions). This one seems to be a magazine launch (there's a stack of them next to the drinks on a trestle table). White walls are hung with large white canvases to which slightly darker white paint has been applied. No one's looking at these, even though the paintings are going some way towards making all these people look, as a group, as I imagine they want to look, that is, definite, expensive, well anchored. The name of the artist, approximately ten letters long, is painted on the outside of the plate-glass frontage in what must be some kind of removable if rain-resistant paint. It is raining outside, and if I wanted to I could decipher the reversed letters of the artist's name.

A good supporting cast, then, a good background; plenty of gilt snaffle, quilted velvet and pouchy suntan moving against the white paintings, plenty of veined and overshaved jowls rearing and barking unamused, plenty of points being made strong and definite through the faint lowered ceiling of smoke; the humidor smell of wet coats and hair, and outside, the slick wet dark.

But none of this in focus, really.

In focus, the amused and reactive line of her mouth as she listens; her eyes, sea-glass pale, her eyebrows dark, darker than her hair, the hair somehow pulled back.

Pale skin, dark clothes.

She is wearing one of those cashmere cardigans that button up to the throat. Ironed, from the creases flattening the sleeves. Charcoal. The top two buttons undone; one side turning at the collarbone to show the black moiré ribbon backing.

She raises her empty glass with a faint, questioning smile (the charcoal sleeves are pulled a short way up her forearms).

She's talking about painting. She's not particularly good, she explains, but she does love it (the smell, the concentration, the little bottles). Out of, I think, a forgivable fear of silence. I've already told her about my work. A television researcher is not, strictly speaking, a television writer, but the Venn diagrams do overlap in places. I do write things for television. What I write is USED on television. I haven't lied.

She says it sounds interesting. I confirm that yes, sure, it can be, and she asks me whether I've always worn what she calls spectacles.

'Tea, Sahib.'

The waiter stood invisible for a moment between my eyes and the whiteness of the sky, before bending and carefully placing the tray on a low green-painted table to the right of my deckchair. He straightened a white jacket which had seen better and cleaner days and which had the club's initials sewn on the top pocket, frowned absently out to sea, and held out the bill.

'Six rupees, Sir.'

I searched through my pockets, looking down at his shoes. They looked wooden, cracked and old. I gave him the coins; he nodded, hesitated, I added a couple more rupees and, limping slightly, he started back to the clubhouse.

I sat forward in the deckchair.

The tea in its stainless-steel pot was tannic, dark, and opaque, the milk was warm, its surface skinned, and the sugar crystals damp and greyish. I poured myself a cup, the silvered alloy handle hot in my hand, and lit a Chesterfield.

Often, when I had thought of Bombay from the other side of the world, when I had let myself sift through the time when I was, I suppose, fully a child, I'd thought of myself here. These memory sequences were uneven, mostly out of focus, but sometimes the vagueness would cut to sudden detail. One such image was of myself half-sitting, half-lying in one of these deckchairs, white cotton sun-hatted, scab-tracked and Mercurochromed knees drawn up to my chin, squinting through my prescription spectacles at the more daredevil children on the diving boards.

For me, as for many other children of Europeans living and working in Bombay before and presumably since, the Nepean Sea Bathing Club had been part of childhood. The poolside had been a safe place for my parents to leave me, and while they'd sat upstairs in the bar or under the umbrellas outside the clubhouse I'd learnt to swim, made myself sick on custard-apples and *fallooda* and sweets from Bombelli's, been bitten by the soldier ants in the stiff grass by the sprinklers, courted sunstroke and prickly heat, and stared fearfully at the Russian attachés in their unfashionable bathing suits.

And here I was again, twenty-three years later, lying back against the damp, salted canvas and facing a neutral sky, neither required nor expected to do anything.

I didn't, I felt, even have to close my eyes.

In front of me extended the sea wall, an empty hundred yards of piled and levelled boulders against which brown and heavy waves were thrown and fell, and rolling back to meet those oncoming, jetted vertically to spatter the cracked concrete.

Overhead, at different levels, the crows curved watchfully. Turning on a wing, one of their number detached itself and swung idly down, landing a circumspect distance from my tray; blinking, it stropped its beak against the grass, and hopped towards me. I had forgotten just how disrespectful these birds were; with a last and longest hop it jabbed a waxy beak into the stainless-steel milk jug and lifted its head to swallow. I waved my arms at it, and it lazily hauled itself from range to settle a yard or two away, the yellowing skin of the milk hanging wet and wrinkled from the blue-black beak.

I lit another cigarette. Better to get on with it, I supposed. From the bag at my feet I pulled a damp copy of *Cinestar*, a Bombay weekly film magazine.

'This month's Star Birthdays' read the opening page: Dina Mehra, Omprakash Rai, Somnath . . .

There were half a dozen 'celebrity' names on the list, and against each was quoted an age, a date, and an address to which admirers could send birthday cards, letters or presents.

Lakshmi Khandekar's name was fifth on the list. Her birthday, apparently, was on 10 April, a week away, when she would be 22, and the address given was #17, Divya Apartments, Colaba Causeway.

The easiest and most direct way of contacting the actress, I knew, would have been to identify myself to a film writer from one of the quality newspapers, preferably one who had earned her favour with good reviews, and ask for an introduction and a telephone number. I didn't, however, want to alert the Bombay film press to any interest I might have in Lakshmi Khandekar. Outside interest created inside interest; withheld knowledge was power.

And, of course, I wanted her to myself. Wanted my approach to be ambiguous, to promise. The press, I was sure, even the benevolent press, she thought of as 'them'; the enemy of her self-possession. The last thing I wanted was to come to her from 'them'.

So first I would write to her. I'd type out the letter this evening and take it down to Colaba by taxi. I'd phone her tomorrow. Or try, anyway. Take it from there.

I turned to the opening pages of the magazine.

'"NO LOVE FOR *Lakshmi*", by Seeta Rao' ran the white letters across the olive-toned black and white illustration. The print suddenly blurred; I laid the magazine on my knees, wiped my face with my towel, and re-addressed the picture. It was, I recognised, a still from *Akeli*, Lakshmi Khandekar's first film. Something about the pose, however, something of its artifice, was more late Forties than late Seventies. Strongly and artificially backlit, the actress was standing in near-silhouette against a tall window. A pale finger of light from some secondary source had been drawn down the long forehead, and moving downwards, had found the fall of the cheek, the tiny dark fan at the corner of the mouth, the oval curve of the chin. Lower, amongst the shadowed falls of a Maharashtrian sari, the same graded light lay along the pale arm which, pressed against the dark beginnings of a breast, reached across to draw the heavy curtain.

I studied the photograph, searching the image for clues as to the woman beneath. Eventually, and with a feeling of dutiful bathos, I turned to Seeta Rao's accompanying article:

Despite beginnings far from the glamour and glitz of filmi Mumbai, soft-eyed Lakshmi Khandekar is quietly taking 'Bollywood' by storm. In six short months, the 'Pyari Pyari' girl, who started professional life as an infants' teacher in Kolhapur, is proving that she has what it takes to compete with the best and the brightest (and to unsettle the crown of a certain other rather longer-established filmi princess). Her story, in short, is equal to anything penned by a Salim or a Jawed . . .

So how did it all begin? I met Lakshmi Khandekar in the Sea Lounge of a certain Five-Star Hotel not one million miles from Apollo Bunder. The ice was soon broken by the discovery of a shared passion for pistachio kulfi, and soon there we were, squealing away like kids!

Not that there was much of kiddish in the looks that several prominent business types were sneaking at the slim girl in the

Indori sari sitting opposite me. In the last eighteen months, though, the 22-year-old Kolhapuri has learnt to take such attention, as she has the plaudits of the crits and the claws of the cats (Miao-o-o-w!) in her stride.

'So tell me about the day,' I asked, 'that your life changed forever.'

'OK, see, what it was, yaar, there was this shooting slated for the village outside Kolhapur where I was teaching in the school there. Ganpat Naiyer was directing Somnath and Devyani in *Khamosh*, and a dance number was being picturised in the village, all very rural – typical Holi sort of thing. So I was there with the kids, who were behaving beautifully, quiet as mice. Actually they're damn cute kids, I really miss them, yaar, Raju, Sonu, Vinod . . .'

At this point I felt I should redivert on course the undoubtedly diverting if diverted Miss Khandekar, Cho Chweet though these kids undoubtedly were . . .

'So sorry, Seetabehn, I know I'm a bit of a rambler, they ought to call me Rambling Rose, isn't it?'

She laughs (she laughs a lot, this young Kolhapuri, despite the stories printed in other, lesser, natch, film mags claiming her to be a bit of a Misery Miss), and a waiter, entranced (and I swear, humming 'Pyari Pyari'), almost loses control of our tray tea.

'Anyway, there we were, on the set, and I had just given each of the kids a piece of paper to ask for the stars' autographs, when Ganpat-*ji* came up to us. At first, Seeta, I thought he wanted to talk to the kids, yaar, he was damn sweet with them, gave them Limcas and Thums-Up and all to drink and sweets and I think they really thought it WAS Holi. And then of course, I realised that it was me that he really wanted to talk to. He called over the stills photographer and asked him to take my Polaroid snap, and then showed it to me. "*Dekho*," he said, "look at this photo. It is the face of the star of my next picture . . ."'

I turned the page. The next few thousand words of Seeta Rao's rosewatered prose described Lakshmi's uncertainty about appearing in Ganpat Naiyer's *Akeli*, the reaction of her liberal Brahmin parents, her and their eventual acquiescence, and (despite her boundless respect for Ganpat-*ji* and her confidence in both his propriety and his directorial abilities) her surprise at the modest but definite success of the film.

Akeli, explained the article at some length, and with much tangential emphasis on the friendship between star and journalist, was followed, under the same banner, by *Zakhmi*. The director, cast and principal theme of wronged and abandoned woman remained unchanged; like *Akeli*, *Zakhmi* showed a profit, which was as much as its producers felt that they could hope for from a picture with no fights, no male star and a female newcomer in the main role.

Then had come Saiyad Ali's *masala* blockbuster *Mera Dost, Mera Dushman*. This was a film which, if no one had agreed about, at least everyone had talked about. To begin with, there had been a considerable buzz of interest, especially when it was announced that the film's star, Sanju Saxena, had insisted on Lakshmi Khandekar, a virtual unknown, as his heroine.

Mera Dost, Mera Dushman had been conceived as the 45-year-old actor's personal vehicle. He had insisted on the casting of Lakshmi, so Seeta Rao managed to suggest in her article, because he had invested heavily in the film himself, and did not want to see a more expensive actress paid lakhs of his own rupees to steal the picture from him.

And then, a fortnight before the film's *muharat* (the ceremony in which a coconut is broken, the venture blessed, and the first shot canned) Lakshmi Khandekar had calmly announced that she had changed her mind, that she was not interested in appearing in the picture after all.

. . . The sloe-eyed *ingénue* [I read on] had decided to stand on her principles, despite the fact that this was a film for which a score of better-knowns were waiting in the wings to step into the Khandekar shoes.

'I will not compromise my principles for anything,' Lakshmi had said at the time, 'nothing.' 'The latest script calls for me to expose in a two-piece bikini, and both my parents and I are not prepared for me to flaunt my body like this. Are you telling me that every actress has to expose to

succeed? Look at Swaroop, look at Dina, do they expose? No.
And don't tell me they're not successful. And to come to that,
what's happened to all those show-it-alls? Where's Pritthi
Puri these days after her famous white-swimsuit scene? She
can't be getting too many offers, isn't it?'

'Do you feel,' I asked Lakshmi with some mounting trepi-
dation (and changing the subject back again) 'that you won
that battle or not?' 'See, Seeta,' replied the composed 23-year-
old, 'what I think is this. I won the battle but I have not yet
by any manner of means won the war. At the time everyone
had cribbed just so much that you put the production on the
line, all this for a small thing like this bikini scene, well, my
answer was that it was not so small for me. *Bas*.'

So, Tinseltown held its breath, and uncharacteristically,
some might say, Saiyad Ali backed down. The white two-
piece was replaced in the swimming-pool scene by a black
one-piece and cut-offs. It was Saxena Sahib, though, who was
most shaken by the whole *tamasha* – he had thought HE was
the one handing out the favours and from that moment on, as
they say, the rest was history. It was Lakshmi's film and the
once-sexy Sanju was nowhere in sight. La Khandekar wiped
the cutting-room floor with him, although she courteously
denies the fact. 'I have the greatest respect for Saxena Sahib,'
she diplomatically insists. 'I learnt so much from him, from
his years of experience, from just watching him in front of the
cameras. Honestly, in my book he is still one of the greatest
evergreens our industry has seen, up there with Dev Sahib,
Amitabhji, Dilip Kumar . . .'

For Lakshmi Khandekar, *Mera Dost, Mera Dushman* (or *MDMD* as
it came to be called) proved an enormous popular and critical success. The bikini controversy had raised rather than lowered
expectations, and whatever reservations the film-going public
might have had concerning Saxena's return from the wilderness
had evaporated in the fever which greeted the release, six months
before the film itself, of *MDMD*'s soundtrack hit song: 'Pyari
Pyari'. It had been played, the article claimed, on every radio,
every loudspeaker, and outside every temple, for almost a year.

The film itself, apparently, by this stage, would have made money however bad it had been. As it was, it had been quite good (as well as having the big song) and made a lot of money.

Lakshmi Khandekar had not, at first, seemed inclined to capitalise on this success. She had made no professional personal appearances, had given no interviews, and for a time, had refused all scripts offered her, claiming, quite simply, that the roles were unsuitable. Finally, and just when all of the film press (with the exception, according to Seeta Rao, of *Cinestar*) were about to write her off as an arrogant and spoilt one-hit wonder, she had signed to play opposite the 25-year-old Rahman Khan in *Khandaan*.

Khandaan was conceived as a big-banner star-crossed-lovers vendetta epic. Its only potential difference from scores of similar 'formula' pictures lay with its director, Sunil Bhattacharaya. Bhattacharaya was thirty-two years old, and had spent more than ten of those years in Hollywood. There, according to Seeta Rao's researches, he had directed several commercials for household products as well as assisting in the direction of a daytime TV series. His film education thus complete, he had decided to return to Bombay, marry according to his parents' wishes, and sink the family fortune into the creation of his own film banner.

His first Hindi movie, *Nuksaan*, had been a modestly budgeted revenge picture and had done respectable business. *Khandaan*, promised Sunil Bhattacharaya via the pen of Seeta Rao, was going to be big.

'. . . See, what it's going to be, yaar,' explained Lakshmi, 'there's these two powerful families, divided by a feud over land. Now one family has a son, that's Rahman, and I'm the daughter of the other family. We meet, neither of us knowing who the other is, and fall in love. And it goes on from there . . .'

'And how do you feel about working with the deadly Khan?' I asked, turning my beadiest eye on the young actress.

'I'm looking forward very much to working with both Sunil-*ji* and Rahman,' she answered sweetly, evading the question that *Cinestar*'s entire readership (and staff!) are desperate to hear answered. I gently reminded the demure

Kolhapuri that Rahman Khan has, not to put too fine a point on it, a certain reputation as a ladies' man (or at least, as a *leading* ladies' man . . .).

Lakshmi swooped with the air of a girl who knows her own mind:

'See, yaar, the moment he meets me he's going to realise that I'm not the outgoing, disco type. I honestly don't go for that whole socialising scene. I'm sure he will behave like a complete gentleman.'

'So is there anyone in your life at the moment?' I asked. 'Anyone special?'

'There's no one,' answered Lakshmi. 'I know what you're getting at, but right now I'm concentrating on my work. I just don't have time to get involved. But I must admit that some-times, just sometimes, there's a lonely place in my heart ready for the right person . . .' 'And what would this person be like?' I probed gently. She hesitates, and the neat oval features take on a faraway look. 'Sometimes,' she finally answered, 'I think that this person doesn't exist at all . . .'

She's silent for a moment and then she laughs, kiddish, playful. '*Arrey,* yaar, I'm hungry. What about some of that kulfi. Looks delicious.'

And so, undoubtedly, is she. But, for the time, it seems, no love in the life of Lakshmi Khandekar. But then, who knows what the future, or for that matter the *Khandaan* set, holds. Until next week, then, M-I-A-O-O-O-W!

I closed my eyes and dropped the magazine. It was a month old and I'd bought it in London. I'd read the article before, twice, every last clotted phrase. Seeta Rao's article had been, effectively, my research. Lakshmi Khandekar held my future in her small brown hands and I hoped, vaguely, that she was at home.

The light was beginning to go. I was still jetlagged.

Later now, we are in a restaurant (Italian, walkable from the gallery, not fashionable), and here is Emilia, three feet away, hair still wet from the rain, beyond the Elixir Spa water, the giant peppermill, and the Villa Antinori in the wire-netted bottle. She's done the ordering (in a rapid and unsmiling Italian which cut straight through the 'bellissima signorina'-and-cummerbund stuff). She goes, she is explaining, raising her eyebrows, crimping the long line of her mouth, and twisting a gold and pigeon's-blood ruby ring on the little finger of her right hand, to acting school. She tells me about it.

She could have told me anything, of course. But by then I'm . . . there are women like Emilia, who no matter what they say, you forgive them, just as you know yourself a fool. Because you know, you KNOW, that they aren't telling you everything and you tell yourself that they aren't because they can't. And what they aren't telling you becomes the thing that you swear you'll forgive if they tell you, that nothing would shock you, nothing, honestly, nothing at all. But they don't, of course, and can't. The thing, whatever it is, is concealed.

Is this going too far? I'm not sure. I've known her for what? Not long anyway. And in that CONTEXT, as my professional colleagues would say, it might seem a bit excessive to talk about concealment. I'm not so sure. There are things she hasn't said which, not having been said straight away, can never be said. This seems to be confirmed physically. She is sitting opposite me, the long pale line of her mouth moving slightly in reaction to what I'm saying. Her eyes are close-set, which gives them a directness, and often a seriousness. At rest her face seems serious. I am already wondering about that seriousness. She has a fine, straight nose, and her silence is articulate, has volume.

'Stanley, you idle bastard.'

I woke with a yelp, dislocated, dry-mouthed, exhausted. It was nearly dark.

'Bit early to be rat-arsed, isn't it?'

I still wasn't sure where I was. Standing over me was the shirt-sleeved, Raybanned, and under the circumstances, slightly menacing figure of John Pearcey, director of documentaries for a rival independent production company. I slowly decided that I was not in London, that I hadn't just dreamed up Pearcey, but that the whole ebullient fourteen stone of him was actually here, and that here was Bombay.

'John,' I managed, 'what a surprise.'

'Small world, Stanley, small world. You here on holiday or . . . errr?'

'Working, really.'

'So I see. So I see. No, just kidding. Look, I've got to see some people up in the ummm, up there. Why don't you come up and join us, tell me about it, yuh. Yuh? Great. See you in a sec.'

He touched my shoulder with the tips of his fingers and hurried tensely off.

John Pearcey was the most exhausting person I knew. He somehow vacuumed all available energy from the air. He was deafening, even in silence. And if he was not actually the *last* person I wanted to see, here and now, he was certainly one of them.

I took the path to the men's changing rooms. These were in a long pavilion surrounded, for decency's sake, by a carefully kept hedge. Inside, under the low beams, the evening air held the sharp, cloudy smell of disinfectant. I undressed, and left my clothes and bag on a bench. Fresh-water showers of pre-Independence design stood at intervals down the tiled centre of the room, but despite the extravagance of their twelve-inch shower heads, I soon discovered that, from each, the water fell only in a single tepid rope, which twisted to a trickle a few seconds after the tap was turned on. By turning the most productive-seeming tap on and off almost continuously, however, I finally managed a single-handed shower and began to feel more awake.

I dried and dressed, avoiding the small enamel footbaths with their puddles of crystallised chemical, and crouched to comb my hair in the reflective surface of a dysfunctional weighing machine.

'Mirror here, Sir.'

One of the club servants was standing to attention by the row of washbasins at the far end of the room, an ironed hand towel over his arm. I walked over, and he turned on both taps of one of the basins. Both were cold. I rewashed and dried my hands.

'Comb, Sir.'

'I have one. Thank you.'

'Thank you, Sir. Nice to see you again, Sir.'

I slicked the wet hair back from my forehead.

'Thank you. Nice to be back.'

I found a note in my pocket. Not that I believed that he remembered me from any time past, but I had enjoyed his attentiveness. I turned to go.

'Excuse me, Sir.'

He was holding up the note. It had a small tear in it.

'It'll be fine,' I said, slightly irritated.

'No, Sir, not fine, Sir.'

'OK, hang on.' I found another note, twice the value.

'Thank you, Sir, thank you.'

He busied himself at the sink. I wondered if he thought me generous or a fool. I lit a Chesterfield, and made for the bar.

'What's brown and has a hazelnut in every bite? Squirrelshit. Hi, I'm Lance.'

He was sweating, pubbish, and inside the knitted shirt, fat. With what looked like exaggerated care he lowered himself, farting slightly with the effort, into a creaking cane chair.

'Whoa-a-ahh, sorry, gents, nearly followed through there; bring me my brown trousers, as Nelson cried at Waterloo. I'll tell you something for nothing, John, those tiger prawns are crucifying my arse.'

'Lance is our sound-guy,' explained Pearcey, who was now wearing the sunglasses suspended round his neck by a black cord. 'Forgive him, Stanley, he's from Watford and knows not what he does. Lance, Stanley.'

'Evening, Stan, how's it pulling? Evening, lads, looks like you've got a bit of a start on me, where's Colonel Gaddafi? COLONEL' (this last word roared into the white interior of the bar). Sweat tracked Lance's gingery, pear-shaped head. The headwaiter, a slender and sad-looking Goan with nothing visibly in common with the Libyan president, started to crab sciatically towards us.

'Ek, do, tin, char five Bulbul Pilsners, please, Colonel,' Lance called to the approaching figure, 'and as the crocodile said to the dentist, make 'em snappy!'

He wiped his face with a damp handkerchief, blew his nose into it, and inspected the result with the air of a connoisseur.

'The thing you get to realise about Lance,' Pearcey told me, winking at the cameraman and myself, 'is that a little goes a fuck of a long way.' Lance laughed. Pearcey hadn't shaved for several days, I noticed, except to shape the stubble at his throat.

As the headwaiter reached the table, the cameraman, a streaky, bony individual whose name I'd forgotten and who hadn't said anything, as far as I'd noticed, in an hour and a half, leant forward in his chair and with his fingertips, nudged a plate towards the stained, melancholy figure.

'Pappadum, Sir? Yes, Sir. Four beers, Sir.'

The cameraman held up a hand, fingers and thumb extended.

'Five beers, Sir?'

The cameraman nodded.

'There's always a talkative one, eh, Colonel.' Lance smiled at the Goan and gestured towards the cameraman, whose eyes glittered behind their steel-framed glasses with aggressive self-consciousness.

The headwaiter remained blankly downcast.

'Yes, Sir. Five beers, Sir. Pappad. Anything else, Sir?'

He started painfully back to the bar with the trayful of empty bottles.

Pearcey had spent much of the last ninety minutes enthusiastically describing his film to me. Its working title was 'The Toothpaste and the Tube' and it was to be a critical examination of the activities of multinational companies in the third world. The fifth person round the table, whose name, I think, was Ian, was actually employed by one of these multinationals and was working, on secondment from London, as the manager of a chocolate plant outside Bombay. Ian had a cricket sweater knotted round his shoulders, and after four months in the country, already spoke of India and its peoples with a proprietorial air. He would be accompanying Pearcey and crew round the plant tomorrow. He had been initially dubious about this idea but Pearcey, with a wink or two in my direction, had smoothed away these doubts with a combination of beer, assurance, and inter-bloke freemasonry.

I knew exactly what Pearcey was going to do. He would show a pretended interest in the 'positive' sides of the factory, pretending to film the happiest workers, the most party-line staff. Actually only Lance's Nagra tape recorder would be switched on, and the

voices thus obtained would ultimately be placed in ironic juxta-
position to lovingly scavenged vignettes of undernourished peons,
scabbed children, fly-blown refuse heaps, and broken safety equipment. I could picture the walkabout; Pearcey energetically shaking
hands and slapping backs, Lance in his headphones, all sound-
checks and disarming smiles, and the hunched, silently turning
figure with the Arriflex camera falling further and further behind.

It was a good technique, and one which had never failed Pearcey
yet. 'Rule One,' as he had said earlier in the evening, when under
full didactic steam, 'is show 'em the Money. And Rule Two is show
'em the Kids. Just remember that and your average commissioning
editor's happy as a pig in shit.'

I'd leave after this one, I thought, before Pearcey remembers to
ask me what I'm working on. The pleasure afforded by Pearcey
and company was not such as to justify the hangover that would
certainly follow a third bottle of Bulbul Pilsner.

At that moment a neat, blazered figure appeared in the clubhouse door and moved towards us.

To my surprise both Ian and John stood up and extended their
hands. Both appeared to know Das by name. I held out my hand
in turn.

'Hello again.'

'Hello to you. I think I said this morning that this was just a
small town?'

'I think you did.'

He turned to Pearcey. 'You and Mr Collinson aren't . . . professional associates?'

'We're professional rivals,' said Pearcey, with the big Pearcey
laugh. 'No, that's not true. We started off together as researchers
at the BBC, many moons ago . . .'

'And now you've both got your own companies.'

'John has his own company,' I answered evenly, 'he is both a
film director and a managing director. I am a researcher with another, smaller company.'

'Vicky,' said Pearcey, 'why don't you sit down. Let me get you
. . . hang on, let me get you a chair.'

The headwaiter appeared behind them with a tray and several
tall brown bottles, and waited patiently as a chair was brought for
Das.

Although Pearcey was behaving towards Das with what looked like normal courtesy, I knew Pearcey well enough to know he only afforded this to the most potentially useful of acquaintances. He soon had Das locked into a lowered-tone and thus exclusive conversation. I wondered what each was after from the other.

A waiter walked slowly round the terrace, flicking on the electric lights above the outside tables. Below, the tide was receding, and was now only faintly audible beyond the sea wall. In the swimming pool beyond the clubhouse lawn, two elderly male figures performed an almost unmoving breast-stroke by the light of a single suspended bulb.

I refilled my glass and turned to Lance.

'How much longer are you in Bombay for?'

'Leave for Delhi tomorrow night, three nights in Delhi, back here for a night, ummm, fly out, week in London to drop off, pick up, and see the rushes, then out to Brazil.'

'Sounds good.'

'Well, yeah. Tell you though, much more of this food and I'm going to start sleeping with a Zoom ice-lolly up my arse. Talk about ring of fucking fire.'

'Try yoghurt, rice, and bananas.'

'What, straight up the ringpiece?'

'I'd try the talking end first.'

Lance leaned towards the cameraman.

'Eh, Laughing Boy, Stan reckons if I feed my Black Hole bananas, I might stop pebbledashing the khazi for a day or two.'

'You have loose stools, Mr Lance?' enquired Das politely, stretching his legs under the table.

'Loose is an under —' began Lance.

'I don't think we want to hear about Lance's stools, whatever their consistency,' said Pearcey, the several large measures of Hercules Rum and the litre and a half of Punjabi lager beginning to take their toll on his directorial tone. He turned to me. 'Stanley, tell us, please, about your project.' He sat back suddenly and expansively in his chair, the beer slopping in his glass, the Raybans bouncing lightly against his chest.

The Ian character, eyes half-closed, leant forward with a kind of bored interest and lit an imported cigarette with a gold lighter. He saw me look at it.

'Dubai, duty-free. What d'you think?'

I hefted its warm weight in my hand, and flicked the cap on its silent hinge. There was the faint hiss of gas.

'Very nice,' I said. 'Don't lose it.'

I placed the lighter on the table and turned to Pearcey. I suddenly, and very intensely, did not want to talk about Lakshmi Khandekar.

'Oh, the idea was to present a portrait of the Hindi film industry by looking at the career of an up-and-coming actor or actress.'

'Do you know which one?' asked Ian, pouring beer carefully into his glass.

'That's what I've come to arrange, really. I'll be talking to several.'

Das raised his eyebrows. He said nothing.

'Do you really understand them?' asked Ian. 'These films, I mean?'

'Our Stanley,' said Pearcey to Ian, raising his glass ironically, 'is by way of being rather an expert in these things. He did a degree in, what was it, Hindi and Sanskrit? Which, as I remember, impressed the BBC considerably more than my humble,' he paused to focus on the swirling yellow beer, 'film-school background.'

'How long did you stay at the BBC?' Lance asked me, interested.

'Oh, eighteen months, two years . . .'

'Our Stanley . . . what was it they said? *Not a team player?* Not, what was it, a *people person*? Something like that, anyway. To that effect. Very much the cat who walks alone, our Stanley . . .'

'And to prove the truth of it,' I said, 'I have to go.'

'Hang about,' said Pearcey, 'it's only . . .'

'I have to go,' I said.

Pearcey made a shrugging, open-handed, be-my-guest gesture, spilling some beer from his glass.

'If I can be any help . . . contacts out here?'

'Thanks, John, OK.'

'Good night, Mr Das.' I leant forward to shake his hand, and he inclined his head with a smile.

'Good night, John, Lance, Ian. Good night, Roger.'

'My name's not Roger,' said the cameraman.

Emilia half-turns, and places the book face-down behind her, next to my glasses, on the faded silvering cornflower and poppy of the carpet.

Tonight she is wearing pink. We are facing each other. Her first two buttons are undone, showing a red facing of ribbon at her collarbone inside the cashmere (close up, I can see everything without glasses; it's the far things).

As I undo the third button there's a nervous bluntness to my fingers. Her dark eyebrows rise slightly.

'If thou think'st I am too quickly won,' she softly quotes from the play that she has been reading, she looks down and the corner of her mouth twitches, 'I'll frown and be perverse and say thee nay . . .'

I am suddenly, acutely embarrassed for her. Desperate for her to stop speaking.

She half-turns from me, crossing her chest with an arm, and considers. I am suddenly unable to risk a change of expression or an audible breath. From the street outside, the hiss of night-traffic, a bus changing gear. Please, not more Shakespeare.

'I should have been more strange, I must confess . . .' She smiles, her pale eyes and pale mouth smile, the arm stretches towards me, my eyes are on hers, I can feel her fingers at my shirt.

I move my face towards hers, and hers retreats the same number of inches.

'. . . therefore pardon me . . .' I reach for her fourth button, the ribbon facing is a narrow red V against the pink. My fingers descend, the V lengthens, her hand is against my chest.

'. . . And do not impute this yielding . . .' I part the red facing, feel a soft contraction of warmth and she gasps, laughs. 'Your hand . . . is so COLD . . .'

III

〜〜〜〜〜

I had always thought of myself as OK-looking, one way and another, but amongst those Indian women I have to say I felt a real cuckoo.

We were standing in line at the top of a flight of steps leading down to the sea. In the brown water below us several launches slopped at anchor; one of these was due, at some unspecified future point, to take us to the island of Elephanta and back. A day trip. An excursion.

'It's historic,' Beth had said. 'The major tourist attraction. You can't just NOT GO.'

There were caves on the island, apparently; rock carvings and things. I wasn't too concerned about what was at the other end, but I did quite like the idea of a drift out into the haze of the Arabian Sea.

It was a hot day, a day of squinting, thumping heat. Most of the people in the queue were women, and had covered their heads against the sun with the trailing ends of their saris; amongst them, surrounded by their hot electric pinks and limes and chromes and peacock blues, I felt colourless, inhibited. From their patience and attitude I guessed that they couldn't have been that well off; rich Indian women wouldn't have been caught dead standing in the sun. And for some reason that I hadn't yet fathomed, only the lower classes got to wear the really gorgeous saris, the ones you could see a mile away, the ones, in fact, that *I* would have chosen. The better-off tended to duller, more muted numbers.

Maybe they were out-of-towners. They were darker-skinned than the women at the hotel who, with their sallow, bruised-looking complexions, looked as if they spent their whole lives indoors. Which, when I thought about it, I supposed they did. These women stared at me, smiling shy, fine-featured smiles. One of them touched my hair. For almost the first time in my life I felt awkward, over-tall. From beneath Beth's hideous straw hat, I smiled self-consciously back.

As we waited, a group of boys in ragged shorts dived and somer-saulted into the sea from the steps; when they climbed out, their footprints dried immediately on the hot stone. A mother-and-child beggar duo worked the queue but were ignored, got nothing. A man failed to sell us peanut-brittle.

Behind us, shadowing the tail-end of the queue, rose the arch of the Gateway of India.

A rope was thrown ashore. At the same moment as one of the launches started to edge itself against the bottom of the steps and the women started reaching for their bags, an insistent, gravelly voice poured over my shoulder.

'Hi, God, SAW you standing there in the heat, thought we were NEVER going to move. Smoke?'

I turned round into the tiny, aggressive eyes of a total stranger. Her eye sockets gleamed with pearly highlighter. She shook the Dunhill packet.

'Go on. They're proper ones, duty-free, not from Nigeria or wherever. Have one. God, that's a nice hat, isn't it. Sort of beach-comber style. Lizzie, isn't that a nice hat? Karen? . . . KAREN?'

She put the wrong end of a cigarette into her mouth.

'They should get themselves proper hats. I'm always bloody tell-ing them.' She shook her head.

'It's my sister's,' I said.

She looked to be in her forties. Unpredictable. Aviator sun-glasses jammed into a corkscrew perm. The two teenage girls hung back awkwardly, dissociating themselves from her.

'Come on, guys.' She spoke with the cigarette between her lips. 'Let's get to the front of the line. Get good seats.' She turned to me. 'Did you say you smoked? I'm Deirdre McConachie by the way. Dee. And that's Lizzie and that's Karen.' She indicated them with a jerk of her head. 'Say Hi, you guys.'

In her Camberley drawl the Americanism was grotesque. The girls didn't say Hi, but smiled weakly at me. One of them, Karen, I think, reached for the wrong-way-round cigarette in Deirdre's mouth and flipped it irritably into the sea.

Deirdre opened her mouth, but Lizzie waved her dismissively to silence. We moved down towards the boat, Deirdre stiff on high-heeled sandals.

'Careful on these dreadful steps, guys, don't wanna ... Sorry, what did you say your name was?'

'June.'

'Can you give us a hand up, June? Thanks. Great. Now quick, under that awning thing, before those damn women bag the seats. Karen, go and put your things there. AND YOU, LIZZIE ...'

'Fuck's sake,' muttered Lizzie, as Deirdre elbowed her way to the front, the prow or whatever, of the boat.

'I heard that,' said Deirdre. 'Fuck you, too. Smoke?'

She snapped her lighter shut and pointed the packet at me.

'I don't,' I said. 'Thank you.'

She sucked smoke out of her mouth and up her nose. The women who had stood in the queue with me watched her in fascination.

'Did you get it here?' she asked.

'I'm sorry?'

'The hat.'

'Oh,' I said. 'No. It's my sister's. I think she bought it in Florida.'

'Love it,' she said. 'God. Miami ... Palm Beach ... Key West ... Boca Raton ...'

'Mu-u-u-um,' said the other girl, I think the Karen one, a warning note in her voice.

'What?' Deirdre flicked ash angrily on to the floor of the boat.

'Leave her alone.'

She dragged furiously. 'I was just telling ...'

'Just leave her alone, Mum.' Karen turned to me. 'She hasn't been to a single one of those places, you know.'

'It's fine,' I said. 'Really. But I might actually just go a little nearer the back. I'm afraid this petrol smell from the engine's making me feel a bit sick.'

It was the best I could think of. I got up before anyone could speak.

'Excuse me.' I smiled. 'Nice to meet you all.'

I always got them.

I supposed I had to resign myself to the fact that whatever it was that made people keep a polite distance from other people, I didn't have it. In the crowded tube train, I'd be the one being interrogated by the derelict with the bleeding eyebrows. At the party, I'd inevitably end up cornered by the dandruffed death-ray theorist. I had only to venture a step on to Tottenham Court Road for Scientologists to start shoving their clipboards towards me. When I had first graduated from the school and joined the company, it had seemed appropriate to try and cultivate a subtle distance from the public, from the non-elect, the unglamorous. It never worked. No one ever got the message.

Maybe it was my Mineola straw-and-freckles complexion. Maybe it was my short nose. 'Breakfast cereals, maybe, or sanitary products. Sunshine stuff, that's your look,' a commercials' agent had once told me.

For a time I'd concentrated on my eyes. Grey eyes, I thought, were possibly rather sad and Russian. I deliberately developed Bolshoi characteristics in my classwork; splashy, yearning jetés, tortured arms, spiky fingers.

What on earth was the problem, asked my exasperated teachers. Arthritis? Thrush?

So finally I had to accept it. I just had that sort of look. It could have been worse. I could have had pale eyebrows.

We chugged quietly over the flat sea. As we left the city behind us, the water darkened. Tankers, oil-platforms and other installations rose from the haze, were clear as we passed, folded into invisibility behind us. Working somewhere out here, I remembered, was Dane, Beth's husband.

Around me, the Indian women chattered quietly, plastic shopping bags on their knees. There was only one male passenger on the boat, a vague, rather fastidious-looking individual sitting with a fat-armed woman I guessed to be his wife. He was accompanying his words to her with languid gestures of his hand. A large metal watch hung loosely from the slender wrist.

Something about the hand and the heavy watch reminded me of my mother, who in the same way that she still wore teenage hairstyles, habitually bought all of her clothes and ornaments in much larger sizes than she needed. When I visited her she was forever pulling the sleeves of outsized sweaters up her forearms or shaking her hands in the air to clear them of heavy bracelets. I had this theory that one fateful day towards the end of her Dorothy phase she had been watching one of those film scenes in which the heroine, possibly Goldie Hawn, is making breakfast in the man's flat for the first time and appears, tiny, scatty and adorable, in one of his great big business shirts . . .

Certainly from one particular school holidays onwards the key to her entire presentation and behaviour had been contained in two words: Little Me.

'June.'

It was Lizzie or Karen.

'Hi, please, sit down. Sorry, you're . . .'

'Karen. Lizzie's over there with Mum. About whom sorry. Mum, I mean. She's a bit of a liability. Going on like that.'

'Oh, please, that's fine,' I said. 'God. Actually it's funny, I was just thinking about my own, a liability if there ever was one.'

'Really? What sort of — '

'Oh, you know, sort of . . . wanting to be one of her own daughters.'

'Oh, all that. Are you American, if you don't mind my — '

'I was born in Texas, but I've actually lived most of my life in London.'

'Oh, right. That explains . . . Because you have this definite American accent at the same time as this, like, completely Brit look and way of saying things . . . Are your parents in the Foreign Service?'

'No, my father's in the oil business, but not here. I'm staying with my sister. She's married to an American; another oil-man, in fact.'

'Lizzie and I are here for the school holidays. Dad's tied up with some engineering project.'

'Do you like it?'

43

'Oh, it's quite fun, isn't it? I mean it's an impossible place and nothing works and the British expats are pretty much a nightmare and once you've done the tourist things and bought the silk and stuff it's really a bit samey, but it is nice to have the heat. At least we think so. Mum, though, really hates it here. I mean REALLY. HATES IT. The food, the climate, the people, everything . . .'

I thought of Dane. Beth had used almost exactly the same words.

'Dad, though, loves it; he's learning the language and has loads of Indian friends and goes to all these Hindi plays and concerts and so on. Actually, I think that it's him liking it, almost more than her hating it, which is finishing things off between them. Their marriage, that is.' She patted the pocket of her jeans for cigarettes and looked over at her mother. 'Better get back, anyway. Just wanted to — '

'Really,' I said. 'It's fine.'

A path led upwards from the jetty towards the caves. At the side of the path were stalls selling religious knick-knacks and, for some reason, Russian badges. At the top of the hill I found an unoccupied bench.

Bombay, I thought, as Deirdre crossly threw her cigarette end to the ground and her daughters looked tiredly at each other, exaggerated your state of mind. Rather like its gin, it drew out your tide, left you exposed.

I would have to watch myself.

We gathered outside the first temple, which had been carved into the solid black rock of the island. It looked extremely old. A small, rather fierce Indian woman carrying a long bamboo pointing stick marshalled us into a group and divided us into English and Hindi speakers. The Hindi speakers were led away by the man with the metal watch and the floppy hat.

'First,' asked the woman sternly of the group, 'is any lady having their period? I am asking because there is bees' nest in the cave and the woman's period is disturbing and causing to sting.'

We darted glances at each other. No one owned up. Would fear of embarrassment mean that we would be stung to death by killer bees? There was silence.

'See, now we proceed to sculpture,' said the woman, briskly, signalling us to follow her into the cave. We stopped in front of a carved relief.

'The principal figure in this compartment,' she began, 'is Shiva Nataraj, performing his mystic dance of creation. He is shown here setting the Universe in motion, while himself remaining unperturbed. Parvati, his consort, was also participating in dance, and she was equally good as Shiva. So Shiva played his special trick which is to raise one of his leg and touch with it to his head.'

I can do that, I thought. Développé in second.

'Parvati,' she continued, 'hesitated to perform this posture due to delicacy of womanliness.'

I could see that it certainly wasn't a position you'd want to adopt without underwear. Parvati's predicament reminded me of an old nightmare. I am informed that I have to dance a royal command performance of *Giselle* at short notice. I arrive backstage to discover that there is no costume, that I have to fashion myself one from flower petals and old cloakroom tickets. I realise that I have forgotten every step of the choreography. I have five minutes before the curtain goes up. I have four minutes, then three minutes, two minutes, one . . .

'What do you think?'

It was Karen.

'I don't know, really,' I answered. 'I know so little about it all. The guide seems to assume you know who Shiva and all these gods are. But the figures are wonderful, even though they're different sorts of physical shapes than I'm used to finding beautiful.'

'And what sort are you used to finding . . . ?'

'Oh, you know, slender women, collarbones and so on, men with a bit of . . . definition.'

'I know what you mean, obviously, but the thing you have to understand around here – God, listen to me, "the thing you have to understand" – is that physical definition's for road-menders. And actually you see these statues and so on and think no man could be that shape, like they're carved from butter and sat in the sun, and you take one and get his clothes off and that's exactly how they are.'

'Buttery?'

'Buttery. I mean broad shoulders and everything, narrow waist, all the things you can see when they've got their clothes on, but no muscle, no definition, at all. Unworked flesh. Barely lifted as much as a teacup.'

'I see,' I said. 'And who are all these butterballs?'

'Oh, you know, just guys you meet. You should come out one evening with me and Lizzie. You're not . . . WITH anyone out here, are you?'

'Umm, no, I'm not.'

At that moment Lizzie appeared beside her sister. 'Where's Mum?' asked Karen immediately.

'She's fine,' answered Lizzie. 'She's got that bloke who was in the boat explaining to her about how Shiva could be half male, half female. Not that she's interested, but having got the entire attention of the only English-speaking man on the whole island, she's quite happy. For a bit at least. Hi, June.'

'Hi, Lizzie.'

'I was just telling June,' said Karen, 'that she should come out with us one night.'

'Mmmm. That'd be really fun. Where're you staying, June?'

It was unexpected.

With an hour to go before the boat left, I followed a narrow trodden path inland, away from the caves and the views of the sea and the makeshift café. Turning a corner, I caught my breath to find the path leading along a really quite dizzying clifftop. A fallen tree lay along its length, and sitting in a line on the trunk, like resting butterflies, were four of the women in the bright saris. As I hesitated, they gestured me towards them, and made room for me on the tree trunk.

'Thank you,' I said, and they laughed. One of them said something in Hindi and they all laughed again and looked at me. Curiously, it didn't worry me that I couldn't understand them. Their stares were entirely free from calculation, from assessment, and their laughter at me had nothing in it of mockery or of advantage taken. They fell silent and the five of us sat looking inland, over the island. Below us the cliff fell away to dusty rocks, a broken reach of jungle, a kilometre of dark green hills. Beyond a headland to our left was the sea again.

It was an uncomplicated landscape but somehow a satisfying one. The Indian women, who were my own age or maybe younger, seemed to find it so, too. They were quite happy to sit there, as they had sat before I arrived, in unmoving silence.

After a while, my consciousness of how near we were to the edge of the cliff was replaced by the knowledge that I was safe with these women; safe from language, safe from judgement, safe from falling. I felt a relaxation, a cautious lengthening of muscles in my eyes, my face, my neck, my shoulders. The silence, for a time, for a long moment, took on almost positive form, before suddenly bursting into a non-silence so complex and prickling and intense that I couldn't believe that I had ever thought of it as silence. With this realisation, this sudden consciousness of the screaming of insects and the minute partings of branches and the accompanying clatter of leaf on leaf, came a sliding-away within me, came the relaxing of a hand at my heart.

Nothing, I knew at that moment, nothing beyond existence was demanded of me at all. I was simply there, above the island and the sea. I found that I could shift, if I wished, into conscious thought, move back again into suspension; I realised that part of what I was feeling was recognition, memory of a time before memory, and that the whole of what I was feeling, for want of a better expression, was happiness.

It seemed longer, but it must have been about forty minutes later that the girl to my left touched my arm and indicated that it was time to go. I rose to my feet, still dazed, and as I unsteadily followed her vermilion sari along the clifftop path she half-turned and took my hand.

She was still holding it, I was still dazed, as we came into the trodden café clearing at the top of the hill. The fierce little woman with the stick saw us on to the path to the jetty with a fierce little smile. Although I had only trailed along earlier, facetiously uninterested, barely listening to her words, I realised that my anti-gravity, soda-bubble state had been prompted, in part at least, by the hour or so I had spent in the caves. That it had been

released by the butterfly presences on the clifftop was equally unexpected; I had spent my life surrounded by blindingly dressed
women, but I'd never been particularly one for letting my guard
down in front of them.

As we started on the path down the hill, Deirdre suddenly
swung in front of us waving a hundred-rupee note.

'June, darling. It IS June, isn't it?' she demanded, ignoring the
girl with me. 'Be an angel and give me some change. That silly
BUGGER at the stall hasn't got any and if I don't have something
wet and chilly RIGHT NOW, I'm going to die!'

As I gaped at her, not immediately understanding her words, I
felt the small hand at my side release from mine, saw a whisk of
vermilion at the edge of my vision.

'Change?' repeated Deirdre, insistently, waving a hand in front
of my eyes as if verifying my reactive functions.

'Umm, yes, hang on,' I managed, 'let me have a look.'

'Thanks, great. Who's your lady friend? Nice frock.'

'Here,' I said.

'Thanks. I'll pay you back.'

'Would you believe,' asked Lizzie frowning at her *Eve's Weekly*,
'that you can get an abortion for fifty rupees?'

By some sort of pre-arrangement, it was Karen who was keeping
the eye on Deirdre for the return journey. Lizzie had attached herself, unsolicited, to me.

'Fifty rupees,' she continued. 'That's about, what, two pounds
fifty?'

'Where do you stay?' I asked.

'While we're here? Dad and Mum's flat is at Breach Candy, just
by the Nepean Club. Do you ever go there?'

'I know where you mean,' I said. I found myself liking Lizzie
rather less than Karen.

'We go there quite often,' she said. 'It's a bit of a Victorian old
dump but it livens up a bit on Sundays. They have a barbeque and
stuff and there's usually a darts competition. I've got quite good,
actually, since I've been here, although I'd never dream of playing
at home, where it's really quite a proley sort of game. But God,
listen to me. Here I am talking to you as if you've never seen a pub

or a game of darts in your life. Sorry. You're probably some sort of an expert.'

'I've never actually thrown a dart,' I said, 'although I've seen it done often enough.'

'What actually do you do?' asked Lizzie after a short pause. 'I mean, for work?'

Here we go.

'I've just retired from being a ballet dancer.'

'Really? Wow. I'm impressed. Where did you dance?'

I told her.

'We went to see *Giselle* last year. With the school. A matinée. Pauline Faull was dancing Giselle. I'm not one for ballet especially, but I have to say she was completely stunning. Do you know her? God, stupid. Don't answer that, you must do, being in the same company. I wonder if I saw you that afternoon? Might you have been dancing?'

'In *Giselle*?' I said. 'Probably, yes.'

'As what?'

'I was usually Queen of the Wilis.'

'Oh, yes. In fact I'm sure I remember you.'

Sure you do.

'Why are you retiring, though, you seem awfully young to be retiring from anything?'

I looked ahead of the boat. The low shoreline of the city was uncertainly assembling itself some thirty minutes away.

'I'm just tired of it,' I said eventually. 'I've had enough.'

By the time we were moored at the base of the stone steps leading up to the Gateway of India, most of the heat had gone out of the day. Lizzie and Karen had extracted a promise, which I intended to break, to meet them at the Nepean Sea Bathing Club for the next Sunday's barbeque.

I hurried up the steps, leaving the girls with their mother. I wanted to say goodbye to the woman in the vermilion sari; Lizzie's insistent presence on the return trip had, I thought, kept her and her friends at a distance.

At the top of the steps I rummaged through my bag, eventually finding what I wanted, an old photograph of myself in costume as

Gamzatti on the supposedly Indian set of *Bayadère*. The curious thing was, the more I looked at the photograph the more similar its landscape seemed to the one that had appeared before me on Elephanta. Not topographically, maybe, but in character, in atmosphere. Then again, of course, that might have been my imagination.

I wrote my name and address on the back, and as Vermilion and her friends reached me, I handed it to her. She looked at the photograph, and pointed at me interrogatively.

'Yes.' I nodded. 'Me.'

She looked at it again, the others gathering round, before placing it thoughtfully and with care in her shopping bag.

Borrowing a ball-point and a piece of ruled paper from one of them, she carefully wrote out her own name and address in Hindi script, folded the paper, and handed it to me.

'June,' I said, pointing to myself again. 'My name is June.'

'Gita.' She smiled, mirroring the gesture.

They waved as they disappeared towards the city. I waved back and looked at my watch. I had to catch the Taj Patisserie before it closed. Beth was having some people over.

IV

~~~~~~~~

To: Miss Lakshmi Khandekar,   BY HAND
#17, Divya Apartments,
Colaba Causeway.

From: Stanley Collinson,
#3, Seashell Apartments,
Nepean Sea Rd.

Dear Lakshmi Khandekar,

I have come to Bombay as the representative of Coldharbour Films (UK) Ltd. Coldharbour Films is an independent company specialising in the making of documentary and feature films for broadcast on British and overseas television.

We are currently developing the idea of a documentary examining the life and career of one of the younger Indian film stars, and having seen and greatly enjoyed your performances in *Akeli, Zakhmi,* and *Mera Dost, Mera Dushman,* I was hoping that we might discuss the possibility of making you the subject of our production.

While I am sure that you are currently very busy with preparations for the *Khandaan* shoot, which I understand begins soon, I would be grateful for the chance to discuss all this at an early date. In that hope, I will try phoning your home number later today or tomorrow.

I can be contacted at the above address or on Bombay 828 1108.

With many thanks and in anticipation of an early meeting,
Yours sincerely,
STANLEY COLLINSON

The morning was already colourless, white, vague.

Anubai, Cuckoo's servant, had opened the doors on to the small terrace overlooking the sea wall. It was low tide, the Arabian Sea glittering listless and dirty a hundred yards away, the rocks exposed, the sand wet.

I pulled the letter out of the typewriter and reread it. It wasn't perfect, but it would do.

Baby, Anubai's nine-year-old daughter, brought me tea, the overfilled cup shaking slightly in its saucer as the small hand slowly carried it to the table.

I sipped at it in silence. Baby sat opposite me on a pile of laundry, watching closely, frowning. She remembered me, even if half her life had passed since my last visit.

This room had not changed in her lifetime, though; it had barely changed in mine. The walls had surrendered their thin distemper to a webbed grey, but the bookcase still held the same yellowing paperbacks; the same silvered portraits watched from behind their flyspecked glass.

But of all the people to run into, John Pearcey. Thank God he hadn't suggested ringing Emilia on my behalf when he got back. On the other hand, maybe that's exactly what he intended to do as soon as he got off the plane, and on his own behalf, knowing that I was safely out here. When I had first introduced them at an awards ceremony (Pearcey, naturally, had been a nominee) he had displayed his slyest, most effortful, charm.

Well, I couldn't worry about that.

I opened Cuckoo's bureau (one of several pieces she had bought cheaply from departing British families in 1947), and found an envelope for the Lakshmi Khandekar letter. Cuckoo herself, her note had informed me on my arrival, had gone to spend a few days with a friend in Mahabaleshwar, it was a long-standing arrangement and she hadn't wished to break it. My letter, in addition (and a touch of asperity detectable here, between the neatly ruled lines), hadn't left time for a reply that would reach me before I left London.

Anyway, until her return, Anubai would be here, and I was to help myself to whatever I needed.

I finished my tea. Outside, beyond the sea wall, washermen

were spreading laundry over the rocks. At each headland, right
and left, stood a Hindu temple, and between them the transparent
forms of tankers at anchor wrinkled in the haze.

There were only two other customers when, fifteen minutes later, I
climbed the steps up to the Breach Candy Men's Glamour Hair-
dressing Saloon; both were being attended to, both had their eyes
closed. No one spoke, the fan whop-whopped overhead, two pairs
of steel scissors snipped, and cut hair fell silently to the shined
linoleum.

A middle-aged barber, his hair skilfully dyed and fashioned into
a centre-parted style popular amongst younger actors, stood up
from his copy of *Screen*. An open hand indicated one of the heavy
Rexine- and chrome-upholstered chairs; in the mirror an eyebrow
raised.

'Short,' I said, 'please.'

The haircut proceeded with surgical seriousness. Scissors were
weighed in the hand, held up to the light and, from time to time,
discarded without apparent reason. Lotions were applied from
bulb-powered sprays. There was much stepping-back and frowning; at one point the barber called over, in Hindi, to a colleague,
'It's beginning to thin. Do you think I should leave it longer on
top?'

'That way he won't get sunstroke,' replied the colleague
seriously, after some thought.

'Please,' I replied in the same language, 'cut it short and I'll
wear a hat.' Both men stopped and smiled, and the barber asked
how I knew Hindi.

'I studied it in London,' I answered, 'and then spent several
months at the University of Varanasi.'

'Varanasi,' replied the colleague. 'Very nice. I took my father to
die there last year.'

After the cut, the barber poured almond-oil on to my scalp from a
pink plastic bottle, kneaded it for several minutes, and then fitted
heavy steel appliances to the backs of his hands. When these were
switched on at the wall, his hands began to vibrate at high speed,
and he clamped them to my scalp. Twenty minutes later, dazed, I
opened my eyes.

The two earlier customers had disappeared, and the other barbers were sitting down flicking through magazines. The barber with the centre parting laid a hot towel over my face, offered me a tea and when I accepted, shouted out of the door to a boy.

We talked about films. He was an aficionado, and went to everything. As much to keep up with the hairstyles as anything else, he explained. If Jeetendra or Dharmendra or Sanju Saxena or the Bachchan appeared with a new cut, well, he was certainly going to be asked to duplicate it within the week. He had a pair of aviator-style graduated sunglasses on the counter so that clients could try out their new haircuts, film-star style.

The glasses of tea arrived.

I offered him a cigarette, which he accepted, and I asked who his favourite film heroes and heroines were. He replied that he was very much a conventional Hema and Amitabh man, himself, but admitted that there were younger actors also who were putting in beautiful work. I asked him about Lakshmi Khandekar. He hesitated, and his eyes flickered to his colleagues. He said something rapid and incomprehensible in Marathi at which they all laughed. He smiled at me, apologetic.

'We were saying that her breasts are too small.'

Outside the Regal Cinema I paid off the taxi and as the car disappeared into the traffic at the roundabout, crossed over towards the sluggishly milling pavements of Colaba Causeway.

It was getting hotter, and I felt unaccustomedly neat after the haircut; I touched the sharp new fuzz at the back of my neck and wiped the bridge of my nose with a handkerchief.

Looking up the causeway I saw that it was a question of either dodging through the traffic on the main road or running the gauntlet of the pavement. The traffic looked angry, so I sunk a hand firmly into each trouser pocket, and swung up on to the kerb. Pushing my way through the elbowing crowds I stepped into the most productively pimped and hustled pitch in the city. Lounging, nutcracker-faced boys turned to me like lovers, and whispered friend, change money, friend, and grass and smack and fucking. Beggars in various states of physical disorder shuffled and crutched towards me, one with a length of orange piping protruding from an

opening in his ribs and taped to his chest, others blinded and club-
handed by leprosy, others again hoop-backed, twisted, trolley-
borne. Smiling stall holders plucked at my shirt (friend, friend),
urgently indicating pirated devotional cassettes, Air India combs
and soapdishes, cellophane packets of henna, cobra-skin belts,
faded shirts with glued-on crocodile emblems.

I shouldered my way through. The tourists mostly looked
bemused, their every dipping step under the awnings a repeating
cycle of curiosity, irritation, and repulsion. Beggar-children pulled
at their clothes, burning *agarbati* sticks stung their eyes, lolling and
senseless monkey-babies were pushed at them by sun-blackened
and eternally pregnant women.

Electively blind to everything and everyone except themselves
and the contents of some of the more expensive shops, three six-
teenish Sindhi girls, all bangles and flash, were marching up the
pavement ahead of me. I passed them and turning, asked if they
knew Divya Apartments.

'Sure, yah, just on the corner there, past Electric House.'

'Thanks. Thank you.'

It was eleven o'clock, and getting very hot. The blisters on my
heels stung.

Around the entrance hung a number of hand-painted boards,
mostly cracked and faded, advertising the venereologists, sputum
analysts and shipping agents within. I climbed the steps, lifting my
feet over a sleeping beggar-child. Inside, unusually for a building
of this size, there appeared to be no watchman. The stairwell was
dark, and smelt of joss stick and urine; elderly electrical cables
looped into the blackness, and the two corners that were touched
by the faint light from the entrance were streaked the dull clotted-
blood colour of spat betel nut.

Opposite me, I made out the vertical iron parallels of a lift-gate;
on the wall, the black square of a board painted with numbers and
names.

The lift, its light broken, started to rise through the darkness
with a gulping hydraulic shudder. A dozen shadowed floors rolled
slowly past before the oiled cables overhead came to an uncertain
rest. Sliding back the gates, I stepped out into a dim corridor with

a single door at its end. Above the door hung a long-faded flower garland. I searched unsuccessfully for an electric bell, and knocked hard on the door. There was a long silence before I heard, from inside the flat, the sound of a closing door.

I hesitated, wondering whether to knock again, when I heard the sound of feet softly approaching. The door opened to the limit of a short security chain; beyond it an unsmiling woman, the *pallao* of her Maharashtrian sari looped over her head and held in her mouth, jerked her head at me interrogatively.

'I have come to leave a letter for Miss Khandekar,' I said in Hindi.

'Name?' she snapped in Marathi, expressionless.

'Collinson. Stanley Collinson.'

With this she disappeared. I pulled the letter from my shirt pocket. It was damp.

Several minutes passed. I returned the letter to my pocket and wiped my hands on the back of my trousers.

The chain was finally unhooked and the door opened by the same straight-backed and unsmiling servant. She led me, not, as I had somehow expected, into a narrow corridor, but into an unlit and pillared hall some forty feet square, dominated, like the dining room of a Cunard liner, by a heavy period chandelier.

I looked around me with surprise, stilled, for a moment, by an edge of recognition; I had accompanied my parents to apartments like this one as a child.

I followed her across the room, the dusty and uneven shafts of light thrown by the tall windows paling her dark-edged sari and reflecting in the dark wood panelling of the walls and pillars. Opening a large door she allowed me to precede her into sudden sunlight. Before me extended a terrace covering, on several levels, the entire area of the building's roof. I was led up a shallow and turning flight of steps to the covered centre of the upper level. From here four colonnades of pinkish stone radiated to the corners of the building, terminating, in each case, in a small, domed pavilion.

In one of these, overlooking the distant crawl of Colaba Causeway, a woman wearing a sari identical to that of the servant was seated with her back to us. Hearing our approach she turned around, straight-backed and expressionless.

She looked, I thought, about fifty.

'Please, sit down.'

I lowered myself into a rattan seat opposite her.

'What can I do for you, Mr . . . Stanley?'

For a moment I said nothing, but stared at her.

'I had actually come,' I began, 'to leave a letter for Miss Lakshmi Khandekar, the actress.'

She nodded slowly.

'Ah. I understand. You are a . . . *Cinestar* reader.'

'Guilty, I'm afraid.'

'Well, *Cinestar* have been helpful neither to you nor to me, Mr Stanley; I'm afraid that they have taken my name from the telephone directory, where I am listed as Miss L. Khandekar. I have received a mountain of letters for Lakshmi Khandekar as well as several telephone calls; unfortunately, my name is not Lakshmi but Lata. I have contacted the magazine and they have apologised, but a little late, clearly.'

'I've wasted your time then, I'm afraid.'

'Not at all, Mr Stanley. Please, stay and have some tea. It's the least I can offer anyone braving that appalling lift.'

'Thank you, that's kind.' I was glad to continue sitting where I was, especially after the heat and desperation below. It was very quiet, and there was a whisper of a breeze from the sea; it plucked and touched at the cotton sari of the servant as she rose from the centre of the colonnade and came towards us, almost silent on bare feet, carrying a tray on which was a covered glass of cold water. She put this at my side, and Miss Khandekar asked her, in English, to make us a pot of *masala* tea.

'I won't bother to explain what that is to anyone who speaks Hindi as well as Leelabai says you do,' said Miss Khandekar, her features relaxing in curiosity. 'Where did you learn it?'

'London University. The School of Oriental and African Studies. At least, I was born here, and lived here until I was seven, as well, and grew up speaking a sort of Bombay Hindi, but I suppose I must have forgotten most of it . . . Anyway I started from scratch again in London, and then managed to spend some time at the university in Varanasi as well . . .'

'It sounds as if you know India quite well.'

I smiled. 'I suppose so, for a foreigner.' It really was very quiet. 'Have you lived in England, Miss Khandekar?'

'Yes, for nearly twenty years. I was an English teacher in Hornsey, in North London. I lived near Alexandra Palace.'

She turned thoughtful eyes towards the sea. Long dark hair, undyed, iron amongst the black, hung in a long queue to the centre of her back. She wore neither make-up nor glasses. On the seat at her side lay a library copy of an American political thriller. We sat for a time without speaking. I half-closed my eyes, and felt the breeze touch my face. After some minutes I saw Leelabai approaching.

She poured us each a glass of tea. It was very hot and very strong. Miss Khandekar watched me levelly.

'Cardamom, black salt, and ginger. I hope it's not too strong?'

'It looks perfect,' I answered her. It was too hot to taste.

'Tell me,' she began again, looking away from me, 'about your time in Varanasi. How you found it. Forgive my curiosity, but as an Indian who has spent time in a British school your . . . reverse of that situation interests me.'

I didn't mind; I was unlikely, I thought, to see her again.

'I loved Varanasi the place,' I started, 'but I didn't feel quite the same way about the university, which – bearing in mind that I was twenty-two and that the year was 1975 – I found humourless and overstructured. Academically, I suppose, I had pretty much shot my bolt in London, and it wasn't long before I was handing in the minimum amount of work necessary to avoid actually being asked to leave.

'At the same time, as I said, I loved the city itself. I felt that my whole life had led up to my arrival there. I would sit on the ghats for hours, gazing out over the river. And, I suppose inevitably, I smoked all the opium, hash, and everything else that was put in front of me, paying for it by acting as interpreter and drugs middleman to Western travellers. Fellow pilgrims, of course, as I saw them at the time.'

I looked sideways at Lata Khandekar to see how she was taking this. She was frowning thoughtfully at her hands, which were folded in her lap.

'I suppose . . . viewed through the haze of that summer, Varanasi WAS nirvana. The temples overrun with monkeys, the stoned priests, the ringing bells, the crowds, the beating sun, the burning corpses on the river's edge. It was just the most . . . EXTREME place on earth. And then of course the dream, as it was quietly but constantly reminding one that it might, turned into a nightmare.'

Lata Khandekar's half-smile told me that mine was an old story, that she already knew its outcome. I blew at the *masala* tea.

'The monsoon came and I accepted a ride to Goa as the pillion motor-cycle passenger of an American heroin dealer. Under other circumstances I'm sure it would have been a fascinating journey. We went, I think, through Nagpur and Hyderabad, but with the dope streaming through my bloodstream I saw nothing of them, or of the journey. I'm sorry.' I interrupted myself. 'This probably isn't quite the story you want to hear.'

'You tell it well,' said Lata Khandekar obliquely.

I hesitated, but she said nothing further.

'Well, my appetite had disappeared, my urine was almost black, my mind was drifting, disconnected for hours at a time; it was all I could do, really, to stay upright and on the bike for all those wet, endless days of road. Finally we arrived outside Panjim Hospital in Goa, and the American ordered me off the pillion and roared away for ever with my money, clothes and passport locked into the pannier of his Triumph Bonneville. I was too weak to stand, by then, and just crumpled into the rain like a sort of . . . sulphurous corpse. The police visited me in the hospital. Was there anyone, they wanted to know, who could pay for the treatment, take charge of me, or should they initiate repatriation proceedings? I can't remember what I answered, but three days later Cuckoo arrived from Bombay.'

I stopped.

'And who,' asked Miss Khandekar, after a moment, 'was Cuckoo? Is Cuckoo?'

'Cuckoo was my parents' Parsee housekeeper when we lived in Bombay. You know I said I grew up . . . She was more than that, though, she joined my parents just before I was born, and just after the early death of her husband. She became . . . you know, one of the family, and so on.'

'What happened to her when your family left?'

'She inherited some money,' I said shortly. 'She came to England once or twice.'

'I'm sorry,' said Miss Khandekar, turning away and signalling to Leelabai, who was hovering near by, to collect the tea things. 'I shouldn't interrupt. You're staying for lunch, by the way. That is, unless you've something more important to do?' She raised her eyebrows interrogatively.

'Well, no. Thank you very much, that's . . .'

'It's nothing of the sort. Fish? Good.'

She asked Leelabai to prepare lunch for both of us, and settled herself expectantly back into the rattan chair.

'At the hospital, they told me, with the air of having said it all before, that I was lucky to be alive. They kept me there for ten days, and then Cuckoo put me on to a coach for Bombay. I could hardly walk, I slept most of the way.

'I spent a further six weeks in Bombay at Cuckoo's flat, convalescing, living on fruit and vegetables and sugar cane. If Cuckoo guessed at the other . . . non-hepatitic causes of my weakness, she didn't refer to them. For myself, I felt sick at the thought of smoking or swallowing anything except the blandest food and drink. I was more depressed than I had ever thought possible.

'A junior consular officer, a nice chap not much older than myself who I was vilely rude to, visited me at Cuckoo's in the wake of the police enquiries in Panjim. He arranged for a new passport and a return ticket to be issued to me against my bank account in London.

'The week before I went, I was able to see a little of Bombay. It was a pretty joyless experience; I found it sadly changed from the city of my childhood, especially around Malabar Hill. The neighbourhood seemed . . . shrunken; the house where we had lived had been condemned, or at least boarded up, and most of the other, older houses had already been bulldozed to the ground to make way for high-rise apartments. All of the local characters that I remembered had been displaced, had died, or moved on. I went to the Nepean Sea Bathing Club, where my parents used to take me. There I saw a couple of faces that I knew, but in the fifteen years I'd been away, they'd . . . I don't know, lived whole lives, they weren't interested in the past.

'Cuckoo, of course, having seen it all happen over the years, was philosophical, but personally I didn't feel like staying around, re-establishing myself. My memories had become less sure, were no longer checkable. For the first time in my life I was aware of the useless passing of time.

'So I went back to London, where, to cut a longish story short, I applied to the BBC as a researcher. My degree and my time in Varanasi, which I described as a postgraduate study course, secured me an interview. I turned up at the White City offices at the appointed time on a cold December morning, and was shown into a room where my hand was shaken by a man whom I'd last seen sitting on the steps of Assi Ghat in Varanasi, picking the seeds out of an eight-ounce packet of Kerala grass.

"Well," he said, when he saw me, "look who it isn't. You've lost weight."

Lata Khandekar, frowning, nodded.

I shrugged.

'That was it, really. A couple of years later I took a fortnight's holiday in Bombay. I felt guilty about Cuckoo, and it was good to see her again. She was pleased that I had a good job but said she would have liked to see me married. I told her that so far I hadn't met the right person, but who knew? Any day I might be writing to say . . . and so on. Once again, of course, I found the city changed for the worse; whole areas were now completely unrecognisable. There was a desperation about the place, too; the certainties of childhood seemed lifetimes away. Only the Nepean Club was there to remind me that I had ever known them, and I spent most of the fortnight there.'

'No Dogs or Indians,' commented Lata Khandekar.

'I'm sorry?' I said.

'That's what the notices outside those European clubs used to say. No Dogs or Indians.'

'Oh,' I said. 'Right.'

'And now you're back again,' she smiled, 'and looking for Lakshmi Khandekar . . .'

'Well,' I said, wondering at her continued interest, 'last year I joined an independent production company called Coldharbour Films . . .'

I took the envelope from my shirt pocket and removed the letter. Handed it to her. She read it in silence.

'I see.' She handed the letter back to me. 'I see.'

'Thank you,' I said half an hour later, 'that was excellent.'

'Leela goes to the market for me every morning. It's only two hundred yards away; all the fish comes in from Sassoon Dock.' As we were eating she had continued to question me with a kind of tactical politeness about television and the various programmes I had worked on. At the same time she had politely evaded my questions about herself.

'When did you leave London?' I asked, after one of her long pauses. As a researcher I recognised the technique. Its purpose was to unnerve the interviewee into nervous disclosure. Anything to break the silence.

'I left London six years ago,' she replied.

'Do you miss it all?'

She turned back to the sea. Leelabai appeared at the top of the steps holding a tray, and seeing that we had finished eating, walked towards us. Lata Khandekar watched her come, watched her take the plates, before continuing in the same tone, as if I hadn't spoken.

'Students, you see, come and go. Either you never see them again or, if you do, they invariably seem older than they ought to be. It is tempting, in teaching, to subscribe to a sort of . . . relativity; to feel, without actually thinking it, that you aren't subject to the same forces of time and so on as your students. But then you wake up one day . . .'

She spoke, I noticed, with very exactly measured pauses, as if in exact correspondence to invisible punctuation.

'Let me add that I am also an Indian, a Maharashtrian. I have family obligations. But, yes, to answer your question, sometimes I do miss it all very much.'

'And now, if you'll excuse me, I am going to lie down. Please stay as long as you like. Ask Leelabai to bring you anything you want. Once again I apologise for not being a twenty-three-year-old actress.'

'No, please,' I replied, getting awkwardly to my feet. 'Thank you very much for your time. And also, of course, for your . . . for my lunch.'

'Not at all. It was the very least I could offer you in return for your most interesting story. But just one other thing: can you come round in two days' time. In the evening? There's someone I'd like you to meet.'

I hesitated.

'About eight?'

I opened my hands in acquiescence.

'Well, thank you very much.'

She turned and walked away, straight-backed, along the colonnade.

I sat for a time. My smile, a response to Lata Khandekar's own, faded. I imagined her elegant and elective solitude turning to loneliness. Cold winters, student indifference.

I thought, too, of Emilia, silent amongst her clothing and her dark brown hair, her face turning slowly from mine, her eyes focusing sightlessly, unreachable. Her body there for me, but her self waiting somewhere else, at a grave-eyed distance. I touch her lips, pale, darker-edged, with mine, but hers are soft, and no more present than her eyes. My mouth touches the hollow between her collarbones, follows the breast's weighted curve. My eyes lead my lips along the translucent line falling from the bay of her ribs, down past the sunken knot of her navel, down to the prickling and softly parted scribble, its parting palely parted, scalloped, darker-edged. She does not move.

I stepped out of the dark stairwell and into the noise and light of Colaba Causeway. The streets were emptier than they had been in the morning, people were sleeping, or had gone inside. Shops were shut.

I wiped my heels on my trousers and stuck new plasters on to the blisters. I looked for a taxi, but I wasn't really in a hurry to go anywhere. And the blisters weren't too bad.

Opposite me, a hoarding announced that *Akeli* was showing at Strand Cinema, a couple of hundred yards away. I supposed that I ought to go and see it again, but almost immediately decided that this was not an afternoon for sitting in the dark. Following my meeting with Lata Khandekar, and her curious invitation, I determined that the day and the city had more to reveal to me. On impulse, I turned off the causeway and into one of the lanes leading to Colaba market. The sun was above me now, whitening the dry ground, reminding me vaguely that I should buy some not-too-daft-looking sort of a hat. The noise of the traffic began to disappear behind me, was replaced by a looping transistor whine and the beating of hammers. I would try and lose myself, I decided, in the dusted gimcrack maze. I would find a mystery.

From the direction of the sea curled the mosquito whine of 'Pyari Pyari'. I followed the sound. Small dark interiors gleamed with stainless steel, lamp-lit temples flickered, tin-panelled stalls offered used car-batteries and bandicoot poison and blouse-pieces and glass bangles. Children squatted in the dust, calling the flies to their eyes and their shit; in the uneven patches of shade, *paan*wallahs and old men chewed and spat and watched, and on the ground, veiled against the sun, women waved the flies from circular baskets of red and green and yellow vegetables.

It was suddenly and immediately clear that there were no mysteries to be found here; it was only a market, selling things that people needed. Fighting back a feeling of foolish intrusiveness, I continued determinedly along the line of the music. Ducking under a washing line hung with faded school uniforms, curious eyes following me, I picked my way between the hutch-like dwellings and towards the sea. Here the roofs were lower, hung with old tarpaulins and plastic sheeting and weighed down by tyres and rocks.

I stopped to wipe my glasses, replaced them, and turning a narrow corner, stepped into a black, blow-flied smear that skidded underfoot and smelt like guts. As I wiped my shoe in the dust a small girl ran out and pulled a staggering child out of my path and into a hut. Inside the hut I heard a slap and a cry. I put out a balancing hand and grasped an unsteady stack of fouled wire cages. White chickens inside. More slaps from inside the hut, and more crying. On the ground below, an old man in a lunghi looked worriedly up at me, wiping his hands on a rag; his arms were as thin and knotted as old wisteria branches, and at his feet, sticky with new blood, a knife and a flat stone gleamed and buzzed with flies. I scuffed a black ribbon of gut into the dust of the path, and as I took a further step other flies lifted blackly from a board laid out with dark and sinewy flesh.

The smell was bad, my neck was beginning to sting with sunburn, and I was way beyond anywhere that could still be described as the market. With determined illogic, I decided to continue. I turned my shirt collar up. A hundred yards beyond me the sea appeared between low roofs, stale and glittering, and I followed the narrowing path through the hutments towards a jetty to which fishing boats were moored and on which a transistor radio was blaring the last chords of 'Pyari Pyari'.

At the near end of this jetty, women were arranging shrimps and fish to dry in the sun, and some way beyond them a number of men were clustered around something that had been laid out on the concrete. I stopped, as the salted rotten stink hit me with a warm thump. The Koli shrimp-women straightened slowly, frowning. The furthest one shouted in Marathi to the men, who raised their heads. The nearest Koli stepped towards me. It was, I realised, the same woman as I had seen fighting on Ridge Road two days before, although there seemed something harder, tireder, more cracked-face, about her.

'What do you want?' she shouted in hoarse Marathi.

'Nothing,' I replied shortly, in Hindi, 'I was looking.'

She continued towards me. Behind her the other women, and beyond them the men, were staring at me. One of the men detached himself from the others and started walking along the jetty towards me. He was carrying something.

'What do you want?' she asked again, more quietly.

'I saw you yesterday,' I said, 'fighting with the Waghre. By the Hanging Garden.'

She frowned at me. I wasn't sure whether she understood me. She looked behind her, saw the man approaching, and started screaming at me.

'Go away. Go. Now.'

She had stained and broken teeth. I stepped backwards. I was suddenly no longer certain that she was the same woman that I had seen. I turned away at the moment that the man started shouting, and started back up the path. I was sure that I wouldn't be attacked but part of me was suddenly not so sure. As I turned the first corner and stopped smelling the fish and starting smelling the gut-pile I heard their shouts behind me and then their swearing and then, a step or two later, something that could have been laughter but was worse than everything that had gone before it.

I stepped out of Kemp's Chemist, avoiding a cadaverous and obviously heroin-addicted Western beggar, and climbed back into the taxi. As the driver restarted the black and yellow car I shook the Calamine bottle and poured a pink, chalky pool into the palm of my hand. Carefully, like a Maxim's waiter supporting a tray, I manoeuvred this hand behind my head and palmed the lotion on to the sunburn. As I leaned forward, the driver switched on a small dashboard-mounted fan whose breeze, exquisitely, found the back of my neck. I closed my eyes.

By the time I opened them again the Calamine was setting in a cool skim and we were moving at speed up Marine Drive between the big Thirties apartment blocks and the sea. I considered. Tomorrow I would ring up and make an appointment to meet the cinema critic of the *Times of India*. Shouldn't be a problem. Not, of course, that there was any desperate hurry about all this; time, I couldn't help smiling to myself, was on my side. Still, it would be nice to have things, well, under way at least, by the time that shooting for *Khandaan* started.

I should have known, of course, that things could not be as easy as they'd seemed. There had to be more to locating someone like Lakshmi Khandekar than riding in a taxi to an address printed on the opening page of *Cinestar*. On the other hand, today had not been entirely wasted; I had met Lata Khandekar, and she seemed to have liked me. Enough, at any rate, to invite me to dinner in that extraordinary ocean liner of an apartment. Was it to be dinner, cocktails? Sidecars and stiff Manhattans over Colaba Causeway? Unlikely. What then, and with whom? Lata Khandekar couldn't have had much time for the whiskied favour-broking and self-congratulatory flatulence of the Bombay professional set. Maybe I would be meeting some sapphically adoring young social worker in a cotton sari or some humourlessly brilliant graduate from the Poona Film Institute . . . For the next fifty hours at least, I had a mystery to enjoy. And of those fifty hours, my thoughts bubbled vaguely, of those fifty-odd hours, I intended to spend at least the next two and a half lying face down and neck up on my mattress, eyes closed, shutters closed, fan moving overhead . . .

'You could be the one,' she whispers, 'you could be him. I think that I've been waiting for you and I think that I, mmmmm . . . that I'm telling you that I . . .'

I kiss her spine, my lips touch the warm crest of her vertebrae, lift the translucent curl at the base of her neck, and I can't answer. I am being short-circuited; a concern has been lodged by some voice within, and my response has been frozen by its logic. Listen, the voice is saying (levelly, as if reading from a book), the point is this. The point to bear in mind at this moment is that *you* went to *her* in the gallery, you chose her, she didn't choose you. And it hasn't been long. There's still a lot she doesn't know about you and your . . . let's call them your circumstances, OK?

Now, if it hadn't been you that evening, if, let's say, someone else had spoken to her before you did, wouldn't she now be saying these same things at this very moment to someone else two miles away, in, say, Camberwell or Fulham or Ladbroke Grove? OK, maybe not Fulham, but face it, this drowsy body that you are now learning in such fretful detail, whose pulsing and unshivered surfaces are, for now, yours to make shiver and contract and weep, could easily be, right now, being smudged and blurred and scoured by some bond-dealer or cardio-thoracic surgeon or, face it, some *director* . . . (Once the voice begins, I have to hear it out, the whole spiel, the whole spool. I have to.)

. . . It obviously doesn't take much, you know. Or much time. Thousands of people could have been hearing the words she's just spoken, moving their lips HERE as they listen, and just because right now you're the one doesn't mean to say that the rest of those thousands aren't out there, waiting, that there isn't the drying saliva of a thousand other men beneath your lips at this very moment . . . (Here it comes, the deep logic.) . . . The question is this. Just how far can you trust the emotional judgement of someone who has put aside the armour of distance as readily as she has. You *know* there are things she hasn't told you . . . we've established that, haven't we, surely? (Nastier, chillier, the voice now. Commoner.) Be honest, and LOOK AT YOURSELF . . . It's for your sake that I'm saying this, OK? Just bale out, hit the clouds face first, flatten out, slide sideways . . .

What I can't understand is why the voice, usually so distinguished, should be so plebeian. It's usually an amiable barrister-like sort of a voice, but what I'm getting now is some nightmare pub philosopher using longer words than he's used to. I cut, blinking, to Emilia, who tells me that just for a moment there I was miles away and what was I thinking about and did I hear what she just said which is that she loves me and that she would ask only one thing of me and that's time, and as she turns to me her breathing is suddenly faster and her breath clouds . . .

By the time I arrived at the club the heat had gone from the sun. On the court by the entrance the volleyball group were just beginning the elaborate pantomime of arm-punching, joshing, and shadow-boxing with which they announced to each other that they'd maybe had enough volleyball for the day.

Very few users of the club, it has to be said, were actively concerned with their health. It would probably not be true to say that the volleyball players were entirely unconcerned for their health, but they were much more concerned for their appearance. Playing volleyball (no girls or women played volleyball) allowed the group to stalk the Nepean Sea Bathing Club premises in a combination of tight bathing costume, socks, and baseball boots, that no other activity would have permitted. There had been a volleyball group as long as I could remember, and they had always dressed in this way and they had always seemed to play more volleyball than they did anything else in their whole lives.

There were the sons, mostly, of Indian fathers and European mothers. Few of them had to work in the sense of having to physically attend a work establishment on a regular basis, but most, if pressed, could lay claim to some notional management position.

They collapsed into deckchairs with the jockish air of good men spent and in need of drinks. Their mixed blood meant that most of them were handsome, and I recognised one or two from the pages of *Cinestar* where they had been employed to advertise cigarettes and deodorants. Inevitably, I suppose, there was a fat boy, and inevitably he was the richest of them all. He was tolerated, carried the cassette tape recorder, and paid for most of the drinks. There had always been a fat boy acting as acolyte to the volleyball players.

As I walked up the path leading beneath the wild almond trees to the clubhouse, I understood the reason why the volleyball players had collapsed into the particular group of deckchairs that they had collapsed into. Sitting in the shade of the trees beyond them a pale clutch of Russian Embassy wives was applying frosted lipsticks and blue eye-shadows and drinking freshlime sodas, and although nothing was going to happen immediately there was a tension between the two groups of the sort that the volleyball players liked to feed off.

Beyond the Russians, and sitting by herself, a woman in a red bikini was reading a magazine. Although she made no sign of being aware of the presence of either the male or the female group behind her, she was unmistakably within their ambit, part of the cat's cradle of mutual consciousness beneath the trees. The club had always had this quiet way of denying complete anonymity to its visitors; Bombay, as Das had said, was a small town.

I'd seen the woman in the red bikini the day before. She had spent the afternoon sunbathing on the far side of the pool, at the furthest possible point from the clubhouse, and as far as I had noticed, had spoken to no one for the whole afternoon. By the time I had been wakened by Pearcey she had vanished.

Now, as I passed her, she removed her sunglasses. Her face, beneath them, was expressionless, and she didn't look at me. She was about twenty-nine or thirty, I supposed, tanned and grey-eyed, her eyebrows and the roots of her hair darker than the pulled-back blonde crop, the body long and brown like a swimmer's. I somehow immediately knew that she was both American and the real target of the noisy pantomime behind her.

Two of the players passed me on the way to the clubhouse. They had a long-focused way of walking that seemed to avoid the eyes of an audience while simultaneously condoning its interest and accepting it as the inevitable consequence of beauty such as theirs.

I followed them into the café on the ground floor, where they ordered half a dozen Thums-Ups and I ordered a Bulbul.

A hot afternoon was turning into a warm evening. In the café the ceiling fans turned, and beneath them the tablecloths lifted and fell in their draught. At the tables men and women sat facing silently outwards, towards the sea. Their cigarette smoke rose thinly above them and was whirled invisible by the fans.

Outside on the lawns, the sprinklers had been turned off. Beyond the darkening grass the pool was still turquoise, although the colour was leaving it fast. A soft purple was banking over the horizon, and beneath it an iron-feathered sea pitched dark and silent.

A waiter brought a bottle of Bulbul to my table. Because of the turning fans it was quieter to sit outside. I also preferred not to sit below the electric lights which, I knew, would be turned on at any minute. I lit a cigarette, the match flashing before my eyes, and listened to the soft electric squeak of the fruitbats. I wondered, vaguely, what I was going to say to Cuckoo when she returned from Mahabaleshwar. I thought about Lata Khandekar, alone with her servant in that sad, grand, oddly familiar apartment. I suddenly decided to tell her the whole truth about my presence in Bombay, but the moment passed; I could only, I realised, move forward alone, and the image of Lata Khandekar was replaced by that of the actress who so nearly shared her name. I saw Lakshmi Khandekar standing at the tall window in *Zakhmi*, looking out into the invisible bank of lights, and saw her turning, reaching out to me. I crushed my cigarette into the ashtray until all the sparks were extinguished and the picture had disappeared. It was essential, I told myself, to remember that Lakshmi Khandekar was real, flesh and blood, and probably less than two miles away from me at this moment. I looked up the coast towards Juhu. She wasn't far, I was sure.

Under the trees behind me, with the usual handshaking, back-slapping and theatre, the volleyball players were leaving. As they went, the fat boy fumbled in his pocket for the waiter's tip and struggled with the heavy cassette player; behind him, the Russian women were moving in the opposite direction towards the clubhouse. The American woman was nowhere to be seen. The wild almond trees were black against the sky.

I turned back. Touched with the last light the diving boards stood between the dying turquoise of the pool and the colder iron of the sea. I sat without moving until there was no longer a horizon, and then took the bottle by the neck and climbed the stairs to the bar.

V

ᔕᔕᔕᔕᔕᔕ

'Film-shooting, Madam? Going to the shooting? This way, please.'

Kimmie Kitzinger and I followed the group out of the hotel doors and into the heat of the car-park.

By now I knew some of the women by sight. Kimmie knew all of them, of course, they met up regularly for this kind of thing. As they climbed into the bus, Kimmie whispered names to me, most of which I immediately forgot.

The film studios, though, I had particularly wanted to see. Beth had mentioned the trip almost hesitantly, but to her pleased surprise I'd leapt at the idea, despite what I was sure would be the breathlessly all-girl tenor of the occasion. I'd never sat through a Hindi movie but I'd heard that they were monumentally kitsch; all glycerine tears, showgirls in wet saris, and overweight Lone Rangers. Definitely worth a visit, if only to describe in a postcard to Grace.

'When I went before,' Kimmie announced as we passed the Haji Ali Mosque, 'we were all asked to be extras; it was kind of fun. Some of the girls went on to a hotel in Juhu to shoot a scene by the pool there, as well.'

'Wow,' said Amy Alvarez, who worked for a bank but acted so dumb I was sure she was really a CIA agent, 'that must've been neat.'

'Abso-lutely,' said Kimmie, 'those actors are not all fat little guys in high heels, you know. Some of the younger ones definitely fall into the gorgeous category.'

Since Amy's husband Benny was a fat little guy whose Cuban heels left little horseshoe shapes all over Beth's hotel suite whenever the couple dropped by, this last was something of a Kimmie classic. Amy went quiet, frowning out of the window at the sea, and after two long beats of silence the consul's daughter, whose name was Biffy or Buffy or Tufty, very quickly and firmly started telling a story about some film-production people she'd met at the Radio Club.

At Mahim Bridge we got stuck in traffic. The smell was dreadful; a rank blend of exhaust and sewage. Nobody said anything, but noses were wrinkled and windows closed.

'Have you ever been in a film, June?' asked Kimmie, when we finally got moving again. 'June was a ballet dancer,' she added to the others.

There were murmurs of 'Oh, how lovely', 'Mmmm', 'Wow', and 'Oh, I used to DREAM of being a — '

'I've been on television a few times,' I answered. 'And I was once in a Tampax commercial.'

'Glory be!' said Kimmie. 'What did you have to do?'

'Well, it was one of those sequences to show that even if you had your period you could still, should the need arise, dive from hundred-foot cliffs, ride runaway horses, or dance the Act Two variation from *Swan Lake* in a white tutu. Which was where I came in.'

'Was it fun?' Kimmie asked.

'It earned me quite a lot of money. I nearly got sacked from the company, though, for doing it without permission. Which,' I smiled, 'I definitely wouldn't have been given . . .'

'And what was the television?'

'Oh just, you know, performances of the classics: *Giselle, Sleeping Beauty, Swan Lake* and so on. Not starring me, unfortunately.'

'But you've given up, now?' asked a woman of about my own age who had a silk scarf from Paris around her shoulders. Embassy, I thought.

'Er, yes, I have, really.'

'Do you know what you're going to do next?'

'Well, that's sort of what I've come over here to think about.'

'Right, right. So where're you staying, June?'

'June's Beth Conroy's sister,' Kimmie answered on my behalf, 'she's staying back at the hotel with Beth and Dane.'

'It's funny,' said Amy Alvarez, 'Beth never mentioned a ballet-dancing sister.'

'Well, there you go,' I said. 'Out of sight, out of — '

The bus lurched through a pot-hole and we clutched each other, disentangling ourselves with apologetic little laughs.

'June, forgive my asking, I don't mean to pry,' the scarf-woman leant forward to me as the bus swayed again, 'but you've got a very kinda BRITISH accent there . . .'

'Well, Lauren,' I explained, suddenly remembering her name, 'I haven't actually lived in the States since I was seven. With ballet school and the company and everything in London, I just sort of . . . stayed put.'

'I see. Well, it's an interesting life you've had.'

'It's not over yet,' I said, brightly.

By the time we passed the airport, conversation had rather flagged. Seeing the road again in the daylight I thought of how unsettling I'd found it on the night of my arrival. Even in the light of day there was something desperate about the windowless concrete towers and the undrained fields.

'Would you rather live in a hut, Kimmie,' I asked, 'or in one of those blocks?'

'Why, June, you do ask the strangest questions. I most sincerely hope I never have to live in either.'

'But which, if you had to choose?'

There was silence for a moment or two.

'How long is it that you've been here now?' Kimmie asked me.

At the roadside a line of camels was being led past a bus-stop. That caused a moment's excitement.

Our visit to the studio had been timed so that there was lunch as soon as we arrived. As we left the bus we were introduced to a group of rather preoccupied-looking film people who had clearly, moments before, been arguing.

A production assistant sat us down in a line along one side of a trestle table, under a tree. Food arrived immediately; all of us refused the water and so cold drinks were brought. Nobody had thought to bring knives and forks, though, so with varying degrees of skill and experience we dived in with our hands. The film people, all smiles now, walked over and sat down opposite us. At my side I felt Kimmie kick my ankle.

'Right hand, June, not both.'

Beth had mentioned this, I remembered, in one of her cultural briefings. Fine, but what was I to do with my unclean left hand, by now dripping with chicken gravy. Fuck it, I thought, and sucked my fingers.

I looked up to find a tall dark-skinned man watching me with sad amusement. I shrugged and held up both hands like a black and white minstrel. He turned his head and spoke a single word to a subordinate who hurried away, returning a minute later with a paper napkin and a single spoon.

'Thanks,' I said, 'I'm not very good at this.'

On my left flank, eyeing me with rather tense concern, was Lauren. Despite the ease with which she was managing the food, I noticed that there was already a spot of gravy on her Hermes scarf. Well, I thought, getting stuck in with the spoon, I hope it was worth it.

As the meal progressed, we made elaborately courteous conversation with our hosts. I discovered that the pretty, intense girl opposite me was called Priya and had the second lead in the film. It was her first *masala* picture, she explained.

'What's a *masala* picture?' I asked.

'That's what we call these big commercial pictures. *Masala* means mixed spice, and these pictures have a sort of . . . pinch of everything in them. *Masala* also suggests that they have steamy scenes in them, although this one doesn't. Or at least if it does,' she laughed, 'I haven't been told about it.'

'Saving the big rape scene till last, huh?'

'June!' said Kimmie, next to me.

Priya laughed. 'Please, don't give them ideas! Although in fact I could always use a double.'

'They have doubles for rape scenes?'

'Oh, yes.'

'Women who just sort of ring an agency and say "Hi, where am I being raped today?"'

'JUNE!' said Kimmie, kicking me again.

Stupid girl. My legs have always bruised easily.

But I liked Priya immediately. She had got into films, she explained, through being a television news presenter. She had been spotted by a director and given the lead, untried, in an art-house picture.

'It was a distinguished failure at the box office. But that's as much as you can hope for, really, in the parallel cinema.'

'Parallel?'

'Means arty, non-commercial-type pictures.'

'People want the *masala*?' I asked.

'People want the *masala*.'

A servant brought a bowl full of mangoes to the table. One by one my compatriots refused them.

'Have one,' said Priya, 'they're Alphonsos.'

'Who's Alphonso?' I asked.

'No, they're called Alphonso mangoes. Go on, try one. They're the best.'

'I'd love one,' I said, 'but I'll get juice all over myself. I'll disgrace my country. I'll be sent home.'

Priya took a mango from the bowl, sniffed it, called for a knife, and deftly carved it into two inside-out halves.

'Brilliant,' I said.

She answered with a smile and an Indian phrase.

'What was that?'

'*Koi bat nahin.*'

'What does that mean?'

'It means: it's nothing, don't mention it.'

'*Koi bat nahin?*'

'*Koi bat nahin.*'

After lunch we were taken into the hangar-like building containing the sound stage. The set had been got up as a bandits' hide-out, with grey-painted papier-mâché rocks rising around a circular dance-floor area disguised as a clearing. A shot was being set up involving the heroine, a big-busted moon-faced girl in a sari, and the villain, a hairy-shouldered giant in a studded leather gladiator's outfit, ginger toupee, and sunglasses.

The director was standing in the clearing, discussing the shot with the cameraman; we all stood around rather awkwardly for a minute or two before being shown to chairs.

'June,' whispered Kimmie, two minutes later, 'I have to find the little girls' room. Will you come with me?'

'Sure,' I said, picking mango fibres from my teeth, 'let's go.'

We picked our way over electrical cables and between stacked boxes of equipment. Outside, in the sunshine, a woman was sweeping the ground in an aimless sort of way. I was sure she wouldn't speak English.

'Toilet?' I asked. 'Bathroom?'

She smiled and spread her hands in incomprehension. At that moment Priya came out of a small bungalow.

'Please,' she said, 'help yourself. In here.'

'Thanks,' said Kimmie. She looked back over her shoulder.

'I'll be fine, June,' she called back to me, 'see you back inside.'

Priya smiled at me and, followed by a woman carrying a basket full of hair-dressing equipment, disappeared into the hangar.

Knowing just how long film set-ups took, I decided to have a look round.

The studio was a dusty and well-trodden area of several acres, surrounded by a perimeter wall, and dominated by the sound stage. Inside a grandiose brick and wrought-iron gateway a line of identical white cars was drawn up. Their front doors were open; their drivers lay asleep across the seats.

Around the entrance were several small brick and thatch bungalows. Offices, I thought, or dressing rooms. All looked deserted. Beyond them stood an exterior set. This must have last been used for some Himalayan scene, but the grey and white painted peaks now hung in tattered folds from the wooden spars. Even when brand-new, I thought, it can't have looked too realistic.

As I watched from near the gate, some fifteen girls dressed in bright peasanty costumes and carrying plastic bags and tambourines made their way over to the set from a long side-building. They were followed by a small bald man carrying a cassette tape recorder.

Dancers, I thought. Know them anywhere.

Without any particular haste they took their places on the floor of the set. The choreographer lit a cigarette and counted them into the routine. I was surprised to see how jazzy the choreography was, especially considering the costumes. While the hips and arms and veils were what Grace would have called your basic Fry's Turkish Delight, the legwork was pure Broadway, and ended in a swirl of skirts with a pirouette to the knee. As the choreographer took them through the piece a second time, I found myself learning the routine.

One girl in a turquoise outfit, I saw, couldn't get the ending, she kept getting on to the wrong foot and turning a count late. The third time this happened the choreographer stopped the tape with a stab of the thumb and made as if to slap her.

Bastard, I thought. I've met YOU often enough.

The next time through, everyone was step-perfect except for the one girl.

Instead of breaking the step down, the choreographer simply pulled her out of the line and ran through the routine once more without her. Then he nodded, picked up the cassette player, and followed by the others, sauntered off towards the sound stage. The girl in turquoise, uncertain whether to follow, stayed where she was. No one looked back at her.

When she saw me walking towards her, she jumped. I saw that she was very young, no more than fifteen or sixteen, and close to tears. Pimples studded her face beneath the thick make-up.

I took her by the wrist. She was terrified.

'Look,' I said, 'watch me. Even if you can't understand a word I'm saying, OK? Slowly now. A-a-a-nd . . . Coupé right and over, coupe second and fourth and en dehors, tambourine and knee. There. Now you do it.'

She did it wrong.

'Look,' I said, 'weight on the right foot to start. No, pet, other right foot. Watch.'

I showed her again. Saw her eyes understand.

'Now you,' I said.

She did it right.

'Again.'

She did it right.

'Again.'

She did it right.

'Very impressive.'

I turned round. It was the sad-eyed man who'd got me the spoon at lunch. He had changed into an all-black outfit. Black shirt, black jeans, black boots. Sunglasses. He didn't look entirely ridiculous.

'Oh, you know . . .' I shrugged, 'just lending a hand. A leg.'

I could tell from the open mouth of the turquoise girl that this suavo character was important.

'You're an actor.'

'I'm an actor, yes.'

'You're the lead, right?'

'I'm,' he smiled ironically, 'what we call a hero, yes.'

Behind the sunglasses he was staring at my breasts.

'Could you do something?' I asked. 'Could you get to see that this girl gets to do the dance number, she couldn't pick it up but now she has and they've gone without her . . .'

'It's OK,' he said, 'I'm in that scene too. I'll see she's there.' Without looking at the girl he spoke to her in Hindi; she nodded, smiling, and, turning to go, touched my hand.

'Thank you, Madam.'

'Don't mention it,' I called after her. '*Koi bat nahin!*'

'You speak Hindi as well as you dance? You should go into films.'

'That's my lot, I'm afraid. Priya taught it to me at lunch. But tell me something. That girl, what would have happened to her?'

'Oh, she'd have been paid,' he shrugged. 'They have unions and all that.'

'That choreographer was pretty vile to her.'

'You shouldn't blame the choreographer. He has one hour's rehearsal and a full routine to deliver. Better a dancer short than a whole production number ruined. Retakes and all. You can't hold fifty people up for one dancer.'

'Is everybody waiting for you, right now?'

He smiled, nodded. 'I expect so.'

'Hadn't we better get over there?'

'It won't hurt them to wait.' He took off his sunglasses and rubbed his eyes. He looked tired. In the distance a line of gladiators, many of them carrying automatic weapons, were making their way into the hangar. 'I'm afraid I didn't catch your name at lunch.' He opened his hands conspiratorially. 'All those people . . .'

'I'm June Webster, what's your name.'

'I'm Sanjay. Sanjay Saxena.'

'Well, thanks for the spoon, Sanjay.'

'I'm sorry?'

'Spoon. At lunch. I was struggling. You got me a spoon.'

'My pleasure, June.' Again the tired smile. 'Do you know what the word is for spoon in Hindi?'

'No, what is it?'

'*Chamchah*. The word usually just means spoon, but it has a second meaning of . . . what's the English word for someone who follows you around everywhere and agrees with everything you say?'

'Creep? Flatterer? Yes-man?'

'A yes-man, yes. See, that's really the trouble with this business. Too many yes-men.' He took a half-step towards me; I moved the same distance backwards.

'Why do the words mean the same?'

'I beg your pardon?'

'Why should the word for spoon and yes-man be the same?'

'I suppose they both . . . A *chamchah*, I guess, is someone who literally feeds you by hand, like a spoon. See, June, I used to have quite a good sense of humour before people started laughing at every joke I made. Now I'm not quite so sure.'

Had I missed something, I wondered.

'Well,' I said, 'if you find you've got too many guys laughing at your jokes, send a couple of them over to me. My jokes need all the help they can get.'

'I'm sure you make wonderful jokes, June.'

I looked over at him. He had applied an actorish curl to the corner of his mouth and there was a patient directness to his stare. Give me a break, I thought, I'm thirty-one years old.

'If ever I think of anything funny to say,' I folded my arms over my breasts as his eyes drifted downwards, 'it's always long after everyone's gone home.'

The closeness of his attention made me feel I was speaking gibberish.

'And where is home?' he asked after a small pause.

'Um, London. Baron's Court. I've had the same flat for fifteen years, actually.' I'm talking too much, I thought. Too many words.

He rocked on his feet.

'Really, is that unusual?'

'Quite, I think, for London. For a single person.'

He digested this. 'And where are you staying in Bombay?'

'With my sister and her husband. At the President, in Cuffe Parade.'

'Everything OK there?' he asked.

'Supposing I said No,' I answered, 'what would you do?'

He laughed. From the direction of the dressing rooms a guffawing, backslapping delegation was approaching us.

'*Chamchas?*' I asked.

'*Chamchas,*' he confirmed, looking tired again. 'I have to go to work.'

'For your sins,' I added.

'I'm sorry?'

'You have to go to work. For your sins. It's one of those things they say.'

'Well, I expect they're right. Come on.'

'You go on,' I said, 'I'll be there in a minute.'

I had just realised, from a drift of sourmash breath, that Sanjay Saxena was drunk. I moved purposefully towards the car-park, to avoid meeting the spoons.

'I'll BET!' said Kimmie, swivelling towards me on her canvas chair. 'You sly old dog, June.'

'I just ran into him outside. I had no idea he was anyone so famous. Besides which, he was pissed.'

'June, why? What did you say to him?'

'No, I mean he was pissed in the British, drunk as a skunk, sense.'

'No, really? Wow. Because this guy Saxena is one of the biggest stars in India. Sort of the voice of the Comman Man, standing up for Decency and Truth against Corruption. He's married to an ex-actress, Shakuntala Karkar, who's regarded practically as a saint, although everyone knows that he's been having a long on-off affair with another actress called Swaroop.'

On the set the lights swooped to near darkness, then powered up to full brightness.

'Kimmie, I just don't believe it that you know all this stuff.'

'Oh, after we came here last time and were, like, introduced to all these stars, well, after that I picked up one of those film magazines and just . . . kind of got interested. It's a real Hollywood soap opera. I buy all the mags every week, now. Ray thinks it's all really stupid, but I like it.'

'Well, I think that's . . . great.'

'That's why I was going on at you at lunch. That girl Priya was supposed to have been raped by some producer in his hotel, somewhere in the South. There was a big *tamasha*, a big kerfuffle that is, but nothing was proved, and it all died down after a bit.'

'Oh God,' I groaned.

'QUIET ON THE SET, PLEASE. FIRST POSITIONS.'

'Forget it,' whispered Kimmie, 'she wouldn't have thought you — '

'ROLL CAMERAS. ACTION.'

The bandit camp sprang to life. After delivering himself of a roaring and unmistakably villainous speech, the gladiator type, attended by two scowling henchmen in shortie leopardskin tunics, tied up his drenched and swooning captive. Despite only token resistance on her part, he performed this task with considerable zeal and very great attention to detail. Gagged, bound to an iron ring set into the rock, she was a helpless spectator of the campfire song-and-dance number that followed, in which, bless her little cotton socks, Pimples danced her heart out.

'Tell me about Lauren Weiss,' said Beth, 'what was she wearing?' Framed by the window opposite her bed, the sun was sliding into the Arabian Sea. Beth was pleased with me.

'Oh, she had just these pressed jeans and little snaffly shoes and a sky-blue Lacoste T-shirt and an Hermes scarf round her shoulders which she got gravy on at lunch and ended up tying round the chain of her handbag.'

'Chanel? Gucci?'

'What?'

'The bag.'

'Fendi,' I said, 'and real, I think. Not from the shop by the Taj where you got yours.'

'Did she look good?'

'She looked gracious. She was introduced to everyone first. She makes me feel slightly boondocky. As if England were a sort of un-fashionable Midwestern state where nothing you achieved really counted.'

'Oh, June. I'm sure not . . .' Beth frowned vaguely at the window. 'But Kimmie. Did she enjoy it?'

'She turned out to be some kind of expert on the whole thing. When I — '

The phone rang by the bed. Beth lifted the receiver from the hook, listened, and covered the mouthpiece.

'Talk of the devil,' she mouthed.

I stood up from the bed and walked over to catch the last of the sunset. It had been a hot day. For no very good reason that I could think of, I felt very slightly depressed. From time to time, as she listened, Beth looked up at me.

VI

〰〰〰

The time by my non-luminous luminous watch was eight o'clock. In the morning. Good. I had woken at a reasonable time, my body-clock was adjusted, and apart from the Bulbul Pilsner beating at my temples and the dry Chesterfield mouth I felt systemically sound.

Cuckoo had returned from Mahabaleshwar late, while I had been at the club. She had gone straight to bed, leaving a note to say that we would see each other in the morning. I had, I supposed, about half an hour before Anubai or Baby came to wake me. I had to do what I had been putting off doing for the last few jetlagged days, and pull the strings of my life together; draw up some sort of mental profit-and-loss sheet.

But which was which? Was Emilia a loss? Or had my actions, apropos of her, been to my (or her) profit? Elements of my present situation, I thought, were equally ambiguous.

Definite profit, then: I was in Bombay with a working visa and a very adequate amount of money at my disposal. My project, the development of the Lakshmi Khandekar film, was comfortably achievable. As soon as I got hold of Lakshmi, which shouldn't be too difficult (Bombay being, as Das said, a small town) I would quickly persuade her of the virtues of the film. I was sure that she would be compliant, enthusiastic, and generally pleased, there being much in it for her (at the very least) in the way of publicity, status, Western connection, and so on.

I was also sure I could make a good film. I had a foot comfortably in both camps; I knew my way around Bombay, and had a very exact knowledge of the requirements of British television. And I could live here at Cuckoo's, I thought, for as long as I wanted.

Loss. Everything to do with returning to England, as would surely eventually be necessary. If the film was made, I would have to return to London to edit it. And in London, for me, there was nothing. London I had cut away.

Would it be better if the film was never actually made?

Loss. Emilia. I had to think about what I had done.

It had been a complete coincidence that we'd both been in the Corporation building at the same time. I'd been called to a meeting with a commissioning editor and had decided to have lunch in the canteen. Maybe, I had thought vaguely, I might run into someone I knew.

It was wondering about former colleagues that had led me to glance at the noticeboard outside the lift. When Emilia's name leapt at me from a long list headed STUDIO 4, 7.30 a.m. *Bacchae* (Maenads), I realised that this was the walk-on part for which she'd left the flat before I'd been awake that morning. She'd mentioned it to me ('some Euripides thing') the night before, and ritually unamused by my 'Euripides trousers' crack, delivered in the Mediterranean English accent about which she was still sensitive, she had gone to bed early.

I'd stayed up late watching a very bad videotape print of *Mera Dost, Mera Dushman* in order to make a final decision about the Bombay project.

Film stars. By two o'clock in the morning I'd been convinced that the couple of million Britons who would eventually watch our film would indeed fall for the sad, dark eyes of Lakshmi Khandekar. There was a glamour about her, an ability to enchant, which made a believable world even of Saiyad Ali's leery, sadistic picture. As I lay in bed beside Emilia, later, her hair and face dark against the sheets, I thought of the other lives that I might have been living. I thought of the corner of Bombay which, until I had been seven years old, had been my whole world. It had been a world of happy confusions and certainties whose fracturing, I was sometimes sure, had been one of destiny's aberrations. That life had been intended to continue. There were even times when I imagined that, in some parallel world, it WAS continuing. Lakshmi Khandekar, or at least her reproduced image on celluloid, seemed curiously familiar; seemed to correspond to someone I might have known in that distant parallel life.

This life, however, was Emilia. She was there, she was love, she was all. I desperately feared losing her. I feared losing her when I should have been loving her, because, the truth was, I couldn't believe that she loved the myopic, uncertain figure beside whom she woke up every day.

And there were the voices which, even here and even now, still spoke behind my closed eyes, still pressed their insinuating logic.

There was an impossibility, I recognised, about the architecture of such jealousy. But I continued, even so, to pace its endlessly repeating parapets.

The light above the door of Studio Four turns green. I push the heavy doorway into darkness; another door, a soft hydraulic wind, and into a further and wider darkness hung with cables, the rearing backs of sets, and further, at a distance, higher, angled lights suspended from a vast, tracked ceiling. A figure, female I think, wearing headphones and carrying a clipboard, passes in front of me, speaking rapidly into a small transmitting microphone which is angled in front of her mouth. She walks with silent and almost dramatic floating purpose over the matt grey flooring and towards the edge of a circular pool of light some distance away, at the centre of the studio floor. At the outside edge of this light, facing inwards, are television cameras with attendants and operators; cables snake into the darkness behind them. Above them a third camera, unattended, is mounted on a crane. Disposed within the circle, not moving, waiting, presumably speaking to each other although at this distance their faces are blank and expressionless beneath the light, are the actors. They are dressed, variously, in white cotton tunics, shifts. None of them is Emilia. There seems to be no set other than the grey of the floor and the blackness beyond. Standing in the half-dark are a dozen or so technicians and several others whose function, even to my reasonably accustomed eye, is unclear. One is smoking, the cigarette held behind his back. From time to time they speak, laugh, nod. They do this soundlessly; I can hear nothing from where I am standing, but even at this distance I am aware of a sense of sluggish technical purpose; a sense that something, before long, is going to happen.

'Sahib?' There was a small but insistent knock on the door.

Baby.

'Sahib? *Aiyey*, Sahib, breakfas'.'

Cuckoo was not yet down. I wrapped a cotton lunghi round my waist, hurried into the small black-and-white-tiled bathroom with its sloping floor, and poured a bucketful of tepid tap-water over my head. Taking my glasses from the shelf holding the Odomos insect repellant and the Ayurvedic toothpaste I polished them with a towel and grimaced at myself in the mirror. The blurred head and shoulders looked reasonably presentable, if a rather unsatisfactory colour. I replaced the glasses and faced a more focused portrait.

As a child I had had a clockwork hedgehog. On its back, to simulate prickles, the manufacturers had glued a silvery-brown fuzzy-felt. My newly cut hair, I thought, now looked exactly like this hedgehog's back, while my face, freckled and pale-eyed behind the glasses, remained a rather foolish sunburnt pink. I had always envied the olive-skinned, the easily tanned.

'If you could see your SMILE,' Emilia had used to say, 'you might see yourself the way that I see you.'

But of course I never had.

Baby brought my tea on to the terrace. It was high tide; a line of washermen sat smoking on the sea wall. Below them I could hear the sea dragging at the rocks.

'Stanley!'

Cuckoo, tiny, permed and pearly-eyed in a faded cotton print dress that she had owned as long as I could remember, walked towards me, arms open. I stood, and bent forward to hold her narrow shoulders and kiss her pale cheeks. She was faintly perfumed, as always, with Lakmé eau-de-Cologne. Behind her, Anubai was smiling in her oblique way; Baby, suddenly shy, was holding her mother's hand.

'You got back last night?' I asked unnecessarily.

'Ten o'clock or so. The coach dropped us by Metro Cinema, and I caught a bus back from there.'

I was suddenly guilty. I could easily have found out what time the coach was expected, been there to meet her, taken her home in a taxi.

'I'm sorry, I should have — '

'Stanley, it's quite all right. These coaches are usually hours late, I deliberately didn't give you the arrival time.'

She looked at me with a half-smile. 'Besides, if I'd needed you I'd have known exactly where to find you. Which table, even. You're a creature of habit, Stanley Collinson.'

I was appalled at myself for not thinking. Thought of her dragging the heavy suitcase from the coach to the bus-stop.

'Stanley, it's all right. Really. Now, how are you?'

'I'm well. I'm fine.'

'You look well. You also look as if . . . well.'

'Look as if what?' I smiled.

'Oh, nothing you won't tell me yourself, sooner or later, I'm sure. Now, sit please. Have some sweet-lime.'

I held out her chair, and we sat down.

'How was Mahabaleshwar?' I asked.

'The weather was good. A nice breeze. Mosquitoes were bad. Very bad. And a strange thing. Do you remember that servant of Bapsi's who used to give foot massage, the one I told you about last time whose daughter married the cook who beat her, well, apparently, all this time . . .'

Cuckoo had an inexhaustible supply of servant stories. Horror stories of servants who kidnapped children, stole the laundry, drank country liquor, prostituted themselves, and poisoned the food. With the possible exception of Anubai, she trusted none of them.

I looked out to sea. It was another hot, blank overcast day. Beyond the sea wall the first laundry of the day was being hung from long lines supported by poles. The tankers had disappeared from the horizon.

'. . . and selling the empty bottles to the bootleggers. She had been systematically robbing them for years!' Cuckoo turned to me triumphantly. I smiled at her.

'You haven't changed, Cuckoo. Still the scourge of the servant classes.'

'Which of us changes?' she asked, suddenly serious. 'Not you,' she smiled again, 'you still only listen to every third word I say.'

'That's not true,' I said.

'I'm only teasing you, Stanley. Really I am. Tell me about this film you're making.'

I told her.

It didn't take long, and she listened attentively, occasionally lifting her teacup to her mouth with a slender pale-blotched hand. Cuckoo had been born with leucoderma, a skin pigment deficiency which caused patches of her face and hands to remain pale pink in contrast to the dark ivory of the rest of her skin. As a child I'd found it fascinating, as I had the dusty shadows beneath her eyes and the blue shingled hair which was attended to once a week by the Chinese beauty salon at Breach Candy, opposite the Nepean Sea Bathing Club. She looked no older now than when I'd last seen her five years ago, but then, to me, she'd never looked young. Nor could I have imagined her, with her Parsee thrift, her elephantine memory, living anywhere else than in this small dusty-seeming flat piled high with trunks, boxes and elderly furniture. (All Parsee apartments are full of boxes, a Zoroastrian novelist had once told me. 'You never get a Parsee household without boxes.')

'Why Lakshmi Khandekar?' asked Cuckoo. 'Even I've never heard of her. Why her? Why not Rekha or someone really well known?'

'I wanted someone starting out,' I explained. 'And I also think there's something special about this Lakshmi Khandekar. Something different, something . . . not so glitzy.'

'I thought glitzy was what you wanted.'

'Well, I wanted to show that it wasn't all like that.'

'I see. Except that I thought that it was all like that. But I don't know anything about films any more . . . I liked the old ones, *Pyaasa . . . Sahib Bibi Aur Gulam . . . Shree 420*. Actresses like Waheeda Rehman, Nargis and Meena Kumari. Meena Kumari was my favourite, you know she died just up the hill?'

'No,' I said, 'I didn't know.'

'She died, just . . .' She shrugged, appearing to drift away on her thoughts. 'These days I prefer gramophone records, anyway.' Looking up, she caught herself. 'You know who you should go and see? At the *Bombay Mail* the film critic is . . . do you remember Nelson D'Mello?'

'Hang on. Yes, I think so. Fat boy. Lived in one of those big houses in Laburnum Road.'

'That's right. He had an accident in his shorts at your seventh birthday party. I had to lend him a pair of yours. His mother never gave them back. And now he writes about films in the *Mail*.'

I laughed. 'Was that Nelson? I'll ring him up and remind him.'

'He could probably help you.'

'I'll ring him,' I promised.

I rang from the club. Once again it was almost deserted. The potted plants, which usually stood in dusty wooden boxes between the tables, had been taken outside on to the lawn, where they were being slowly watered by a peon. At the other end of the bar from where I was standing with the phone to my ear, a cleaner was making slow-motion movements with a broom.

The phone crackled. I had now been on hold for several minutes. 'D'Mello.'

His voice was a distant thread, as if from another continent.

'Nelson,' I half-shouted, 'you probably don't remember me, but it's Stanley. Stanley Collinson. We were at Don Bosco School together.' A waiter raised incurious eyes towards me. The earpiece roared emptily. 'Nelson, I've come over from London to research a documentary on the Bombay film industry. Could we meet? If you've got time?' The roaring became a hurricane, then abruptly stopped. The voice was suddenly close at hand.

' . . . name was?'

'Sorry,' I shouted, 'bad line. Collinson. Stanley Collinson, we were at — '

' . . . I know, I know, it's great to . . .'

'Can we meet, Nelson. Hello. HELLO?'

' . . . this evening. Sorry, this is a terrible line. Where . . .'

'The club?' I shouted. 'The Nepean Sea Bathing Club? Eight o'clock?'

' . . . o'clock. See . . .'

The line went dead. I replaced the Bakelite receiver and dropped two rupees into the tin.

On the far side of the swimming pool a tall blonde figure in a red bikini was picking her way between the deckchairs. As I watched, she arranged herself on a towel on the grass, face down, looking out to sea.

I went back down the path under the wild almond trees to the changing room. When I returned she hadn't moved. I dropped my clothes, towel, watch and glasses into one of the deckchairs on the lawn and lowered myself into the pool. Because of the salt water I was wearing goggles; the water itself was tepid, clouded, unrefreshing. I swam beneath the surface for a few strokes, examining the cracked and magnified base of the pool ten feet below me. Nelson D'Mello, I thought, would at the very least be able to put me on to somebody who was in touch with Lakshmi Khandekar. It would be interesting to meet someone who had known me then, to see what time had made of him. In my mind he was still a fat, rather worried-looking boy who carried his school books in a little tin suitcase.

I had to make this documentary, I thought; it would be self-destructive to think in any other terms. As I drifted through the blood-temperature water, elements of a plan began to form by which I could both edit the film and remain here in Bombay.

On the bottom of the pool my shadow crossed that of the single diving board. I pondered the logistics of the plan; it would certainly save Coldharbour a fair amount of money.

I wondered how I'd feel after I'd been here a month or two. I knew just how quickly, in India, curiosity could become torpor, optimism turn to irritated depression. When I'd made my last two departures, I'd been glad to leave. But this time was different. My life was restarting. I was determined for it to be so.

Salt water was trickling into one of the eyepieces of the goggles. Lifting my head from the water I pulled them away from my face and saw that I was no more than a yard from the edge of the pool. The woman in the red bikini was lying on her towel, face down, a short distance away. Without my glasses I could not see her clearly; her head seemed to be resting on her folded arms, her hair pulled back in some way from her face. I could not tell if her eyes were open or closed.

I turned away from her, treading water, adjusted the rubber strap of the goggles, and kicked off from the edge into an almost stationary backstroke. Above my head the crows turned in endless circles against the white sky.

London, with its sleeting streets, its emergencies, its early darkness, seemed incalculably distant, irrelevant.

*

'Beer?'

'Mr Das!'

'Victor, please. Or my friends call me Vicky.'

'Good. Yes. Let me get them. It's my turn, I think. Bulbul?'

'Thank you.'

We settled ourselves at a corner table. In front of us the large, un-evenly shaped pool was empty except for an elderly woman and the small child she was teaching to swim in the shallow end. The child's gasps and splashes reached us only faintly, damped by the still air.

We lit cigarettes.

'John Pearcey, I believe, has left,' began Das.

'You're probably right,' I said.

'Forgive me for asking, but you're not exactly the best of friends?'

I shrugged. 'How did you meet him?'

'Oh, just here at the club,' replied Das, smoothing his hands over his neatly barbered hair. 'You know how one does.'

'I suppose so. Whereabouts do you work, Vicky?'

'My office is near VT Station. One of those buildings there. I know why you're asking.' He smiled his elegantly amused smile. 'You're wondering how I have time to sit around drinking beer in the middle of the day?'

'No, not really,' I said. 'It hadn't occurred to me.'

He replaced his glass on the checked tablecloth with precision. 'A lot of foreigners come here, Stanley. Many of them, sooner or later, want to do more than just spend their foreign exchange in the tourist shops. They look for a little adventure. And they come un-stuck. John Pearcey, for example, last week, thought he'd change some money on the black market. About seven hundred pounds sterling, to be exact, and the transaction was performed just a stone's throw from here. Well, the scenario proved to be as well worn as a *masala* movie. The rupees had just been counted out in front of him in return for his pounds, when the group was inter-rupted by a lookout shouting "Police". The bundle of rupees was thrust into Mr Pearcey's top pocket, and he was advised to make himself scarce. All very well, except that when he came to count the money later, it turned out that not all the notes were there. Nine-tenths of them, in fact, were missing.'

'Did John tell you this?' I asked, trying unsuccessfully to look concerned.

'No, he had no idea I ever knew.'

'How did you know?'

Das didn't answer me, just looked out over the pool. 'Did you know he tried to bribe me?'

'What!' I was amazed. 'To do what?'

'He wanted to film in a public hospital. The victims of industrial accidents, apparently.'

'And he tried to bribe you to fix it for him?'

'He said it would be worth my while, yes.'

I tried not to laugh.

'See, Stanley, there are rules to these sorts of . . . negotiations. One of the first is that the opening player plays low. A high bid makes for nervousness on all sides. Unfortunately this is one thing that isn't taught in British public schools.'

'Pearcey never went to a public school,' I said, rather more sharply than I had intended.

Das looked at me levelly.

'But you grew up here, did you not, Stanley? Before you went to a British public school. You know how things work?'

That phrase again. I wasn't quite sure what he was getting at. I nodded.

'See, all I'm saying is that if you ever need anything, assistance . . . out of the ordinary,' he frowned at the beer in his glass, 'it's possible that I may be able to help.'

'I've been at the club,' I told Cuckoo, 'and I rang Nelson D'Mello. We're meeting this evening.'

'That's good.' She broke a Britannia biscuit in half, and dipped it into her tea. 'Ask him if his mother still has those shorts. Thank you for the gramophone records, by the way. Very nice recordings. Sweet of you.' She placed the half-biscuit into her mouth and chewed absently. 'You know Zubin Mehta played here in December? It was at the Cricket Club. Just wall-to-wall Parsees, you can imagine? But nice, yes? I went with Bapsi Wadia, and she was telling me, you know how these Christians drink? Well, she had this boy called Jude, whose family was from Panjim, and you remember, the cook was called Anthony, well this Jude was his nephew or something. Anyway, she, Bapsi, had gone with her husband to some big wedding at Mahalakshmi, you know, at the race-track, I think it was one of the Antia girls, Hofrish was it, was marrying one of the Billimorias, the Poona Billimorias, and anyway, they decided to come home early, they were third sitting for dinner, and her legs were bad. Well they got back to Cuffe Parade, Pallanji Mansions they live now, just above the Siddhwas, and she opened the front door on to this extraordinary scene. There was an empty fenni bottle on the table, you know that smell fenni makes, and these two Macca Pao Goans, drunk as lords, dressed in their Sunday best, all over her best couch, posing for some photographer they had called over. Tripod and all. This Jude had his arm round a marble bust of Goethe, and the cook was toasting him with one of her husband's old badminton trophies . . .'

I smiled. By the terrace door Anubai was ironing a pile of clothes. The warm, slightly stifling smell of steamed cotton filled the room. From outside came the faint transistor wail of a film song. Cuckoo looked through the open doors towards the horizon, her eyes slowly losing their focus.

'Tell me about this girl,' she said suddenly, quietly.

'Lakshmi Khandekar?'

She was silent.

'You mean Emilia.'

She nodded.

'It didn't . . . I don't know.' The moment she had spoken, I had wanted a cigarette, but knew that Cuckoo hated the smoke. 'It didn't work out. She was an actress, I think I wrote to you that that's what she did. When I first met her she was still studying. But then she started working and . . . wanted to go her own way. Career and so on. I don't know.'

My heart was thumping in my chest. I lifted my teacup, saw that it was empty, slowly and soundlessly replaced it.

Cuckoo's eyes seemed to remain vague. She continued to face away from me.

'In twenty years, Stanley, this is the only girl you've ever mentioned in your letters. Twenty years. You didn't say much, but you said enough. And I was happy for you. Your letter made me . . . happy.'

My dread evaporated, and to my horror I was suddenly aware of a tear glistening, running down one cheek. I chewed at my lip; didn't trust myself to speak. At that moment Anubai looked up from her completed ironing. Seeing the expression on my face she slowly lowered her eyes, her question unasked, and carefully and unnecessarily refolded a sari whose peppermint green starred, streaked into the white of the sky as my eyes began to swim. I covered my face with one hand; as Cuckoo turned to me I shook my head, and sniffing loudly, tears running down my wrist, managed a hopeless heaving shrug of my shoulders.

She held out her arms. I fumbled for a handkerchief, but couldn't find one, and standing, stumbled awkwardly out of the room. In the black and white bathroom I palmed warm tap-water over my face. It was as much Cuckoo's undemanding love as anything to do with Emilia that had set me off, I thought blearily to myself. Over the years I had done so little, God. I hadn't thought of her for months on end; just a dutiful letter from time to time when I had nothing better to do. And she'd always been there for me. Always.

I looked in the mirror at my puffed and reddened eyes, took a deep breath, and returned. Cuckoo looked at me with thoughtful concern. She took both my hands in hers.

'I'm sorry, Cuckoo, really. I don't know what . . .'

She silenced me with a squeeze of the hands.

'I'm sorry, it was really none of my business.' I shook my head, meaning, I suppose, that of course it was her business. She imposed a firm smile on her features, realising that, at this moment, I couldn't take too much kindness.

'I'm sure you shouldn't worry, Stanley dear, everything will be . . . what was it your father used to say? Hocus . . .'

'Hunky-dory.' I smiled sniffily. Behind the pile of ironing I saw Anubai smile. At this moment Baby walked into the room, carrying her satchel from school. Anubai crossed in front of us, shunting her daughter outside again by the shoulders. Cuckoo stood, and looked at me with concern.

'Why don't you lie down for a bit.'

'I think I will.'

I heard her switch on the fan by my bed, and wondered whether to smoke a cigarette on the terrace first.

*

I don't think any of the actors can actually see anyone standing
outside the circle of light. I can walk quite close and not be seen by
them; I can also see the people standing around in the half-dark of
the studio. Two figures, one tall, leather-jacketed, the other in a
white tunic, slight, are walking through this half-dark from some
completely unlit area; maybe from some far entrance. His arm
easily circles her slender shoulders, they walk in step, heads down.
With a sick thump of recognition I see it is Emilia. There is movement around the cameras, she walks into the light, the technicians
outside it defer to the tall figure. Instructions are given. I am closer
now, but for some reason can still hear nothing. Positions are
assumed in the light, camera movements essayed. Emilia stands at
the centre of the circle, peers squinting outwards, smiles, a hairdresser attends to her, then hurries from the light. There is a
sudden intensity to the silence.

She stands, arms outstretched, facing the cameras. From behind
her, four male figures take her arms. A fifth, horned like a satyr,
approaches her. My heart is beating hard, painfully; my mouth is
dry. For a moment he stands in front of her, then he puts his hands
to the top of her tunic and, with deliberation, tears downwards,
hard. The fabric, torn, falls from her shoulders; her breasts, exposed, lit, shudder slightly.

A television camera, like a giant reptile with young clustered
about it, moves silently towards her; its lens snouts and probes at
the offered body. I neither believe that I am watching any of this
nor am able to stop watching. In front of me other watchers move
slightly; there are covert smiles, speculatively raised eyebrows. The
satyr, mouth opening, eyes closing, sinks to his knees, lies his head
against her belly. Slowly, in her turn, she kneels too, her breasts
flattening against his chest, her hands clasping his back, her eyes
closed. He bears her to the ground and the shot is cut. As the
cameras retire, Emilia and the satyr climb to their feet. She allows
the torn halves of her tunic to hang from her waist as she speaks to
him. Her breasts are shining with the sweat from his chest. He
nods, frowns; she speaks to the darkness. Leather-jacket appears in
the light; she is baby-faced as she lifts a scratched breast for his inspection. As they examine the breast together they are very close;
Leather-jacket kisses his index finger, and touches it to her nipple.

Better? A baby nod. Briefly, Leather-jacket turns, frowning, to the satyr, who raises his hands, he will be careful in future. Leather-jacket nods, winks at the satyr, and a woman in cowboy boots with a pin-cushion attached to her wrist moves to resew the front of Emilia's tunic.

All withdraw, the shot is tried again. This time the tunic has been sewn too securely, the stitches will not tear, she is almost pulled off her feet.

Again. This time it looks too easy, as if the fabric is already torn.

Several more takes. They can't get it right. More spectators have gathered, now, although of course most are carefully retaining the air of being there for a reason. The satyr-man is getting visibly short-tempered. Finally a tunic is taken from another actor. Emilia changes in the half-light, she is naked for a moment, there is a hard obstruction in my chest, in front of me the hand of a man wearing a tool-belt goes to his groin. The shot is retaken, the clustered insects move in, she is stripped, handled, the take continues, her whole body shining for the nosing, tracking lens, her movements un-choreographed now, and murderously familiar. At last the camera is still. The satyr is climbing from her, a little uncomfortably now that his performance is done. The skirt of Emilia's tunic has ridden up her parted thighs to her stomach; her crotch is also parted and, beneath the lights, paler than I know it. She doesn't immediately move, but allows him to rise from her before slowly half-sitting, bringing her knees together, and pulling the torn tunic over herself. Leather-jacket is moving into the light now; he is carrying a towel, wraps her possessively, like a baby at bathtime. Little-faced, she looks up at him. I see that, around me, there is sudden movement; some people appear to be clapping, but, dead, utterly betrayed, I can hear nothing.

'The answer to your question,' said Nelson D'Mello, pouring Thums-Up and Old Monk Rum into his glass in equal measure, 'is yes. I have contact numbers for Lakshmi Khandekar. And I can let you have them. No problem. But two things, yaar. One, I think you are making like MAXIMUM *dukha* for yourself by having everything depend on someone as, like, FLAKY as Lakshmi, when I can put you on to several chicks who would give you like one hundred and ten per cent access and co-op. And I mean big names, like Poonam or Meenakshi. Two, brother, I have like this VIBE about *Khandaan*, that it's going to be, like, a real fucking downer. Nothing I can put my finger on, I just have this bad feeling. See, yaar, I can see that this Lakshmi is like DAMN cute, but I've also heard that she can be one right *kharab* bitch. Think, yaar. If *Khandaan* bombs, then she's dead. She hasn't exactly won the industry's love with *MDMD*; not that she gave Saiyad Ali too much trouble on the set, she wasn't as stupid as to piss HIM off, especially after all that bikini *natak*, but from the moment the picture was canned she started giving herself this, like, unbelievable *bhao*, no interviews, all that shit. So take my advice, man; use someone else. If you've got the hots for Lakshmi Khandekar, then just give her a ring and fix to meet her. Say you want to interview her for some UK publication. But, for your own sake, man, don't risk fifty grand of the BBC's — '

'Channel Four's.'

' . . . cash trying to get laid. And I'm assuming that that's what's behind all this because, unless you know something about this three-picture *ghatan* that I don't, and in this town that is DAMN unlikely, there can be no other reason that you want to stake your career on her.

'Having said all this, and even though I'm half-pissed, I mean it. Ring me tomorrow at the office and I'll give you the numbers I've got for her. And if you decide to make the picture about someone else, then, *chalo*, let me know, and we'll talk again.'

He belched comfortably into the darkness. Below us, in the pool, the two elderly male figures performed their unmoving breast-stroke by the light of the single bulb.

'It's just,' I said, 'that she's the only actress whose entire output I've seen. I can . . . get a handle on her. It makes the whole thing infinitely simpler if we only have to look at three films, only deal with two producers for clips and so on. And I do really think she's got something special . . . she has to me, anyway.'

'Look,' said Nelson, removing his baseball cap to scratch at his thinning scalp, 'the whole point about most successful Hindi film actresses, as well you know, is that behind that whole Goddess of Virtue-type façade, behind all those like, lowered eyes and oiled plaits and chasing round trees and shit, is a chick who has started her professional life flat on her back under some sweaty-vest producer, been signed up for some piece of crap opposite a star old enough to be her father, and hung in there. Thirty or forty pieces of crap later, she has a bad-taste apartment in Bandra, a gangster boyfriend with three jealous wives, and a weight problem.'

He shook one of my Chesterfields from the packet, lit it, exhaled. 'The image and the reality, man, that's the story. Lakshmi Khandekar's just closer to the beginning of this process than most of them, that's all. She'll end up the same, though. As to whether you're planning a scene with her, don't confirm or deny, man, that's cool.'

I laughed. 'It's good to see you again, Nelson.'

'It's damn good to see you, man. Twenty years, man; it's a trip. And it's Saturday night. We can celebrate. I don't have to go to any screenings. So what d'you say?'

'Fine by me,' I said. 'Another drink?'

An hour later we were hunched over a small, battered tin table.

'I promise you, man,' said Nelson, articulating with drunken care, 'I PROMISE. This is going to be like the BEST meal you've ever . . . in your LIFE.'

'I believe you,' I said.

'*Chalo*,' said Nelson, 'your glass.'

In his lap he poured Old Monk into our tumblers of Thums-Up. I hoped vaguely that no one had seen. Alcohol was not sold at Mirza's. At the other tables the customers were all men, dark and thin and with the knotted build and faded clothes of labourers. All were Muslims. Those who were facing us watched and murmured speculatively, others turned to us from time to time. Mirza's Kebab House, of which, in the club, Nelson had spoken with serious reverence, was actually no more than a black, trodden area off a narrow gully joining two streets of brothels. At its centre stood a heavy oven attended by two cooks in holed and fat-spattered vests who alternately pressed handfuls of greyish minced meat around heavy iron skewers and laid and turned these over the red coals of an open grill. Stinging smoke and the thick smell of goat mutton rose from this grill and circled the twenty or so crowded tables gathered around it. Above these, supported by poles like a nomad tent against the black sky, hung an ancient tarpaulin canopy; the area was cramped, close and irregular, bounded by the grim exteriors of other buildings.

Our table was in the angle of two brick walls. Nelson looked uncomfortable on the small metal stool. He was a big man, thickly bearded, and heavy at the waist; as I watched, he hauled himself into a position from which he could be a less effortful spectator of the cooking operations.

In the normal way of things I would never have recognised him, nor he, I am sure, me. Earlier in the evening I had been the only European male in the club, and so we had identified ourselves easily enough, but in truth the large easy figure in the crumpled kurta-pajama and the Atlanta Braves baseball cap had born no resemblance to the worried-looking little boy I thought that I remembered. We had had friends in common, though, we discovered, as we undertook the cross-questioning that the situation had seemed to demand. One rather spiteful little boy had become a doctor and gone to live in Toronto. A toothy girl we had called Ratty had become a television news presenter. The school's prize athlete was now a film editor. Nelson still saw several of them. In reality, he and I had hardly known each other at school. I had enjoyed my time at Don Bosco, but had made few real friends. They, I supposed, had wondered briefly about my disappearance, and then, as children do, had put me from their minds. Nelson had done well. He had married a girl from Santa Cruz called Bobita who was now seven months' pregnant with their second child and to whom, as he explained to me, he was routinely unfaithful.

In return for his easy confidences I had found myself recounting a rather incoherent history of my time with Emilia. He had listened without comment or movement, and then his attention had seemed to drift entirely to thoughts of food.

A boy in a dirty skullcap shimmied between the tables, stainless-steel plates balanced along both arms. All six of these clattered to our table. There were kebabs, a chutney of mashed chilli, crisp oily parathas, handfuls of fresh mint leaves. The boy returned with a stainless-steel jug of water and splashingly refilled Nelson's beaker. The food, as promised, was delicious; the alcohol had made me very hungry. We ate in silence.

'What do you think?' Nelson asked eventually, belching.

'*Burhiya*,' I replied, copying the belch, 'damn good.'

'You still speak?' he asked quickly, surprised.

'I forgot it all,' I said. 'Relearnt it at university.'

'Fuck, man, you're crazy, you know that ... Go on about this chick. What happened, you're in the studio, she's broadcasting her pussy ...'

I took a deep hit of Old Monk and Thums-Up from the steel beaker, and leant back against the brickwork. Lit a Chesterfield.

'As I said, I just knew, somehow, that she was having an affair with this director or whatever he was. Anyway I got myself back to my office and my heartbeat down to a rate where I could actually speak, and rang the channel about the Lakshmi film. They confirmed that they were sending the development money, and I left with the company chequebook. My first stop was a travel agent, where I ordered an open return to Bombay, and my second was to the bank, where I ordered a couple of thousand pounds-worth of traveller's cheques on Coldharbour's account and stuffed my current account on deposit. Now, I had never bought a flat, always rented. I had an OK deal, and rather than take out a mortgage on a place of my own I'd kept the rented one on. For someone in my situation in London that was unusual; paying out dead money, people called it. But in the short term it was cheaper.'

I passed my beaker to Nelson. Without speaking, he refilled it with rum and Thums-Up.

'Anyway, after I'd done all this I went back over the river to the flat. I rang up first to make sure that Emilia wasn't home, and then went over, picked up my passport, and packed a bag of clothes. By the time I got back to the office everyone had gone home. I worked until midnight, answering letters, filing documents, tying up loose ends. I rang the flat several times to see if Emilia was back; I would have put the phone down if she'd answered, but there was no answer. I slept that night, eventually, stone-cold sober, right there at the office.'

The string of bulbs hung above the tables suddenly flickered and dimmed from a yellow to a brownish light. I hesitated. Nelson raised his head an inch, indicating for me to continue.

'Early the next morning I took a bus to the Indian High Commission. I was one of the first in the queue, and by eleven o'clock I had completed the visa application. I rang the flat again, but again there was no answer. When I eventually got round there, about two o'clock, I found a note from Emilia. They'd finished shooting very late, she hadn't got in until the early morning, where had I been, another night edit? The good news, the note went on, was that her contract had been extended, she now had a featured part, there was some location shooting, she'd had to leave early, it would probably be another late night, she would ring me, she missed me.

'Another late night, I thought, sure. She missed me. Again, sure. The worst part was that the whole thing corresponded to the edge-of-consciousness nightmares I had had ever since I met her. The only course of action open to me was to cut myself away. Cauterise. Leave no trace.'

Nelson was watching me from beneath the blue peak of his cap. His features seemed blurred, but the eyes, dark, were acute.

'I went back to the office late that afternoon, and presented my *fait accompli*. It was important, I explained, to get this project under way. I had cleared my desk and was going immediately, the Channel Four cheque would be here any day, and would exactly cover the amount I had drawn for my ticket and expenses.

'There were nods and shrugs. If the others felt dubious about doing things this way round, nobody said anything. They also agreed not to release any details of my whereabouts to anybody who might ring. When I said that that included Emilia they looked surprised, but again, nobody said anything. I did some shopping, spent the evening in a pub, and eventually slept in the office again.

'The next day I went back to the flat. No Emilia, needless to say. As soon as I arrived, I set about removing all trace of myself. I took all my cold-weather clothes to the charity shop and threw two carfuls of possessions on to an unattended skip a mile away. I filled a rubbish bag with papers and left it in a dustbin outside a nearby apartment block. I took my record player and all my records to a second-hand shop and accepted the first price offered; I did the same with all my books. I rang a local furniture dealer and had a lorry sent around to take away the few pieces of furniture that I owned. Again, I didn't bargain, but took the first figure they offered. By that evening I was left with nothing except a few clothes, a handful of documents, a wad of used banknotes and the canvas suitcase that I had arrived in England with, twenty years before. The flat, oddly enough, looked very little different. Even though it was me that had originally lived in it alone, it was Emilia's presence and possessions that had brought it to life. It looked emptier without my things, sparer, but it didn't look gutted.

'I cleaned the place behind me, pretty much wiped it free of fingerprints, and left enough money to pay the quarter's bills in an envelope under the phone. Then I walked out, pulled the door closed behind me, and got into the car. On Waterloo Bridge I stopped, and got out. You're not supposed to stop there, but there wasn't too much traffic, and on a clear evening, with the lights, there's the most wonderful view. It was my favourite place in London. I threw the keys of the flat as far as I could, into the river.

'I spent my last night in England in a boarding house near Paddington Station. The next day I collected my passport, my ticket and my traveller's cheques. If there had been a delay I don't know what I would have done, but there was no delay. I drove my car to the garage in Ladbroke Grove where I had bought it twelve months earlier, and sold it for cash.

'By midnight I was in the air.'

For a long minute Nelson didn't move. Eventually, shaking his head, he laughed.

'You're mad as a fucking snake, man. *Ekdum pagal*. On the other hand I do, like, sort of understand your thinking.' He shifted uncomfortably on the small seat and flipped his cigarette butt into a black ditch which ran past our table, where it hissed briefly. 'But what are you going to do long-term, man? Meaning, can you work, can you earn, what about visas, all that?'

'I'm here,' I said. 'I've got a project, I've got a brain, I've got time, and I've got a little money in my pocket. I've spent the last seven years ticking over, being sensible. Now I want life to surprise me. I'm thirty this year, presumably like yourself since we were in the same year at Don Bosco, and I want to find myself on a new track. While I was with Emilia I was prepared to toe the line, but now . . . fuck it Nelson, you know what I mean.'

Nelson looked at me sadly. He seemed ten or twenty years older than me. He suddenly smiled.

'First thing you've got to do, man, you've got to get that bitch out of your system. I think we might just take a walk down the road.'

'I didn't mean anything as . . . literal as that. I'm drunk, Nelson, and I'm not in the mood. Really.'

'Listen, little brother, listen. I haven't seen you for twenty years, but I know you better than you know yourself. The words of yours that I'm hearing now are the ones that you're not saying.'

He threw a couple of notes on to the table, and got unsteadily to his feet.

'Nelson,' I said, not much later, 'I'm really not sure that I want to do this.'

'Just take a look, man. Think of it as a gift from an old school-friend. Besides, there's something I want you to . . .'

He stumbled noisily up the narrow stairway behind me as two tight-shirted South Indians pushed their way past us. As I stepped on to the dark landing behind them I was met by an unexpected scene, and stopped dead. The planking floor, instead of turning into more narrow stairs, extended as far as I could see in both directions; the back of the entire row of houses had been opened up like a stage set, and only an unsteady-looking guard rail stood between the long corridor and the empty darkness beyond. By the light of a string of low-powered bulbs I could see several stalls along this corridor selling tea, *paan*, *bidi*s, and watermelon slices; between these, *chai-pao* boys threaded a hurried path, children played vacant games, pimps gestured, hesitant customers clutched and whispered at each other, and matte-painted girls with powder-burn eyes stood tight and watchful. It was a thoroughfare; grey, tense, and silent.

I stood for a moment. Nelson arrived beside me, took my arm and led me along the corridor. To our left was an entrance hung with dirty plastic strips. Parting these, he gestured me inside. Around the wall ran a cracked Rexine banquette, whose colour, in the dim light, was unclear. Opposite us, at a window, sat a boy of about twelve, jaws moving rhythmically as he stared into the street below. Seeing us, he removed the gum from his mouth, stuck it to the window-frame, jumped to the floor, and ran from the room. I saw that he was carrying a stick. A few moments later a line of women entered, and started to take their places on the banquette. The boy returned after the last one, whom he hit hard on the thighs with the stick before collecting the gum and returning it to his mouth. The women sat there in a line, awkward and expressionless. I saw that they were Nepalese, their round, rather simple features flattened by dead pink foundation, small Mongol eyes blackened into permanent surprise. As I watched them, I felt the balance shift beneath my feet. The women blurred. When I opened my eyes there was bile in my throat and a waiting boy with a stick.

'Nelson,' I said, 'please. Let's go.'

One of the women nudged her neighbour as I spoke, and they both smiled, showing *paan*-reddened teeth.

'I guess I see what you mean,' said Nelson. '*Chalo*, then.'

'I'm going in the opposite direction,' I said. 'I'll be fine. I'll just get another taxi.'

'Are you sure, man?'

'Nelson, I'll be fine, really and truly.'

'Well, OK then. Don't forget to ring me tomorrow.'

'Tomorrow's Sunday.'

'Oh . . . well, OK. Call me Monday. Cool?'

'Sure.'

I reckoned that I knew more or less where I was. If I could get on to Grant Road, which couldn't be far, I could walk all the way up to Kemps Corner and from there to Nepean Sea Road. It would take about half an hour, walking fast, and it would clear my head. I was glad that we'd called it a night; I liked Nelson for his blowsy generosity and his Calangute Beach hippyspeak, but I wasn't quite ready to be his whoring partner.

At a street corner I asked a policeman the way to Grant Road. He narrowed his eyes and indicated the direction with a nod of the head.

Despite the time, and it was after midnight now, the pavement was tightly crowded. I was jostled by beggars, rag-pickers and drug dealers as well as other, less identifiable types, but fine and drunk, I was unworried. It was as hot as day, and the faint scent of rosewater overlaid the heavier stench of urine and open drains. I continued past a series of small overhanging alleys which led off both sides of the road. These were unsurfaced, puddled, and tracked by ditches; outside each entrance knots of prostitutes lounged and shimmered in cheap metallic saris and *salwar-kameez* while others lay fanning themselves on the charpoi beds which were laid out in rows along the gulleys. Stray dogs nosed the ground; strings of fairy lights hung from the buildings above. There was a sudden sweet burning smell on the air and although I didn't slow my step I was conscious of a crawl of desire.

After a time the pavement crowds thinned and the brothel-warrens gave way to larger, unlit buildings. For a moment I was tempted to turn back. I looked around, hoping for some indication that I was approaching Grant Road. On the pavement ahead of me I saw that a small boy was leaning against the broken pillared upright of a gate, smoking a *bidi*. Seeing me he ran up and caught my hand.

'*Aiye*, Sahib, *aiye*.' He pulled me urgently towards the broken gateway. I saw that, set back a short distance from the street, was a small, dilapidated pavilion within which a single pinkish light shone. I wrenched my hand from his grasp, and looking up at me, the boy stepped back, uncertain. Looking beyond the boy to the single pink light I felt sudden curiosity, and beyond the curiosity, a dredging, fearful desire. I hesitated for a moment.

'What is inside?' I asked him in Hindi.

'Girl, Sahib,' he answered, simply.

I followed him towards the pavilion.

VII

~~~~~~

The shadow that was Dane frogged towards me under the water and surfaced, thick and brown of shoulder, six feet away.

'Couple more yards . . .' he gasped, blinking the salt from his eyes. 'Couple more yards. Two lengths.'

'Pretty good,' I said. He might have tried to swim two lengths underwater if I hadn't been there, but then again he might not.

'You coming in?' he asked.

'I might leave it for a bit,' I smiled. I wouldn't have thought twice about it, normally, but with Dane things were always complex. He wasn't a man I'd have asked to rub sun-cream into my back, for example.

'Can I order you something?' I asked.

'I don't know . . . Yeah, beer.'

I nodded and moved away towards the counter.

He launched himself into a ferocious butterfly stroke.

Every evening since Dane had returned from the oil platform we had ordered up room-service at eight p.m. He and I, watched by Beth, had eaten at the coffee table, while Beth, wrapped in a dressing gown, had eaten her specially prepared meal in bed.

These had not been easy occasions. Despite his surface good-old-boy manner I had always found it difficult to be relaxed around Dane. He liked to roll his shirtsleeves over his biceps and crumple beer cans in his fist and throw them at the wastepaper basket.

When he missed, which was not often, for he was a man of some physical authority, the twisted can had the power to silence us all.

He rubbed his eyes with a towel.

'God, that's better.'

He shook his head like a dog.

'Little moody last night,' he offered. 'I apologise.' He took a pull of his beer and wiped his moustache with the back of a large hand.

'I guess it can't be much fun,' I said. 'Wife stuck in bed; problem sister-in-law to entertain . . .'

'You're no trouble, June.' He leant forward on his elbows. 'None at all. Hell.'

'Beth'll be up soon,' I said, looking away. 'On the wagon for a few months, special diet and so on, but up.'

'I know that.'

Beth wanted a child. Dane apparently wasn't ready. I'd got this from Alma Benson. Hadn't yet checked with Beth.

Did Dane's behaviour mean he was planning to bale out? Yesterday at seven o'clock he had hauled himself into the hotel suite like a man condemned to death. He had spent most of the evening staring out of the window with a magazine on his knees, pouring himself glass after glass of beer, throwing them back with measured precision. At first I had tried to include him in the rather aimless conversations that were the best that Beth and I could manage in his presence, but the alcohol had seemed to release a sour and silencing fury into him.

If Dane was planning to leave Beth, her illness had come at a bad time for him.

I'd had a letter from Beth two years ago in London. The good news, she had written, had been Dane's promotion; the bad news had been Bombay. Bad because Dane had wanted Galveston so badly. Beth hadn't minded, really, except on Dane's behalf. Con-Oil, she wrote, had come up with a real proper job for her. That'd been a first.

And I'd got the impression that as a team player, flying the flag, Beth had been almost happy. She'd felt more American in India than she ever had in the States.

'Do you really hate it here?' I asked Dane, and instantly regretted the question.

He snorted, uncrossed his legs, and for a while said nothing.

'What I don't know . . .' he eventually began, 'is just how much is the place, and just how much is . . .' He shook his head tiredly and unbelievingly, poured the last of his beer into the glass, and swung it back.

'What do you think?' he asked, replacing the glass.

'Well, I haven't really thought what I think. It's all so different.' I stirred at my tepid tea. 'Although you come across unexpected things you recognise. Like at the film-shooting we went to yesterday. The way everyone was behaving. Desperate to be paid the proper professional respect. Behaving as if all people junior to themselves were invisible, and so on. I recognised all that. And I could tell the difference between those who thought they might get somewhere if they played their cards right and those who knew that this was as good as it was going to get and were grateful just to have the work.'

He nodded.

'You know June, if . . .'

I waited. He looked up at the crows. Don't tell me anything, I thought, I just don't want to know.

'If what?' I asked eventually.

He lowered his head. Lifted his hands in a pacifying gesture.

'Forget it. Gotta make tracks.'

I forced myself to exhale as he loped heavily off towards the changing rooms.

Alone. With the crows and the sunshine. I'd save *The Lotus and the Flame* for the evening. I wasn't sitting through another scene like last night. Talk about Pinteresque.

It was high tide. As the waves broke against the rocks of the sea wall they spattered the concrete walkway between the sea and the salt-water swimming pool. The sea was an opaque brown; the water of the pool a cool, controlled blue. However hard the waves broke against the sea wall they would never reach the pool. I lay on my towel on the grass, face down, listening to the waves on the rocks.

I felt the sun on my back.

The sequence begins, as always, in the studio, Sandrine Decourcelles suspended in the air, mid-jeté.

It is the *Swan Lake* entrance, chassé, pas de bourree, flick jeté; Sandrine, a toothy, rather chinless girl from the Paris Opéra, has tacked it on to the end of the allegro exercise set by the teacher. The pianist is playing a circular waltz which is so grindingly familiar as to reduce itself to non-music, to a basic count of three. Sandrine is in the air, legs fully split at the height of the flick jeté, arms rounded above her head en couronne, the sun behind her. She is a guest artist, and as far as Pauline and I are concerned, at least, an unwelcome one. She opens with us at the Opera House, tomorrow, in the *Swan Lake/Sleeping Beauty* season.

Sandrine Decourcelles, then, coming out of the sun; twelve o'clock high. My own movement, away from the piano and towards the back of the studio, has already begun. My eyes, turning, photograph Sandrine at full extension, full flick. Her eyes are already streaking with fear. She's misjudged the distance. Or, as she will forever afterwards tell it, I've moved, foreshortening her landing.

Her mistake, of course, was going for the allegro exercise in new pointe shoes. I could have told her about this studio floor.

Or if I spoke French I could have told her.

The whipcrack snap of Sandrine's Achilles tendon silences everything except, for a bar or two, the piano. It's her scream that stops that. I find that I've caught her, that I'm holding her to me like a lover and that she swallows the scream but her mouth stays open and moving as I lower her, white-faced, shuddering with shock, to the floor.

Everybody gathers round, most of them open-mouthed too. Jean Dazat, Sandrine's Parisian partner, tears over from the other side of the studio; terrified, he waves us away from her, kneels, lifts her head, gabbles what I assume to be French. Someone starts shouting about ice.

It seems as good a moment as any to fix my leotard. Sandrine, *en passant* as she would probably say, has pulled open the little safety pin I use to ruche the front into a nice line.

I look up, eventually, into the eyes of Pauline Faull. Neither of us dares an expression.

We are sitting in the dressing room, class aborted; several people are telling me that I mustn't blame myself, that it was an accident, just one of those terrible, terrible things. Otherwise the room is quieter than usual. We hear the ambulance siren fading southwards towards the river; it is still just audible as a full-company rehearsal is called over the tannoy. The dressing-room phone rings almost immediately after the announcement, summoning Pauline and myself to the ballet office.

We are alone in the cold upper corridor, Pauline Faull and June Webster, newly promoted to principal dancers, jittering, squealing, shusshhing, triumphant. The best, worst and oldest of friends. Friends since Golliwog's Cakewalk days, since pink-hairband and Sunshine Competition and tap and acro days. Bliss and wonder. Blood and satin. Sweat and tears.

At last.
Now it starts.
Pauline has *Lac*. Odette-Odile.
I have *Beauty*. Princess Aurora.
Sandrine Decourcelles has a private room and a view of the Thames.

That night, the night before her first Opera House *Lac*, we are alone in the studio, Pauline in a practice tutu and an advanced state of tearful panic.

Pauline Faull, of course, famous for fear; famous for retching in the wings of the Bradford Alhambra in her Nikiya tutu. Right now all of her fears are concentrated into one forty-five-second sequence from Act Three of *Swan Lake*.

Fouettés. Fouettés are a pretty basic step, really. At school we used to finish every pointe-work class with them. Fouetté, a word that I'd guess crops up (ha) pretty often in the works of the Marquis de Sade, means whipped. Fouettés are whipped turns. In fouettés to the right, and most of us turn better to the right, you whip your right leg from the front to the side and turn on your left foot. In the Black Swan pas de deux Odile performs thirty-two of these turns on pointe without stopping. The sequence, the enchaînement, takes between half and three-quarters of a minute.

Fouettés are a pretty basic step.

But.

Killing, utterly killing, on the supporting leg.

With each turn you bend at the knee and ankle as you face front, rising to full pointe again as the working leg whips you round. Bend, rise, bend, rise; fondu, relève, fondu, relève. Sheer muscular exhaustion can finish you after twenty-four turns or less. Locking the supporting leg for those last eight fouettés with your calves and your thighs and back cramping can take a certain amount of what the school used to call character.

The blur, the sheer seasickness.

The trick to overcoming giddiness is spotting. Each time you hit the front and face the audience you find the same point in front of you and for that split second, focus your eyes on it. The best thing to spot on in a dark auditorium is a lit-up exit sign. God help us if they ever phase them out. Because your spot, your exit sign, is all that you see for the whole of that forty-five seconds. The rest, as you turn, is a blur. Lose your spot, lose it for one second, and you're lost. You're on your ass. Or your arse. Depending. But either way.

And what they call travelling.

You're dancing on a stage which, to give an impression of depth, is raked, angled towards the auditorium. You start your fouettés centre-stage and with each turn find yourself edging forward or sideways. Your spot is no longer in front of you, and the tireder your supporting leg becomes, the faster the stage seems to move backwards beneath you. Velocity is it? Momentum? As always, my education deserts me. But what do you do? Sink to one knee for the rest of the music? Or fouetté on towards the orchestra pit, shit or bust?

Your choice. You're wearing the tiara.

At the school, as I say, we used to whip off our thirty-two fouettés at the end of every pointe class, hairpins and barrettes flying. And as we ran to the front of the studio in our pairs there wasn't a one of us who didn't see ourselves in the mirror, just for a flash, as the Black Swan.

But the classroom is not the stage, and if you're Pauline Faull and your eyes are skidding everywhere and your throat is raw from dry-heaving and your toes are bleeding from the Act Two pas de deux and the audience haven't paid to see you, anyway, but a *Grande Étoile* of the Paris Opéra eighteen months your junior, then that walk to centre-stage in the black and gold tutu, that cool preparation, is something quite else.

'Break it down,' I am saying. 'Fondu. Second. Retiré. That's all it is. Breathe. Wipe your eyes. Blow your nose, pet, you don't want snot wrapped round your face. Here.'

She blinks, blows, wipes, prepares.

'Fondu. Second. Retiré. Just that. Do it without the turn. Calm down. Give me a smile, even.'

She sniffs. Frowns. Concentrates.

'Fondu. Second. Retiré. Relax your eyes. See yourself in the mirror. Shoulders.'

Relaxes. Her shoulders fall.

'Fondu. Weight on the heel. Hips and shoulders square. Second. Relevé. Hold. Don't tuck. Retire. High on the passé, working heel forward. Good. Now turn. Spot. Use your head. Relax your eyes.'

Slowly we build it all back up.

1. 2. 4. 8. 16. 24. 32.

The truth is that fouetté turns are a technical trick, and like most tricks, they're easy if you can do them and a nightmare if you can't. Fonteyn, for example, hated them.

And Pauline knows. Like the rest of us she's seen ballerina performances broken in those forty-five seconds. She knows, I know, everyone knows that this moment in Act Three is where the informed audience holds its breath, where the critics smell blood.

A single drop of salt water landed, at that moment, on my left eyelid; I opened the eye.

A yard from me, in the pool, a dark-haired man was treading water and pulling a pair of racing goggles away from his face. I thought for a moment that he was about to climb out, drip all over me, force me to open the other eye.

Since the club was all but empty this seemed like a bit of an invasion. For several moments he just stayed there, hair plastered to his face, blinking as if unsure of where he was, before turning and launching himself away.

There was a cast to his neck and shoulders, though, in the instant that he turned, which I recognised.

Body-lines, postures, the disposition of limbs. Things I could read. Things I knew.

I closed the eye.

The fire curtain rises; the house lights go down. There is a settling-back, the smell of perfume, a slight creaking of seats. Gets me every time.

'Due to the indisposition of Miss Sandrine Decourcelles, the role of Odette-Odile will be danced by Miss Pauline Faull.'

A sweeping murmur, a spattering of applause, instantly stilled. Leaning forward, arms folded on the velvet lip of the company box, I am as nervous as if I was dancing. On the other side of the curtain, less than twenty yards away, I imagine Pauline pacing the dark, wide stage, claiming the space, making it hers.

But not in full costume yet, I pray. The secret of these long ballets is pace. Odette, the Swan Princess, doesn't appear until Act Two, so the trick is to warm up during Act One and get into the tutu at the last minute. Not that I've ever had to do it in *Lac*. But I do know that standing around in the wings for half an hour before you go on in a new role chills the nerves as well as the legs, and most especially so if you have nerves like Pauline's.

'Do you think she'll be all right?' I whisper to Charlie, beside me.

'She'll be just fine. She's tougher than you think, June.'

'Well, you should know.'

'Very funny. And not true.'

'It's OK, Charlie.'

He sits back, ever so slightly irritated, as the overture starts.

I watch Jean Dazat closely in Act One. He is to be Prince Florimund to my Aurora, and although we have run through Act Three of *Beauty* a few times in the studio and once on stage, I have yet to see him in performance.

He is a dark Nureyevian Siegfried, all cloak and nostrils. A deliberately self-conscious, slightly ironic stage manner. There is a moment of sudden unsureness when the Queen Mother hands him his birthday present, a crossbow. He doesn't appear to know how it works.

'Looks as if he might have preferred a cashmere dressing gown,' whispers Charlie. Guest artists have been eating into his perform-ances, too.

Lac isn't easy on either of its principals. Siegfried has to stand on stage freezing his legs for at least twenty minutes before getting to crack so much as a posé arabesque. It doesn't seem to worry Jean, though; his solo, when it comes, is very centred, very balanced. Which is good, of course, because when push comes to shove there's nothing worse than a flaky partner. Especially one who doesn't speak a word of English.

In the blackout between acts, I run out of the company box to the toilet. Nervousness for Pauline and too much coffee have left me all but incontinent. It's so long since I've watched a perform-ance, since any performance has been more than a broken sequence of last-minute adjustments, desperate adrenaline surviv-als.

The curtain rises on Act Two. A lakeside. Night. Swirling mists, swans everywhere (there, but for the grace of God, and so on), Grace camping it up a storm in the bat frock as Von Rothbart, Jean prowling around with his crossbow, sucking in his cheeks as if for a photo-shoot on *L'Uomo Vogue*.

Act Two *Swan Lake*. Our job. Our work.

And then.

And then Jean Dazat as Siegfried sees something off-stage, a swan, perhaps. He kneels, raises his weapon, and slowly, carefully, aims.

Chassé, pas de bourree, flick jeté.

Pauline Faull, pale, whippety, worrying Pauline, her legs a sud-den fluent line, the moment split, suspended.

A desperate, captive fear. The audience sees it, feels it im-mediately. As Pauline's arms seem to disjoint behind her and her leg unfurls high into arabesque, the fear holds them in absolute silence.

But the fear is no longer Pauline's.

The fear is Odette's.

I've felt it myself once or twice, on good nights, and I know it when I see it. The moment when your technique is finally all there for you, part of you, steely and flexible as a Capulet rapier. The moment when you know that you can trust everything to a bunioned toe's width of darned, shellacked satin; trust everything to the art, if you like to call it that, and know that the science is there to carry you.

That's what they count on, of course, when they lie you down on to the cold floor in your knickers at eight years old, measure your spine and your legs and rotate your hips and the rest of it. That when your day, your night, finally comes, you can clear your thinking mind for your role and leave the technique to physical memory.

The trouble is that fear, real fear, freezes you, blocks your body's access to its memory. Your thinking mind jams up with thoughts of fouettés and falling and forgetting.

Pauline, though, streamlined neurotic Pauline, has finally grasped her fear. Its edge is still there, in every balance, in every quivering, attenuated line, but she knows it now for what it is; she has turned its blade.

The killingly long pas de deux comes to an end; Pauline, unsupported, holds its final arabesque for a moment, and then, followed by Jean, runs to the wings. As she returns to centre-stage the swans are taking their lines behind her. They do this more slowly than usual, because they know from the roar of applause, the shouting, the bouncing-shut of seats as spectators rise to their feet, that they have a little time yet, a little more time than usual.

As Pauline stands there for a breathless instant, the lights catching her white glittering tutu, I feel a blade of the coldest, purest jealousy slide beneath my ribs. She kneels, arms winging behind her, and bows. In the stalls people are clapping with their hands held above their heads, turning to each other. As she and Jean finally leave the stage and the four little swans run on I feel Charlie's eyes on me. I don't look at him.

I don't watch the little swans either. Those ditsy, noddy little entrechats always make me want to slap them.

As the act comes to a close and the curtain falls I stand up in the box.

'I'm just going to see Pauline into her Black Swan things,' I say to Charlie.

'Are you sure that's a good idea?' he asks, doubtfully.

'Look, Charlie, Pauline and I have known each other for fifteen years,' I answered. 'If I can't hook her into her frock for her first Black Swan, what the fuck can I do? Besides, we were here until ten last night going through the fouettés. I just want her to know I'm here for her. When I dance Aurora next Saturday I'll want her there for me, too.'

'Well she won't be there for you before the Rose Adage, if that's what you're thinking, because she'll be on stage. Dancing Lilac Fairy.'

This I didn't know.

'Pauline's dancing Lilac Fairy on Saturday?'

'She's replacing Sandy.'

'Oh, great. Fucking great. Wonderful. Look, Charlie, I'll see you in a minute, OK?'

On stage there is the usual inter-act hammering and chaos as the lakeside is struck and the court scene reset. There are no dancers in the wings.

I cross the stage behind the cyclorama and make my way out to the door with the ironic little tinsel star pinned to it, and knock. Pauline is wearing grey track-suit pants over her performance tights and an old cardigan of mine.

'For luck.' She twitches at it, smiling.

For a moment I just stare at her. The nervous tramlined eyes, the slightly uneven mouth, the pale pancaked skin; everything the same, but not the same.

I don't know what to say. 'You look great,' I say, fatuously.

'Was I all right?' she asks. There is sweat at her temples.

'All right? You were stunning, Pauline, just so lovely. I don't know what to say. Just keep going like that.'

'You're an angel, June. I'm glad you're out there. It's sort of weird, Jean not speaking any English, twenty-six swans watching me out of the corner of their eyes, desperate for me to skid or fuck up.'

Behind her the dresser is running stitches through the bodice of the Black Swan tutu.

'They're not doing anything of the sort, Pauline, they're just

116

leaving you alone. They want you to be wonderful, that's the whole point, they want it to happen for people like us who've gone through the school and bashed our way up through the corps.'

'Mmm . . . suppose so.'

'Rather than little chinless rats flown in from France, for example. Talking of which, how's himself?'

'Sweet, actually. He knows I'm terrified.'

'After-shave?'

'Slightly too much, but, you know . . . copable-with.'

Old jokes. We both manage a smile.

The five-minute call comes over the tannoy. She turns to face me. 'Help me into the tutti?'

'I always promised I would.'

'Well, here we go. Act Three. God, Junie.' She turns to me as she steps into the black tulle tutu and pulls on the elastic shoulder-straps. 'I'm just so shit-scared. I can't believe I have to go out there and do those fucking fouettés.'

I concentrate on the hooks and eyes. There is a pulse beating behind the sweat at her temple.

'You'll be fine, Pauline, I promise.'

'I wish I was so sure. Honestly, June, I think right now I'd rather jump out of an aeroplane or have a baby.'

'Well,' I say, 'first things first.'

'God, Junie . . . I'm sorry. I know I'm talking too much, it's just nerves. Tell me to shut up.'

'You'll be fine, I promise. The fouettés will be fine. Just take a good relaxed preparation. Spot. Relax your eyes. Get your working heel down. Usual shit.'

The tannoy calls beginners for Act Three to the stage.

'Oh, God, June.' She lifts a heel with her hand, stretches the leg up to her side.

'I should get back, Pauline,' I say. 'Or do you want me to stay with you till you go on?'

'No, go on back. I'll be all right.'

'Promise?'

'Promise.'

In fact it is almost twenty minutes before Grace, as Von Rothbart, leads Pauline, as Odile, down the ballroom staircase. The mime unfolds, Siegfried is deceived by Rothbart into thinking that Odile is Odette.

Pauline's first solo, in deliberate contrast to her dancing of Odette, is icily scientific. Jean, walking slowly to his opening position in order to give Pauline time to recover her breath, follows with his own rakishly Parisian version of Siegfried's solo. The crowd enjoy it, sit forward in their seats, and as the conductor whips the brass into the blaring Black Swan coda, Jean launches into a manège of grand jetés.

For some reason that I've never understood, audiences always clap a manège.

Pauline watches his leaping approach with something that, from where I'm sitting, looks like amusement; she allows him to complete his penultimate jeté, then steps unhurriedly to centre-stage and takes the preparation for her thirty-two fouettés.

There's a German word I've got written down somewhere which means that awful guilty pleasure you get from seeing your loved ones completely screw up. What would its opposite be? Is there a word, I wonder, for the equally guilty, equally awful pain in seeing them excel?

I'd have died, really died, if Pauline hadn't survived those fouettés, but I could see right from the first that she was safe; that I'd made her safe; that adrenaline and physical memory had kicked in. But safety, for Pauline Faull that night, was not enough. She wanted, as they say, more.

I had thought during Act Two that what I felt was jealousy; jealousy of Pauline's besting of her fear, jealousy of her fragile, lovely Odette, jealousy of her capture of the audience's hearts. But later, and especially after those fouettés, I wondered. Mixed in there, of course, complicating things, was my own apprehension about my debut as Aurora and envy at Pauline for surviving her first ballerina role, but I was feeling something else, something harder and less sickly familiar than jealousy.

Part of it was anger at my own misjudgement, of having taken Pauline's febrile, bewildered persona at face value, while all the time, underneath, was this steely ballerina, waiting her day. And part of it was a dawning sense of having been used.

Pauline Faull, famous for fear. Well, maybe. But maybe all the tears and the retchings and the wide-eyed, fucked-up rehearsals were just little numbers. Maybe we had all just become supporting players in the heart-stopping drama of Pauline Faull.

I thought I knew her.

She let me think so.

I thought she needed me.

She let me think so.

OK.

Fouettés.

If you're going to get smart with your fouettés, if you've danced at least a couple of dozen good *Swan Lake*s and it's a really 'on' night for you and your solo's gone well and you're feeling really centred, really bang to rights over your pointes AND you've tried the whole thing successfully in rehearsal, then, and ONLY then, you might, you JUST MIGHT, consider dividing your thirty-two fouettés into four blocks of eight and doing something nifty with every eighth turn. Remember that you don't get any extra music; there isn't any, so if you're going to add anything, step-wise, you're going to have to cheat the counts. Don't even consider talking to the conductor about it. Musicians don't tend to be very amused about bending Tchaikovsky to dancers' needs and these little collaborations always either end in tears or with the orchestra racing ahead like a runaway pram. Just do it.

But just be very, very sure you can deliver. Don't start anything you can't finish. Because if you decide to swap your eighth fouetté turn for, say, a pirouette in second en dehors, then that commits you to a similarly cute variation for, at the very least, your sixteenth and twenty-fourth turns; thirty seconds and a cramping calf muscle later you might not be feeling quite so clever. It might be as much as you can manage to finish at all, in which case that turn in second will have made you look a right little twat. And I've seen one or two.

Did I say that?

I said it and I'm glad.

Pauline, that night, basically brought the house down. She went into the fouettés straight as a blade, eyes as calm as if she was eating éclairs in the Patîsserie Valerie. There was a gasp as she replaced her eighth fouetté with a double pirouette en dehors in attitude (a bitch of a step at the best of times) and the same gasps as her sixteenth became a straight double; for her twenty-fourth she went back into attitude and finally pulled up out of her thirty-second into a perfect quadruple.

Poor Jean had to start his own turns in a roar of applause that completely drowned the orchestra. He put a brave face on it, all things considered.

To this day I don't know where she found those fouettés. Of the two of us I was always the one with the killer technique.

Pauline, of course, had the collarbones.

I opened my eyes to the glare, reached for my sunglasses. I felt displaced, of nowhere.

I was in India? Impossible.

That was the attraction of the performance life, that it was unnecessary to be of anywhere, that it lifted you from wherever you were into that simple sphere where all that was important was physical. That the show went on.

Why did the show have to go on?

The answer is that if the show did not go on we would all have been revealed for what we were without the show.

My name was June Webster. I was thirty-one. I had grey eyes, and dark blonde hair that needed attention.

It wasn't that we NEVER read the newspapers, we did. But in reading them, in discovering events around us, we hugged to ourselves our separation, our dissociation from those events. Dissociation? We were different. Grasshoppers. Storing no grain. And now. The hot white sky, the brown sea, the turning crows.

The London weather, of course, was essential to us. The contrast of gloom without, glamour within. Glamour in its Scottish rather than its Marlene Dietrich sense, meaning misty subjection to a spell, to seeing what isn't there. The essentially misty nature, too, of crappy backstage surroundings, weird plumbing, and of that smoky, well-darned atmosphere, rain streaming down discoloured windows.

But all that was a by-product. Hardly formed us.

Oh no?

You saw the ballet girl at some reception, some first night. Knew her, of course, by those pronounced little apples of calf muscle, by the turned-out stance, the flat-ironed shoulders, the scraped, pinned hair, the big shapeless bag from which trailed the solitary grubby pointe-shoe ribbon. But did you understand the other mute messages?

Why, for example, was that coat so shapeless, that dress so wilfully unfashionable? And as for those shoes . . .

The point is that they were the costume; that when you saw her face to face, the ballet girl (a.k.a. the sprite, the *sylphide*, the *wili*, the *bayadère*) was dressed as a human being, for the performance of real life. And her costume, well, the costume couldn't be too perfect because it might have been mistaken for a real person's clothes. That coat, for example, the one that could have doubled as boiler lagging or as a duvet, was really just a sly reference to the hard and supernaturally unpadded body beneath it; a joke, of course, that only the ballet girl could have gotten away with completely.

Ha.

Conversation stuttered over the still air of the pool. I fastened the clasp of my bikini and turned over on my towel on to my back. The splashing man was with the good-looking Indian in the blazer whom I'd seen at Naaz. They were sitting together over a couple of bottles at a corner table, smoking.

After a while they left, and I wandered round to order something to eat.

It wasn't until much later that I left. I had slept, dreamlessly, under one of the shade trees. I hadn't meant to drop off; I knew that I would find it that much harder to sleep later. Once again it was the breeze that signalled me to dress, to comb my hair, to wander, yawning, along the path, through the last intensity of evening light.

I stepped out between columns of hedge into the sudden layered blare of Nepean Sea Road. The woman who sold mirrored embroidery on the pavement outside the club was folding her fabric panels into an old cardboard suitcase. A dog nosed at my knees. There was the smell of trodden fruit; baskets of it were being packed away into trucks or on to trolleys. In front of the shops opposite, to the serious inconvenience of the traffic, a team of men with picks was excavating sections of the road.

I stood there for a brief moment before hurrying through the horn-blowing traffic towards the trenches and the piles of rubble on the other side. One of the gridlocked cars was a taxi.

'June,' said Beth, irritably, as soon as I walked in, 'where have you been?'

'At the Nepean Club,' I answered, 'like I said I'd be.'

'It's just that I've been trying to ring you. They said you left hours ago.'

'Well, only half of one hour ago,' I said. 'There was bad traffic on Malabar Hill, the roads were up, stuff like that. Why, though, what's the panic?'

'No panic, it's just this Sanjay Saxena, you know, the . . . er. You met . . .'

'What on earth, Beth, do you mean?'

'Well, he's here. At least his car's here. Downstairs, look out the window. That big white Ambassador with the flag.'

'So, big deal. Maybe he's having some — '

'June, you don't understand, the car's here for you.'

'For ME?' I squealed. 'To go where? What's he sent a car for me for? How do you know it's for me?'

'Here.' She held out an envelope. 'I opened it. Sorry.'

'That's . . .' I pulled out a sheet of writing paper, headed with his name.

'Dear Miss Webster,' I read, 'I wonder if you would do me the honour of dining with me tonight. My driver will bring you when you are ready. Yours respectfully, Sanjay Saxena.'

Beth nodded at me slowly.

'This is crazy,' I said. 'I mean, I only talked to him for two minutes. What's all this sending cars and assuming I'm just going to climb in and be driven to God knows where?'

Beth gave me a long look.

'Well,' she said, 'aren't you?'

'No. And I mean, what would I — '

'I rang Kimmie about that. She says just a jacket, skirt sort of thing. I've got some things you can ... But if you don't want to go,' she shrugged, 'no problem. Just send a note down to the driver.'

She looked away as if the matter was finished with, and reached for her book.

'If you're going to the phone, though,' she said, without looking up, 'could you ask them to send up half a dozen bottles of Bulbul for Dane?'

There was a long silence.

'That Italian suit of mine,' said Beth, eventually, still not looking up, 'it's on the back of your door.'

VIII

〜〜〜〜〜

By the time the black and white clock above the clubhouse read eleven o'clock, I was beginning to feel a little better. I'd forced myself out of bed for breakfast with Cuckoo after what had seemed no more than minutes of sleep, but with all the heavy cargo sliding around the deck of my brain, hadn't managed more than a cup of tea. Nelson, I'd told Cuckoo shortly, remembered her well. We'd stayed up talking at the club, I explained; had eaten somewhere near Gwalior Tank, where his family still lived.

If Cuckoo had noted my queasy state, she had said nothing.

I told her that I would be out for the evening again, that I was having dinner with Lata Khandekar, and explained the misunderstanding which had led to my meeting her. Cuckoo was interested. She knew of some Khandekars from Solapur, was Lata Khandekar one of those? No more than half-listening I replied, vaguely, that I wasn't sure. Cuckoo said she supposed there were several families, it was one of those big upper-caste Maharashtrian names, there were some living in Bapsi Wadia's building at Teenbatti. I had nodded; felt the floor dip sickly away.

A swim, I thought, was probably a good idea.

I dived in. By the time I reached the far side of the pool I was not so sure. I kicked tiredly back towards the clubhouse, and pulled myself out, gasping. Grabbing my towel and glasses I all but ran over the hot stones and hard grass to the changing rooms. These, thank God, were empty; I fumbled with a blurred bolt, locked myself into a lavatory stall, and, hands on knees, heaved up a brownish acid stew in which, when I had finally straightened up and unsteadily wiped my eyes, mint leaves were clearly identifiable. The lavatory, needless to say, would not flush, so, wiping my eyes and nose on a tap-wettened towel, I chased the vomit

down the pan with a mop-bucket full of shower water and disinfectant. Returning to the clubhouse, I bought a bottle of mineral
water, and out of sight around the back of the building, washed my
mouth out with half the contents and poured the rest over my
head. I felt better, and for the first time, noticed that it was a
beautiful day.

Sunday at the club was barbecue day and was something of a
tradition for British expatriates and diplomatic staff. Others came
too, but a beery British presence predominated. As I emerged from
behind the clubhouse I saw that the first families were beginning to
arrive, and moved to secure my deckchair.

Nelson, I mused behind closed eyes, had not given me his home
number. I had not asked for it, but then, neither had he offered it.
More than ever I was glad that he had left when he had, although,
curiously, I felt at ease, my conscience unsnagged by the later
events of the night.

A rattle announced the arrival of my coffee-tray. I found a note
in my trouser pocket, handed it to the waiter who stood between
my eyes and the sun, and squinting as he stepped from my vision,
turned to the side-table and poured hot water and milk into the
cup over the thimbleful of coffee powder. As usual, the milk delivered itself of a bluish skin and the water, which had been
standing for some time on the counter, was not quite hot enough to
dissolve the coffee. Once a spoonful of grey sugar had been added
to the warm mixture, however, I had a reason to light the day's
first Chesterfield.

I must have been drunk, I thought, dropping the match into my
saucer, I must have been very drunk. Kamatipura at one o'clock in
the morning. Not wise.

I remembered a peeling film poster, *Zakhmi*, on the crumbling
face of the little pavilion, and the arched entrance with the heavy
curtain which the boy had parted to admit me. I had stepped inside, heard a whisper of film music, 'Pyari Pyari', but seen nothing
until suddenly a movement had translated a pattern of shadows
into a figure on a divan, a square of light into a chromed transistor
radio; slowly I had made out watching eyes and a rolling, toad-like
mouth.

'Mr Stanley, I presume?'

I opened my eyes.

It was the cricket sweater that reminded me. Ian Something-or-other, the chocolate manager. I shaded my eyes with the hand that wasn't holding the cigarette.

'Ian. How are you?'

'Oh, not too bad. All parts bearing an even strain.'

'How's the chocolate?'

'Actually, it's proving pretty interesting. Listen, I'm just going up to the bar. Can I get you a beer?'

'I might,' I said, 'scrub round that one. On this occasion. I'm still rather recovering from last night.'

'No problem. How's the film?'

'Oh, preparatory stuff, you know, there's always lots to . . .'

He straightened, and looking away with the air of one shifting to a regrettable subject, dragged the long fringe back from his forehead.

'I . . . that bloke Pearcey filmed at the factory the other day.'

'Yes, I meant to ask you about that. How did it go?'

'He seemed, I don't know, pretty happy with it.'

'And what did you think?' I asked.

He frowned, hesitated. 'Do you think he could be trying to stitch us up in some way?'

'Probably,' I said, 'but I wouldn't worry about it. It's only television.'

'He seemed like such a nice bloke.'

'They always do.'

He nodded his head in silence for a moment, then, pulling his gold lighter from a trouser pocket, began to toss it from hand to hand before suddenly bringing it close to his face, frowning at it knowledgeably, and with a nod, re-pocketing it.

'D'you fancy a game of darts, a bit later? I said I might meet up with some of the consulate lot.'

'Maybe later.'

'OK, leave you in peace.'

As he moved away I could hear the barbecue being assembled behind me. I called a waiter and ordered two freshlime sodas. The alcohol had left me with a raging thirst that I knew would be with me until evening. Once everybody started arriving it would take at least forty minutes for orders to be filled; even when the club was deserted it took twenty.

As I stood silently in front of the toad-mouthed woman on the divan, my eyes gradually made out details of the place. I was in a small marble-floored chamber, decorated in filmi-Moghul style. Time, poor building materials, and the salt air of the city had caused much of its plaster ornamentation to fall away in patches from the walls; these were now hung with framed texts in Urdu script and cheap film-star portraits. It was hard to tell what the purpose of the building had originally been, a chamber for nautch-dancing, perhaps, or the folly of a rich man with a sentimental nostalgia for the Lucknow of the nawabs. I felt, for no very good reason, in control of the situation. I forced myself to enjoy its tension and my own beating-heart apprehension. I told myself I would go along with whatever scenario presented itself.

The woman lifted a fat arm, which, I noticed, was tattooed, and beckoned to the boy. When she spoke it was from a mouth so full of red saliva and masticated *paan* as to reduce her words to grunts. The boy seemed to understand, though.

He led me through a doorway to a dark area at the foot of a curving flight of steps. I followed him upwards, feeling the way with my feet, towards the pinkish light I had seen from the road. At the top of the steps a thin blue curtain was suspended at head-height from a rail. The boy parted this, and beckoned me through. I ducked beneath the rail and into a small circular area containing nothing except a single mattress covered with a dark bedspread. Above my head hung a clutch of weakly illuminated pink light bulbs. To the curved wall was taped a *Cinestar* centrefold pin-up of Sanju Saxena. I was, I realised, inside the building's dome.

'Wait here,' said the boy. He hesitated. 'And listen. The girl will ask you for a hundred rupees, because you are a foreigner. The fat *khutmal* below will order her so. But she will take less.' I found a five-rupee note by the light of the pink bulbs. '*Shukriya*, boss,' he smiled, and disappeared.

I sat for several minutes on the thin mattress. It occurred to me, belatedly, that maybe a couple of *goonda*s were being sent for and that I was to be beaten up and robbed. I stayed, nevertheless.

After a time I heard soft footsteps climbing the steps beyond the curtain.

I'm not quite sure what, or who, I was expecting. Probably not another of the stolid moon-faced Nepalese or overpainted Maharashtrians I had seen earlier in the evening. I had a feeling that they probably came a lot cheaper than a hundred, or even fifty rupees.

The figure who slipped through the blue curtains was small, dark and thin-armed. She was wearing a sari in some dark material whose colour, in the pink light, was hard to determine. Its free end was arranged over her head in such a way as to completely conceal her features. She looked like a bride. She held out a small hand wearing a digital watch.

'A hundred rupees.' The voice low, insistent.

I put my hand in my pocket, and squinted at the small roll of notes. There were three of them, each for a hundred. I could hardly, I thought, bargain her down and then ask for change. Any more than I could ask to see her face before agreeing the price. At least I could, but it would remove even the pretence of pleasure from the whole exchange.

I gave her a hundred, which, turning away, she pushed into her tight, high choli.

I kicked off my shoes and half-sat, half-lay on the mattress, my feet streaked dark with sweat and dust. She remained standing for several moments, then stiffly lowered herself into a sitting position beside me. Her face was still turned towards the curtain, away from me. Distantly, I could hear the whispering thread of the transistor at the bedside downstairs.

I placed one hand on her slender bicep. It was bisected by the silver-banded sleeve of her choli. Her skin was cool, and very soft. As I tried to steer her shoulders towards me she turned her face further away. Reaching beyond her, I lifted the end of the sari over her head, and saw immediately that despite the heavy matte foundation she was very young, probably no more than fifteen. Behind the black *kajal* her eyes were nervous. Small tribal tattooes showed through the make-up on her chin. Beneath the small tight-skinned features I could see the shaped hollows of her skull.

This was not what I had expected. I had expected, wanted even, greasy professionalism, sweat, cheap perfume. A filmi-harlot.

'Give me back the money,' I said, 'and I'll go.'

'No,' she said in the low gravel voice, 'wait.'

She stood, and her narrow hands went to one hip, beneath the sari. Standing too, I saw that she was struggling with a large safety pin which was holding the pleats of the sari in place. I withdrew her hands, which were shaking slightly, and undid the pin myself. My own hands, I noticed, were steady; curiosity was fast replacing lust. I saw that she had a large scar tracked across her lower belly. I sat down again on the mattress, and watched her drop the sari to the ground and step out of the black underskirt. Beneath this, she was wearing an ugly pair of high-cut knickers in some dark-coloured synthetic material. She sat on the bed, pulled these down her legs, and kicked them away. They caught between her toes, and as she kicked, wrapped themselves round her foot, pale gusset outwards. Raising her eyebrows in a tight, apologetic smile, she leant forward to free them. Before she drew her knees back towards her chin, I saw from the stubbled crease between the Caesarean scar and the pubic bone that she had been shaved. Presumably, I thought, some venereologist's diktat, to facilitate weekly inspection. She hugged her knees to her chin and, warily, watched me. I could see that she smelt the alcohol on my breath, knew that drunks were trouble, unpredictable.

Still fully clothed, I drew her to me. Physically she didn't resist, but I could feel her unwilling. The palm of my hand found a breast; it was hard, not flesh, not a breast at all, and beneath my fingers, something crackled inside the choli. Propping myself on one elbow, I quickly undid the buttons at her front. She shook her head, muttering at me with suppressed force to stop, pinching at my hands. As I pulled the last button open, my hundred rupees and several smaller banknotes fell to the mattress; she gathered these fast and thrust them into one of her shoes on the floor by the mattress. I could see that, beneath the choli, the cups of her nylon bra had been stuffed with rolled-up fabric of some kind. I smiled. Angry, embarrassed, she reached behind herself, unhooked the clasp, and threw the bra and its stuffing after the pants. Around both dark uneven nipples were the darker puckered scars of what looked like cigarette burns. She lay back, lowered her knees, and, simultaneously resigned and irritated, looked up at me.

'What's your name?' I asked.

She hesitated for several seconds. 'Gita,' she replied, finally.

'What happened?' I touched one of the burn marks with my finger.

'My boyfriend,' she smiled, using the English word.

The smile faded, and reaching absently between her legs, she scratched at the dry, plucked-looking vulva.

'I'm not going to hurt you, Gita,' I said. 'I just want to smoke a cigarette.'

She shrugged.

I pulled out a Chesterfield, lit it, and for a few moments, smoked in silence, tapping the ash on the floor. I offered her the cigarette; she took it doubtfully, sucked at it, held it away from herself like a Thirties vamp. I really shouldn't encourage her to smoke, I thought vaguely. I lay back and closed my eyes. My feet seemed to rise as my head tilted backwards. Beyond my eyelids the cluster of pink bulbs swam, swung, spun. Acid rose to the back of my throat.

I opened my eyes, swallowed the sour taste. A line of volleyball players was passing between myself and the sun. One of them spoke, turned, presented a palm. Behind him another made movements of laughter, slapped the proffered palm. At the back of the line the fat boy carried the heavy cassette player, a thumping bass line shivering its tinny speaker.

They settled around a table, threw themselves into deckchairs. Soft drinks materialised fast, Thums-Up, Limca, Mangola. For the beautiful, all was immediate. They wouldn't drink beer, of course, with its heavy, glycerined taste and soporific effect, but accessorised themselves with the smaller bottles, the bright straws and gassed-up lolly-waters that, in the advertisements in which they themselves appeared, signified Good Times, Young People, Carefree Summer Days.

Beside me, on a rug, two teenage girls in bikinis were slowly applying an English brand of suntan lotion to their still-pale legs. Both were smoking imported Dunhill cigarettes, as was a woman I took to be their mother. A few yards away one of the volleyball players removed his baseball boots and socks, walked to the diving board with easy self-consciousness, executed a perfect swallow dive, surfaced, flicked water from a well-controlled head of layered hair, and swam to the side of the pool. Eschewing the iron steps, he placed two palms on the hot paved edging, and in a single turning movement, pulled himself from the water to a standing position. Immediately dry, he started to walk back towards the group.

'Cute,' said one of the teens on the ground at my side.

'But can it count to ten?' wondered the other to her sister.

'Does its IQ ever exceed room-temperature?'

'Well, frankly, did Jason's?' asked the first.

Their mother threw them a dismissive glance before returning to a narrow-eyed assessment of the volleyball players. Her face shone with sun-oil except for the area around her eyes which showed the duller nacreous sheen of cosmetics. It was hard to tell if the stare that she was directing at the volleyball players was lascivious or myopic.

She and the girls were joined by a stout, uneasy figure carrying a tray of drinks.

'Right,' he said, 'who's for what?'

The smell of smoke and barbecued meat drifted across the lawn, joined that of Virginia tobacco and suntan lotion and, more distantly, seaweed. Beyond the wall the tide was low, a white line crawling over dirty sand a hundred yards away.

The fat boy fast-forwarded the cassette. It was hard to tell what the music was: a recording of an Iowa local radio show, perhaps, or a countdown of the Canadian top twenty. What was certain was that the cassette was in some way exclusive; unobtainable in Bombay. He started it again, apparently at random. The ball players instantly resumed the tiny nodding movements which, combined with very slightly closed eyes, served as their reaction to all music, then suddenly stopped as they realised, too late, that they were conceding rhythmic acknowledgement to a commercial.

'Two freshlime soda, Sir.'

I paid him. The exchange attracted the flickering attention of the teenage girls; I polished my glasses on the end of my shirt and, feeling the sun's burn at my hairline, touched my forehead with the cold glass. The girls looked away, uninterested.

This evening, I thought, I am dining with Miss Lata Khandekar in the sad, dark luxury of her 1930s apartment. I will dress with untypical care, for I am to be introduced to a person or persons unknown. The outcome of the evening is unknown. The outcome of my life is unknown.

I recited these facts to myself because something in the dismissive glances of the girls on the rug had, perversely, made me think of Emilia at her most vulnerable. A doubt dragged at me about what I had done, about the deliberate contraction of my life that I had engineered, about the way that time passed here and nothing ever changed except that people got older and the salt air and the monsoon made ideas seem pointless and turned clothes and rooms and buildings damp and old before their time. I looked up at the white sky. The crows turned. I looked at the coarse grass and the dusty potted plants between the tables and the crates of empty soft-drink bottles (Thums-Up, Limca, Mangola) and the movement of smoke and pale limbs and paper plates and hot expatriate faces. I thought of the lines that I passed every day outside the American Embassy, the combed, tight-shirted figures clutching the cheap bags and rehearsing the lies that would be so familiar to the officials before whom, a morning or two later, they would stand with such insistent hopelessness. This was a city to leave, and I had just arrived.

I checked myself, aware of the old pattern, the old reaction. Excitement and disorientation followed, on acclimatisation, by irritable lethargy. Short temper. The thing was to keep busy, swim often, and go easy on the Bulbul. And, of course, to think of England, to think of sour pubs on the edges of council estates and dark Sunday afternoons and men shovelling snow from motorways. And of Emilia, naked for Leather-jacket.

I decided to swim before drinking the freshlime soda or acquiring a paper plateful of smoky meat and hard foil-wrapped baked potatoes. I folded my glasses and placed them on the ground next to the packet of Chesterfield. As I picked my way over the spiky grass I saw Victor Das going into the changing rooms.

It was a beautiful evening. Conch-pink sky and a late breeze coming off the sea. Distantly, the sound of the sea. Myself, shaved, cool, and, for me, very adequately presentable in a linen jacket and trousers from which the suitcase creases had had time to fall, goodish white shirt, and a tie which Lata Khandekar might or might not recognise. Shoes were a pair of hand-made desert-boots, now somewhat battered, but still, I told myself, showing evidence of decently cobbled beginnings (it already felt curious to be wearing socks). In my jacket pockets were cigarettes and lighter; in my trouser pockets, money. If I appeared to be overplaying the part of the Englishman Abroad, well, there were worse parts.

The taxi was a fast one. I opened both the windows as far as they would go (two-thirds) to let in the rushing night air. The driver, I saw from his skullcap and his unadorned dashboard, was a Muslim. He had just had the cassette player fitted, and to a swooping, pleading arrangement of 'Pyari Pyari', we raced past Chowpatty Beach, past the *bhel*-puri and *kulfi* stalls, past the giant figure of the diving man at the Hindi swimming baths, past the Tarapoorevala Aquarium, past Charni Road Station and the Gymkhana, with green lights all the way. The driver smiled at the music and the speed and the ease of it. I closed my eyes and smelt the sea. At the Air India Building the driver threw the wheel to the left and we swung away from Marine Drive towards Colaba; three minutes later I was standing outside Divya Apartments.

Lounging in a chair outside the entrance, watching me without interest, was a bored-looking security man in an ersatz khaki uniform, splintered cane balanced across his knees. He nodded, feeling in his pocket for a *bidi*, as I stepped past him.

The light in the lift had not been repaired, and once again it was in darkness that I rose on the small shuddering floor through the silent layers of flats. As I stepped out, gates clattering behind me, there was a dim light beneath Lata Khandekar's door; I knocked, and a half-minute later Leelabai admitted me with a shaded look which was almost a smile. I stepped past her into the hall. A faint sandalwood smell overlaid that of floor-polish and damp furniture. The heavy elliptical chandelier suspended from the ceiling's centre had been switched on; it was dimly reflected in the floor, and the pillars and panels and tables stood dark in its yellowed gleam.

Once again the apartment, with its residue of earlier lives, earlier luxuries, seemed pressingly familiar, but it wasn't until Leelabai moved to one of the tall windows to correct a curtain's imperfect fall and a taxi driver's film song began to replay itself in my mind that memory shifted and I suddenly and finally knew exactly where I was.

When Leelabai silently led me out on to the roof and along the colonnade towards one of the domed pavilions, this time one of those overlooking the sea rather than the causeway, it was with curious unsurprise that I saw that the small dark figure who stepped into the moonlight to meet me was the actress Lakshmi Khandekar.

IX

〜〜〜〜〜

Beth's fake Fendi bag, somehow, made me feel vulnerable and off-centre. It lay beside me on the broad, unyielding back seat of the Ambassador and reminded me that, whatever kind of Barefoot Contessa I might have been going as, I wasn't quite the real thing.

In front of me the driver was wearing sunglasses. Inadvisably, I would have thought, given the fading light.

Several things at that moment, as it happened, irritated me quite a bit. I was irritated at the intense disadvantage I found myself at, with the silent driver in the sunglasses throwing the big uncomfortable car all over the place; I was irritated that I was not going to be able to tell the middle-aged hero at the other end of the journey that the only reason that I had turned out for him was the thought of the alternative, i.e. another evening of Dane's beer-can crumpling and Beth's awful bright transparent unhappiness; irritated that I hadn't been able to manufacture a third independent choice for myself; irritated that Sanju Saxena thought that all it took to hook me, or at least summon me, was two minutes' chat and a twenty-year-old limo; irritated that that was all it HAD taken; and most of all, irritated to feel, somewhere behind my ribcage, a prickle of anticipation.

The driver pushed a cassette under the dashboard. The car speakers, for once, were good, sounded expensive, and I recognised the film tune as one I'd been hearing everywhere. I closed my eyes, and against my better judgement, almost to my embarrassment, allowed myself to be carried away by the amplified sitars and the sugared, dark-eyed yearnings of the singer. The song was somehow the perfect song for the evening, for my uncertainty, for the fading light. Without understanding a single word of it, I understood it, and knew that I had longed, myself, for the same unreachable time, for the same faceless love that danced just beyond the reach of memory.

There had been a time at the school. A moment when I'd caught sight of my teacher's face, reflected in the classroom mirror. In her eyes, as they followed me, I had seen the quickening, quickly suppressed, and the thoughtfulness which followed. That had been the moment when I had first allowed myself to hope; had started to dream, night and day, asleep or awake, of performance. I knew that on the stage, somehow, somewhere amongst the painted leaves, I would find the lost time, the lost place.

There had been a birthday. My parents had bought me, in Aberdeen of all places (we were still living in the awful house in AWFUL Girdle Ness) a book of photographs of Galina Ulanova teaching the nineteen-year-old Ekaterina Maximova the role of Giselle, at the Bolshoi. I had pored over the photographs for months, searching their grainy details, distant mirrors and darkest corners, dreaming myself the broad-faced Maximova, Russian, cat's-eyed, and an enemy of the West. Maximova had already been a soloist in the company at the time the photographs were taken, but it was the Giselle debut that had brought a Moscow audience to its feet and a curious knowledge and a change to her eyes.

Most of my dreams, though, were London dreams. London was nearer to Scotland than Moscow, and could be reached by train rather than defection.

And my dreams, my half-way London dreams, had come true; I had made my first entrance with the company as a *Midsummer Night's Dream* fairy and the moment had been lost in streaking fright and a panic about shoes and the smell of deodorant. Only when I was replacing the moth-silver tutu on its hanger, thankful for my survival, worried how my parents would behave if they ran into each other backstage, had I remembered that I had forgotten to remember.

And somehow, over the years, even in my best and my iciest and my most dangerous moments, as first girl down the ramp in *Bayadère* or as Myrtha ('June Webster's BALEFUL Queen of the Wilis', as *The Times* described me) the unreachable time and place had remained unreachable.

There had been everything else, of course – fear, elation, tears, pain, moments when beauty unfurled itself for me like a banner, moments when nothing was there for me at all – but time, not giving a damn either way, had remained time. Hooks and eyes had cut into my back, faithless partners had bruised my ribs, pancake had baked to my face and my toes had bled.

I had just . . . danced.

Only now that I had stopped, had left, did I think that maybe I understood. Understood that only afterwards, only in uncertain memory were these times touched by anything more than was really there. And by then of course, they were unreachable.

I opened my eyes and the car window, and the warm evening air poured over my face. The light had gone, the driver's sunglasses finally been removed, as we raced past the Haji Ali mosque. On the pavement, faces turned to me silently, recognising the heavy white car as belonging to someone of wealth, importance, status. Mahalakshmi Racecourse swept past to our right and the driver turned off towards the sea. As we left the main road behind us, the character of the area changed. Shorefront hutments stood dark against the water, there were flickering lamps and the smell of fish, of mud, of the bay. At the roadside a huge hoarding surrounded by bamboo scaffolding rose out of the black lean-tos. A man was perched on its topmost crossbeam, painting by the light of a small lamp. As we left the hoarding behind us it resolved itself into the portrait of an actress, rapturous with either bliss or pain, her shoulders and shredded blouse rising from eight rock-carved letters forming the single word: *Khandaan*.

There had begun to be something proprietorial of the place in the driver's manner, and I was nervously aware (and angry at myself for the nerves) that we were close to wherever we were going. Sure enough, only minutes later, we turned into a lane and stopped outside a scaffolded and apparently uncompleted building several storeys high. There was just enough light to follow the driver up a narrow path through an area of tangled weeds and rusted spars to the entrance, where a watchman leant, dozing, against a pyramid of solidified concrete sacks. The driver led me up a dark staircase to the first floor, and rang the bell. A servant woman looked me up and down and nodded me in. Behind me, the driver retreated down the stairs.

The floor of the flat was white, new-looking marble. I supposed I should take off my shoes. It was cool underfoot, but I felt uncomfortable in the tight Italian suit, clutching the gilt-strapped bag.

Beyond us was the sound of gunfire, distant shouts and air-conditioning. I followed the servant down the corridor and into a large pale room. In the centre of its marble floor a woman of about sixty sat in a Rexine-covered recliner chair opposite a giant television and videotape machine. She did not look up as I came in. On the flickering screen, three feet away from her face, Sanju Saxena thrashed a policeman with a length of heavy chain. The light from the screen touched her white hair and her white cotton sari. The volume was on maximum.

I looked around; inside the room there didn't seem to be anywhere to sit. A heavy air-conditioning unit shuddered and dripped from one of the walls, and beyond it the room opened on to a balcony, overlooking the white car and the abandoned garden below. As I looked down, I saw the driver light a cigarette, flip the match into the darkness, open the front doors of the car and lie down across the seats.

The servant reappeared with a stainless-steel beaker of water, and looked questioningly at me. Nothing for it, I thought, and lowered myself to the hard marble floor in front of the TV. Minutes passed. On the screen Saxena, in jewelled turban and armed with a scimitar, made a speedboat getaway past the Gateway of India. Behind him, out to sea, stood the oil-platform on which Dane was working.

An intermission in the film was announced by a commercial for peanut-oil. At my side, a pale hand reached for a silver bell. The servant returned in answer to its ring, an unsteady finger was pointed at the set, and the videotape halted. The screen continued to roar at us, though, a black and white blizzard, as the servant retired and my hostess turned to me with a vague smile. Her lips were moving, and I realised she was speaking to me. Half-crouching, I moved closer, but could hear nothing. Eventually I found the volume control, the roar of the set gave way to the quieter shuddering of the air-conditioning unit and I could hear the words that she was saying.

'British Home Stores,' she was quietly repeating, 'British Home Stores . . .'

'British Home Stores?' I asked, not understanding.

'British Home Stores,' she confirmed sadly, and fell silent, her eyes wandering.

I thought for a long moment.

'Marks and Spencer?' I suggested.

'Marks and Spencer,' she nodded, happy again. 'Littlewoods,' she added after a slight pause.

'Freeman, Hardy, Willis?' I offered, and when there was no reaction, 'Dorothy Perkins?'

But the sad, unfocused look had returned. I thought hard, determined to retrieve the smile.

'Berkertex?' I queried, 'Saxone? Dolcis?' But I was losing her. One last try. 'John Lewis?'

The smile returned instantly, gentle and calm. 'Selfridges,' she whispered, and reached out a pale, ringed hand to me from her lap. Uncertain, I took it, but she lifted it from my grasp, and touched my hair.

Of course, I thought. 'Boots?'

We both smiled. I had her there.

'Miss Webster. June. How's things?'

Sanju Saxena was preceded by a cloud of citrus Cologne and the clip of Cuban heels on marble. The man himself was steaming slightly from the shower and dressed in his trademark black.

'Things,' I said, 'is just fine.' I was very slightly irritated by his not having been ready. Maybe I should have had the driver sit around another hour or two. Maybe, on the other hand, the actor would simply have headed for the bathroom when he saw the car arrive, however late.

'Come out on to the balcony,' he ordered, patting softly at his damply layered hair. 'I see you've met my mother.' He bent to the control switches on the television. The film resumed, but at a very slightly lower volume than before. Mother Saxena was instantly re-immersed, if now forced to crane forward slightly to catch the dialogue. 'I've given her all this,' said Sanju with an expansive wave of the hand. 'Everything you see. This flat. Everything. I had it built . . . It gave me great pleasure.'

A male servant, whom I had not yet seen, appeared behind us.

Sanju spoke a few words to him and he withdrew, reappearing moments later with a tray holding three bottles of Johnny Walker Black Label whisky and, joy, a cold bottle of Asti Spumante.

Sanju smiled at my surprise and steered my elbow towards a seat on the balcony. I stepped into the slight, fishy breeze.

'For you,' he said, hefting the Asti, 'la Champagne de la France.'

'Well,' I said, 'since you twist my arm . . .'

'I've hurt you?'

'Not at all,' I replied. 'Just an expression.'

'I'm glad. I wouldn't wish to . . . Bottoms up?'

'Mmmm, absolutely.'

As it happens, I know exactly how much Asti Spumante I can drink before my judgement is, as they say, impaired, because drinking Asti Spumante is something we used to do quite a lot of on tour and I know that my safety limit is somewhere around about the bottom of the lower label. Having said that, of course, Pauline and I once whacked down a bottle each between matinée and evening performances of some triple bill in Nottingham that neither of us had much to do in.

'Aren't you married?' I asked Sanju. He took a deep breath. Exhaled. Seemed to consider.

'I'll tell you,' he said. 'I'm married. I have two sons and a daughter whom I love very much. I have a mistress who my wife knows about. I have an unofficial mistress who my mistress knows about but my wife doesn't, and I have a girlfriend who noboby knows about.'

'It sounds very complicated,' I said, 'how do you keep them all apart?'

He frowned at the whisky, which he was drinking without water. On the screen behind us I could hear another fist-fight. The noise of punches landing was mechanical, each smack identical.

'See, June,' he replied, 'there's a balance. A balance, see, between possession and knowledge. Look at it this way. The more they have of me, these women, the less, in a way, they know. So my wife, who has more of me than any of the others, knows less ABOUT the others than anyone else. My girlfriend, who has less of me than all of the others, knows more about my situation than any of them.

Which, if you think about it, is a kind of intimacy which is unique to her. It's a trade-off, really, isn't it? Time against knowledge; presence against intimacy.'

'It sounds hard, though,' I said. 'The further up the scale you are, the more in the dark you are. I don't envy your wife, for example.'

'I honour my wife. Shakuntala has a beautiful home, her children go to the best schools, she has security, and she has the respect and admiration of all. We have a good marriage.'

'And she's happy?'

'Define your terms, June. This is India. My wife was a film actress at a time when not many film actresses made good marriages.'

'Well, the official mistress, then. Whose name, unless I'm very much mistaken, is Swaroop. *N'est-ce pas?*'

He laughed at that, a real laugh, and for a moment, behind the residue of the irritation, I found myself almost liking him.

'I'm sorry, June,' he shook his head, 'I don't mean to laugh, and it's not directed at you. It's just the way that the whole world knows my business ... Price of stardom, I guess. Here, let me fill that. Please. And yes, her name is Swaroop.'

'Well, it can't be so great for her; your wife has the kids and the home, the girlfriend has the secrets, the unofficial mistress is banging at the door, what's in it for Swaroop?'

'Swaroop has a definite position in my life. If I have to go to a film party, five-star thing, reception, *muharat* ...'

'A what?'

'A *muharat*. It's when a film venture is blessed. A priest comes, a coconut is broken, a prayer is offered, and the first shot canned. And for good luck, they say, that shot should always be used in the final film.'

'Right. I see. What's the word again?'

'*Muharat*. And what I was saying was that Swaroop has a very definite status as my ... companion. It keeps the *masala* magazines happy, gives them a long-running, what, soap opera, to add a twist to, every week, the rows, the reconciliations, and so on. And the truth is that she really rather enjoys the role that the film mags have given her of . . .' He rolled his eyes, drank, '. . . of "tigress", "sultry temptress", and so on. And although my wife doesn't allow Swaroop's name to be spoken in our house and would never acknowledge her existence, I know that, deep down, she can actually live quite happily with the IDEA of Swaroop. Swaroop is, how to put it, the devil she knows. And she equally knows that Swaroop's a devil I'd never leave her for. It would be too . . . hazardous. Too much furniture would get broken; we're too similar. Both ageing, both vain, both chronically faithless . . .'

'I'm surprised you've survived without one of these women shooting you.' As if to confirm my words, a volley of gunfire rang out from the television.

'Well, you'll probably misunderstand this, June, but my behaviour to all my "women", as you call them, is entirely honourable. *Accha*, OK, yes, I keep them separate and all, but I don't play one off against the other, I don't tell them each other's secrets, and for the time that I'm with any particular one I am entirely hers, there for her . . . so I'm faithful actually, in that way, to each of them. But how did we get to be talking about all this, about me? Tell me about yourself, June.'

It was an order I'd been given before. I stared out over the bay looking for some idea as to where to begin.

I have to say that he was a good listener. It turned out that he had actually seen the company when they'd visited Delhi some years ago. I hadn't been there of course, I'd been immobilised with my knee, in and out of hospital, and had missed the whole tour. But when Sanju discovered that I had been with the company there was a subtle shift in his angle of attack. Slightly more gloves off. Performer to performer. Glamour to glamour. Or something.

The Asti level crept downwards. Bits and pieces were brought to eat, some of them spiced. I remembered to use my right hand. At one point the film ended on the video, the roaring blizzard returned, and the silver bell was rung. I watched as the servant removed the cassette and replaced it without another from a large pile.

'She loves my films,' said Sanju. 'Excuse me.' He moved over to have a word with her before the next picture began. They spoke in

Hindi until the peanut-oil adverts finished and the main feature began.

He returned to the balcony and poured himself another generous slug of Black Label.

'Nectar,' he said, indicating the shot glass. 'In Hindi we say *amrit*. Amritsar means City of Nectar. And I remember once flying to do a show in Nairobi with Poonam and Dimple and Raj and some of the others – I'll never forget – there was this very . . . enthusiastic Sardar in the first class with us all, damn sweet guy, big film fan, wanted to buy us all drinks, had already had one or two himself, of course, was shouting to the stewardess, "Miss, Miss, bring us some Walking Johnny, Walking Johnny all round."' Sanju nodded his head and sniffed at his whisky with sad amusement. 'Sweet guy . . .'

'Your mother,' I began. The Asti Spumante had reached the bottom of the lower label.

'My mother,' he replied, beginning to articulate his words with care.

'What exactly does she think I'm doing here?'

'In Bombay?'

'In this flat.'

He lifted first his eyebrows, effortfully, then his eyelids. Looked out over the bay.

'My mother never liked Shakuntala, my wife. She disapproved of my marrying an actress.'

'But you're an actor.'

'I am a Saxena first. If I am an actor, well, I was educated for better things, and in my mother's view, for a better wife than a middle-class Maharashtrian.'

'Do you bring . . . the others here? Swaroop, and so on?'

'My mother adores Swaroop. She's a big fan.'

'But Swaroop's an actress?'

'Of course she's an actress. But she's not my wife. My mother loves the film crowd, her only regret is that I'm married to an ex-member of it.'

'Your wife doesn't see film people any more?'

'Of course not . . .' He emptied the glass in a swallow, grimacing, '. . . she's a married woman. But tell me something, June, you speak Hindi? Because my mother, who never speaks English, was saying that you were talking about shopping in London.'

'Oh, only in the most general terms . . .' I said, vaguely. 'But you tell me something.'

'Yes,' he replied.

'What's your girlfriend's name?'

'Ahhh . . . Gita.'

'Does Gita know I'm here?'

'No. No she doesn't.'

'So I alone have the whole picture?'

He smiled. 'You alone have the whole picture.'

He looked at me. I looked away. From the television came the unmistakable swirling announcement of a big song-and-dance number. I was suddenly aware that, somehow, I'd switched things to my disadvantage. The Asti bubbles rose to my throat.

I'm with Charlie de la Tour for what I have the feeling is going to be one of the last times. We are where, Oxford? Bristol? On the way back to London, anyway, to families, own flats, real life. Wherever we are, Charlie, as a principal, has a proper hotel room – mournful, darkish, with plastic ferns in a dry vase and a plaster-board partition bisecting the ceiling mouldings – but a proper hotel room.

What have we just danced? Probably the hated *Nutcracker*, given that it is cold, and slush-stained suede boots are standing by the door and the three bars of the electric fire are sputtering and giving off the smell of burnt dust. If it was *Nutcracker* then we are approaching the Christmas break, always, of recent years, a depressing time for me. With Beth and Steph both in the States I have to split my holiday between Dad and his bosomy Moira in Aberdeen, and Mom and the frankly unsavoury Phil in London. The whole thing, the whole seasonal schlep, always ends up with me longing for spring, sunshine, and an end to it all.

Anyway here I am, glad to see the end of *Nutcracker* ('Of the minor roles, the measured sinuosity of June Webster's Arabian Variation deserves mention . . .'), but depressed at the same time, as always, by the season's end. Not everyone will be returning in January, and to greet those of us that do return there will be the usual deadly little crop of eighteen-year-olds from the school, all private jokes and wonderment and secret calculation.

Meanwhile, snow has closed several roads and restaurants. Ten of us have tried to make a go of it in an otherwise empty steakhouse, but despite heavy ordering of wine and brave efforts at rowdiness, the meal has ended in near silence, the staff standing around checking their watches. Even Charlie is affected.

In the hotel room I draw the heavy liver-coloured curtains over the falling snow, and climb into bed in my track suit. There is a radio console built into the veneered headboard. I twist the knobs; there is a single station, playing lounge-bar arrangements of Christmas carols. Lifting a corner of the curtains I look out on to a blurred, snow-piled window-ledge.

Leaving the electric fire on, Charlie turns out the light at the door and the bedside, and gets in beside me. The radio crackles into silence.

'Are you really going to SLEEP in this lot?' he asks, and I feel his hand at the drawstring at my waist.

I wriggle on to my stomach. 'Turn the bedside light on again,' I ask him.

Sitting up, I pull the track-suit top over my head.

'Why?'

'Please, Charlie. Just because.'

'Because what?'

'Because because.'

He turns, reaches, and turns back, frowning, in the light.

'What's up, Junie?'

'Just want you to tell me something.'

'What?' Warily.

'How do you think I look?'

'What d'you mean, look, it's . . .'

' . . . I mean just, starting from the top, how do I look. Out of ten?'

'June, give us a . . . OK, you look, bearing in mind the time and place, great.'

' . . . Eyes?'

He blinks, and rubs his own.

'Ten. I love grey eyes. Aren't you cold?'

'Mouth?'

'OK. A good mouth. A Balanchine rather than an Ashton or a MacMillan mouth, but still . . . a very nice mouth. Seven.'

'Breasts?'

'You have perfect ballet tits, June. Ten marks to each of them. I'd better turn that fire out, or we'll burn this place to the ground.' He rolls from the bed, and hobbles to the switch. 'God, it's cold enough, though.'

'Forgetting ballet.'

'Forgetting ballet what?' He hauls the bedclothes back over himself.

'That they're ballet tits. As you so sweetly put it. Them.'

'Can we drop this, them?'

'No. Tell me. Against your absolute ideal. In terms of shape, size, definition, colour . . .'

And so on. Outside the window the snow falls.

As an item, really we've pretty much run out of steam, although he's been as faithful to me, I guess, as he's ever been to anyone. I half-suspect that he's had a crack at Pauline. I don't blame him.

I had no idea where we were, except that it was somewhere below Malabar Hill and I thought that I could still smell the sea.

We had left Sanju's mother nodding in front of the video and the bottles standing on the tray; in the rusting garden, a shout had woken the driver, who had been snoring gently, hands cupped over his crotch. The drive had taken no more than a few gliding minutes. Or so it seemed.

'Some friends, we're going to see,' Sanju had said. 'Very, very sweet guys.'

The door, implausibly studded, like the entrance to a Hollywood castle, was opened by a male servant. We were shown along an unlit corridor and into a bright, white-pillared area in which a dozen men lounged in casually watchful attitudes on pillows arranged at either side of a long carpet. Spot-lights angled from the pillars through cigarette smoke, touched whisky glasses, large ashtrays, elaborately layered hair. Eyes flickered between Sanju and myself as I blinked in the hot light and smoke; there were tight smiles, nods of recognition, gripped palms. One man stood up; a lean, bearded figure in a striped, floor-length shirt arrangement whom Sanju unsmilingly embraced.

'Haji,' Sanju indicated me, 'June Webster, from London.'

'*Salaam aleikum*,' said the bearded one.

I held out my hand. 'Hi,' I said. 'Nice to meet you.'

He smiled at me, dark-browed, and spoke, not in English, to Sanju. Sanju smiled in turn, did not translate, answered in the same language. I found that the nails of the hand holding the handbag were cutting into my palm. My high-heeled ankles ached on the marble floor.

'The Haji is a very dangerous man,' Sanju said, turning to me with whiskied pride. 'A killer.'

'I'll bear that in mind,' I answered, feeling myself sway.

June Duprez. That was the name I was trying to remember, at least I thought it was. The Hollywood actress who Grace always said looked so like me; the star of *The Thief of Baghdad*.

June Duprez.

It was a hot night. Above us, an electric fan whopped round, billowing the sugar-pink silk curtains which hung, at intervals, from rails and screens. Room had been made for Sanju on the cushions, and I had arranged myself, not particularly comfortably, given the Italian skirt, on a sort of bolster arrangement behind him.

I was still being fairly frankly examined by all the men in the room. Amongst the younger, Western-dressed ones, there was a certain amount of joshing, dry laughter, palm-slapping. Although these routines weren't, apart from the odd word, conducted in English, I was very much aware that they were being worked through for my benefit. Which is a thing, of course, that men do, but that didn't make me feel any better about being the only woman in the room.

Opposite me was an overblown type who I thought was probably an actor. Catching my eye he raised a heavy eyebrow and jacked the linen sleeves up his forearms to show the gold watch and identity bracelet. I looked away, expressionless as I could manage. This is how the volleyball boys would end up, I thought; jowly, red-eyed, but casual unto death.

'Drink, Madam?' said the voice of the servant at my elbow.

'Sherbet,' I replied facetiously, half-curious. He nodded, and returned moments later with a plate of powdery sweets and a Bohemian crystal glass of what I immediately recognised to be Asti Spumante. Sanju turned to me, smiled briefly, and helped himself to one of the sweets.

From the air of idle expectancy, some kind of entertainment seemed to be about to kick off. At the far end of the long carpet, on a sort of mattressed podium, four musicians sat with their instruments. Beyond them, in the darkness, high walls enclosed the gleam of water and the silhouettes of bushes and palms. Against the furthest wall was a frangipani tree, and above it reared a vast neon hoarding, bathing the garden below in alternate rose and violet.

Conversation faded. From the interior of the house, up the carpet, came a heavily made-up woman of about forty. She was dressed in a mauve chiffon sari and her low-cut bodice was picked out in sequins. Huge gold earrings framed her chins, false eyelashes batted at her cheeks. She passed me in a dizzying wave of perfume.

Arranging herself in front of the musicians, pausing briefly to dimple at the Haji, she picked up a radio microphone.

The musicians, serious-looking men in white cotton, started to play. There was a stringed instrument with a bow, a tall thing like a sitar, a kind of boxed accordion, and finally, the one thing I could name, a percussionist's *tabla* set.

The singer started slowly, with a series of sustained, almost experimental notes. Her voice was unlike any I had ever heard. It was the voice of a child, abandoned, but at the same time, infinitely controlled. It hung over the instruments' accompaniment like a bird, falling away at the breath's end into a series of diminishing spirals before, at the last moment, finding itself again. It was a much lonelier, less approachable sound than the film music I had been listening to earlier, and seemed curiously at odds with the appearance of the singer.

The tempo quickened. The *tabla* player waited unmoving for several minutes, before, holding a silent beat, he bowed, and his fingers became a blur over the skins. I tried to count it through, but was almost immediately lost, and gave up.

The singer closed her eyes. I was impressed; she had her audience where she wanted them, and personally I wouldn't have had these swingers marked down as a pushover. But they seemed to love it, and from time to time, when she delivered some phrase of particular subtlety, they opened their hands, nodding and murmuring their appreciation.

I felt a pluck at my sleeve; it was a servant girl. Crouching, as if leaving a cinema, I followed her across the marble floor into the corridor and through a pair of carved wooden doors.

'Welcome to the *zenana*. Thought you might like a break from the chaps.'

It was a moment before I recognised her. The actress from Film City.

'Priya!' I said, surprised. 'Hi. Wow. Am I glad to see you. God, I must sit down.'

The room was broken up by dark screens, again in carved wood; against one wall was a large divan, surmounted by a portrait of, if I wasn't mistaken, Dolly Parton. Priya, expensive-looking in turquoise, was sitting with her feet up on an elaborate Versailles-style dressing table, smoking. She looked older than she had on the film set.

'Help yourself,' she said, indicating the divan.

I helped myself. 'God, my feet. That's better. What are you . . . What was it you called this place?'

'The *zenana*. Women's quarters. The whole building, as you've probably noticed, is a sort of bad-taste exercise in Moghul revival. The fantasy of a rich man who was born poor. And based, needless to say, on the movies. Smoke?'

'No thanks, I don't. But it's good to see you again; what exactly . . .' I hesitated.

'. . . what exactly is this place?' prompted Priya, 'or what exactly am I doing here? Well the answer to the first question is simple.' She lowered her voice. 'This is the house of one Haji Ibrahim, who is basically, I suppose you would say, a godfather, a crime don. These guys, his guests, a lot of them from the film business, are here to receive his hospitality, to pay him respect.' She looked at her hands. 'I, on the other hand, came here with one of those guys and his . . . girlfriend, to, ummm, see Sanju. Who, please don't be offended, June, seems to have come with you, if you see what I mean.'

Above my head revolved a chandelier. It was sparkling, I thought, rather more than was strictly necessary.

'Sorry, Priya, I'm afraid you'll have to take it very slowly. I've poured the best part of a litre of wine into myself tonight, and I'm not feeling very clever. What is it I'm not supposed to be offended about?' The chandelier was still. Now it was the ceiling which was revolving.

'OK, hang on a minute.' She turned, and left the room by a side-door. The sound of a television, which I had vaguely registered as coming from the next room, abruptly ceased. At some further distance I could still hear the singer, and the thump of the *tabla*. My head swam.

'This is Sima,' said Priya. 'Another actress.' A heavily blushered and eye-shadowed creature appeared in front of me, trailing a cigarette.

'Hi, Sima,' I replied, squaring up my gaze. 'I'm June. Forgive me if I don't get up.'

'June,' said Priya, thoughtfully, 'would you like something to eat? Have you . . . ?'

I suddenly realised I hadn't.

'Oh, please, yes, that would be wonderful.'

She pressed a bell, and the girl came.

'See,' said Priya, 'this is how it is.'

She, Sima and I were sharing the divan with an ashtray and at least a dozen stainless-steel food dishes, now cooling. I was picking Alphonso mango fibres from my teeth.

'Sanju, like Sima's boyfriend, Amar, is married. You probably know that Sanju is married to Shakuntala Karkar, who was once an actress. Well, Amar is married to a woman called Swati,' she looked at Sima, who smiled, 'EQUALLY dreadful, and neither of them is about to let their husbands go. OK so far?'

'OK.' I was beginning to feel slightly better.

'*Accha*, good. Now, Amar had said to Sima, as Sanju had said to me, that if he was free he would marry her.'

'Sanju has told you he would marry you?' I asked Priya, amazed.

'I'm afraid so,' she said with a smile.

'Don't be afraid on my behalf,' I said, 'I think that sounds great. I mean, there's no question of any . . .'

'Between Sanju and yourself? I know that. In the same way that I knew he'd ask you out. In that way, he can't help himself.' She smiled absently.

I'm not hearing this, I thought.

'So, anyway,' I said, 'go on.'

'Well, the point is, there IS a way in which Amar can marry Sima and Sanju marry me.'

'Which is?'

'Which is that they become Muslims.'

'You're kidding.'

'I'm serious. Muslims can have more than one wife, and the Haji knows people who can sort the whole thing out. Amar and Sima were invited tonight, knew Sanju would be here, so we were all going to talk about it tonight. And then, no offence, Sanju brought you along.'

'But isn't there someone else in the picture? Swaroop, isn't it, her name?'

'Oh . . . Swaroop, he just drags her around these boring filmi parties. See, he doesn't love her, or anything, she just keeps him in the film mags.'

The unofficial mistress, I thought, the words bursting slowly in my brain like bubbles, Priya is the unofficial mistress.

'You're not upset?' asked Priya, anxiously.

'Not in the least,' I said, 'really. Not even,' I closed my eyes, 'a . . . SPECK upset.'

'Thank you, June. You're very . . .'

' . . . Can we go outside?' I asked. Closing my eyes had been a mistake.

'Sure, yaar,' said Priya. 'We'll have to parade past the heroes to get there, though.'

'I'll try not to fall over, I promise.'

We arranged ourselves in the mirror. My hair, needless to say, had died on me, and I knew it must reek of smoke. We waited for a break in the singing, and trooped through. Hundred-year-old eyes followed us. Walking Johnny. Only the Haji looked as alert as when I had first seen him. Sanju, unfocused, frowned as we passed, but otherwise gave no reaction to Priya's presence. The actor type who had been sitting opposite me nodded at Sima.

'That's Amar,' whispered Priya. 'His name means Immortal.'

I raised an eyebrow at her. She smiled.

The garden was cooler; there was a faint salt breeze, and the sweet, cloying scent of frangipani. We leant against the plaster of the wall, as the neon hoarding turned us from pink to blue and to pink again. Inside, a new singer had begun.

'What are the words?' I asked Sima.

She told me. 'It's Urdu,' she said. 'A *ghazal*. A love song.' She moved out of the sightline of the men inside.

'. . . What is my heart?' translated Priya, arranging herself cross-legged on a stone slab. 'Take my whole life . . .'

'"*Jaan*" means life?' I asked.

'"*Jaan*" means life.'

A shooting star raced across the sky; they were common here, I'd seen several.

'You're thinking,' said Priya, following my gaze, 'that for an educated woman, I'm really pretty . . . naive?'

'I wasn't thinking that,' I said. 'Really. It's just that, to me, it doesn't seem like much of a deal.'

'When does it ever seem like a deal?' asked Priya.

We stood in silence.

'I think I should go,' I said.

'Take Sanju's driver. There's no need to explain to anyone.'

'You're staying here?'

'I'm staying here.'

A gate in the wall led out to the front of the house and the cars.

'Good luck,' I said. 'Ring me at the hotel and tell me how it goes.'

'I promise,' said Priya.

'Mom, please!' I say, 'Put it on PROPERLY.'

The scarlet bobble-hat is perched jauntily on the back of her head, showing off the full Dorothy fringe. She looks like the robin

in the Christmas card, the one that wears the scarf. Outside the car
the heath is grey, the snow tracked and patched with mud.

'Come on,' I say, 'for God's sake. Pull it down over your ears.
They'll freeze. We're going for a walk. I'm not sitting in this horrible van all afternoon.' I curl my toes inside my socks and boots.

'What's wrong with this van?' she asks.

What's wrong with the van, of course, is that it is Phil's van, and
it has dark, worn places where he and his friends have sat in their
overalls and cardigans and farted out their curries.

'It smells of Phil's body,' I say, 'and it's full of disgusting things.'

'It DOESN'T. And whatever do you mean, June, "disgusting
things"?'

'I mean old insoles and spare parts and grease from the back of
people's necks, I don't know what I mean, it's just GHASTLY and
. . . I don't know, this just isn't the way that we've EVER lived our
lives. I'm sorry, Mom, but it just . . . it just ISN'T.' She clutches the
steering wheel. This too bears the dark residue of his touch. She
purses her lips. They are chapped, and ever since a cosmetic make-
over in Selfridges some years ago, have been faintly outlined in
white pencil. She takes a deep breath through her nose.

'I don't know, June, ever since you've been in that ballet company you have just been so, I don't know, so UNLOVING, so . . .
SNOBBISH. We're ordinary folk, June. You think that because YOU
don't have anyone special . . . you just don't seem to understand
that I have . . . needs.'

'I'm sorry, Mom, but NOBODY could have needs involving Phil. I
mean he keeps MAGGOTS in the FRIDGE, Mom. How gross is that?'

'Millions of men, June, like fishing. It's good for a man to have a
hobby.'

'I'm sorry, Mom, I just don't think he's good enough for you
and that's a fact.'

'What you mean, June, is that he's not good enough for YOU.'
She roots around in her handbag and finds her briquet lighter and
a packet of the slimline cigarettes she occasionally smokes. She is
wearing fingerless pink angora gloves.

'Do you think he doesn't know what you think of him?' she asks.
She thumbs at the lighter, shakes it, thumbs it alight.

'Can we walk,' I ask, 'if you're going to smoke?'

She snaps her head back as she exhales. Looks at me sideways. 'You never miss a chance, do you?'

'What do you mean?'

'Oh, to criticise, to show superiority. You see, June, you don't remember, you're too young ... how things were, then, in Mineola. You have some idea that everything was, I don't know ...'

Long silence. Shaking and lowering of head. She sniffs, her chin trembles.

' ... a wonderful time there, well, we DIDN'T ...'

She bites her lip. There is lipstick on her teeth. A single mascara tear rolls down her cheek. She lifts her hands from the steering wheel, and spreads her fingers. They too tremble. She lowers them back to the wheel.

From the dashboard Phil's spare pair of glasses watch me. They have yellowing, fake tortoiseshell frames and have been repaired with insulating tape. Next to them is a packet of man-size tissues. I pluck one and offer it, and at the same time wipe the condensation from the window with my coat-sleeve. A gum-booted family trudges past.

She blows her nose, and leans across me to check her eyes in the mirror.

'I'm sorry, Mom.'

She sniffs, dabbing at her eyes with angry strokes of the tissue.

' ... NOT sorry, June, I know you, and you've NEVER been sorry ... Born with a GOD-GIVEN gift ... developed at the cost of GREAT SACRIFICE by your father and me ... you think that that makes you special. Well it doesn't. It DAMN well doesn't. And if one day — '

' ... you have children of your own ...' I complete the sentence for her ' ... you hope that they're not as ungrateful as I've turned out to be. OK, I know, let's walk.'

Heads down, not talking, we take the path towards the ponds. The cold makes my eyes water. On my coat I am wearing Mom's Christmas present, which is a wooden brooch painted like a rainbow.

Children carrying trays and makeshift toboggans push past us; a slushy snowball bursts at our feet.

'How's the work going?' I ask, judging that enough silence has passed.

'Oh, you know,' she hesitates, 'OK.'

'Are they going to send you on that course, do you think?'

'They might. They might not.'

'But they can't keep you as a secretary for ever, surely?'

'They can. And I'm NOT a secretary, I'm a PA and systems operator.'

'Sorry.'

She stops dead, hauls the pink angora hands from the pockets of her coat, balls them into little fists, and punches downwards at the air.

'You're NOT sorry at all, June. You make an absolute POINT of implying that I do some kind of . . . brainless, unskilled work, so that you can be proved right. So that you can all say: she left her husband for what, for this? Well, if you want to know, I'd have retrained even if it HAD only led to being a secretary. For all that you look down on Phil because he doesn't . . . drive a fast car or dress in the latest styles or . . . whatever. He's a brilliant man and he was a wonderful teacher. Brilliant in a way that none of you, and most especially not you, June, with all your fancy ways, will ever understand.'

I am impressed. This is fighting talk. There is colour in her cheeks which, for once, owes nothing to the make-up counter. In front of us are the ponds. And there is Phil in his jaunty Breton yachting cap, surrounded by equipment, by flasks, by Tupperware containers. As we approach, I notice that one of his tackle boxes, filled with particularly vicious-looking lures, is the same model that I use for stage make-up.

He turns round. His toothy smile steams in the cold, reminding me of the radiator grille of his van. In one hand he holds a frozen herring, in the other, a treble hook on a wire trace.

'Ladies,' he says, indicating a pair of folding seats, 'sittee down.'

X

∽∽∽∽∽∽

Early morning. Too early to switch on the fan.

Head singing, mosquito bites at my ankles and the tiny black-curtained room packed hot and heavy round me.

I have always, I suppose, been an addict of beginnings. Slates and souls wiped clean, limitless potential, an unhorizoned future. I envy the Californians and the Catholics that.

Maybe I should have allowed that the night I met Emilia at the private view was a beginning, that Emilia herself was a beginning; maybe I should have taken less Elizabethan measures in ending things.

All that I knew was that I had to survive, had to cut her away. That cutting-away was, I can admit it now, something of a flaying for me, despite its private drama, finality, and night-flight. But flayed, cut away, I brought no bad baggage to Bombay, to new life, to Lakshmi Khandekar; I came with nothing.

A beginning.

I billowed the single sheet, let it fall like a shroud, but there was only the heat. My hair was damp and my mouth dry.

Flayed, I suppose, I had been susceptible. My sleep, since my arrival, had been shallow; exhaustion had never been far, and sensual memory had unbalanced me, shifting the heavy edges of knowledge that had been lashed down for years.

But elated. My heart racing, streaming with morbid, opiate need; I could have run for miles.

I turned my pillow over, as if the other side was cooler.

Lakshmi.

'Pyari Pyari', her song.

Separated by only a moment, the recognition and the proof. The

156

recognition that I HAD visited the flat above Colaba Causeway, more than once, but through the cinema screen.

It was those very curtains that she had been drawing at the moment of the *Akeli* film still (the photograph that I had scanned so minutely, as I had all photographs of Lakshmi, searching always for the uncontrolled, the unintended physical detail) and it was in that very apartment that much of the film's action had unrolled. It was not surprising, really, that such a dramatic location had found its way into a film.

And her first words, words of apology. Which I half-heard, half-recorded, but mostly, of course I was seeing her, seeing Lakshmi. Snapshot details. In crumpled black cotton. *Salwar-kameez.* Eyes, dark, flicking outwards to the corners as if knife-cut. Dark eyes, with the small black *tikka* painted between. Earrings, gold, small, oval loops. Eyes, mouth, dark, her mouth almost purple in the heavy, yellow electric light, and her nose, more curved in profile than her cinematographers had allowed, and the diamond at her nostril.

She had been there, in that place, with me. Nowhere else. If I had looked out over Bombay she would no longer have been out there, somewhere in the haze; she had been there, with me.

Her first words, words of apology.

The deception, of course ... Lata, my aunt ... sorry that had been necessary. Guardian of my privacy, and so on. You understand, in this film line ...

But, the perfection of her.

The perfection of her.

I had found the words. Listened to myself, almost impressed. I hadn't had time to prepare a word, but the fluency, or some kind of fluency, had been there.

The answer to the Coldharbour film project had been a provisional yes, as I'd been sure it would be. We had drunk a sweet and completely unbelievable Indian champagne.

I explained that I knew the films, *Akeli, Zakhmi, MDMD.* That I had made one or two myself, of course, and that although I was an admirer of her work I wasn't one of the creeping legions of FANS, but an insider. Them and us, and as you know, Lakshmi ... I had spoken to her in Hindi, quoted passwords, pressed on to her my confident knowledge of my subject, my knowing, easy way with the city. All this dust-kicking on my part slightly unbalanced her equipoise. Which is what I intended, of course; I had to avoid being just the Documentary-maker, the *Firang*. But then you always have to do that, one way and another.

When I left.

She'd begun to look tired; everything had gone so well that I'd almost leapt to the suggestion that I leave. She knew as much about me, when I finally got to my feet, as I did about her. I'd known a lot of what she told me, of course, from Seeta Rao's article, but I listened to it all again as she told it back to me. I didn't ask about relationships. I feared a withdrawing, an association of myself with the Seeta Raos, the Nelson D'Mellos.

So we had sat in the pavilion on the roof, Leelabai had brought the food and the sweet, implausible champagne, and for hours, high over the city and the winking ocean, we had talked.

And when I left.

There had been an uncertainty that had begun from the moment I rose to my feet. Maybe before. Holding a sheet of her aunt's writing paper (contact numbers, secretaries, location managers) I had followed her from the roof pavilion to the front door.

'So,' I had said, 'Lakshmi.'

'So. Stanley.'

I had leant towards her, seen as I did so the flash pass through her eyes, the momentary beat before she had inclined her neck, and I had sworn at myself. And then, for a moment, our cheeks had touched, coolly. And then, straightening, I had met her eyes, and she was smiling, and I was unsure.

'*Phir milenge*,' she had said, quietly. 'We will see each other again.'

'*Phir milenge*,' I had replied.

Beyond the black curtains there seemed to be a lightening. Or maybe it was my eyes. The still air pressed me to the bed.

Lakshmi.

It was impossible to remember the evening in order. She'd been asleep just before I arrived, I suspected, and her first smile had been sleepy. She would be sleeping now, the oval loop earrings at her bedside.

She would sleep, I knew with certainty, deeply and easily.

I knew I would not sleep.

I woke to Anubai's knock. It was ten o'clock and Baby had gone to school. Apart from the Chesterfield dryness at the throat, I felt fine, briskly cheerful. All in all I had had no more than three-quarters of a bottle of champagne, and there were no missing sections from my memory of the evening.

'She was charming,' I told Cuckoo, who looked dubious.

'So what was all this dinner-pinner?' she asked, handing me a cup of mint tea. 'Why couldn't this Lata simply have told you, *accha*, you come to eat and you meet my niece Lakshmi?'

'I think that she didn't want me telling any press people that I was coming, and maybe me selling them the story in advance, something like that . . . You know what these film-magazine people are like. They print any old thing. Although I think that Lata did trust me. I'd told her my life story, after all. She was just making sure. Maybe she had to check with Lakshmi, I don't know. But most of all I think she enjoyed the intrigue of it all. Enjoyed imagining the look on my face when I saw who was there to meet me.'

'And there was no one else there?'

'Just the servant, Leelabai.'

'Yes, but there was no one there apart from you and this Lakshmi Khandekar?'

'No one else.'

'I must ask Bapsi about these Khandekars. I'm sure she'll know. She knows a lot of these rich Maharashtrians.'

'There's no reason to suppose they're particularly rich any more, Cuckoo, the place wasn't in the best repair.'

'That means nothing.' She picked up a magazine from the window-sill and fanned herself thoughtfully. 'I'll ask Bapsi. You're seeing her again tonight, this Lakshmi?'

'There's a *muharat* for *Khandaan* this evening at Lakshman Studios. I might go along to that.'

'Who'll all be there?'

'Well, her, I suppose, and Rahman Khan; the director Sunil

Bhattacharaya, and . . . I don't know, various others. You know how these things are.'

She was silent. Could it be that she wanted to come? Surely not. I'd better not ask, though, because inside every Bombayite, ultimately, was a wide-eyed film fan. And at the back of my mind was the thought that maybe, after the *muharat*, I could extract Lakshmi from the group, take her out to dinner. Somewhere expensive, with flowers and maybe a balcony. Somewhere I could spend Cold-harbour's money with impunity.

'Morning, Chatterjee!'

'Good morning, Sir. All tickety-boo?'

'All tickety-boo, Chatterjee. Tell me, how long do you think we have until the monsoon?'

'I think it will come this month, Sir.' He frowned at the hard, even blue of the sky.

I believed him. My father had always been fond of Chatterjee; they had both served in Burma, although without knowing each other at the time, and both had been wounded in the same month at Imphal. After discovering this fact, Chatterjee had got into the habit of snapping to attention and saluting my father whenever he arrived at the club. My father would dismiss him with a breezy 'Carry on, Chatterjee', and ask after his leg. 'Mending well, Sir' would come the inevitable answer. 'Mending well.'

I watched a peon in brown shorts pouring a bucket of neat chlorine into the pool. Another passed a desultory rake over the lawn.

'The place is looking very nice,' I said.

'Morale is high, Sir.'

I couldn't quite bring myself to tip him. Maybe when I left I would give him a decent amount, rather than initiating some kind of embarrassing routine now.

But then, of course, I wasn't leaving.

I managed six lengths, my eyes protected with goggles against the chlorine. I dried off in a deckchair, lit a cigarette, wondered about a cup of tea, and started to rough out a possible structure for the Lakshmi film.

A portrait of the actress would be meaningless, we had agreed at Coldharbour, unless it was a portrait in context. For the documentary to make sense we had to show how the Bombay film industry worked, how a Hindi movie was financed, cast, publicised, distributed and the rest of it.

The best way to achieve this, filmically speaking, would be to follow a production through from Day One, making ourselves an invisible presence (on the set, in the dressing room, at the parties . . .). We would then intercut this 'process' footage with details from Lakshmi's life. Perhaps from a single day in her life, so that we had a double timescale . . .

My eyes flickered as the heat dragged at my concentration. Lakshmi, too, as my memory endlessly recreated her in double exposure to the rest of my thoughts. A detail was enough: a crease at her throat, a soft dark eyebrow, a tiny fan of shadow at her mouth. As the sun forced down my eyelids these details grew outwards, shuddering like soap-bubbles, into whole projected forms of her, vanishing at the moment of their completion.

And behind it all, behind the endlessly re-forming images, the suspicion that if the film, my film, were to bring her to me, then the film, my film, might also send her away.

And in my film, which film to film?

Focus thoughts. Open eyes.

If its *muharat* was tonight, then *Khandaan* would be pretty much in the can by the time our finance had been mobilised. Too late to focus on *Khandaan*. With a bit of luck, though, and if the budget was approved and the contract pushed through by the cost controllers at the channel, we could follow Lakshmi's next film from the start.

I made a written note. My recommendation to Coldharbour would be that an Arriflex camera and film stock be despatched from London and that I employ a local crew. Recording the entire process of the making of a Hindi movie would take months, rather than weeks. We couldn't possibly afford to accommodate a British crew for that period of time in the five-star hotels their union would certainly demand. Nor did I want to be responsible for repatriating them with dysentery, or worse. And for our fly-on-the-wall intentions, for invisibility's sake, a local crew was essential. Nothing would attract more attention than a bunch of British sparks and gaffers lurching around with their arses falling out of their trousers.

So, a local crew. I underlined the words.

Pre-production: 1 month.

Production: 4–6 months, min.

Post-production: 3 months.

Say, overall time: one year. This I underlined too. My fee would be stretched to the point of negligibility in British terms, but here, would enable me to get by. Coldharbour wouldn't miss me. One well-reviewed prime-time documentary and a twenty-grand production fee from the channel would make any grief accruing to them worthwhile, I was sure. No crocodile tears.

The sheer amount of time involved would still chew up the budget, though, rough-hew it how I would. That and the stock ratio. We would end up shooting at least thirty hours of negative to get the footage we needed. With this distilled to a final seventy-eight-minute print, we would be shooting at a ratio of more than 20:1. The channel would have to be persuaded. It wasn't just a matter of buying the stock, all thirty hours of it would have to be processed, synched-up with the sound, rubber-numbered, sorted, stored . . .

And if I wasn't going to return to London, I would have to edit the film here in Bombay. That was possible, and would certainly cut costs in a big way. The exposed stock could be processed at one of the film labs, a work print made, and an editing suite hired here at one of the studios. The final print could be air-freighted, with the thirty cans of negative, back to the UK.

Quality, though.

Even big-banner Hindi feature films often ended up looking as if they had been developed in sheep-dip. The city's major laboratory was known, not particularly affectionately, as the dhobi-ghat, after the laundry-yards in which, like the chemicals at the labs, the same filthy water was endlessly re-used.

Storage of the negative and the print would also have to be thought about. Refrigerated storage didn't exist; the cans were stacked, as often as not, in hot, airless laboratory cellars. And as for the colour-grading . . .

'Can I take this?'

I looked up. 'Sorry?'

'This deckchair. Can I take it?'

She was standing between me and the sun, her arm resting with proprietorial impatience on the canvas shade on the top of the chair.

'Um, yes, go ahead. I'm not using it. Please.'

She didn't move. Inclined her head to one side.

'You were here on Sunday. Was it Sunday? At the barbecue?'

I shaded my eyes with my hand. 'Probably, yes, I was.' It was one of the English girls with the mother. A lunghi round her waist. Bikini top.

'I'm Lizzie. Hi.'

'Stanley.'

'That's an unusual name. It's like . . . a National Serviceman's name. Nice.'

'I'm glad you like it.' From the posture, the awkwardness, she looked about sixteen. Her shoulders, narrow, very fair, shone with sun-oil. I couldn't see her face.

'I do. It's a nice name. Stanley. Definitely nice. I'm interrupting you, though. You're writing a letter.'

'It's not a letter. Just some work. Quite boring. I'm happy,' I said, 'to be interrupted.'

'Actually, Stanley, don't be cross, but we were having bets, my sister and I, what you were doing here. 'Cause you obviously aren't on holiday.'

'Why do you say that?' I asked, squinting. Her face was still between me and the sun.

'Because you're by yourself. And you don't behave like you're on holiday. Smiling and buying lots of drinks and so on.'

'So what conclusions did you come to?'

'What . . . Oh, right. Well. Karen thought you might be French, in fact, from the Alliance Française, and I thought that, um, I know you're not from the chocolate works because I know the guys that are, but . . . that you might have something to do with that razor-blade factory, working there . . . No?'

'Wrong on both counts, I'm afraid. By miles.'

'Do you want to join us and tell us what you do do?'

'Um . . . yes, why not?'

'We're over there.'

For a moment I stood in front of them, unexplained.

The other sister slouched low in the faded canvas of her deck-chair. She toasted me, minimally curious but no more, with a freshlime soda, and was introduced by Lizzie as Karen.

The third pair of eyes regarded me grey and level from beneath the brim of a ConOil baseball cap. Lizzie didn't immediately introduce her, but turned to me.

'How much do you know about ballet, Stanley?'

Opposite me the eyes rolled, exasperated, and the freckled arms folded in protest across the red bikini top.

'Now, shush, you.' Lizzie waved her, unnecessarily, to silence.

'Stanley, sorry, how much? *Swan Lake* and all that?'

'Pretty little. Although I have in fact seen *Swan Lake*. And modern things here and there. In London.'

'Does the name June Webster mean anything to you.'

'LIZZIE!' Pulling the ConOil cap down over her face, but irritated rather than really embarrassed.

'Er, no,' I answered, getting the drift, the ConOil girl's long, well-defined legs and overall sense of physical fluency making sudden sense, 'but then it wouldn't, if it's anything to do with ballet. I don't know the names even of the most famous dancers, I'm afraid. Or not more than one or two.'

'What my sister is saying, in her roundabout way,' Karen spoke for the first time, 'is that June here is a famous dan-soos . . .' She waved her thin pale arms in an undulating Bali-Hai motion.

'WAS a ballet dancer. And NOT such a very famous one,' said June apologetically. 'Hi.'

The accent was American South, but re-routed via Shaftesbury Avenue.

'Did you dance in London?' I asked.

'Yes. I was with the company at the Opera House.'

'I met Pauline Faull once,' I said, 'at the BBC.'

'Really.' She smiled.

I clipped the shade attachments on to my glasses. Noticed her callused feet, the small white scar at the knee.

'Are you on holiday?' I asked.

'She's our discovery,' said Lizzie. 'We found her in the sea. And now you have to tell us why YOU'RE here.'

June smiled in silent concession. I beckoned to a waiter in the clubhouse, who acknowledged me with a nod.

'Well,' I said, 'I've come over here to put together a TV documentary on Indian cinema. So that's what I'm doing. Seeing people, and so on. Working out production details.'

'You're in television,' said Karen, flicking an ant from her foot, 'that's unusual.'

'Indian cinema,' said Lizzie slowly, her attention drifting to the club's entrance and the day's first volleyballer. 'You should ask June about that. She has something of a . . . personal interest in the Indian cinema.'

'I do NOT, Lizzie. HONESTLY.' She pulled off the baseball cap and turned as if to swat Lizzie. But Lizzie's gaze was innocent, distantly focused. June turned back to me. 'This,' she began, 'is about me going to a shoot at Film City — '

'. . . and there,' Lizzie interrupted absently, 'catching the eye of a certain big star . . .'

It was obviously well-trodden ground between the three of them.

'Tell me more,' I said, eventually.

'Oh, it was nothing really, I just got talking to an actor called . . . um, Sanju Saxena. No big deal.'

'Sanjay Saxena,' I said, interested, 'what's he actually like?'

She shrugged. 'Oh, all right, I guess. You know these heroes,' she smiled, 'and their Old-Fashioned Values . . .'

'Tell Stanley,' said Lizzie, deliberately, 'about the date.'

There was the sound, minutely delayed, of an inflated volleyball being bounced, hard, on the pool's paved surround.

'It wasn't a date,' said June. 'Not like you're thinking. He just took me to meet . . .'

But neither sister was listening. Lizzie stretched, yawned, got to her feet, ran a finger under her shoulder-strap, and wandered off towards the diving boards. Karen, with a quick apologetic smile at June and myself, followed her. Both sisters had the same long schoolgirl backs.

'Sir?' said the waiter. 'Madam?'

'Tea,' I said, 'and . . .' I raised my eyebrows at June.

'Club soda, please.'

On the highest diving board Lizzie and Karen were running through a fairly acutely pitched I-don't-dare-yes-you-do push-and-pull routine. The volleyballers, now present in force, didn't actually look up, being fully occupied with their own mime of threatening to hit each other over the head with the ball, but they did know that the sisters were there.

June raised her eyebrows.

'Nice girls,' I said.

'They're sixteen,' said June.

She could have been twice that age herself, although it was hard to be sure. Physically she looked in her twenties, in her late twenties perhaps; there were tiny lines tracking the freckles on her forehead, and there was something drawn at her collarbones, a tiredness at mouth and eyes. Where Lakshmi, I thought, was soft, physically serene, June, even in relaxation, was somehow held by a series of physical oppositions. The apparent calmness of those sea-grey eyes was deceptive.

'You were saying about your date with Sanjay Saxena . . .'

'Oh . . . Nothing really. We went to the house of someone called Haji Ibrahim and sat around listening to some singing, which was beautiful . . .'

' . . . You went to HAJI IBRAHIM'S HOUSE?' I had heard about Haji Ibrahim.

'There were lots of people there. I gather that the Haji's quite a big cheese in the Bombay crime world.'

'He certainly is,' I said, 'although apparently he spends most of his time dallying with a buxom young actress named Pritthi Puri. So you must have had quite a rare sighting.'

From the furthest deckchairs came the thump and whisper of the volleyballers' sound system. Karen was pursuing Lizzie, or possibly Lizzie, Karen, on a squealing and pointless circumference of the pool. From the clubhouse I could hear the rattle of cutlery on a tray.

'Look,' she frowned, 'it wasn't really a date. I mean there wasn't a single instant, for example, when Sanju and I were alone. The whole thing fascinates Karen and Lizzie, who . . . but I shouldn't have gone, anyway. And I don't think I'll be seeing him again.'

I said nothing.

'And sorry about those two,' she continued, nodding towards the pool. 'They get bored easily. You know how it is. Sixteen?'

'I think I can just about summon up the distant memory of those years, yes. How about you?'

She smiled. 'You were working when Lizzie dragged you over. Don't let me stop you.'

The waiter brought our tray over. As we re-arranged ourselves I noticed that June had a thick paperback in her lap, with her place marked by a pink satin ribbon.

'I just have to make some notes,' I said.

And I might, I thought, ring Lakshmi. Thanking her for dinner would be excuse enough.

June smiled again, opened her book, and pushed on her sunglasses.

Lakshman studios was in Andheri, one of the suburbs beyond the airport. As the taxi stop-started its way up the hot rush-hour highway, I wondered if I was doing the right thing in going to the *muharat*. I had called the numbers Lakshmi had given me several times over the course of the day, but none had been answered.

The evening had brought no breeze, no reduction in the heat, and my earlier optimism had become uncertainty. The shirt was sodden between the Rexine seat and my back, and for reasons I could not immediately isolate, I felt physically ill at ease.

And then slowly, as we crept forward, a hot imperative hand began to tighten its grip on my bowels. For a mile or two I forced myself to ignore the sensation, but as we passed a food-stall and I felt the nauseated wrench of my stomach, I realised that I'd better face it.

What had I eaten at the club?

Masala prawns, I remembered. Mother of God.

I lit a Chesterfield. For ten minutes, staring hard at the dusty roadside and forcing myself to count backwards from a hundred in Urdu, I kept my gut at bay. The grip relaxed, and slowly I allowed my sweat-soaked back to straighten.

'Andheri, Sahib. East or west?' The driver spoke in cheerful English. His neck was swollen by a large goitre.

'You said you knew the way. You promised me.'

He smiled, showing large *paan*-stained teeth.

'Sorry, Sahib, I am coming from Dhaka.'

As he spoke I was seized by a churning need so acute as to reduce me, for several long moments, to silence.

'Well ASK someone,' I eventually gasped, thighs quivering as the muscles tentatively unclamped.

'Not speaking good Hindi, Sahib,' he confessed.

'Say . . . Lakshman Studios.'

He wound down the window. Called over an elderly kerb-dweller, naked except for a loincloth and a pair of ammunition-boots.

'Lakshman?' asked the driver, dubiously.

The indigent turned. 'I'm not Lakshman,' he proclaimed in angry dialect.

'Lakshman Film Studios,' I called after him. 'Please, friend.'

The kerb-dweller considered. For several minutes, during which I was again robbed of the power of speech and sight, he gave the driver a flood of instructions.

I opened my eyes.

'Did you understand that?' I asked the driver.

'Yes, Sahib . . . No, Sahib.'

I leant over and opened the front door of the taxi.

'Get in,' I ordered the kerb-dweller. 'I'll pay you. Show this sister-molester the way to the studio.'

He climbed gingerly into the front, beside the driver, and indicated the road ahead. Again my back hooped and my eyes closed. This time there was no falling away, it went on and on, and in the single unclenching moment it took to draw breath, I knew a hot, hopeless release.

We bumped ahead. I was appalled.

'This is a very smelly fellow, Boss,' observed the driver, uneasily indicating our new passenger.

'God loves the least of us,' I answered, worried as to my next move. We drove on, the driver unhappily following the violent hand-signals and hoarse imprecations of our guide. Reaching a decision, and praying that we would not meet a red light, I moved forward behind the seat and surreptitiously removed my trousers and underpants. The kerb-dweller's face suddenly turned to within inches of my own. I noticed with relief that he had well-developed cataracts in both eyes. I wondered vaguely about the accuracy of his directions.

'This *babu*,' he muttered in Hindi, 'has the stink of a black dog.'

'He lies with pigs,' I agreed, forcing a smile as I gingerly hoisted my trousers back up again. At the next traffic lights I bought a *Times of India*, and folding the finance page, slid it between my legs like a crackling nappy. Behind the cover of the rest of the newspaper, as the lights turned green and the taxi shuddered forward, I released my underpants and their warm burden into the evening traffic.

We eventually found Lakshman Studios. I rewarded the kerb-dweller handsomely and the taxi driver less so. Despite the fact that I had paid for our near-blind guide to be returned to his highway home I saw the driver unload him, with much swearing and waving of fists, at the first corner. But I was already hurrying through the gates, waving my invitation at the security guards. My condition was returning with renewed urgency.

'Bathroom,' I gasped to the first peon I saw.

'*Kya?*'

'*Peshab-ghur.*'

He pointed to a flight of stairs. I pushed my way upwards past a detachment of elderly extras in Pathan costume. At the top was a door bearing male insignia. I burst into a small pissodorous chamber containing a urinal and a washbasin. For a desperate moment I eyed the washbasin, then tore back out and flung myself into the Ladies.

A small crowd had gathered around the main exterior set when I finally emerged. Not, it was immediately clear, the major players, but *chamcha*s, minor guests and technical ancillaries. Battered black arc-lights stood top-heavy around a cable-snaked clearing across which fifteen yards or so of track had been laid. As I watched, a pair of *bidi*-smoking camera attendants secured a 35-millimetre film camera to a wheeled dolly, pushed the ensemble up and down the track a couple of times, essayed a whip pan, flicked a duster at the lens, and moved into the shadows.

A tray trembled at my side.

'*Chai*, Boss?'

'Thanks,' I said, 'yes.'

I sat down on a coil of electrical cable, settled the cup and saucer at my side, and lit a cigarette. My hand shook. I felt gutted, overwrought from lack of sleep.

The light was going fast. Along the wall surrounding the studios, loops of coloured bulbs flickered idly and prettily into life. An obese and glittering family arrived, and assumed the front row of canvas seats. The attendants re-entered, dusters in hand, followed by an elderly cameraman. Hitching up the knees of his trousers the cameraman seated himself carefully on the dolly and was wheeled slowly along. A tracking shot with pan, I noted, shifting in gassy unease.

Several things happened simultaneously. The dusk turned to darkness as the arc-lights bloomed, a large white Ambassador car drew up at the side of the building, and Nelson D'Mello slapped me on the back.

'*Kya hal-chal*, hero?'

'Nelson. Hi. Good, thanks. I've made contact with Lakshmi Khandekar. She invited me here this evening.'

'Great, man. Chick in the hand's worth two off the wrist. There's Rahman Khan.'

A liquid-boned young man, sculptural but unmuscled, grooved into the pool of light. He was followed by a balding, astigmatic figure in a Hawaiian shirt.

'Sunil Bhattacharaya,' nodded Nelson.

At the centre of the lit area Rahman Khan swivelled on a toe, dropped his head, and assuming the attitude of Cellini's *Perseus*, raised his palm for slapping.

As Bhattacharaya, blinking short-sightedly, walked straight past him, Rahman segued into a philosophical hip-roll and fingertipped the bouffant layers of his hair. A slap to his rolled T-shirt sleeve found a packet of State Express 555s and initiated a few swift seconds of Zippo choreography. Braced like a gunfighter, he smoked.

Outside the light the driver opened the door of the white Ambassador.

'Here we go,' whispered Nelson.

'What's happening?' I asked.

'Watch,' said Nelson.

From the Ambassador stepped a tall, sad-eyed figure I recognised immediately. Sanjay Saxena was dressed in nationalist white cotton, and as he stepped from the dusk into the light he executed a courteous '*Namaste*' to the spectators. As he clasped Rahman in greeting there was a multiple popping of photo-flash. 'Reconciliation time,' explained Nelson. 'Have you heard of Swaroop? Well, she and Rahman have recently been enjoying something of a shag-fest. Now that the Khan's back with Najma the Moti Peanut-Oil girl, harmony rules again. That's why there's so much press here, not for the *Khandaan muharat* . . .'

I realised a sudden and sharply renewed need.

'Give me a couple of minutes, Nelson.'

I wasn't back for twenty. By this time the disposition of the scene was different, and there was something approaching an atmosphere of serious technical intention.

A second white Ambassador was drawn up next to Saxena's. The back door was open, the interior obscured by a large woman emerging with hairdressing equipment. She moved away through the slanting lights and inside the car, against the dark upholstery, I saw a matte, patient profile. As I stood there Lakshmi turned her head towards me.

I may have smiled. I saw the beginning of her reaction; noted, at the corner of my vision, Rahman's delinquent slouch against the white coachwork.

'Stanley! Hi.'

Not Lakshmi, though. I pulled to a closer and unwilling focus. The ConOil girl.

'June. Hello!'

'We meet again!' She stepped, calculatedly it seemed, between the car and myself.

'What brings you here?' I asked, with less of a return smile than might have been expected of me this far north of the expatriate beat. Her face was amused; presumably that neither of us had mentioned the *muharat* to the other, earlier in the day.

'Well, Sanju very kindly – you said you knew Sanju, didn't you?

No? I'll introduce you – anyway, asked my friend Kimmie and I, this is Kimmie by the way.'

The friend threw a peach-fuzzed smile and a hand across the half-light.

'Kimmie Kitzinger, hi, isn't this just great to be here, like BEHIND THE . . . June was telling me, it's you, isn't it, that's making this film about Hindi cinema?'

'Stanley Collinson. Yes, that's right.' She was wearing a ging-ham hairband. Hard to tell its colour. Behind her I saw Bhattacharaya moving towards the white Ambassador.

'I'm just FAScinated by the whole thing . . . are you going to interview anyone tonight? Have you met Sanju?'

Lakshmi stepped from behind June. Midnight-blue sari. Moved towards the light between Rahman and Bhattacharaya, hesitated, peered back.

'Er, no,' I said vaguely, desperate.

She stepped into the light's hard focus, and was lost. I spooled in my attention. Both Kimmie and June were watching me.

'I'm not going to interview anybody, no,' I caught up. 'I'm just here as a guest.'

'Sanju sent a car to June's hotel. She was going to send it back but I'm afraid I made her accept. And he is j-u-ust SUCH a pussycat . . . Are you a guest of Rahman Khan's?'

'Actually I was asked along by Lakshmi Khandekar.'

'The love interest, right?'

'Something like that,' I said. 'Excuse me a minute.'

Hobbled like a marathon walker, I forced my way through the gawpers to the front of the building and back up the stairs to the tiny, stenching oven of the ladies' room. It seemed impossible that there was more to be voided, but more there was. Mosquitoes whined, and I held my shirt to my face.

After several racking minutes there was an imperious rapping at the door. It was repeated, and this time followed by a stream of Marathi imperatives. I tried to ignore it.

'Coming out. PLEASE!' reiterated the voice, female, in English this time.

For several Krakatoan moments speech became impossible. The concrete chamber displayed powerful qualities of acoustic magnifi-cation. Sweat ran into my eyes. The rapping was renewed. I thought of the Mutiny, of the massacres at the Satichaura Ghat and the Bibi-ghur ...

'Fuck's SAKE!' I gasped. 'Just wait.'

Finally I was able to reach for the plastic water jug that stood beneath a dripping tap. My thoughts flickered to the Indian soprano who was unable to face a European audience in the knowledge that they all employed shiny paper ...

'PLEASE COMING OUT, GENTLEMAN.'

Plastering my hair down with water from the tap I straightened my trousers, squared my shoulders, and followed a rolling gust of fouled air into the corridor. Outside waited the double-decker hairdresser, grim-faced. Not on her own behalf, though.

There was a hurried swirl of midnight-blue sari, and the lowered, embarrassed gaze of Lakshmi Khandekar swept past my feet.

I stood silent for a moment. Felt the last residual optimism drain.

'Madam is waiting long time,' said the duenna, reproachfully. She had arms as thick as my thighs and splayed, cow-catcher teeth. 'Unit is waiting also.'

I considered my reply. Hanged for a sheep as a lamb.

'Why don't you just fuck off?' I asked her.

She stared back at me, expressionless.

The shot was a straightforward one. Lakshmi and Rahman were walking slowly along. The camera, tracking, followed them at a slightly faster rate, panning as it passed, eventually coming to rest facing them. As it did so, Lakshmi delivered her single line of dialogue to Rahman. Cut.

They ran through the shot twice. Silence from the spectators.

Third time was a take.

'First positions,' called Bhattacharaya, glancing at his watch. 'Action. Roll camera.'

Star-cross'd cowboy and child-bride moved through the globe of light towards where I was sitting. They halted, and Lakshmi raised her head.

'*Hum phir nahin milenge.*' We will not see each other again.

They held their positions and expressions.

'Cut,' said Bhattacharaya without emphasis. 'And print.'

The lights faded and the dismantling started immediately. There was a pause as eyes adjusted to the lower candle-power of the coloured bulbs. I opened my eyes in time to see Lakshmi disappear round the corner of the building with the cow-catching hairdresser.

'They've just got to do some photographs,' June walked up to me, 'and then everyone's going to dinner at the Oberoi. Sanju says you must come.'

She was sharing the back seat of Saxena's car with Kimmie. Both were fanning themselves with publicity handouts.

'That's kind,' I said. 'Thanks. I'll see you there.'

'Are you OK?' asked June. 'You look a little . . . wired.'

'I'm fine,' I said. 'Really. See you at the Oberoi.'

She smiled. Kimmie gave a little ticker-tape wave and showed me her teeth.

Nelson D'Mello's 250cc Enfield India roared us to Marine Drive and the Oberoi Towers Hotel in an unhelmeted and streaming-eyed twenty minutes. There, pulling a jacket from his pannier and loosening a shirt button or two, Nelson explained that he had an assignment with a Singapore Airlines stewardess in the nightclub in the hotel's basement; I said I would walk for a bit, see him in the restaurant in an hour. By that time the others would have arrived.

I crossed the road. To my right the road swung round the three lamp-lit kilometres of 'The Queen's Necklace' to Chowpatty; to my left, as if in a falling-away of interest, the sea wall and the pavement became the idle bouldered spray of Nariman Point.

Below me the water slapped at the breakwater blocks. The sound of it in the hot night, the rocking silver of the street-lights, held everything of easy familiarity. In the daytime the Back Bay was a fan of flotsamed cess, but at night, like so much else in Bombay, it became more than itself, became the ocean, drawing whorish and metaphorical at the sensibilities.

Maybe, I thought, I hoped, Lakshmi was not lost to me. She was a Bombay*wali*, after all, and no one understood better than they about shit and need. They grew up surrounded by both, and learnt, as I had learnt myself as a child, how not to hear, how not to smell, how not to see. And it was just possible (stretching probability a bit) that my obviously unwell state might have touched some sympathetic nerve in her, cancelling out in her eyes (and nose, and ears, Oh God, Oh Montreal!) the ghastly rest of it. Women, I had once heard my father remark to a colleague, were damn queer cattle at the best of times. Maybe we would survive the incident. It was, though, a little early in the day, or the evening, to . . .

Again.

The gripping imperative.

The absolute and immediate need.

Traffic on Marine Drive. A possible several-minute wait for a red light before crossing the road to the hotel. There, explanations, requests, and THE NEED, NOW. WITHIN, LITERALLY, THIRTY SECONDS. The pavement empty.

Over the wall, scramble down the boulders out of sight of the road, barking knees, drag down the trousers and hunker, braced, feet clear, against a salted concrete rock.

Only with the blessed release of the next few minutes did my subsequent requirement occur to me. Water. I saw the soprano peering, appalled, through the curtains at Drury Lane, and started to crab downwards over the wet boulders towards the sea, belly up, hands behind my back, trousers round my ankles.

The boulders are WET, the message dragged at my brain as the gravel receded, and then a warm, stinking ton of sea water crashed noiselessly over me, filling my mouth and eyes, lifting me lazily from the rocks, punching other moving rocks at my head and chest, rolling and scouring me over the muddy shingle.

I spat, and stood. I was knee-deep, and there was a street-lamp above my head. Trousers round my ankles, though, I immediately fell; I pulled up the trousers, the zipper jammed with sand, and I fell again before staggering through the swirling coconut husks and discarded garlands to the blackness of the boulders. I fell gratefully against them, and painfully, my clothes heavy, slipping wet shoes against shit-wet rock, climbed the rocks towards the road.

Hauling myself over the sea wall I paused, dripping, for breath.

One lens of my glasses was starred and I could feel blood running down my cheek. There was a black stain at my knee which could have been anything and my watch had stopped.

Opposite, outside the hotel, a deputation headed by two white Ambassador cars was drawing up under the lights. I watched June and Kimmie climb from the first, followed by Saxena and Bhattacharaya. As they disappeared into the hotel the doors of the second Ambassador were opened by the sardar and the slight figure of Lakshmi was escorted up the steps by Rahman Khan. None of the party looked over towards the sea wall.

Turning, I threw the watch as far as I could, into the bay.

XI

⚇⚇⚇⚇⚇

Beth was getting better.

It wasn't that I didn't want her to, it was just that spending the last few weeks on my idle lonesome had been something of a luxury, and I'd become someone here that I wouldn't have become as Beth Conroy's sister. With Beth up and about I was going to be seeing a lot more of the Almas and Laurens and Kimmies.

Actually I was quite fond of Kimmie who, for a grown American, had become quite touchingly star-struck by all the Hindi film *tamasha* I'd become involved in. For all his *nakrah* (listen to me!) I'd also grown to like Sanju. And for his part, because I refused to take him entirely seriously, I think he liked me, too. For a time, and on the Everest principle that I was there, he had felt that he owed it to himself to try and drag me into bed. Now that he knew I wasn't playing I think that he was glad to have a woman he could actually talk to.

The Priya saga continued. For a clever girl she was being very stupid, and from time to time I told her so. The truth was that, although she would have died rather than admit it, Sanju was what Grace would have called her bit of rough. For all Ma Saxena's pretensions and distrust of Maharashtrians, Priya came from a much better-educated and more sophisticated family than Sanju did and I think that the difference amused her. Certainly the fact that he was a notorious womaniser didn't put her off.

I'd hear the latest *gup-chup* today, anyway. We had a date for a girls' lunch at her flat.

Beth was getting better.

The tyrant tones were returning with a vengeance.

Dane, on the other hand, was getting worse. He went to bed swearing-drunk every night he spent at the hotel, and I was sure that he spent other nights ashore that he didn't tell us about.

Beth, I'm sure, was worried.

What to do?

Well, I'd had my hair done; a very good girl in the Taj Arcade. And I'd had a couple of frocks run up. Quite nice. A little man of Alma Benson's (Alma, like Snow White, has all these LITTLE MEN . . .).

One thing, though, that I felt slightly guilty about was the fact that I'd made no real effort to explore Bombay, or at least aquarium, art-gallery and antique-market Bombay. The trouble was, in it's time-standing-still way, it was just so blissful to stretch out at the club and not be sticky and hot and on foot and surrounded by people staring.

And in a way I suppose that I WAS seeing Bombay. Priya lived on Malabar Hill, Sanju in Bandra, I'd been up to Juhu and Film City, seen a couple of nightclubs . . .

But my days were spent here at the Nepean Sea Bathing Club. For the first time that I could remember I was living every day in the luxury of real time. No more scouring of schedules, no more desperate stuffing of the career meter. I made no plans. From time to time I felt the regretful pull of the past, but mostly, as the sea rose and fell beyond the wall and the crows turned in the pale sky, I basked in the warm extended present.

On the other side of the pool I saw Stanley walk for the hundredth time to the phone by the bar. This was a terrible old Bakelite thing that took one-rupee pieces and connected you to random numbers all over the State of Maharashtra.

Stanley and I hadn't spoken since the *muharat*, but I had seen him at the club every day, radiating that particular strain of Brit unapproachability which, because it involves everyone for miles around, completely defeats its own purpose. And once again, even at fifty yards' range, I could sense the frustration in his heavy lowering of the receiver. I looked away, but not before the whole business had begun to annoy me, to jam up my radar. All that I wanted, after all, was loose shoulder-muscles, drifting consciousness, and the sun on my eyelids.

An edge of curiosity, though, was preventing the drifting. I would have got out a book, but *The Lotus and the Flame* had been corralled by my pulp-hungry sister. I would probably never know what happened to Captain Harry (he of the walnut-stained skin and the effortless command of Pathan dialect) and his almond-eyed, mango-breasted Anjali.

As Stanley folded himself back into his deckchair I saw that Karen, oiled and laid out to fry on the springboard, was watching him over her sunglasses. With the strap of her bikini undone, she couldn't actually raise herself on an elbow, but she was definitely watching him. I don't think she quite fancied him, not yet anyway, but as a consequence of his utter non-interest in her, she was definitely beginning to feel the burn. He was quite presentable, after all.

If far too old for Karen.

And not gay. When your corps-de-ballet dressing room has a notice marked 'CAPULET Girls (Friends of Juliet)' pinned on the door and your male colleagues opposite have one that says 'MONTAGUE boys (Friends of Dorothy)' you kind of get a nose for these things. Stanley, I was sure, didn't walk the Walsingham Way.

I did wonder what he was up to, though. I knew that film producers were supposed to spend half their time lying by swimming pools and the other half on the phone, but surely, not Channel Four documentary producers.

Not by this pool.

Not on that phone.

'June,' said Priya, 'hi! Come in.' She was wearing a crumpled cotton kurta over jeans, and her hair was wet.

The flat, vast, anciently disordered, wasn't hers, but her parents'. Her father was a career Foreign Service officer, presently posted to the States, so for another year at least, Priya had the dusty run of the place.

I kicked off my shoes and enjoyed the feel of air-conditioned marble beneath my feet. Feet, I noticed, which, for the first time in years, were beginning to look civilian.

'How are you?'

'I was just thinking,' I replied, 'that for the first time in years, I'm beginning to feel like a normal human being.'

It wasn't just my feet. Aches that I'd taken as much for granted as the London winter had departed my knees and lower back. Despite cautious eating I'd put on half a stone. The muscles of my thighs and calves had started to smooth out.

'You look well,' said Priya. 'Sit, yaar.'

I sat. The boy, Rajan, brought water, and in response to a nod from Priya, switched off the air-con. It coughed to silence, and for a time we stared comfortably into space.

'So,' I asked, finally, 'what's the *gup*?'

'He rang,' she answered, and we were off.

Her rationale was as follows: Shakuntala was the arranged wife, dutifully busy with motherhood and running the household; Swaroop was a rouged old buzzard who would do or say anything to keep her picture in the magazines and her name on the film contracts; the rest were just *chokri-log*. Chicks. Sanju was the prisoner of his birth, of his past, and of his emotional generosity. The love they shared was something above and beyond all this. The two of them were spiritually, if not civically, wed.

From a sensible, even calculating, professional who'd made a career of portraying independent women, this was pretty amazing stuff, and once more I told her so.

I was right, she said, BUT . . . And she went all Hindu on me. Other lives and stuff.

I was torn as to whether to reveal the existence of this 'girl-friend', this Gita. I supposed that I shouldn't, that I had been told about her in something like confidence, but I was tempted. On the other hand Priya would dismiss the whole thing as an irrelevance. She might suffer a bit, but her illusion wouldn't.

'But tell me about you,' she demanded, when the subject of Sanju had reduced us to silence. We often had these Indian silences.

'I don't know,' I said eventually. 'There's . . .'

What I'd been about to say suddenly sounded ridiculous.

'Go on,' said Priya, 'there's . . .'

'This sounds really silly, but you know that *muharat* I went to for . . . what was it called?'

'*Haveli*? No . . . *Khandaan*?'

'That's the one, *Khandaan*. Well, ever since that particular evening . . . this sounds REALLY silly, I know, but . . .'

Priya watched me. This was the lady, I consoled myself, who talked with such ease about being spiritually wed to a male nymphomaniac. I pushed on.

' . . . but since then I've felt this SHIFT, this sense of something moving into place. Or out of place. And I'm not sure if it's anything to do with that particular evening, it's just that something in me has changed. Physically . . . physically I'm feeling more relaxed than I can ever remember feeling, but there's just this SOMETHING, hovering at the edge of my consciousness, something like a bruise. A dangerous bruise that you can't resist touching although you know you shouldn't because there's a dangerous injury beneath it. Well my sort of equivalent of . . . well, of TOUCHING THE BRUISE is to think of that evening, the whole evening, because somewhere in there, beneath the surface of the evening, or maybe only triggered by the thought of the evening and actually nothing at all to do with that PARTICULAR . . . I'm talking nonsense . . .' I floundered.

'You're not, June yaar, really not. Try and go on.' Priya disposed her legs beneath her on the sofa and felt for her cigarettes.

'It's just that I . . . When I used to dance, even when everyone else on stage was behind me, I always had this sort of . . . spider's sense of what was going on, where everyone WAS. There's this ballet called *La Bayadère*. It's actually an Indian mythological story with Viennese-style music composed by a Russian. Very much the *masala* package, in fact. Anyway, there's this section in Act Three – The Kingdom of the Shades, it's called, sounds like a Rayban commercial, I know – where the whole female corps-de-ballet comes on in a series of . . . I won't go into it technically, but it goes on for about five minutes, thirty-two girls doing the same fiendish little sequence, very slow, very controlled, again and again, endlessly repeating it, a new girl coming on each time. And this snake of girls in these pearly chiffon-sleeved tutus just grows and grows and grows and if it's done perfectly, not a slip, not a wobble, then it's stunning. Brings the house down.

'But if anything goes wrong, and it very easily can, then it affects all thirty-two of you and suddenly you can feel the audience praying for you just to get through it at all, just to survive. Well anyway, being Miss Sang-Froid – and I'm not just rambling, there's a point to this story – I used to lead the corps on in *Bayadère*.

And I can admit it now, although I used to joke about it at the time, it was utterly terrifying.

'You start, OK, in the wings, upstage right, and there in the dark you climb this bank of steps. Behind you, backed up close as if you're all going to parachute, are the second, third and fourth girls, and you just huddle there in the dark, hearts thumping away, and listen to the twenty-eight others behind you treading the rosin into the soles of their pointe shoes.

'As the music slides closer – it's by Minkus, pure glycerine – you pull up into your preparation, weight on your left leg, right foot behind. In front of you is a long ramp, falling away downwards, but you can't see it in the dark, can't see anything, and then the split second before the music reaches you, a little red light on the floor flashes and you posé out of the wings into the blackness.

'No set, no music, nothing. Absolute blackness. And then there's a blinding spotlight in your left eye . . . you can't quite see but you can hear again, your working leg's already high behind you in arabesque, beneath you the rosin's gripping the sole of your pointe shoe on to the ramp, your mind's a blank but your body's counting out the music, and you're holding the arabesque, lifting it higher, and your eyes are following your hand down into the penchée . . .'

I refocused my eyes and relaxed my stomach muscles which had pulled themselves up taut. Opposite, on the sofa, Priya was watching me, her cigarette unlit. I suddenly felt ridiculous. All those posés and penchées. She couldn't have understood a word of it.

'You really loved it all, didn't you.' She smiled. Her voice had a lilt to it that was almost Welsh and, at times, almost irritating.

I shrugged, trying to recapture the drift of what I was trying to say. She looked at me quizzically, still smiling, and lit the cigarette.

'Anyway,' I went on, 'from that moment onwards, as the brain caught up with the body, the whole thing became an exercise in pure concentration, pure science. But – and this is what I was getting at – there was something beyond the science, a sort of instinct thing that I've always had, that told me, even though most of the time I couldn't see them, exactly where all the others were, how they were all doing.

'And its the same sort of radar thing that's telling me now that . . . something's happening, something's begun.'

I tailed off. I had the feeling that I was telling the wrong person the wrong story.

Priya turned her head and blew smoke.

'You know, you're funny,' she said. 'So many *firang*s come here to India from the States and Europe and they have two basic reactions. One is that they just, like, freak out completely at the poverty, the beggars, the slums and all and think they're going to drop dead if they eat anywhere outside a five-star hotel; the other is that they go completely and uncritically gaga about the place and start quoting Gandhi at you.' She nodded absently at Rajan, who was hovering with the lunch things.

'But you're neither. You just behave as if you were – I don't know – ANYWHERE. As if the life that we lead here was the most normal thing in the world. That's why I think you get on with us all, because you're not open-mouthed about anything. You don't set us up against what you know.'

'I suppose I just find it easier to concentrate on similarities rather than differences,' I said, although the thought hadn't occurred to me before.

'The other thing,' I added, 'is that I've switched cultures once in my life already . . .'

The room was suddenly flooded with the smell of food. Priya jabbed her cigarette into a vast onyx ashtray surmounted by a dancing Shiva.

'Tell me,' she said, carefully crushing out each spark, 'about this Stanley.'

At about seven o'clock the breeze came; I felt it at my cheek, at my hair, heard the high tide breaking and dragging at the rocks beyond the wall. It had been an hour since I'd been aware of the last gravelled volleyball bounce, the last distant hi-fi thump, and as I opened my eyes, lifted my head from the salt-damp towel, I felt the goosebumps lift on my back.

Arranging my towel over my bikini like a sarong I walked through the cool sprinkle-damp grass to the changing rooms, pins and needles prickling at the hand I'd slept on. The rooms were empty, the tepid shower reduced itself to a burping trickle before I was able to rinse the salt from my hair, and my cotton dress, when I pulled it from my bag, was crumpled.

Outside, the breeze sounded in the trees. In the previous weeks, when it had come at all, it had come like a remission, rising and falling, dying in the early hours; but this was different.

This was steady.

I looked out to sea. Above me the trees were black; to my right the pool was a darkening turquoise. As I approached the club-house, I heard the whop-whop of the fans. I climbed the steps. The lights had not yet been switched on and although there were people sitting at the tables, they weren't moving. Pulled by the fans and the breeze the tablecloths were moving, and in the light-alloy ashtrays the ash and the matches were moving and between the tables the dusted yellow and dark-green leaves of the plants were moving. The people, though, were still, and faced away.

'June.'

I hadn't heard him behind me on the grass. It was Stanley, polishing his glasses on his shirt.

'Hi,' I said, neutrally.

'Hi. I ummm . . . owe you an apology.' He hooked the glasses behind his ears. They looked uncomfortable. 'That dinner thing that you . . . that Saxena asked me to. After the *Khandaan muharat*, I was, I'm afraid, a bit sick, and couldn't make it. I've meant to . . .'

'Oh, that's OK. Don't worry about it. You were asked along anyway, weren't you, by er . . .'

'By Lakshmi, yes, sort of. And looking forward to it. But,' he spread his hands, 'you know how these stomach things are . . .'

'When you gotta go . . . ?' I suggested.

'Precisely. All that. I had a rather *mauvais quart d'heure*. Above and beyond all of which, why don't you let me buy you a drink?'

'I've heard worse ideas,' I said, rooting in my bag for a cardigan.

'*Chalo*, then.'

Upstairs, the bar was pretty much deserted.

As we sat down the barman leant to pull a switch, and lights looped on around the balcony.

'Bulbul for me,' said Stanley. 'June?'

'Bulbul,' I said, 'will do just fine.'

I was glad we'd got the ballet stuff out of the way earlier. People tended to get a bit stuck on the subject, which was fine if they knew what they were talking about, but they never did. What I tended to get were the detailed interrogations (discipline, foot-binding) and the smirking confessions (usually fantasies about Pauline Faull). Either way one didn't end up with a conversation.

'I see you here most days,' he kicked off, arranging cigarettes and matches at his elbow. 'What do you do. Read?'

'I used to read,' I said. 'I've stopped now. I don't seem to need it. I just drift. Something about this place does funny things to time. Sometimes it crawls, sometimes it races. I'm never sure which is going to happen. I lie there and wonder whether it's been an hour or a minute since I closed my eyes.'

The beers arrived in huge cold bottles, labels sliding around in the condensation. Stanley signed for them, and asked for glasses of water. There followed a curious routine of up-ending the bottles into the water to pour out the diesel fuel or some such.

'So how about you?' I asked, when the physics lesson was complete and he had expended half a box of matches lighting a cigarette under the fan. 'How's the motion picture?'

He hesitated, seemed to consider.

'To tell you the truth,' he eventually said, 'I'm kind of . . . at an impasse.'

The beer tasted weak, pointless.

'How so, an impasse?'

He examined the burning tip of his cigarette.

'Well, the trouble is that the actress who's supposed to be at the centre of the film has, well . . . disappeared. Disappeared to me, that is – I'm not saying that she's been kidnapped or anything – but I can't get her on the phone for love or money, I've been chasing around the studios and around town for ten days now and nobody, absolutely bloody nobody, seems to know where she is.'

'Can you get someone else? Make the film about someone else? Time being money, and so on.'

He lifted his jaw in a tiny despotic gesture.

'I could. I could find someone tomorrow. Pick up a phone. But the thing is that Lakshmi and I have discussed all this in . . . really some detail, and she was completely . . . on for it.'

'So she lied. Kick her into touch. Pick up the phone.'

In one of his sudden thespian gestures he allowed his head to drop a degree or two. He should get together with Beth, I thought, they could compare Stanislavskian disapproval techniques.

His jaw and his attention lifted away. 'She would have been just so . . .' His hands clawed as he exhaled smoke into my face. I jerked backwards. He blinked.

'I'm sorry, I . . .'

'Do I detect, by any chance,' I interrupted him mildly, batting away the smoke with my hand, 'a broken heart? An ulterior motive? A director who has become involved with his subject.'

I immediately regretted the questions.

'No,' he said uncertainly, 'you don't detect that.'

Liar, I thought. Interesting, though.

'You could always,' I suggested, 'make a film about my friend Priya Bhoopatkar. She's interesting and gorgeous, she started out in art movies, and then crossed over to . . .'

'How do you know Priya Bhoopatkar?' he asked, accusingly.

'Oh, we met at lunch,' I said vaguely, irritated at his proprietorial attitude. 'She goes out with a friend of mine.'

'Another Saxena leg-over?' he asked spitefully.

'No,' I protested, mock-cross, 'she isn't. Really, what a question.'

Evens, I thought. A lie each.

'You're not a bit like I imagined, just from seeing you.'

'Really?' I said. 'And how did you imagine me from seeing me?' We were each on our second bottle of Bulbul. This time I'd decided to sink the whole thing, chemicals and all.

So, seeing me doing so, had he.

'I don't know, you have this very . . . controlled-looking way about you, very self-contained, those grave grey eyes, always by yourself . . . I mean, for example, I can't imagine you really enjoy hanging around with those brainless . . . Lizzie and whatever-her-name-is?'

'And why not?' I asked.

'I'm sorry, I shouldn't have said that. I'm sure they're both racing towards Oxbridge research fellowships. Have you, though, just as a matter of interest, ever met their mother?'

'I have, in fact,' I said. 'The lovely Deirdre. She's quite a girl.'

'She's got this nightmarish way,' said Stanley, 'of stoking up, within seconds of meeting you, this kind of . . . spacious intimacy. Of leaning forward close to your face, lighting your cigarettes, touching your arm, using your name all the time, keeping her eyes locked on to yours so that you suddenly feel, mid-sentence, that you're talking complete . . .'

'. . . How did you come to meet her?' I asked. 'Stanley?'

'Oh, just here, a few days ago,' he answered vaguely, and then realising what I'd said, laughed. He had one of those tense, rather introverted faces that a laugh or a smile transformed. If he'd known this, he might have delivered a few more of them. But that, I guessed, was beyond his control. At least, though, what you got was real. God save us from all those showbiz crinkle-cut 'laugh lines'. And haven't I become, I thought, quite the little Puritan Brit . . .

'I've seen her here once before,' he went on, serious again, 'with the girls and that fat, frayed-looking father of theirs. This time, though, she was alone. And sort of on the basis that our eyes had at one point, a fortnight before, actually MET, she sort of . . . moved in, with all this . . .'

'If you had been born female,' I smiled, 'you'd find all that sort of thing pretty much of an everyday experience.'

'You're right,' he admitted. 'I'm sure I would. As long as I was born as a half-way ATTRACTIVE woman . . . because, don't you think the thing is, I mean,' he gestured broadly, 'you can say the world's divided into North and South, rich and poor, right and left, communist, Moslem, whatever, but isn't the real truth that the world is divided into those who ARE and those who AREN'T . . . ATTRACTIVE to the people that THEY find attractive. Divided into those who end up with the people they really fancy, and fancied BY THEM, and those who end up making do . . . I mean that you can have two people – one lives in a Dharavi slum and one lives in Beverly Hills – and they can actually have more in common with each other in this . . . significant respect than with their neighbour crouched in the next *bustee* or lounging by the next-door swimming pool. If you see what I mean . . . ?'

'Sounds to me,' I replied cautiously, 'like something of a loaded question.'

'It is and it isn't. I mean, OK, I have my reasons for pondering all this, but it's still ...' he shrugged ' ... discussible in general terms.'

He waved over the waiter. Another Bulbul for him; a club soda for me. Boring, I thought, but not as boring as a hangover.

'Tell me,' I said, 'about this Lakshmi.'

He thought for a bit and then told me. It took him the whole bottle. I'd been right, of course. He was nuts for her.

'And tell me,' I said, when he had finished, 'about this Emilia.'

He told me that, too. It took him another bottle. By the end his eyes were shining with the beer and the honesty and the tragedy of it all. And the bar was full.

'I have to say I'm ... slightly amazed,' I admitted, when he had finally fallen silent. 'Let me get this right. You've left your girlfriend and your country ... FOR EVER? Because she got stuck rather too enthusiastically into a ... BBC DRAMA?'

'If you'd been there ...' he began, without turning to me, 'you'd've ... I mean you should have seen this guy, director or whatever he was, with his leather jacket and his haircut and his fucking Rolex.'

'How close to him did you get?' I asked.

'Close enough to know that he had a Rolex.'

'If I gave you a Rolex,' I asked, 'would you wear it?'

'Of course I'd wear it. And as it happens, I need a watch. So should you have one about your very lovely person I'd accept it with touching gratitude. But what I wouldn't do is buy one, telling myself that I'd arrived at that stage in my career when, frankly, only the very five-grand best and most rugged would do. Especially if I had a face like a fucking newt with eyes on the side of my head. I mean, where's he going that ... that presents more hazardous extremes of temperature than the White City? King Solomon's Mines?'

'I think we're going out on a limb rather, with the watch,' I said, doubtfully.

'Well, let me tell you about some of these guys. There's one fast-track bastard called John Pearcey, who was out here recently. A year or so ago Emilia and I ran into him in an Indian restaurant in Westbourne Grove and he and some other indy-prod hustlers asked us to join their table. Anyway Pearcey manoeuvred himself next to Emilia and told her, in his seasoned expense-account traveller way, that the first time he'd stepped into a real Indian village he'd wept at the simple ordered perfection of it all. Then he started eating with his hands. And then, then he leant a bit closer and told her, and these were his actual words, that he'd like to give her an orgasm. I mean . . .'

'But she told you about it. And she didn't say yes?'

'Of course she didn't say yes, but . . .' He shrugged, Hamlet-like.

'Well, she's gone now,' I said. 'History. For better or for worse.'

'For better,' he said. 'Definitely. John Pearcey, God.'

A thought occurred to me.

'Don't you have family in Britain?' I asked. 'Parents?'

'No one,' he said. 'Actually. My parents died . . . were killed . . . the day they arrived in Britain. They'd always lived here in India.'

'That's . . . I mean, I'm really sorry, gosh, don't tell me if you don't want to, but . . .'

'It's fine. It was years ago. I was seven and a half. They were killed in a car-crash on the way in from Heathrow. From London Airport, as it was then.'

'That's just . . . awful. God.'

Silence. Noise around us, though, at the other tables, at the bar.

'So what happened?' I asked. 'Who looked after you?'

'I grew up with elderly relatives of my father, in Worthing. Careful people, if you know what I mean. Religious but unimaginative, and quite often ill. Endless south-coast waiting rooms . . .'

He looked away. It was too dark to see the horizon. A single bulb illuminated the empty swimming pool. Taking my silence for a continuation of my question, he continued.

'My father had been a banker, so when he died there was a fair amount of insurance and so on, for my education. I went to a local prep school, one of those high-walled suburban country houses with a crunching drive and acres of sodden rhododendrons where I was actually, when it came to it, no more than routinely unhappy. The fact that I was an orphan rather impressed the other boys, and the couple that ran the school became sort of secondary parents to me. Much more so, in fact, than my great-aunt and uncle, and I often stayed at the school for the holidays. He, the headmaster, was a linguist and a Sanskrit scholar; she, curiously enough for the day, a photographer. Walter and Milly LaFrenais. Kind people, no children of their own. And one way and another, they managed to keep me reading and thinking and occupied.'

He smiled faintly, took the last cigarette from the packet and finally, despite the fan, managed to get it lit.

'When I was twelve, letters arrived in Worthing from London indicating that, contrary to expectation, the money wasn't going to last for ever. After passing my Common Entrance I was sent to a very cold and very minor public school in the Midlands which had been set up for foreigners and the sons of officers from second-rate regiments. It was called, appropriately enough, given that scrumming and buggery were the two subjects it taught best, Manley Hall. I kept my head down, avoided games, stuck to the classics that Walter had got me started on, and became the school projectionist. My 'A' levels were adequate; good enough to get me into London University, anyway. At which point my great-aunt and uncle, their duty done, released their tremulous hold on life and keeled within weeks of each other from their respective nonconformist perches. Merciful release for all concerned, etcetera . . .'

He raised his eyebrows. 'How about another drink? Hercules Rum and Thums-Up can help make a good time great.'

'Oh . . . OK. What the hell.'

I was interested. He told a good story, but I had the feeling he'd clam up any moment. 'So what followed university?'

'Messed around for a bit. Came out to India. Went into television.'

'Just like that?'

'Just like that.'

I'd been right about the clamming.

After the soda the Hercules was sweet, cold and potent. Stanley's own drink, the ice fast turning to fine white scum, stood on the beer-damp tablecloth in front of his chair.

He had gone out across the lawn and into Nepean Sea Road to find a cigarette stall.

A sad, funny guy. A loser, one part of me said, but then another part understood only too well the hatefulness of winners. And all that unsaid stuff. The moments when it was impossible not to see the distraught child in the man.

Worthing. The Connaught Theatre. I remembered the place, now. Chilly sunshine and a stony beach. Shopping arcades. The old. A floral clock.

God, to go from this, alone, to THAT . . .

'Well, well, well . . .'

It was Dane. With a fat buddy. Both drunk. I'd been spotted. Inside me an alarm screamed.

'All alone? Mind if I . . .' He waved Fatso towards the bar, swayed, narrowed his eyes and planted his fists on my table.

Hot acid beer-stink. Beefy sweat.

'I'm with someone,' I answered, as steadily and tonelessly as I could manage, gradually leaning the chair away. 'He's gone out . . . actually just coming back.'

His brow lined as if at a problem of immense complexity.

'So . . . you're with someone.' His voice was a phlegmy growl. 'Well, that's really . . . really GREAT for you. Now don't tell me, let me guess, Miss . . . Miss ACTUALLY . . .'

Teeth suddenly showed in the beef.

' . . . Yeah, that's what I'm gonna call you. Miss ACTUALLY. Because you know something, Miss fucken' ACTUALLY, wait, answer me this . . .'

I neither spoke nor moved, couldn't have done so, but he suddenly held up the palms of his hands as if to calm me, as if it was me that was threatening him, as if this was a two-way dispute. I could smell the sweat on his hands. I wanted to turn away, but I knew that it was only my eyes on his that were keeping him from moving closer and that my chair wouldn't tip further back without falling.

Breathe, I thought, breathe. I lowered my eyes to where they could focus, to the flaked chrome longhorn buckle of his belt.

'Lemme put it like this,' he lowered the iron-breath still further, 'when you're ready for a . . . real . . . not some fucken' Hindi pornomonkey or some Brit fucken' queer, well, there'll be a real fucken' American ready for you. You little cunt.' The last three words were a whisper.

'Hey dude, beer time!'

I sat, paralysed, my heart thumping sickly at my ribs, the chair still at full stretch, as Dane's face pulled slowly away.

'Evenin', ma'am. We joinin' your fair self?'

Slowly I exhaled. Fatso, dimpling wetly, was lowering two brown Bulbul bottles to the tablecloth.

'I'm waiting for someone,' I managed.

'You two 'quainted?' he asked me, nodding at Dane.

'Oh yeah,' said Dane. 'Acquainted is JUST what we are.'

At that moment, beyond the two of them, and hovering in a state of some anxiety, I saw Stanley. I looked away, but Dane had caught my line of sight, and turned his head.

'You sittin' here?' he asked.

'Thank you,' said Stanley. 'Yes I am.'

Dane didn't move, forcing Stanley to push past him. Slowly, his eyes screaming questions at me, Stanley sat down.

'Well?' asked Dane.

'Well, WHAT?' I asked. Shock and fear were receding and anger kicking in.

'Well, ain'tcha gonna ACTUALLY introduce us to your pussy boyfriend?'

Stanley's expression blanked. He forced a smile, half-turned to the table behind him and spoke for a few seconds, still smiling, in very rapid Hindi. For the first time I noticed several solidly built Indians in sports clothes. One of these, a bearded man in a track suit, rose immediately to his feet.

'I think it might be time to leave,' he said gently to Dane.

'You talkin' to me?' asked Dane, incredulous, his fingers extending towards the nearest of the beer bottles on the table.

'Please,' said the man, almost sadly. 'Please. Just leave.' Several of the surrounding tables had fallen silent. The cassette recorder at the bar was playing a film tune.

'And who the fuck might you be?' Dane's fingers touched at the wet neck of the bottle.

'Jaswant Singh. Bombay CID,' he answered. 'You want to argue, argue outside.'

'Dane, man.' Fatso's chins were wobbling in increasingly moist concern. 'Let's go, come on, let's just go.'

'Take your friend's advice, Sir. Leave now.' Jaswant Singh indicated the exit. A heavy steel bangle circled his thick brown wrist.

A long freeze frame.

'Hell,' Dane eventually managed, surveying the silent tables, 'I'm not drinkin' here. What is this place, anyway? Bum-fuck Egypt?' He spat brown phlegm at the tablecloth. 'Shit on y'all. C'mon, Hoyt.'

As he moved past the table, his hand reached out and tweaked my nipple, hard, through the cotton of my dress. 'See you later,' he winked, 'sugar.'

The pain was so sudden that for a moment I could only gasp and, hands pressed to my breast, rock backwards and forwards. Then to my fury, my eyes filled with tears and my nose began to run and I didn't have a tissue.

Nobody seemed to move, and then a paper serviette was pressed into my hands.

'Here,' said Stanley, and I blew, wiping my eyes.

'Drink.'

I drained the Hercules. Everybody watched.

Stanley's pale hand was shaking a larger, browner one.

'No problem,' said Jaswant Singh, courteously.

'Well,' said Stanley, 'we were damn lucky to find a CID officer at the next table . . .'

'I hate to disappoint you, but actually I work for Tata Perfumes.'

'Nothing to do with the police at all?'

'Absolutely nothing.'

'You should be in films,' said Stanley.

'You were brilliant,' I confirmed.

'There appears to have been a dividend,' smiled Jaswant, passing Stanley one of the abandoned bottles of beer.

At the hotel, Stanley did all the talking for me, smoothed out all the stuff about passports and so on. Despite the Bulbul he seemed to be thinking fairly clearly.

'I've just booked the room for one night,' he said, pronouncing the words carefully. 'There's a phone, you can ring your sister, whatever.'

'Thanks,' I said. 'Really thanks. Kind. You know, I was only thinking this morning that something like this was . . . I . . . he's been so weird lately. I feel so bad for Beth, though, I really don't know what I'm going to tell her.' And I didn't.

'Well, I'm sure you'll think of something . . . apposite. Anyway, I'll call in here tomorrow morning.' He aimed an unfocused smile beyond my shoulder, and at that moment – and from nowhere that I could identify – something seemed to wobble to the surface of my consciousness, and, soundless and amazing, burst.

'Hey,' I said, 'tomorrow.'

'Sure,' he said. 'Ten o'clock OK? Give or take . . .'

'No . . . what I meant was, tomorrow . . . Let's start looking for Lakshmi.'

'OK,' he said. 'Let's.'

He stumbled out into the street, and I stood for a moment holding the heavy room key.

Of course.

No.

Yes.

Impossible.

XII

∽∽∽∽∽∽

Face down, twisted into the sweat-damp sheet. At the bed-end, my ankles bitten, white-bumped, clawed. It was bright day. I could hear the washermen outside, and I knew that if I opened my eyes or even moved my head I would be letting myself in for all kinds of responsibility.

For a start, that of finding out what time it was. Without a watch this would mean getting up to check the clock in Cuckoo's kitchen. Which meant that I had to get dressed, even though all the clean clothes were piled outside on the terrace by the ironing board.

The whole exercise seemed unmanageably complicated, given how desiccated and mosquitoed and generally thumping bloody I felt. And the added thing to the usual was that, surrounding the leaden brain-sponge, wrapped around the pounding haggis like an arterial gut-lining, was a kind of guilty apprehension. Just what had I said to the ballet-girl. Exactly what?

Too much, certainly. And I'd said I'd meet her at . . . what time? I opened an eye on to another still, white, dry-mouthed day.

'Porter . . . Walton . . . ? Look, I really can't remember. Her first name's June, and she booked in just before midnight last night.'

'I'm sorry, Sir, we can't . . .'

'Please, just show me the book, I'll recognise her name.' I reached for the register. The hotel clerk, faintly alarmed, released it.

'Stanley. Hello.'

She was standing behind me, slightly pale, in last night's clothes.

'June, hi. I was just . . . I'm afraid I'd forgotten your surname.'

'Webster.'

'Webster. Of course. How are you?' I pressed my hand to a yawn.

'I'm fine.' She smiled. 'You, on the other hand, look terrible.'

'I feel not too bad actually, all things considered. Having said which, is there somewhere here we can get a cup of coffee?'

'I think there's a dining room.'

The dining room was dark, deserted and, as a result of its roaring air-conditioning, ice-cold. Something told me that coffee might be some time in arriving. And that by then we might have hypothermia.

'The club?' I wondered.

'Why not,' she agreed, and then hesitated. 'Look, you go on. I'll see you there in an hour and a half. I could use some clean clothes. And I should reassure Beth.'

'Did you ring her?' I asked.

'I said I was staying at Priya's. I'd rather talk to her properly. Face to face.'

'Is our good ol' boy going to be there?'

'Dane? No. Not in the day.'

'Well, mind how you go.'

'I will.'

Two club sodas, a Chesterfield and a tepid Nescafé later I was ready for a few desultory lengths of the pool. I had rung all the Lakshmi numbers, as per, but no longer with any expectation. The numbers, as always, had rung desertedly, crackled, broken off, splintered into crossed lines, dialects, impossibilities.

I pushed the cigarette packet into my shoe. The day was overcast, and there was no difference in temperature between the air and the water.

The warm salt blur streamed past my face. What had I said to June last night? What had we agreed? The formless apprehension remained. The goggles pulled at my eyes.

Maybe some company, an ally, wouldn't be so bad. I had no real reason to be defensive about Lakshmi. Or about anything. So what . . .

There had been a vulnerability about June this morning, in her crumpled clothes, in the mark of the clutched sheet across her cheek. It wasn't something I wanted for her, though. I wanted her as she had been before, strong-limbed, grey-eyed, remote. I wanted there to be things I didn't know about her.

The truth could be that June was right. That Lakshmi was never going to come to me, never going to bypass the professional courtesies.

I, or as it now seemed, we, had to go to her.

Maybe, though, on the basis that nothing easily won was worth having, she wished to be journalistically courted, investigated, pursued. Maybe she had decided to be hardly won. Maybe she wanted to play.

Fair enough.

This time I approached the bar telephone with some hope. Nelson answered almost immediately. The line, as usual, was poor, cutting out intermittently.

'Lost . . . Everyone's lost her, man, she's gone to ground. Her secretary's . . . usual *chutia* . . . No one on *Khandaan*'s . . . Rahman's shooting in Kashmir with . . . find someone else.'

'How can I get hold of a journalist called Seeta Rao?'

' . . . Sunita?'

'SEETA,' I shouted, 'SEETA RAO.'

' . . . have her number, wait.'

I waited, hoping my rupee would not run out.

' . . . find her number, but I . . .'

'WHAT?'

' . . . Building, Shantisthan Colony.'

'Which building?'

The receiver died in my hand. I ordered a third club soda. Exchanged a note for some more change. Redialled.

'Mr D'Mello is out of station.'

'I was speaking to him thirty bloody seconds ago.'

' . . . out of station. Not available.'

The same voice answered when I rang a second and third time. After that the phone must have been taken off the hook.

At the club's entrance I asked Chatterjee if he had a telephone directory. He had; there were eleven pages of Raos, several hundred S. Raos, a score of Sitas, four Seetas, and none of them at Shantisthan Colony.

'How do you get to Shantisthan, Chatterjee?' I asked.

'Proceed by bus to Santa Cruz, Sir. Thence by rickshaw. Not far.'

I tried Nelson again.
No joy.

'I don't really eat lunch,' said June.

'What happened with your sister?' I asked.

'I didn't say anything,' she answered. 'She was in a bad mood. Martyred. Supposedly about having to drink carrot juice instead of coffee, but really because I've gone and made a whole lot of friends that she doesn't know.' She squinted at the sky and checked in her bag. 'If you want to eat, I might just swim, and then . . .' she lifted a questioning eyebrow, '. . . on to the scent, perhaps?'

She hadn't forgotten.

'If you're interested,' I said, 'I'm going up to a place called Shantisthan. To find the only journalist that's written about her, about Lakshmi, recently. Called Seeta Rao. The journey's by bus to the middle of nowhere. It'll be your average nightmare.'

'It'll be an adventure,' said June. 'Do you think my shoes are all right?'

The moment she lowered herself into the pool I realised that I'd never actually seen her swimming. Maybe it was because I'd seen her by the pool so often, long-muscled and lazy in the red bikini; I'd had this picture of sleek scapular power, smooth-cleaving arms, water-dark hair.

Nothing, as it happened, could have been further from the truth. Her physical fluency departed her utterly, she thrashed, laughed helplessly, choked and got nowhere. A small doggy-paddling circle returned her to the edge.

'You're honoured,' she eventually gasped. 'Only a very privileged few have ever seen La Webster afloat. La Lobster. It just isn't . . .' she coughed, wiped her eyes apologetically, '. . . my skill.'

'You're frightened of the water,' I said, 'of getting it up your nose, in your eyes, in your hair.'

'I am,' she said. 'You're right. But knowing all that doesn't make it any easier. Not after being alive for thirty-one years. I find it hard to . . .'

'Think of it,' I suggested, 'like a pas de deux, perhaps.'

'A pas de deux isn't a step,' she smiled. 'A pas de deux takes two.'

'Trust the water,' I said.

'Maybe I should.' She smiled, looking away.

The sprinklers were making rainbows around Chatterjee's office as we walked out into Nepean Sea Road. At the bus-stop, repositioned to accommodate the abandoned roadworks, we stood in dusty silence. Most of the cars, I noticed, already had their bumpers painted with thick waterproofing varnish against the approaching monsoon.

It wasn't until twenty minutes into the journey that I was able to squeeze on to the slatted wooden seat beside her.

'Tell me again,' said June, turning to me with some difficulty, 'why we're going to see this woman?'

'Seeta Rao. Well, she wrote a long interview piece with Lakshmi in a magazine called *Cinestar*, and ... It's possible that she has some kind of access, and as a journalist – but not an immediate competitor – I might be able to swing a bit of help. She might not give us anything, of course, or then again she might demand some sort of quid pro quo ...'

June smiled. 'English public schoolboys aren't terrifically good at bribery, are they?' she asked. 'I mean, it's not one of the things they teach you, is it?'

'Well, I didn't quite mean that, but no, you're right. We were taught to get what we want by force of character, moral or otherwise, psychic dignity, whatever ... None of which works for a moment, of course, as I discovered the day I went into television. But it's funny, actually, that you should say that, because I was talking to this Indian bloke the other day and he said exactly the same. He said that we Brits always offer too much, scare people off.'

'Would that have been that very pukka-looking type you were with at the club a couple of weeks ago?'

'You noticed,' I said.

'Well, there's not THAT huge an amount to notice there ... And most women would remember a man as deadly-looking, as Priya would say, as that. Who exactly is he?'

'Well, he's in fact some sort of policeman. Very much all over the place. Rather frighteningly well informed. He sort of picked me up just after I arrived – I think he sort of keeps tabs on foreigners – and implied that he would like to keep in touch.'

'Weird.'

'This is a weird place, though. I mean, people like your brother-in-law think they can ride into town and just behave how they like here. But it's not actually like that at all here. You want to play, you play by the rules of people like Das.'

She frowned. 'What kind of rules do you mean?'

'Rules is the wrong word,' I answered, and thought for a moment.

'It's more a question of being prepared to play the long game. Supping with a long spoon, and so on, but dining with the devil nevertheless. Look at Saxena and Haji Ibrahim. What I'm saying is that . . . this isn't a place you can crash about like a wounded tiger, roaring about right and wrong. And I mean, torture prostitutes all you like in private, but don't kick tables over in restaurants. That's the ethos.'

In the aisle a man lit a cigarette, held it at the level of our faces. The smoke swung behind my glasses.

'But you don't actually believe that, do you?' asked June, 'and – '

'. . . I don't believe,' I interrupted her, rubbing my eyes, 'that it SHOULD be like that, but on the other hand it's unrealistic to – '

'. . . all this about torturing prostitutes, anyway?' She batted her hand vaguely and leant her head back against the window; a lurch through a pot-hole immediately cracked the sharp metal frame against her head.

'Just something I read about in the papers,' I said. 'Are you all right? That looked painful.'

'Fine,' she said, squeezing her eyes closed, turning away.

'Aren't you being just a little TOO cynical?' she tightly addressed the window. 'Just a little TOO much the . . . Mightn't directness count for something? I mean, you as much as told me . . .'

'Told you . . . ?'

'That . . . well, that you want to find this Lakshmi for more than just professional reasons, that you're – ' She had to raise her voice to be heard. I was aware of others around us listening.

'. . . I just have to find her,' I cut in. 'Unfinished business, if you like, but I just have to . . .'

'Fine,' said June, shortly. 'Let's just find her, then.'

The bus shuddered in and out of neutral as we stop-started through Mahim. Beneath the dreary noon whiteness our progress was slow. At the roadside silver bracelets and mirrored saris briefly resisted the monotone haze as women head-loaded dishes of mortar towards an area of cement dust and rusted spars. On the hoardings over the lean-tos, I recognised Sanju Saxena and Priya Bhoopatkar. They had been painted from stills no more than a week ago, but the anguished faces were already fading, had already been there for ever.

The journey lasted over an hour and a half. June's silence made it seem longer, but eventually we climbed stiffly out of the bus at Santa Cruz Station and joined the back of the rickshaw queue. A further hour later we arrived at the edge of what looked like a vast construction site.

'Shantisthan,' gestured the ricksaw driver.

June looked at me dubiously. Two ranks of uncompleted high-rise blocks, a dozen in all, rose from a broken plain strewn with building waste, rubbish and abandoned machinery. A road joining the buildings extended fifty yards in front of us before deteriorating into a series of littered tracks.

The driver jerked his head at me interrogatively. I found his money and watched uneasily as the rickshaw turned the corner and disappeared, leaving us with the silence.

'Xanadu,' said June finally. 'Perfumed breezes.'

'Quite,' I said. 'Shall we give it a go?'

'Absolutely.'

We followed the track. At the base of each building was a painted board naming the tenants. Beggars and watchmen sat motionless in the shade of the stairwells, watching as we read the boards.

'It'll be the last one,' said June. 'In these situations it's always the last one.'

I don't mind if it's the last, I thought, as long as it's one. And as long as it's in her name.

'Are you OK?' I asked, as she picked her way over a revetment of solidified cement sacks.

'I'm fine,' said June. 'This is NOT slingback country, but I'm fine.'

We were past the road now. Red earth, mechanically excavated and sprouting dry weeds, banked at each side of the track. Uncertain plank bridges crossed drainage channels from which, as we crossed, the mosquitoes rose blackly. At the base of each building was a large skip around which crows and dogs and children worried at strings of refuse.

'It's strange to think,' said June, wrinkling her nose, 'that this is all these kids have ever seen. Poor babies. They must think that the whole world is a shitheap.'

'I'm not so sure,' I said. 'I bet they've seen a film or two. Even if it's only a blurry tenth-generation video or some old thing projected on to a sheet. And they know their stars. They can all sing "Pyari Pyari" and disco-dance like Jeetendra. They know there's more than this. What's unlikely is that they'll ever see it.'

'Doesn't it make you wonder about living here in India?' she asked. 'All this, I mean. All that?'

'What depresses me about this place in particular,' I said, 'is not the shit and the flies and the dogs. It's the architecture. The fact that this is the future.'

We were half-way along the line and the going was getting worse.

'Oh, God!' said June, freezing. 'What's that?' A questing brown head the size of a small dog's was watching us from a parapet of broken earth.

'Bandicoot,' I said. 'Giant Indian Rat. From the Telugu *pandikokku*, meaning — '

'. . . Stanley, PLEASE!' she gripped my upper arm. 'Make it GO. PLEASE!'

'It won't bite,' I said. 'It's vegetarian. Vegan, even.'

'Make it GO.'

I waved vaguely at the bandicoot, and shied a stone at it. Twitching, it watched me with interest. The head of a second, larger bandicoot appeared.

'Oh, God, Stanley, please.' June's voice had dropped a register; she manoeuvred herself behind me, put both hands on my shoulders. I lifted my heels and peered over the bank. There were about twenty of them, black, scurfy, hairy of tail, gorging themselves on the contents of an overturned dustbin.

I turned back to June.

'Look,' I said, 'we're just going to walk straight past them. Just look at your feet. I'll walk between you and them, OK?'

She nodded miserably.

I put my arm round her waist.

'Walk. Look down. Now.'

Slowly, matching my step to hers I walked her, resisting, past the inquisitive sentries. Under her cotton dress her waist was tense and drawn. I rested my palm on her hip, felt knicker elastic and ligaments nervously articulate beneath my fingertips, remembered her swimming.

'We've passed them,' I said eventually, lifting my hand.

'Have they gone?'

'They've gone,' I said.

She raised her head. There were tears trapped in her eyelashes. She smeared them, shook her head.

'Sorry. It's just a thing. Rats. Stupid.'

'Are you all right?'

'I'm fine. They just panic me.'

'Sorry I was flippant.'

'That's OK.' She sniffed, rubbed her eyes again, laughed. 'God, you must think I'm a right girlie.'

'There are worse things to be than a right girlie.'

'Well, I'm not any of them. It's just rats. They just . . . I imagine them, their yellow teeth, those scaly tails . . . just . . . yuck.'

'They're mucky,' I admitted, 'but not dangerous. People eat them.'

'That's DISGUSTING.'

'It's like a rather fine-textured, gamy pork. Dark meat, of course, with little grey bones. We had it at school a lot.'

'Very funny. And don't tell me there aren't things YOU'RE frightened of.'

'Oh, there are, lots. Dentists, for a start. Coastal towns in Sussex. Dark furniture. Tapeworms. Plum-coloured carpets. Anglicans . . . The list is endless.'

We stepped into the dark of another stairwell. Another painted board. No Raos.

'Press on?'

'Press on.'

'How did you feel,' asked June a minute or two later, 'don't answer if you don't want to, but when you were told that your parents were . . . had been killed?'

I bent down to shake the earth from my shoe. Ahead of us, several small boys were squatting sociable and fly-blown at the side of the path, their shorts round their ankles. I replaced the shoe and lit a cigarette. June watched me.

'I was called to the headmaster's study – it happened in term-time – and arrived there terrified that, for some obscure reason, I was due to be beaten. I knocked and went in and to my enormous relief saw that Milly was in the room as well as Walter. He told me as kindly as he could what had happened, and the awful truth is that the relief of being off the hook myself was so great that for a moment or two I didn't begin to understand what he was saying. And then for a VERY short time I minded more terribly than I could begin to bear before realising that of course the whole thing was a complete scam and that Mum and Dad were still alive and living in Bombay.

'And so I pretended to believe Walter and Milly, although I couldn't make myself cry in front of them, and that night I ran away, heading for India.'

'Did you get there?' asked June, worried, as she picked her way through the debris in her unsuitable shoes.

'I got to a place in the dark that I told myself was India, would be India when I woke up, and then in the morning the farmer rang the police and the police rang the school saying that they had a very cold seven-year-old in their custody who would only speak some strange foreign language and they were buggered if they understood a word of it.

'After that I don't remember very much. I remember the school's white isolation room, nights running into day. Not going to lessons. Praying that no one would make me cry by remembering my eighth birthday. Helping Milly with her photography. Her showing me how to burn a hole in the newspaper with the lens of my glasses. I also remember – curiously, given what they say about children – the silence and respect of the other boys.

'The truth is that most of that year was quite simply wiped from my memory. My last year in Bombay I can remember quite clearly, but not the year that followed.'

'We forget so much,' said June, after a time.

'I wonder if this could be it? It just says Rao.'

'Ninth floor,' said June.

'Seeta Rao?' I asked the watchman, who was nodding in a chair, his cane balanced on his knees.

He raised his eyes to indicate up.

There was no lift. Work on Happy Home seemed to have been abandoned at an earlier stage than on the other blocks, and rotted sacking and bamboo scaffolding still clung to its grey exterior breeze-blocks. We spiralled up the raw concrete stairwell from floor to floor, past a succession of faded election posters and steel-barred doors. On the first few landings, goats and hens had been tethered by string; as we passed, they nosed at us with gentle pessimism.

The ninth floor was cool and silent. A minute after my knock, a servant admitted us, with a long expressionless stare, to an ante-room smelling strongly of disinfectant. The walls were an uneven grey plaster skim. There was no decoration and no furniture.

'Nice place,' said June, looking around the pictureless walls. The servant re-appeared, handed us steel beakers of water, and gestured us to follow her.

The bed looked as if on loan from an institution. From her writing style I had imagined Seeta Rao as aggressively young, but this woman was probably fifty. She was propped up against several pillows; her hennaed hair had been neatly back-combed and draped with a pink chiffon dupatta.

'Hello,' she said quietly.

At the foot of the bed was a steel trolley on which stood a small tin of powder, a plastic comb, and a paperback romance from a circulating library.

I introduced June and myself, explained the purpose of our visit. As I spoke she smiled. Her eyes, darkened erratically with *kajal*, were dreamy, almost babyish. I noticed that the fingers plucking at the pink dupatta were knotted with arthritis. Surely, I thought, she couldn't type.

'You're making a film?' she asked.

'A documentary,' I said. 'For British television. I read your piece in *Cinestar*, so . . .'

'I have been ill,' said Seeta. 'For a long time I'm . . .' She frowned.

'What has been the problem?' asked June, gently.

'Yes,' said Seeta. 'Problems. They don't know what it is, of course. Doctor Davar at Breach Candy, others say Moolgaonkar in Pedder Road . . . See, I was one of the last to see her alive.'

'Who was that?' I asked.

'Meena. Manju, he called her. At the flat in little Gibbs Road.'

'Lakshmi?' I said.

'She died. The cemetery is near the railway.'

'Lakshmi Khandekar is dead?' I asked.

'She died also? I didn't know.'

I had the article folded damply in a trouser pocket. I pulled it out and smoothed it over my knee, a look from June braking my irritation. I handed over the pages, and an arthritic hand rose uncertainly. June took the article from me, and following the direction of Seeta's eyes, handed her a pair of clouded spectacles.

'*Akeli*,' smiled Seeta, 'means "alone",' she told June.

'Did you meet Lakshmi Khandekar in the Taj?' June asked her.

'They use my name,' explained Seeta. 'I write the pieces,' she indicated the instrument by her bed, 'on the telephone. They use my name. I've been ill, you see . . .'

The telephone at the bedside rang. The servant appeared in the doorway, and hovered briefly as June handed Seeta the receiver. Seeta listened in silence, her eyes vague, and eventually handed back the receiver.

'Rahman Khan,' she said sadly, 'passed last night with Swaroop.' Slowly her expression cleared. She indicated a small brass bell next to the telephone. 'Please ring.'

When the servant reappeared, Seeta spoke to her in Marathi. She left the room and returned a minute later with several typed sheets of paper, which she handed to me. It was bald list of facts, written in English, and had clearly formed the basis of the *Cinestar* article.

'Where did you get this?' I asked.

'It was sent,' answered Seeta, surprised at the question.

'By who? Is it true?'

'True?' asked Seeta. She turned her head to the square breeze-blocked gap that was the window.

'You don't know where I can find Lakshmi Khandekar?' I asked, exasperated. 'You can't help me?'

Seeta, her face still turned away, rang the bell; the servant returned to the bedside.

'I think we should go,' said June. The arthritic hand had released the bell and was twitching at the sheet.

'Thank you,' I said. But Seeta Rao's focus was distant.

'That,' I said, as we passed the goats again, 'was what I would call an opaque personality.'

'Do you think she ever gets out?' wondered June. 'I mean, nine floors up, no lift?'

'There wouldn't be much to go out for,' I said, looking out of one of the uncompleted windows at the lunar desolation below. A man dressed in rags was slowly leading a camel heavily laden with hi-fi equipment along the earth track.

'We're some way,' I went on, 'from anywhere she could possibly want to go . . .'

I felt a strong need to leave the place behind me, to return to the Nepean Sea Bathing Club, to float, eyes goggled and closed, in the blood-warm water. For a moment, lassitude overcame my desire to find Lakshmi. It was just all too exhausting. I was getting nowhere.

'There WAS something . . . about her.'

'Seeta?' I asked.

'No,' said June hesitantly, 'about Lakshmi.'

I stopped.

'What do you mean, June, there was something about her?'

June looked at me, embarrassed.

'I talked to her.'

'When?'

'At that dinner thing.'

'You didn't say.'

'Well, I'm sorry, Stanley. Nothing she said then could help us find her. I just talked to her. Is that a problem?'

'Of course it's not a problem. It's just that if we're going to trail half-way across Greater Bombay looking for her I'd have said it made sense to pool our information, no?'

'OK,' said June, folding her arms and raising her chin. 'Let's REALLY pool. Tell me why, for a start, you want to find her.'

Fuck it, I thought. Give us a break. I leant back against the concrete wall.

'OK. I'll tell you why. Because I have to find an explanation. Because I was elaborately set up. Because, and I'm not imagining this, we really liked each other. And I can't just let her disappear without . . . some explanation.'

'Do you want the explanation? Or do you want the lady?'

'I was hoping that one might lead to the other.'

'Well, maybe she doesn't want to be found. Maybe she's changed her mind.'

'What did she say to you about it?'

'Nothing about any of that. We talked about, I don't know, people, the way that they are with you when you're a performer. Men. General stuff.'

'And what was her, ummm, line on men?'

'She didn't . . . take them too seriously.'

Hardly surprising, I thought, working with guys like Saxena and Rahman Khan.

'And,' she went on, 'I know you're the media expert around here, but how much can you believe of a story when your only source is the subject of that story. If Lakshmi's planting no-check stories about herself in the press, I mean, up to you, but . . .'

'But . . . ?'

'BUT, Stanley, it's been the best part of a fortnight. I mean, OK, maybe she wants some elaborate game of hide-and-seek, but frankly, she didn't strike me as that kind of girl. If she hasn't contacted you in all that time, if no one ever even ANSWERS the numbers she gave you . . .'

It's true, I thought, she has my address, my number.

We stared at each other.

'Do you know something I should know?' I asked her.

She frowned at me for several long seconds.

'I don't think so,' she said, eventually.

*

Replacing the glass on the table I leant back against the faded canvas of the deckchair and closed my eyes. The cigarette smoke ran hot up my trailing fingers. I flicked the butt over the sea wall.

A typically, pointlessly knackering Bombay day. I felt in my back pocket for the article, the *Akeli* still.

Damn. I'd left it in Shantisthan with Seeta Rao, its nominal authoress. Bugger. Still, I had the information, for what it was worth, in my mind. I could summon Lakshmi, of course, at will. I did so. She was wearing the black *salwar-kameez*. Freeze-framed. Smiling.

What do you want of me? I asked her, after a time. Where are you leading me? Remember, *meri jaan*, I understood you. I alone. Trust no other.

Trust, I thought. June. She'd taken the taxi on to Cuffe Parade. Happy Families. I couldn't say I envied her, but then we'd probably seen enough of each other for one day.

The breeze came.

Lakshmi.

It was street-light dark by the time I climbed from the taxi.

As I counted out the notes for the driver I felt the beat of my heart, hard and dry. Orienting myself, I walked away from the station and up Grant Road. It was late, but the crowds still pressed and murmured around the shop-windows, around the stalls where the lottery tickets and the plastic wallets and the used watches were laid out.

I walked as fast as the crowd allowed. As the station fell away behind me, the displays of clothes and bright alloy vessels gave way to darker premises, to dim-staircased entrances and cell-like bars. On the pavement, smoke lifted pungent from coal grills, pans of oil. Cigarettes glowed and eyes followed me as I passed. I almost missed the turning, saw the sign at the last moment. Except for an uneven necklace of low-wattage bulbs strung around the mosque, Suklaji Street was unlit. At first glance the pavements were deserted, and then, as my night-vision cleared, the shadows shaped themselves into sleeping forms. Some were shrouded like the dead, others, the children, open-mouthed and akimbo as if flung there. None moved as I passed.

Beyond the pavements, in the dark sheds and yards of the rag-pickers and the welders and hammerers of scrap, night-trading continued. Bowed and threadbare figures unshouldered stinking gunny-sacks, sifted through the waste. Others poked at small fires below blackened walls, smoked *bidi*s through cupped hands, and watched.

The road curved. I followed the curve and saw, on my right, the broken gate, the small pavilion, the pink light. I stopped for a moment, my heart thumping painfully, and crossed the road. As I reached the pavement the boy stepped from the shadow of the gatepost. As I jumped in surprise, he laughed.

'*Phir aye, Saab.*' He slapped his knees and fell back against the wall. '*Phir aye.*'

'I've come again.' I smiled, looking around. We seemed to be alone. 'Do many come?'

'People come,' he answered obliquely, and laughed again. 'People come. But my sister will be happy to see you.'

'She's your SISTER?' I asked.

'Sister,' he confirmed. 'Beautiful, no?'

'Beautiful,' I agreed.

He took my hand.

On the divan, the toad-mouthed woman seemed to be asleep. But as my eyes refound the framed texts, the film posters, and the cassette tape recorder, I realised that her chins were slowly working, that at one corner of her mouth was a dark dribble of betel, and that the small unblinking eyes were watching me.

I switched my gaze from hers. From above us came a scraping and the laughter of the boy. He came half-way down the steps and beckoned to me. As I climbed the steps the cloying aniseed smell that surrounded the divan was replaced by the sharper *masala* of cardamom, turmeric and coriander. The boy parted the blue curtain, and I ducked under the rail.

'She is eating,' he said unnecessarily, and with a quick squeeze of my hand, vanished.

Before I had taken a step, his head reappeared through the curtain. 'Give her fifty,' he said. 'No more.'

I found him a note. He smiled, an arm reached out, and he was gone. I handed another to the slender figure on the mattress, who turned, briefly, to thrust it somewhere behind her. She was propped on one elbow, eating rice and mustard-seeded vegetables from a banana leaf. The small-domed room with its clutch of pink lights was heavy with the smell of food and I realised that I hadn't eaten since the morning.

Her mouth full, the girl gestured interrogatively at the banana leaf. Swallowing, she wiped her tattooed chin with the back of a thin hand and gave me something that I took for a smile.

'Eat,' she said.

I lay down facing her, the food between us, and we ate. From the wall, in his white suit, Sanju Saxena smiled down at us. The girl sucked her fingers, which were yellow from the food, and I watched the narrow cheekbones working beneath the fine, hollowed sockets of her eyes. Between her eyebrows I noticed another small tattoo.

'Water?' she asked, and I nodded.

As she picked her teeth with a small stick, I rested on an elbow and smoked a cigarette. One of her incisors was a darker colour than the others, the nerves dead. At intervals she took the cigarette from me, tapped the ash neatly into a brass pot containing the burnt out stalks of several joss sticks, sucked at it dubiously, wrinkling her nose, and returned it to me. She was wearing earrings of twisted silver wire. Finally I leant beyond her and crunched out the cigarette against the mouth of the jar.

Lakshmi.

XIII

∽∽∽∽∽

There'd been no sign of Dane for two days. Not a call, nothing. In her clothes, Beth looked terrible. She'd lost over a stone and her jewellery looked too big. Next to her I looked like one of those hearty sweater-blondes from the Fifties cigarette ads.

Beth wasn't allowed out of the hotel, doctor's orders, but that didn't mean I couldn't take her down to the hairdresser for some vanity therapy. I had said nothing about the other night except that Dane had looked in on the club.

In the lift, though, Beth wouldn't meet my eyes.

'Do you FEEL better?' I asked. Any conversation, rather than none.

Her shoulders rose in a shrug under the woollen jacket, and in the moment before she turned away I saw the tears shining at her lower eyelids. Only sheer, bloody-minded, elder-sisterly determination can have seen them off before they fell to her cheeks.

'FUCK him,' she said quietly, frowning into the mirror. 'Fuck him, fuck him, FUCK HIM.' As the lift gulped to a halt and the doors slid open, she turned to me uncertainly.

I steered her out before the doors closed again, and our heels clattered over the marble. As we passed the banquette arrangement in the centre of the floor, she paused, braked me with a hand on my wrist. 'You would tell me, June, if anything, I don't know, between . . .'

'Beth . . .' I was appalled. 'You couldn't possibly think that I . . . ?'

'No, of course not. Although I know that he does quite . . . I mean, weirder things have happened.'

'Look, just put it out of your mind. Besides,' I smiled brightly, 'he ain't my kinda guy.'

'Crass and alcoholic, you mean?' she asked, raising an eyebrow.

I shrugged.

She walked to one of the bronzed wall-mirrors and frowned at her troubled reflection.

'Forty-eight hours,' she said, finally turning round, 'and then this girl is outta here.'

'Fighting talk!' I said. 'I like it.'

She put a thin hand on my shoulder. 'I'm glad you came, Junie.'

'Me, too,' I said. 'Now what are we going to do about this hair of yours?'

An hour and a half later I was ready for my lunch appointment.

'Who ARE all these grand friends of yours?' Beth had asked, more her old self after a shampoo and set. 'You MIGHT ask Kimmie Kitzinger along just ONCE or TWICE, you know, she's absolutely DYING to meet all these film people you've been . . . hanging around with. It really is her particular interest. You really can be quite thoughtless, June, do you know that?'

'Not at all,' said Priya. 'I'm really glad you're here. See, I'm not sure about this script at all. These directors always promise whatever you want to hear.'

'Then hit you with the wet-sari scene at the last moment?'

She laughed. 'Oh, worse than that . . .'

We were in the Sea Lounge, with its cool aqua walls. From time to time the people at the other tables sneaked looks at Priya. They all knew who she was. She ignored them quite elegantly, not pretending they weren't there, but not allowing them to distract her, either.

'You look great, though,' she went on. 'He'll probably offer YOU the part! Here he is.'

At the entrance, Sunil Bhattacharaya peered short-sightedly round the tables. A waiter led him over.

'Ladies,' he said. 'Priya.'

'This is my friend June Webster,' said Priya. 'She's a famous British actress.'

I smiled nicely, and kicked her.

'How do you do,' I said.

Sunil Bhattacharaya had a beard but no moustache. In contrast to his Hawaiian outfit of a fortnight ago he was dressed entirely in porridge-coloured homespun, and carried a Congress cap made from the same material.

'Cool,' he said, turning my hand and peering at it. 'Didn't we meet in LA? At Rod's?'

I gaped for a moment. Priya beamed at me.

'Well, you know LA . . .' I managed, shrugging.

'Believe it.' He nodded sagely, dropped my hand absent-mindedly on to the tablecloth and rubbed at his eyes.

As he held his heavy glasses up to the window, I stuck my tongue out at Priya. On the other side of the room a bearded man, whom I recognised from the *muharat* as a reporter, made a note in a notebook.

The waiter drew up alongside our table.

'Ah,' said Bhattacharaya. 'Friend.'

'Sir,' said the waiter.

'Do you have . . . let's see . . . just a very simple rice and dal. And maybe a little fresh coconut water?'

'Er . . . Yes, Sir. Of course.'

'I'll have the same,' I said, remembering the robust figure that had faced me in the bathroom mirror that morning.

'Madam?'

'I'll have, to start with,' said Priya thoughtfully, 'the Lady Curzon soup. With French bread and butter. And a *chickoo* milkshake. After that the quail, sauté potatoes, and spinach. Then the *badam kulfi*.'

'Certainly, Madam. Anything else, Sir? Ladies?'

'I might . . . just try a very little clear soup,' said Bhattacharaya. 'And possibly . . . the prawns are fresh?'

'Yes, Sir. Madam?'

'Maybe an Alphonso mango,' I said.

'Vegetables, Sir?'

'Of course, vegetables,' said Bhattacharaya. 'India,' he turned to me, 'has the richest selection of vegetables in the world. I could live off nothing else. Most of the time I do.'

'Anything to drink, Sir?'

He sighed. 'You have a wine list?'

'Certainly, Sir.'

'What I have to do,' explained Sunil Bhattacharaya to me, 'is to persuade this very . . . charming young lady to allow me to make her a star. A bigger star than she already is.'

Priya smiled and said nothing.

'As I've explained,' said Sunil, squinting at his wine, 'it's basically a traditional campus picture. But the social element also is there.'

With the Soave bottle nearly empty, his West Coast accent was beginning to unravel.

'It's a Romeo and Juliet theme,' he continued. 'Young love. College boy. Feminist girl. The picture opens in the graduation disco of a social-science department. Big picturised song. The heroine in a one-piece leopardskin costume.'

'And then what happens?' asked Priya.

'The boy passes away.'

'Why, exactly?'

'He is beaten by negative forces. Lightly only, but he perishes.'

'And the girl?' asked Priya. 'Who I assume is to be me?'

'She is humiliated.'

'Lightly raped? By the negative forces?'

He nodded. 'But tastefully shot. All you see is the bound wrist. The hand opening and closing. Very simple. Moving.'

'And then?'

'She is tied, helpless, under a waterfall. But she escapes. With other feminists she takes revenge on the gang. One by one they are killed and fed to leopards in Borivali Park. Finally the smugglers are all dead but victory is bitter-sweet because the heroine is dishonoured. No man will have her. She becomes a leopard.' Bhattacharaya turned to me. 'What do you think?'

'I think it's a perfectly lovely story,' I said, 'with a theme that will appeal to women everywhere.'

'See.' He opened his hands. 'Think of what this could do for your career. It won't be just another formula *masala* picture.'

'Who will play the college-boy hero?'

'I am in discussion with Sanjay Saxena.'

'Sanju,' I said, 'but he's . . . he's nearly fifty.'

Priya crossed her eyes at me.

'Old is gold,' shrugged Bhattacharaya, pouring himself the last of the Soave.

'Mr Bhattacharaya?'

It was the journalist with the beard, notebook poised.

'Nelson D'Mello. *Bombay Mail.*'

Bhattacharaya looked up, a little bleary.

'Two minutes of your time, Boss. Can you confirm the line-up for *Tendui*?'

'Means *The Leopard*,' whispered Priya.

'I can confirm that I am in discussion with Mr Saxena and Miss Bhoopatkar here. No signings have taken place, *bas.*'

'And *Khandaan*? We have been informed that shooting has been postponed.'

'*Khandaan* is in the process of rescheduling.'

'Can you give us any information on the whereabouts of Lakshmi Khandekar?'

'As far as I am concerned she has not informed me that she has disappeared. It is not impossible she is in Nairobi. Our relationship is harmonious. I have great respect for Lakshmi as an artist.'

D'Mello scribbled furiously.

'And the story-line for *Tendui*?'

'Basically is boy meets girl. Script is of Akbar, location shooting at Kanheri Caves and Alibagh, dances to be picturised in Kulu and Nilgiri Hills. Dance-master is Moisin. Songs are of Mohandas. Sets are lavish. And now Mr . . .'

'D'Mello.'

'. . . Mr D'Mello, if you would allow us to finish our meal?'

'One last question, Sir?'

Bhattacharaya nodded.

'Can you comment on information we have received that the shooting of *Khandaan* is to be recorded as a BBC Channel Four documentary production? Subject of Lakshmi Khandekar?'

'I have received no official request from BBC in respect of any such project. No permission for such a project has, to my knowledge, been issued. And now, Mr De Souza, please . . .'

Still scribbling, the reporter backed away.

Bhattacharaya watched him out of the room, laughed, and patted his pockets for cigarettes.

'*Khandaan*, man . . . Those BBC-wallahs have got one L-O-N-G wait.'

'What is happening there?' I asked. 'After that *muharat*, and all?'

'Put it this way,' said Bhattacharaya, applying a shaky flame to his State Express 555. 'The nominal producer, Ghosht, is one wealthy guy from Solapur. Sugar-cane. He has a daughter. Despite her elevated caste she is dark-skinned, and her complexion is somewhat . . .' He exhaled at the window. The sea was the dull glittering grey of bazaar silver; the Elephanta ferry traced its slender wake into the haze.

'Let me fill in the gaps,' said Priya, resignedly. 'And Sunil can correct me if I'm wrong.'

Bhattacharaya's eyebrows lowered. He released a smoking *masala* burp.

Priya continued. 'Ghosht has the parents of a suitably wealthy boy nibbling at his dusky daughter. A show of wealth and connection is necessary. Ghosht finds himself gently led, like a *bakra*, a goat, in the direction of film finance. A considerable deposit is made, and a well-known director, hero and heroine are signed. The press is informed. There is a lavish *muharat*. The *bakra* and several members of his large Solapuri family are photographed arm-in-arm with well-known stars like (just for the sake of argument!) Lakshmi Khandekar and Rahman Khan. These photographs, along with details of the production, are published in the filmi press. The prospective in-laws are *ekdum* impressed. Their son, who is taking a quick fortnight off from his dental practice in Des Moines, Iowa in order to procure a bride, is also impressed.

'Stage Two, of course, is when the *bakra* is informed that much more money is needed. The first payment has secured, in advance, the services of stars, co-producer and director, possibly even bought a song or two, but now the production needs REAL funds. At this point the *bakra*'s feet begin to get a little cold. Not to worry, he is advised, there is no urgency, things can be . . .'

'Rescheduled?' I asked. 'Indefinitely?'

Priya smiled.

Bhattacharaya smiled.

'Very elegant,' I said.

'And absolute nonsense, of course,' added Bhattacharaya.

'Just as a matter of interest,' I asked, 'DO you know where Lakshmi Khandekar is?'

He turned to me and made as if to slap his forehead.

'Lakshmi? Why, all of a sudden, is everyone asking about Lakshmi Khandekar? I've got no idea. I've always done everything through the aunt, what's her name, Lata.'

'Is it true,' I asked, 'that Lakshmi Khandekar was discovered by some director when she took some schoolchildren to . . .'

Both Priya and Bhattacharaya laughed.

'Who told you that old *jhoot*?' asked Bhattacharaya. 'Ganpat Naiyer, a damn good friend of mine, and this is true, told me that she just turned up at his office one morning with a portfolio of modelling stills and demanded a screen test. And he thought '*kyon nahin*, what the hell?', I mean, pretty girl and all, one of the richest families in Southern Maharashtra – sugar-cane again, as it happens – shot the test and next day found himself negotiating for dear life with Auntie. Why do you ask?' Both of them looked at me.

'Oh, I'd just heard about this documentary . . . Nothing, really.'

'Shlockumentary,' dismissed Sunil Bhattacharaya, waving his cigarette for the waiter and the bill. 'I've heard nothing.'

Priya raised a single eyebrow.

It was almost four o'clock by the time I reached the club. The meal at the Taj had left me overfull, obscurely guilty. I was beginning to understand that no objective here was achieved by moving towards it in a straight line. I had spent most of my life locked into a system whose rewards were an exact function of physical pain, denial, effort. Here, as Lizzie or Karen had said, sweat was for road-menders.

In my stomach the butterfly prawns fluttered a warning. There was more to my unsettlement than worries about fat.

The crows turned.

'Thanks for telling me, anyway.'

Stanley looked despondent. His nose and his collarbones were peeling. There was a damp crumpling at the thighs of his trousers where he had wiped the palms of his hands. With the tan, the paling of his eyebrows, his features had taken on a more fatalistic cast.

'I guess there's no business,' I started, 'like . . .'

'Thanks, June. Thanks a lot.'

'How did you spend the morning?' I asked.

'I went round to Colaba to try and knock up Lakshmi's Aunt

Lata. She wasn't there, only her servant Leelabai who seems to have retreated into some state wherein she understands no language, Indian or otherwise, spoken by man. But now that you tell me that Lata's Lakshmi's, I don't know, MANAGER . . . ?'

'Well, that's what this Bhattacharaya said.'

'Well, he should know, I guess. And to think that I thought she was some kind of retired bloody academic . . . God, she certainly picked MY brains.'

'Maybe she's both,' I offered.

'Both what?'

'Both an ex-teacher and Lakshmi's manager. I mean it's not impossible, is it?'

'Look,' said Stanley, 'are you sure that when you saw her that evening she didn't say anything about this project? ANYTHING?'

'Lakshmi? Not to me. Really. Not a word.' I cast my mind back and was suddenly flooded with something like apprehension, something streaming through the bloodstream, dragging at the sternum, flattening the ribs, that I suddenly, impossibly, recognised as stage fright, but the best sort, the sort when you know you've got it cracked, know, cold-bloodedly, that the science is there for the taking, that you're going to be REALLY good . . .

'. . . understand,' said Stanley, 'I really can't.'

I need the guys from Silicone Valley, I thought. My chips are fried. My reactions are scrambled. The wrong bells are ringing. I'm all over the place.

'. . . I'm sorry?' I said.

'. . . whether you fancied a Bulbul?'

'Share one, maybe?'

'OK.'

'Is it that she LIED to you?' I asked, some time later. 'Or is it that she lied to YOU?'

He smiled (first of the day).

'The second.'

'Because you see it as a betrayal?'

'More of a disappointment.'

'Can't you let the whole thing go?'

'I could.'

'But?'

'But.'

'I'll bet you one thing,' I said.

'What's that?'

'That the moment you decide to forget about her she'll re-appear.'

'Why do you want me to forget her?'

'I think . . . I think you're wasting time.'

'I have time.' He smiled. 'More Bulbul?'

'Yes. Truth or dare?'

'Dare.'

'OK. Forget Lakshmi. Make the film about Priya and Sanju and *Tendui*.'

'Pass. Truth?'

'Why did you really leave Emilia?'

'I told you.'

'You told me that you thought she was seeing this guy.'

'Right.'

'If she was, why did that necessarily have to be the end of everything. I mean, you could have put up a fight.'

'I could have. But I've always felt that to actually . . . DO IT with someone else is to go thermo-nuclear, to move beyond the possibility of negotiation. At which point, for reasons of sheer self-preservation, one bales out, moves to Mars, whatever. No?'

I said nothing.

'Just answer me one thing,' he went on, folding his arms on the stained linen tablecloth. 'Which of the following would you prefer to happen. That your lover comes to you and says I'm desperately in love with someone else, worship the ground etcetera, but haven't so much as touched her, or that he says that there's this girl and she and I have systematically munched our way through the entire Kama Sutra salad but having said that I've now come to my senses and had enough of paying for drinks with paper umbrellas in them and it's you I love. Which, truthfully, would you prefer to hear?'

'Well.' I sat back. 'Let's see. As the lesser of two evils – and forgetting for the moment that I'm quite the paper-umbrella type myself – I'd have to say the second. You?'

'Well if it was . . . you mentioned Emilia, so let's say Emilia, if she came to me and said there's this bloke, etcetera, well, I'd honestly much prefer if it was the first option. Worshipping the ground and the rest of it.'

'This is turning into one of those conversations, isn't it?' I said, warily. 'One of those ones, you know that thing, where you say afterwards, well, I'm REALLY glad we ... OK, why. Why Option One?'

'Because bad as it is to be told the news, at least neither of you is diminished by the situation. Pain, sure, but at least you can keep your chin up, refuse the handkerchief, enjoy the last cigarette and so on. At least the thing's in the realm of full-bollocked tragedy.'

'Trevor Howard?' I asked.

'Exactly. Trevor Howard. But Option Two says, well, OK, these things happen, they might conceivably happen again, I mean, after all the purpose of sex is SELF-realisation, and this other sex that I've been having, my leisure sex, is nothing really to do with you at all. So let's put it behind us – although not denying its validity as an experience – and get back to ...'

'Need it all be quite as ... ?'

'Look, the language isn't the problem. The problem is: how is one going to accommodate interference with one's *mehbooba* by a known, seen, cowboy-booted other. You can say, OK, for a short time her emotions went walkabout, there was a degree of jiggy-jiggy, but now it's over. It was one of the things that, like it or not, made her the person she is today, and it is the now and the future that is important, blah, blah, blah. If you can say that, and believe that, fine. Except that the mind, or at least MY mind, doesn't quite work like that. Because a physical thing has happened whose physical effects, even if only to a microscopic degree, will always, physically, chemically, biologically, be there in her. They won't always be there in him, the cowboy-booted other, but they will always be there in her.'

'You've lost me,' I said. 'I have the vague feeling that I disagree with every word you're saying, but ...'

'What I'm talking about,' said Stanley, 'is, I guess, sustained physical jealousy. If you really concentrate, for example, you can even be jealous of yourself. Yesterday, you can say, and from a purely cellular point of view, I was a different person. How could you have loved this other person then and now love me?'

'These are Bulbul arguments,' I said. 'And if we're going to have any more of them I think we should also have some food.'

'OK,' he said. 'But rational or not, let me finish. Think of any penetrative image you like, the wasp and his sting, the drill and the rock-face, anything . . . The penetrator, having penetrated, remains the same, the penetrated is changed for ever.'

'I think,' I said, 'that if we're talking dirty, I'm definitely going to need a drink with a paper umbrella in it. Possibly even a cherry. And what about the bee, anyway?'

'What bee?'

'The bee and his sting. If he stings, he dies. He leaves his guts behind with the sting. Try telling HIM nothing's changed.'

'You're concentrating on the wrong end of the bee. Look at the front end, the end that penetrates the flowers. Rose, as the poet said, thou art sick . . . the flying something that somethings in the night and doth your dark something destroy.'

'Oh, phoooey!' I said. 'Don't give me poetry. And don't talk to me about roses.'

'Why not?'

'Ummm.'

'Long story?' he asked.

I nodded. 'Ballet.'

He considered for a moment, the fan snatching at his smoke.

'If I invited you back to eat at Cuckoo's,' he wondered, 'would you tell it to me?'

'I just might,' I said.

'Have some more jelly,' said Cuckoo.

Once again I was too late telling her to go easy on the condensed milk.

'She's a darling,' I said to Stanley when she had gone back inside. 'And she clearly adores you.'

'She likes you too,' he said. 'In fact she's dangerously over-excited that I've brought you back.'

'What nonsense. I've never had rosewater jelly before, though.'

We both watched in silence as Baby, the servant's daughter – routinely adorable – brought us out cups of tea. There was just room on the tiny terrace for the two of us to sit at the table. Below us I could hear and smell the tide washing and dragging at the rocks, and through the dusk, five hundred yards away, I could see the lights of the club.

'It looks close,' I said, to break the silence. 'Spitting distance.'

A thread of smoke rose from the mosquito coil on the parapet. Stanley smiled. 'I think you owe me a story.'

'Once upon a time ...' I began, and stopped. From beyond the northern horizon came a pale electric flash and a distant growl. For several seconds we were held by a breeze, but it fell away, and a minute later the smothering heat had returned.

'How long do you think we've got?' I asked.

'A few days,' said Stanley. 'At the very most.'

'What day is it today?' I asked.

'Saturday, I think. I'm not sure, though. Why?'

'Just that it was a Saturday. About ten years ago. I was down to dance my first ballerina role. Princess Aurora in *Sleeping Beauty*. It was a spring day, cold. A guest artist had injured herself and Pauline Faull and I had been allocated her roles.

'There was a big thing in ... *The Times*, I think it was, photos and everything. "New Flowers for the Garden" was the headline, I remember. Anyway, it was our big break, Pauline's and mine.'

I turned to Stanley, who was staring out to sea.

'Are you sure you want to hear all this?' I asked.

'I want to hear it very much,' he said.

'OK. Well then.'

'As I said, I remember that it was one of those really cold days. March. I woke up in my flat in Barons Court having dreamt about it all night and thought for a moment that it was over, that I'd done it, and then realised that I'd just been dreaming and that actually I had twelve whole hours before the curtain went up.

'Anyway, we had class at ten, usual thing, and then, as you do when you're doing a principal role in the evening, I had the day free. So at 12.30, thereabouts, I wrapped up to go out for a walk, just to get out of the place, sort of thing, and there at the stage door was my mother with her awful, awful boyfriend, Phil. I won't go into Phil, but you have to take it from me that for various reasons he's just the utter terminal pits.

'Now I hadn't actually told my mother that I was doing this Aurora role, but she'd read it in the paper. The reason that I hadn't told her was that the last time I had had a big part on the Opera House stage, at the School Performance, she'd behaved really badly. It had been one of those really make-or-break things and I'd really flogged myself through the part – *Sylphides*, it was – and done well and everyone from the company had been watching etcetera, etcetera, and after the show people were congratulating me at this sort of reception thing they hold and I just think that she must have been ... I don't know, JEALOUS of me, or something, because she got totally drunk and in front of everybody started crying and saying that she'd given up her chance of a career so that I could have mine and now here I was suddenly far too grand to spend time with her and why didn't I just go off and leave her alone if I was so ashamed of her and so on and so forth ...

'Anyway, the last thing I wanted was a repeat of all this, plus the fact I'd invited my father and his ... wife she was, by then, they were coming down from Scotland, and I didn't want them – my parents – running into each other.

'Now, one of the things you get as a principal, or used to get then, was a pair of comps, of guest tickets. I'd already sent these to my father, and there at the stage door my mother went into this big routine of having had to PAY for tickets to see her own daughter dance and added to this the fact that the performance was all but sold out so they had had to buy these like REALLY EXPENSIVE SEATS ...

'So I said, look, let's just go out and get some lunch. Phil is there with her but so far he hasn't said a word, just stood there in his awful car-coat smoking his pipe and grinning like, what are those fish called? The ones with those long snouts that live in the Norfolk Broads and eat swans and babies?'

'Pike?'

'Exactly. Pike. He was grinning like a pike. He was a communist and smoked this horrid sort of wheezing pipe. God knows what manner of sex he went in for.

'Well we went out for lunch and my mother insisted on going to this foul sort of greasy-spoon place off the Strand – not that I don't adore greasy spoons or that I haven't eaten in them for weeks at a stretch on tour, just that this was a PARTICULARLY greasy and horrid one – the message of course being that the tickets had cost so much that this was all they could manage. I ended up eating quite a lot to get my blood sugar and stuff up for the performance and then of course Mom insisted on paying for it on the basis that if I can't take my OWN DAUGHTER out to LUNCH ... everyone in the place turning round at this loud Texan voice, of course, most of them stage hands who recognised me, and me remembering that as a principal my salary had been upped and, far too late, offering to pay for the tickets. Anyway the whole thing being just a nightmare.

'As soon as I could I escaped, ducking into Fox's saying I had to get eyelashes and stuff for the show and that I'd see them after. I didn't actually need more lashes but I got some anyway, to be safe. I went on to Boots to pick up some Eyelure, which is eyelash glue, and then got the tube home.

'Needless to say, I couldn't sleep. The flat was cold, someone from the *Evening Standard* rang up and asked if they could interview me so I told them not today and then got stuck as one does into a very depressing play on the radio about a riot in an old people's home and before I knew it it was 4.30 and time to walk to the station. In the tube somebody recognised me – there are a lot of ballet people round Barons Court – and wished me luck. When people wish you like that it's very bad luck to answer or to thank them, so I just smiled dumbly at her and I could see that she was longing for me to thank her, but I didn't say anything, just smiled at her, and eventually she got off. I wasn't feeling nervous at all.'

I stopped. Stanley flipped his cigarette-end over the sea wall, and I wiped the sweat from my eyebrows with my sleeve.

'Go on,' he said.

'Not boring you?'

'Not boring me at all. Quite the opposite.'

'When I got into the Opera House I went down to the canteen for a cup of tea because that's what I always did. There were other people there from rehearsals but nobody really said much. People know to leave you alone.

'I went up to the stage where a new girl from the school was learning the Garland Dance from Act One. It was going to be her first performance on the Opera House stage. She must have been about seventeen and looked very young and very scared. In a tray at the side of the stage I found myself a lump of rosin, which you crunch up under your shoes for grip, like sugar. Sometimes between acts the red light is on, meaning you can't go on stage because the scenery is being shifted, so you can't get at the rosin in time. Which is why I liked to swipe a bit for the dressing room.

'As I picked it up I caught the eyes of the new girl. She looked at me sort of curiously and I realised, God, to this, like, semi-transparent, veiny little creature I'm really someone. I'm what she wants to be. I smiled at her and she smiled back, but . . . kind of respectfully. Four or five years ago that'd been me and I wondered just how long it would be before I had to watch out for her – the girls they pulled out of the school mid-season were always dangerous.

'Anyway, I found my dressing room. The principal dressing rooms are all at stage level and there are five of them. I had Number One; it had a tinsel star on it. I just stood there for a bit, looking at the door and the star and the little drawing-pinned card with my name written in biro.

'June Webster. Unbelievable.

'Inside, I unpacked my stuff and checked my Act One shoes. I had chosen these specially as having an especially broad balancing surface in the toe. The reason for this is that Act One of *Sleeping Beauty*, choreographically speaking, has a very nasty little sting in its tail.

'What happens is this.

'Princess Aurora comes on, does her entrance solo – pas de chat, pas de bourree, attitude, blah blah blah – and is introduced, usual fairy-tale thing, to the four princes who are her suitors. They each present her with a rose, and she dances with them in turn. So far so good. *Nada problema*.

'And then, on the end of this sequence, comes the hard part, the most bitching, knackering series of balances in the whole classical repertoire. It's called the Rose Adage. And it goes like this.'

I stood up.

'You take an attitude balance on pointe. This means, basically, on your toes on one straight leg, the other leg lifted high behind, like this.' I showed him the position, felt my back begin to protest.

'Slowly, taking your hand, the first prince walks in a circle round you, revolving you on your pointe until you are facing front again. You lift your hand from his, and unsupported, continue the balance.

'The second prince comes. You place your hand in his, he performs the same promenade, brings you round to face front. You lift your hand from his, continue the balance.

'The third prince comes, you place your hand in his, he performs the same promenade, brings you round to face front. You lift your hand from his, continue the balance.

'At the end of the FOURTH promenade, and by then you're ready to give a year's salary just to get off pointe, the last prince releases your hand. This is your big flash finish, the moment that all the photographers wait for at the dress rehearsal, and somehow you've got to find a smile and a last ten seconds of balance and then at last, just before the music ends, you come off pointe and into this sort of scrambled pirouette thing and you're done.

'Physically speaking, it's very, very tough. And you never quite know how you're going to find it. I remember watching one girl just whacking into her first attitude and refusing to move for the whole thing. She just stayed up there on pointe in this perfect balance, beaming, while the boys walked round her like pet poodles. It was stunning. All the crits and the ballet-queens went berserk for her, of course. They love stuff like that.'

'Where was I? Yes, in the dressing room.

'I checked my Act Two and Three shoes. They had smaller pointes than the others – pirouette rather than balancing pointes – and were new. I checked the sewing on the ribbons. I checked the hooks and eyes on my tutus and the grips on my head-dresses, I turned the volume on the tannoy up and down, arranged my telegrams round the mirror, and laid out my make-up and the earrings for each act. I checked everything again, changed into practice clothes and put on my make-up. My hands were completely steady and I got my eyebrows how I wanted them in one. The eyelashes went on straight, and stayed there. I pulled on a pair of old demi-pointe shoes and crunched the rosin into the floor.

'It was 6.30. I was ready to get ready. I went backstage, found a barre, and slowly warmed up. Twenty-five minutes later I went on stage. The curtain was up and the auditorium was dark, empty except for the front-of-house staff. The stage, though, under the working lights, was crowded, completely deafening. Stage hands with hammers picked their way between the dancers, shouting to each other over the rehearsal tape which was playing because there had been a last-minute placing call for the new girl. Usual bumper cars, in fact.

'So I found a corner, and practised my attitude balances and pirouettes. No problem. Hands still steady, breathing normal.

'I still hadn't spoken to anyone.

'At 7.00 exactly the half-hour was called, and the curtain fell.'

Stanley's feet were crossed and his eyes closed. He was no longer smoking.

It had been a long time since I'd thought of that day as a whole. Details of it, though, little blocks of time, had revisited me endlessly; still did.

Had the day started differently, I wondered, would it have ended differently? And which was the exact . . . Pointless stuff, I know, but you still wonder.

The rush to the dressing rooms leaves the stage empty of all but the new girl and a single hammering figure, and it is at that moment, when the heavy velvet curtains close away the auditorium and the world outside, that the sick, icy fright comes stamping in.

When I see Pauline I'm still just gaping, silent, clutching my ribs. She's already in the Lilac Fairy tutu and although it's some time before I can understand the words that she's saying I eventually realise that she's holding my arm and repeating that it will be all right, it'll be fine, this always happens, it'll be fine, you'll be wonderful, just breathe, June, breathe, you'll be fine.

We're in the dressing room, and I'm drinking tea. Pauline's forcing me to smile and the terror has receded to the point where I am now just badly, raggedly scared. No thought of excellence has survived, all I want to do is get through.

I am called over the tannoy to the stage. Pauline comes with me. There's been a cast change; a new prince for the Rose Adage.

All I need.

The first two princes are the Finucane boys, Grace and Davina. The fourth and principal, at my particular request, is Charlie de la

Tour. The third, unfortunately, is no longer Colin Jones, who has just done something serious to a hamstring, but a venomously ambitious little minx named Pat Fuller.

We mark through the Adage. With Pat, who has never partnered me before, I do the promenade on pointe. We get by, but I don't trust him. I tell Charlie to have a word with him about locking his wrist and forearm, all the technical stuff.

Pat asks for another run-through. I don't want to kill the pointe shoes, so we walk it. I don't trust Pat; he's a clever dancer, brilliant, even, but he flinches from me, clearly doesn't like touching women.

Still, it's got me moving, and slowly the confidence is beginning to seep back.

Pauline is sharing a dressing room with Teazle Ferris, who is dancing her first Bluebird. Teazle, of course, is exactly the sort of girl who WOULD have a name like Teazle, being slappably petite, a Snoopy fan and much given to clever little polo-necked leotards.

As we walk in she is grooming her lucky panda Odette-Odile (Black. White. Get it?) with Pauline's hairbrush. I lift an eyebrow, but for some reason Pauline's not playing.

I'm very slightly speechless at this. Apart from a fouetté or two, Lilac Fairy really has very little to worry about and at this moment I could really use some of Pauline's time. At twenty-five years of age, even making allowances for a mental age of nine, Teazle Ferris hardly needs her hand holding, Bluebird debut or no.

Beginners for the Prologue are called to the stage. I find myself alone in Pauline and Teazle's dressing room and realise I haven't remembered to wish Pauline '*merde*' for her Lilac Fairy. I chase after her and catch her in the wings. She smiles at me.

The dresser helps me into the pink Act One tutu and head-dress, checks me. I'm very nervous but the dresser makes it clear that her job is to see me into the costume, not talk to me. I go to find Jean Dazat, my Prince Florimund for the evening. He is in the next dressing room but one, I knock on the door, he shouts '*entre*' and I walk in to find him standing in his dressing gown, pissing, to the great amusement of Pat Fuller, also present, in the sink.

'*EXCUSE MOI*,' I say, retreating. 'Shouldn't you be on stage?' I ask Pat.

'Oh, I've a minute or two,' he assures me. I decide to catch Jean later. He's not on until Act Two. I hope he washes his hands.

I'm not enjoying myself.

The moment the curtain comes down on the Prologue, there is pandemonium. The entire corps has a quick change from the heavy court costumes into garlands. MAJOR hair-changes. Everyone's also been sitting for half an hour, giving their muscles the perfect chance to seize up, so they're desperate to get into the garlands costume in time to get in a few quick pliés and relèves. The new girl tears past me. Act One *Beauty* is a corps-dancer's nightmare but it's also a good thing to start with because you don't have time to think.

The only person not moving is me. People shout '*merde*' in my direction, blow vague kisses. They have their own worries.

The curtain comes up on Act One. In the wings, during the mime sequence, I keep touching my head-dress, worried that it will come loose. Eventually I really do loosen it and spend the garland dance jittering around the wardrobe girl, who eventually fixes it.

'Just don't TOUCH it,' she says, but by then I'm counting myself in, surprising myself by noticing that there is real applause as I run on stage, and that even if my brain's still somewhere up there with the pins and combs, the rest of me is slap-bang on the music.

The entrance ends with a manège of jetés round the stage. I pace it out, finishing neatly, not throwing it away. Around me the rest of the cast are standing frozen, smiles fixed, sweat trickling down their cheeks from the garland dance. By the end of my applause the princes are smiling courteously if slightly apprehensively at each other as they move into their opening positions and I just have time to think that the four of them look more like the Versailles branch of the Judy Garland fan club than any kind of serious candidates for my hand in marriage when the conductor brings down his baton and we are into the Rose Adage.

It starts well. Grace and Davina whisper encouragement as I scoop the roses off them, Pat Fuller, damp-handed, manages a tight little smile and Charlie is as cool as ever. 'Breathe,' he reminds me, his hands confident at my waist as I bourrée into my pirouette, 'Enjoy it.'

First and second stages complete.

Breathe, I remember. Focus eyes. Opposite me in the wings Pauline stands watching me in her lilac tutu.

Here we go.

As the music builds and modulates, Grace presents me his hand. Dead on the beat I lay mine over it, grip hard, and step into attitude. He feels me on balance and as he starts the promenade I focus long, beyond him, finding the exit sign for when he lets go. I am unsupported for a breath and then Davina is there, and I lower my hand to his.

'Smile, June Duprez,' he reminds me as we go round. I realise that I have been concentrating so hard on the balance, on the attitude, that I have forgotten about my face completely. When did I last smile? I smile. He brings me round and I lift the hand for the second unsupported balance.

Good.

But the instant I lower my hand to Pat's I know I'm in bad trouble. As I commit my weight to him his wrist jags and his unlocked elbow chicken-wings. He tries to step into the promenade, but feeling my hand plunging downwards on his, leaves it a fatal beat too late, panics, then tries to drag me round behind the music. Forward of my balance I can't move, I gasp out loud, see Pat's eyes skidding away, see the conductor slowing the orchestra to a crawl, and then I lose the music, can't find Pat's eyes or my balance, I've missed out a whole promenade and then at last Charlie is there and he takes my hand, somehow I am still in attitude, still on pointe, and he is moving me back over the screaming hyperextension of my supporting leg, my nails are clawing into the back of his hand and, incredibly, Charlie is smiling.

Charlie squares me up, takes me into a last, fast promenade in which I am too shocked to be anything but passive, and standing there, lines me up for the last big balance. All I have to do is raise my hand from his. Just for a second.

All I have to do.

My eyes find Pauline in the wings, lock on to her. She lifts her arms, shows me the balance. With her movement I lose my focus. I can no longer feel my supporting leg.

'GO!' whispers Charlie.

I can't lift my hand. Can't feel my body. Anything.

'GO!'

The orchestra is sustaining a single note.

I can't lift my hand.

'GO, JUNE!'

Charlie stands there, holding his smile. My nails are clawing into the back of his hand. Beyond him in the wings, Pauline.

I can't lift my hand.

There was rain on my face. I opened my eyes, tilted my face towards the darkness but as suddenly as the rain had come it passed, along with the breeze that had carried it. On the tiled parapet of the terrace there was no more than a spattering.

'Maybe less than a week,' said Stanley. 'What happened?'

'Where was I?' I asked.

'About to go on stage in *Sleeping Beauty*.'

'Ohhh . . . Well, OK. I lost it, basically. My nerve. I mean I got THROUGH it but . . . not so well. And even though I stayed with the company for the best part of ten years after that, I never got any more first-cast ballerina roles.'

'But that's awful . . . I mean, isn't it?'

'Oh, I thought so for a long time, that it wasn't my fault and so on, but . . . Eventually I think I realised that they probably made allowances for nerves, bad partnering and stuff and that it wasn't necessarily . . . I don't know. I mean they didn't freeze me out or anything, I always got plenty to do, sort of Good Old June, chuck her on at ten minutes' notice, sort of thing. Lots of matinées, schools' shows, stuff like that, it just didn't . . . happen for me in the big way it did for someone like, say, Pauline Faull.'

'I told you I once saw Pauline Faull dance?'

'You told me you once saw Pauline Faull dance.'

'She was wonderful.'

'I know,' I said.

After a long silence we both spoke at once.

'Go on,' I said.

'I was just wondering if you felt like a drink. I haven't got anything here, but we could walk back to the club . . .'

'I should get back,' I said. 'Why don't you come back to the hotel for a drink? Meet Beth?'

'OK,' he said, after a moment, and I could tell he was wondering about Dane, 'that'd be nice.'

In the taxi we didn't speak. In places the road showed signs of the rain.

Beth, who, from her shining face had just removed her make-up, answered the door in her dressing gown. I should have rung first, I thought. The place, clothes everywhere, smeared pulls of cotton-wool on the carpet around the waste basket, looked not great.

I introduced Stanley, and Beth made a decent stab at looking glad to meet him.

'Dane?' I mouthed to her, as Stanley sat down, patted his pockets and scanned for ashtrays, but she shook her head.

I knelt to fix the drinks. At that moment it occurred to me that Beth had foreseen Dane's leaving months ago, had wanted me here, invited me here for just such a time as this.

'We'll talk,' I whispered, and squeezed her arm. To my amazement she winked. I frowned at her, and turned round to Stanley.

'Bulbul for you. And *pour moi aussi*, Bulbul. And for my dear *soeur*, a club soda. Mmmmm.'

'June was saying . . . Oh lovely, thanks,' started Stanley, 'that you've just . . .'

'Hepatitis,' said Beth, cheerfully. 'Unbelievably boring.'

'Ghastly. Do you mind if I . . . ?'

At that moment the phone started ringing and we all stared at each other. Eventually Beth crossed the room.

'It's for you.'

'Who is it?' I mouthed. Beth shrugged.

I took the phone off her and retreated into a corner.

'Hello?'

'Hello? June? The voice was casual, anxious, female.

On the sofa Stanley, frozen as he speaks, lights a cigarette. Beth in frozen laughter.

I pressed the receiver hard to my ear.

'It's Lakshmi here. Lakshmi Khandekar.'

XIV

~~~~~~

Sunday, and the sky like lead. Low tide. No sprinklers. From the clubhouse, the hissing smoke of barbecued meat; from the pool, the season's last desperate screams and bellyflops.

It was only a short walk from Cuckoo's to the club but already my shirt was holding to the small of my back. I genuflected for a moment to scratch at the dusty, sweat-slick bites at my ankles. I had been spotted, though; above the thicket of deckchairs a pink-shouldered torso was waving at me.

'Stanley!'

'Ian. And Karen, Lizzie. How are you?'

Ian dropped heavily back into the canvas of his chair.

'Damaged goods, in my case, I'm afraid. Bit of a heavy night in the Library Bar with the lads from the bank. Certain amount of food moving through the air.'

'Have you seen June?' asked Lizzie, innocently.

'Not,' I said, 'since I dropped her off last night.'

'Just good friends, eh?' smiled Ian, cocking a quick eyebrow at Lizzie. 'Your story and you're sticking to it. God, just look at that sky.'

'Why don't I get some drinks?' I suggested.

At the bar a young Sindhi with the sleeves of his raw-silk suit pulled up his forearms was explaining to a squinting Deirdre that he'd just had polythene covers made for the units of his German hi-fi.

'I think you're wise,' she said, leaning forward in order to run a thumb under her bikini-top. 'That's a nice watch.'

'The movement is Swiss, Dee,' he explained, 'but the styling is Canadian.'

'I love Canadian things,' agreed Deirdre. 'The Great Lakes, beaver, everything. Smoke?'

A yard away her husband craned over the bar and feigned happiness.

When and if June turns up, I decided, I'm going to ask her to put me on to Priya Bhoopatkar. I wouldn't end up with the film I had originally had in mind – the pre-Saxena Priya having starred in some of the dullest and most socially aware epics ever committed to celluloid – but at least I would have a film. Face of liberated Indian womanhood and so on. Good multicultural stuff. Perhaps, of course, if I was going to stay here, it might just be more tactful not to mention the Saxena connection . . .

If I was going to stay. The next six months would tell. Six months of dreary drenching rain, of flooded streets, drowned cars, backed-up sewers.

Time, though. Time to find Lakshmi Khandekar.

There was no sign of June. I drank most of a bottle of Bulbul, smoked, and let Ian do the talking. The shouts from the pool and the distant thwacking of the volleyball hung in the humid air and the beer quickly became warm. Bored, the girls wandered off.

I opened my eyes to see Victor Das, in shirtsleeves and well-pressed whites, removing a cigarette from his case. Following his amused gaze I saw that Deirdre had joined the Sindhi boys at their table and that the boys were watching Karen and Lizzie.

Ian shook his head at the cigarette case, and Das turned to me. 'Stanley. How about some TT?'

'OK,' I said, without particular enthusiasm, and poured the residue of the beer into the grass.

I followed him into the clubhouse and past the bar. The games room held the powdery, eruptive smell of neglect, of old monsoons. In recent years it had been used for storage, and stepladders, poles and netting leant against the bleached panelling of the walls.

Das closed the door behind us and flicked a switch, yellowing the pale light admitted by the single shuttered window.

'I learnt to play in this room,' I said, as we clamped the net to the table. 'Twenty-two years ago.'

'So you're a player,' said Das, offering me the less degraded of the two bats.

'Not really,' I said, slicing an exploratory shot towards his backhand, the impact of ball and table sharp in the closed room. 'Not any more.'

From the first lazy descent of his arm I knew that Das WAS a player, that I would win only those points that he chose. For five effortful minutes I dived and lunged as, immobile, he pulled my wild returns from the air, floated them easily back to me.

'Best of three?' I suggested eventually.

'How is your film project?' he asked.

'Coming along,' I answered.

He allowed me to win the service and, for honour's sake, the first point, and then quickly dispatched the next four past my forehand. His thoughts appeared to be elsewhere.

'Have you any locations in mind?' he asked, serving. My return spun away, finally coming to rest behind a dusty stack of board-games.

I knelt.

'Film City, mostly, I should think.'

'Not Suklaji Street, then?'

My stomach fell away. I stared down at the collapsed boxes of Halma, Ludo, and L'Attaque.

Smiling, Das held out his hand for the ball.

'No,' I said slowly, 'not Suklaji Street.'

I threw him the ball, and he trapped it between bat and palm.

His shots became harder to counter, lower, more oblique. At times, drifting with spin from his slicing bat, the ball appeared to stop moving altogether, at others it became a flickering blur, cracking against the panelling behind me.

'Why, exactly,' I asked, 'have you been following me?'

'I don't need to follow you, Stanley. And it's your service.'

We played two games. Each time Das allowed me to win the first point.

Finally he replaced his bat and the ball beside the half-dozen tarnished and listing trophies on the mantelpiece, and turned to me.

'There's someone I think you should meet,' he said, flipping open the cigarette case.

This time I took one. He handed me the heavy silver lighter, and I weighed it expectantly in my hand.

'Have you, by any chance, heard of Pritthi Puri?'

'The actress?' I asked. 'Haji Ibrahim's . . . protegée?'

'The same,' smiled Das.

He picked up one of the silver-plate cups and peered, frowning, at its inscription. I lit the cigarette.

'. . . It occurred to me,' he continued, 'that Pritthi Puri would make an excellent subject for a documentary. I am informed that the idea pleases her greatly. And it is the Haji's wish that she should be pleased.'

He watched me.

'Think about it, Stanley. Lakshmi Khandekar, I understand, has . . . lost enthusiasm for the project. The Haji would deliver you anyone you wish to interview, any facilities. You would have, as they say, Access All Areas. And as well as showing on BBC . . .'

'Channel Four,' I murmured.

' . . . on BBC Channel Four, the Haji would ensure that the network here bought it.'

'Pritthi Puri's film career,' I said, 'is hardly, well, ILLUSTRIOUS. I mean it would take a bit of cranking-up . . .'

'Stanley, be realistic. Think of your situation. The day will come when you will need help. In the matter of a visa, for example. Many, many things. And here you have a chance to please the Haji. A rare chance. Take it, Stanley.'

'I'll have to think,' I said.

'Tonight,' said Das. 'Come to Naaz Cafe. Seven o'clock.'

'OK,' I said eventually.

'You'll be there?'

'I'll be there.'

I let him leave. There was the noise from the lawn outside and then, as the door closed, a new silence. I was considering the implications of Das's suggestions when my eyes, panning absently across the dusted lumber, were halted. Behind the furled cricket netting, its dull brass finial resting against the cornice, was an object like a curtain-rod or an ornamental spear.

I recognised it immediately.

Where, I wondered, was the rest of it. Two minutes later, sneezing, I was hauling out a long rectangular box by its rope handle.

Inside, folded into a neat oblong on top of the croquet mallets and the chipped wooden balls in their faded reds, blues and yellows, was the banner. Against a frayed grey background that had once been sky-blue leapt a threadbare dolphin. Above it, in cut-out letters, were sewn the initials N.S.B.C., and below, the legend 'FIDELITUR'. The tapes that had attached the banner to its brass pole had perished.

It is New Year's Day, and my seventh birthday. Because the club's Sports Day is always held on New Year's Day, and I have just become a Junior Dolphin, it is probably the best day of my life. The best day I can remember, anyway.

I have not actually WON anything – I have never thought of trophies and so on as being within my reach – but today, along with Salman Bux, I have succeeded in passing the swimming test (one length freestyle and a springboard dive to retrieve the sixteen-anna coin).

This changes everything. Because, along with the award of the Dolphin patch which I will have Cuckoo sew to my navy Speedo trunks, I am now allowed to swim in the deep end, the clubhouse end, of the pool. I can swim with the others.

Facing us, Mr Bux is crouching over his box-camera. Behind me, in the back row, arms folded beneath the banner, are the Senior prize-winners; there are Mohan and Jagjit in their turbans, identical and lightly moustached, there are the Carmichael brothers, Tom, I think, and Andrew, and next to him Klaus, the club's Victor Ludorum, and on the right, his turning head a blur, the Parsi boy we called Froggy.

In the centre row, seated, are the girls; I recognise Deepti Sampat (with whom I am in love), her white rubber bathing cap poppered together beneath her chin; I recognise Jaswinder Kaur, a spotty Sally Padgett, and the Scottish girl whose name I've forgotten (Judith something?) who swears a king cobra once watched her peeing behind the clubhouse.

On the ground, legs crossed, are Salman and I. The truth is we shouldn't really be sharing the photograph with the prize-winners, but then it IS Mr Bux who is taking the photographs. Mr Bux works at the bank with my father.

At the end of the day I will have a sunburnt neck and shoulders and my mother will apply calamine lotion. I will be lying in bed, face down, under the fan, when they come to kiss me goodnight. They are going to a dinner. My mother is wearing perfume, pearls and a pleated skirt, my father, in a dinner jacket, smells of Bay Rum.

I hear the car leave.

At my bedside the fan turns.

In the corridor outside the white room I hear footsteps approach, the door open. I pretend sleep. The door is softly closed, the footsteps fall away.

I open my eyes. On the locker at my bedside is a folding leather frame. In the left-hand compartment is Mr Bux's photograph, the sixteen-anna coin safe behind the cellophane, and to the right my parents stand rather self-consciously in front of Flora Fountain. The photograph has been badly taken; they are on a slant, and squinting into the sun.

Next to the photo-frame is a glass jar which once contained Shippam's Meat Paste. It now holds a clouded mixture of Dettol and water, with a blob of cotton-wool cushioning the thermometer's mercury-bulb against the glass bottom of the jar. Behind it a chipped enamel kidney dish contains Disprin in metal-foil blisters.

There is a single picture on the white walls: a faded reproduction of Utrillo's *Street at Sannois* with a large white border between the print and the pale wood frame.

And beyond the locker and the picture is the window and the white Sussex sky.

By the time I came out of the games-room, Das had disappeared. I ate a barbecued chicken haunch in a bridge roll and walked down to Grant Road.

Three and a half hours later I left the Mars Picture-House. The air-conditioning had broken down, the fans had proved noisy but ineffectual, and the low power of the projector's bulb had lent the picture a brownish cast. By the intermission, flea-bitten, I had found myself scratching compulsively at my scalp.

Love '81 was two hundred minutes of bad cinema. Even Saiyad Ali himself had admitted it. The plot was incomprehensible, the technical standard wildly uneven, the continuity non-existent.

None of which altered the fact that the picture had run in Bombay for twenty-two months without a change of title, broken records in several territories, and made more money for Saiyad Ali and his investors than any of those pragmatic men had dared hope.

In 1980, Pritthi Puri had been an unknown, hefting a portfolio of test shots around the production offices. Eventually, or so the legend continued, she and her mother had talked their way into Saiyad Ali's presence. Something about the rather blowsy eighteen-year-old had caused the director to frown, to ask her to turn round, and round again, and to book her for a screen test. Pritthi's family were Kashmiri, and her puppy-fatted complexion was exceptionally fair, her eyes pale, and her hair auburn.

Watching the test, the slow zoom-ins on the babyish, suggestible face, the full-screen close-ups of the big anxious lips, Saiyad Ali knew that he had found his heroine. She was spoilt-enough-looking to be believable as a 'college girl' (and apparently possessed of all the concupiscence that those two words implied), yet 'ethnic' enough to lay final claim to the natural and traditional virtues of Indian womanhood.

The thirty-second scene that jacked the film into the multi-crore league was the last to be canned. Unlike the others it was perfectly lit, filtered, and metred, and shot on registered, rather than black-market, stock. It duplicated beautifully.

Sanju Saxena, as the hero Vijay, has come to Lonavla, a hill-station, to search out his childhood friend Pratik (Omprakash Rai). The gates to an extensive property are open. Approaching the house he rounds a corner to discover (in wide shot) Pratik's baby sister Sita – at least, she used to be a baby, but as we and Vijay see, Sita is quite a big girl now – snoozing on a lilo in the swimming pool . . .

Recognising Vijay, Sita rolls off the lilo and swims to the edge of the pool to greet him. She is wearing, we note, a white one-piece bathing costume. Magically dry-haired she smiles (tight close-up), tells Vijay she will go and find Pratik (cut to mid-shot), places the palms of both hands on the lip of the pool, and slowly, facing the camera, straightening her arms, taking her time, HAULS HERSELF UP ON TO THE SIDE. The white bathing costume (furnished, the credits will inform us, by Harvey Nichols of London), is sheer, without upholstery. It clings, semi-transparent, to Sita's biggish breasts; water streams from her body as she pulls herself to a sitting position and thence to her feet. From behind her, from Vijay's point-of-view, the camera follows the wet footprints and the languid progress of her pale, unworked thighs into long shot and the family home.

The thumping backhander that had ensured that this scene was ignored by the censor had, I had read, consumed nearly twenty-five per cent of the production budget. The risk, however, had paid off, as was proved to me when half of the stalls audience left the cinema as soon as Sita exited the shot. They had seen the film before, but had just dropped in for a quick repeat of the 'white scene'. Saiyad Ali had calculated that this would be the case and ensured, on their behalf, that it was only five minutes into the picture.

I walked home, handed Anubai my shirt, and stood for ten minutes beneath a blood-temperature shower.

'Tell me,' I said to Anubai afterwards, as she ironed, 'about Pritthi Puri.'

'You know about the White Scene?' she asked.

'I saw *Love '81* this afternoon,' I said.

'And what did you think?' Anubai smiled.

'I thought it was not such a great film,' I answered. 'What did you think?'

'She's very beautiful,' said Anubai. 'Green eyes and all. Very pale.'

'Do you think she's a star?'

'She's given only flops since *Love '81*,' answered Anubai. '*Disco Ki Ladki* flopped, *Satyanath* flopped, *Love '82* flopped, *Campus Ki Rani* flopped. All have flopped. I think maybe she is more of a star than an actress.'

'What do you think?' I asked Baby, who was folding the clothes. 'Is she a star?'

'Of course she is a star,' said Baby.

'Do you want to meet her?' I asked.

The taxi dropped us at Naaz at exactly seven o'clock. It was too hot a day to walk uphill. There were three levels to the café, and when I asked for Das, Baby and I were shown up to the topmost of these, which had been closed to the public.

Das had changed into a blazer, flannels, and something that might or might not have been a Wykehamist cravat. He stood, smiled courteously at Baby, and made the introductions.

Pritthi, in white stilettos and a rhinestoned jeans suit, was much smaller and rounder of face than *Love '81* had suggested. She presented me with a nervous smile and a tiny limp hand which I squeezed and replaced at her side.

The fifth member of the party was an unsmiling Pathan of about seventy with a hennaed beard. One of the Haji's team, I thought, here to keep an eye on the Boss's property. Probably armed to the teeth. Baby stared at him warily before allowing her gaze to lock on to Pritthi. The whole thing, of course, was a set-up, a complete *fait accompli*, but I was curious to see where it led. Below us lay Marine Drive, the ocean, and the last of the light. Das ordered. Coffee for himself and for me, as if in proxy respect to the Haji's sensibilities, nothing for the Pathan, large Royal Falloodas for Baby and Pritthi.

'Pritthi-*ji*,' Das started, in Hindi, 'Mister Collinson has expressed a very particular interest in making a film about yourself and your film career. He has a long and distinguished record of film-making for the BBC and has come to India in search of her greatest actress. His path, of course, has lead him to your door.'

Pritthi nodded, expressionless.

'I was explaining,' Das turned to me and spoke in English, 'about your project.'

'I see,' I said. 'And does Miss, er, Puri think that this is a project in which she would be interested in, um?'

'Miss Puri,' explained Das, 'speaks excellent English. I'm sure she would be happy to tell you herself how she feels about this-all.' I waited. Pritthi turned away and frowned out over the city as if to give the impression of retaining a measure of control over her life.

At that moment the elderly waiter re-appeared at the top of the steps accompanied by a swart, cross-looking woman in a cloth-of-gold sari.

'Srimati Puri,' exclaimed Das, as if Indira Gandhi herself had appeared, '*Kya* pleasure!'

'These taxi-wallahs . . .' the woman announced to her daughter, lowering herself into a seat, finding a damp toothpick in her purse and commencing deep buccal excavation. '. . . From Juhu only.' She coughed experimentally and slapped her throat. 'Sun-n-Sand. Ninety rupees.' She coughed again, insistently and at length. 'Thieves. A Muslim.' She turned to the Pathan. 'And one very dirty fellow.' With a last phlegmy gag she extracted a lump of gristle on her pick, examined it critically, returned it to her mouth and swallowed it.

Das, still smiling, if a little tightly, watched the Pathan. The Pathan remained both silent and expressionless. Baby stared at Pritthi as Pritthi, pained, closed her soft, pale eyes.

'Please, Mummy-*ji* . . .'

Das beckoned to the hovering waiter. The mother seized the menu impatiently from the elderly Irani, squinted furiously, and eventually allowed a single chipolata finger to come to rest on its buckled plastic surface.

'Army Dish,' she commanded. 'Chips. Mangola.'

'Yes, Madam, right away.'

'So,' she turned to me as the waiter retreated, 'you wish to make a film for BBC about my Sweetie-Pritthi.

'It's a possibility,' I said, 'yes. And for Channel Four, not the BBC.'

'Have you signed anything?' she asked Pritthi in Hindi.

'No, Mummy-*ji*,' she replied in the same language, troubled, 'and please . . .' Her mother waved her to silence and turned to me.

'What will be my daughter's fee?' she asked. 'Her signing amount. BBC is a big-banner company?'

'Er, this is a documentary film, Mrs . . . Srimati Puri. No money passes hands.'

From the other side of the table, Pritthi watched me. She was recognisably her mother's daughter, but somehow presented the characteristics that they shared – the chins, the bosom, the mild hirsutism – in a docile, benign form.

At that moment, and to my absolute surprise, she delivered herself of a shaded but unmistakable wink. I looked round at Das and at the silent Pathan, but they were still watching me. Only Baby had seen. She added a wink of her own.

'So where is the profit for my daughter?' asked the mother, twisting irritably in her seat to see if the food was on its way. 'I am Sweetie's manager,' she added. 'The only person she trusts.'

'Listen,' I said in Hindi, 'if I decide to make this film about your daughter, then the profit to her would lie in that the film would be shown in the UK, in India, and . . . and all over the world. The publicity would be unlike any other. And let me say also that if I DO decide that Pritthi is the right actress for this film then I deal with HER alone. No managers, no mothers, no secretaries, no *chamcha*s, and most importantly of all, NO MONEY. *Samajh?* Understand?'

The furred chins of the mother moved in incoherent anger. She made as if to rise and then, treading on the hem of the gold sari, fell back heavily into her seat. The ghost of a smile touched the passive features of the Pathan.

'It's all right, Mummy-*ji*. Please. Mr Collinson is right. I wish to appear in this film. Others wish it. *Sab thik ho jaega.* Everything will work out.'

There was a long silence, Das staring out over the darkening city with his customary deep amusement.

'Tell me,' I said to Pritthi, 'your daily programme.'

Pritthi smiled. At that moment some unseen hand turned on the café's lights, illuminating the studs and jewels at her denim lapel. She looked up at me thoughtfully.

'See, if I'm not shooting I'm not such an early bird. Mummy brings me some breakfast, milkshake, some sweet thing, at maybe eleven o'clock but see mostly I like to lie in bed and read fanmail and talk to my phone-pals Pooja and Farah. I have a special telephone by my bed in the form of one hamburger. Also what I like to listen to some sounds. Not so much of film music but more of Dolly Parton who I very much admire. I freak on Dolly. Then also I have to look after my hair which Mummy says is one bird's-nest only. Then afterwards the *malish-wali* comes to massage my thighs which one reviewer of *Cinestar* has said are unshapely and also to oil my feet. If I'm hungry I take some *wada pav*. I freak on *wada pav*.

'In the afternoon often I have a dubbing or some fitting. Sometimes the dance instructor is coming also. Shopping is there. Videos are there. So, full day, and then bed only. I'm not so much of a raver type, not so much for that disco scene. I freak on sleep.

Early to bed, early to rise, makes a girl healthy and wealthy and wise, isn't it?'

'It is,' I said. 'What films will you be shooting over the next six months?'

'Actually I am signed for several, but biggest banner is of Sunil Bhattacharaya.'

'For *Tendui*?'

'No, for *Love '84*. See, it's like a college picture with that theme of Romeo and Juliet . . .'

'It all sounds perfect,' I said.

Das slapped his pockets and found his cigarette case.

Soft but insistent, Pritthi Puri's eyes held mine.

In the early morning, a waking dream of green eyes, pale lips, fatted softness. My reaching hand, though, touched hard ribs, fell to a stubbled, scoured pelvis. As my fingers traced the long raised scar she half-woke and waking, turned away.

Distantly, towards Grant Road, the sound of hammering.

XV

〜〜〜〜〜

'So, when I rang, who did you say it was?'

'I said you were Priya Bhoopatkar.'

'Priya Bhoopatkar? You know Priya?'

'Oh, I met her at some shooting we all went to in Film City, and then again . . . It's a long story.'

'Tell me.'

'I'll tell you later.'

'I'm jealous already. Tell me now.'

'Nothing to tell.'

'Promise?'

My lips smoothed her eyebrows outwards, left and then right.

'I promise.'

Lakshmi moved back from me, lifted herself on to one elbow, and smiled.

'So tell me again.'

'Tell you again which?'

'Everything.'

'Everything which?'

'When we met.'

'It's so hot,' I said.

'I'll turn the fan up.'

Naked, Lakshmi walked to the door. The whirr of the electric ceiling fan became more insistent, and the sheet flattened to my body.

'The sky,' she said. 'Just come and look. Don't worry, we're on the top floor. No one can see us.'

I stood, and walked over to her. She pulled back the sliding glass and aluminium doors on to the balcony. Far below us was Juhu, the brown sand, the green tops of the palms, the brown sea. Around us the sky was colourless and still, but above the horizon hung a flickering curtain that was almost black but at the same time the source of an intense and hard-edged light.

'We're looking south,' I said.

'This is the tallest building for miles,' said Lakshmi. 'I always try and get this room.' She turned to face me and I put both arms around her waist, felt the warm small of her back beneath my hands.

'Tell me again, June,' she said, 'about . . . when we met.' Our foreheads touched; I was maybe an inch taller than she was.

'You tell,' I said. Her forehead was damp.

'You told me so beautifully before. And my English is funny.'

'How many languages do you speak?'

'I speak fluently, let's see, Marathi, Hindi, English; Urdu also, I suppose. And some Punjabi. I've done plays in Gujarati and Bengali. How many's that?'

'Plenty,' I said. 'But I love your English.'

'I suppose,' I said, 'I didn't really notice you at the whatsit, if I'm honest.'

'The *muharat?*'

'Yes. I mean it was dark, you were in your car most of the time, I was there with my friend Kimmie and neither of us was too sure exactly what was going on and anyway you were flirting like MAD with that Rahman Khan . . .'

'I was NOT flirting, how can you say that? Just . . . *natak*. For the press.'

'. . . And Stanley was there too. At the *muharat*.'

Her gaze lifted from my face to the ceiling.

'Actually I feel quite bad about that-all. Especially after you said he went on phoning for WEEKS . . .'

'You didn't tell me why you changed your mind.'

She shrugged.

'Oh . . . *Khandaan* was cancelled . . .' She looked away. 'Also this Stanley, I think he . . .'

'Liked you?'

'It was my auntie, actually. First she said to meet him, then two days after changed her mind and said definitely not to. Changed my number and all.'

'Why did she change her mind?'

'She was ordered, actually. There's this man called Haji Ibrahim . . .'

'Ah,' I said.

She turned back to me, traced a finger between my breasts. 'Go on about us, *jaan*.'

'Ohhh . . . I'm not sure if I should.'

'Why not?'

I kissed my finger and touched the end of her nose.

'Because.'

'Because what? And if you touch my nose I have to touch yours. There. Otherwise we'll fight.'

'Because you'll think . . . I'm a pushover.'

She smiled. 'In that case I'm a pushover also. Who rang who, after all? So tell.'

'OK. I guess.' I rolled on to my side.

'Well, it was at the dinner after. At the hotel. There was this moment when you and Rahman were having one of those filmi conversations like you all do where half of each sentence is in English and half in Hindi and I was sort of listening in, because the English bits made me think I could understand what you were saying although of course I couldn't, actually, at all. And then Rahman reached for his drink and you sort of looked at me as if . . . as if your eyes had been on their way somewhere else but you'd decided at the last moment to stop there, and . . .'

'My eyes weren't going anywhere else, *jaan*, I promise you.'

' . . . and my heart, quite literally, missed a beat. I shouldn't be telling you this, but that's exactly what it did. For a beat, stopped. And for the length of that missed heartbeat I couldn't move or hear anything at all and then I looked away and you looked away but I guess too late, too late for me anyway, because by then there'd been some sort of . . . shift, inside me.'

Her hand moved down my stomach.

'Anyway there I was with my knife and fork sticking in the air and I just couldn't BELIEVE that no one . . .'

'And you've never . . . ?'

'No,' I said. 'Really, really never.'

We were sitting at a table by the swimming pool, waiting for coffee. Although it was only four o'clock the light was poor and a steady breeze was breaking the surface of the water. I was wearing one of the hotel's white towelling dressing gowns.

'The thing is,' I said, 'even after that evening, and talking, and swapping telephone numbers, I didn't realise, I really didn't. Something IN me realised, of course, and kept, I don't know . . .'

'. . . And then I rang.'

'And then you rang. And then you rang. But before you did, as I said, it was really strange. Because every time I thought of that evening at the hotel, or Stanley mentioned you, or whatever, I felt this sort of . . . nervousness. Sort of like stage fright and anticipation and physical hunger rolled into one. But because, each time, I never really . . . examined it, or someone changed the subject, it sort of evaporated, each time.'

Smiling, she closed her eyes, shook her head. I reached over the table and took her hand, stroked her knuckles with my thumb.

'I'm glad you rang,' I said.

As the waiter approached, Lakshmi withdrew her hand. I pulled the dressing gown tighter around me.

The breeze pulled at the waiter's white jacket. As he placed the rattling tray between us, he looked quickly out at the sea and the dark horizon.

In the first photograph Galina Ulanova, rather incongruously, is wearing snowshoes and an elegant, Paris-cut suit (in the late Fifties the Bolshoi toured both Europe and North America. Possibly Ulanova bought the suit then. Then again, perhaps the suit is Russian and it is her sheer physical elegance which transforms it. At sixteen years old such questions, of course . . . exercise me).

Ulanova is standing with her back to one of the windows of the studio. The window is enormously tall, twenty, maybe twenty-five feet in height, and covered by curtains. Well, not exactly by curtains, but by a dusty fall of that black material that hangs in the wings of theatres. It doesn't reach the ground, but has been looped up over the barre which runs along the side of the studio.

Behind Ulanova, and presumably reading the music by such light as is admitted by the tall window, a pianist in a long black skirt sits at a grand piano.

Ekaterina Maximova, frozen at the height of her leap, cannot actually see Ulanova; Ulanova is behind her, speeding the nineteen-year-old Maximova's flight with the inclination of her body, with a half-extended hand.

Maximova's face, in this photograph, I can't see; it is turned in the direction of her flight, shadowed and half-concealed by one arm. The light is behind her, with Ulanova. Before her is nothing, her flight is into a grainy incomprehensible blackness. In the second photograph Maximova, in her Act One costume from *Giselle* (it is the night of her debut) is in a backstage room in which are stacked chairs and what looks like lighting equipment. Possibly it is the corner of a dressing room, but it does not look like one; there are no costumes or dressing tables. Maximova, her fingers touching the lacing on her bodice, has just relevé-ed on to pointe in fourth position in front of a mirror angled in the corner of the room. She is checking the shoes she will wear for Act One, moving her weight from foot to foot (I have tried Bolshoi pointe shoes – very low-vamped and uncomfortable – and in that respect I don't envy her the evening ahead). In the mirror, facing me, facing her, is her reflection. But she is not staring at her reflection, she is looking beyond it, again, to a place which the photograph can only register as a blackness. Her reflection, in turn, looks some distance past me.

At the club the bar was closed, its windows battened shut. On the verandah below, however, and despite the wind, the fans still turned. Amongst the half-dozen silent figures watching the sea from behind their drinks, I recognised Deirdre McConachie and Victor Das. A single waiter stood motionless behind the counter. The clock showed half-past six.

I didn't see Stanley until he stood, waved. He was in the place I had liked to lie, on the end of the headland furthest from the clubhouse. Carrying my shoes, I walked towards him over the cracked concrete, beneath the dark scaffold of the diving boards. Beyond the wall the tide was high, and an oily and uneasy flotsam of coconut husks and discarded garlands moved over the rocks.

Stanley was making notes in a notebook with a silver propelling pencil. A glass and two Bulbul Pilsner bottles stood beside his deckchair. I pulled over a chair of my own.

'I was going to call you,' he said, not looking up. 'I wanted Priya Bhoopatkar's number.'

'Did you call?' I asked. 'I haven't been home.'

'I changed my mind,' he said, absently. He made a small entry in the notebook, and his face cleared. 'Let me just read you this.' He held the book out at arm's length.

> *'Aaring, birring, longa chirring*
> *Longa chirta dub-dub baja*
> *Gai gopi uttala raja*
> *Sati tara lombdi bara*
> *Lombdi combda bil-bil gonda*
> *Nairi naura kanchan phul.'*

He lowered the notebook to his lap, turned to me.

'What is it?' I asked. 'A poem?'

'It's a nursery rhyme. A Marathi nursery rhyme. When I was born my parents had this ayah called Bai. She taught it to me. And I've always remembered it, even if I've never actually written it down. Before.' He picked up one of the bottles by the neck and poured the last of its contents into the glass.

'What does it mean?' I asked.

'Mean,' he answered. 'Well. The answer, in one sense, is that it doesn't mean anything at all. But in another sense . . . the words, individually, mean things. They're real words, words for kings and cows and brides and flowers, even if they're only put together for their sound. They can mean, I guess, as much or as little as you like. Maybe they meant something very specific to Bai, I don't know.' He lit a cigarette, its tiny coal glowing as the wind whipped away the smoke.

'What I'm wondering,' he said, allowing the propelling pencil to describe an erratic trace over the page, 'is if our lives are like that. Sequences of utterly disconnected events which are only given meaning by our need for them to have meaning.'

'Probably,' I said, but sleepless, elsewhere, I wasn't really listening. My head was singing and I was wearing yesterday's clothes.

'Look.' I pointed.

The darkness between sea and sky had pearled, was drawing a

wavering curtain over the headlands ten miles to the north. Stanley drained his beer. For a flickering double-beat the towers of Juhu stood pale, then the curtain twitched and they faded into the sheeting grey.

'I might get under cover,' said Stanley. 'Return these bottles.'

'Have you found your actress?' I asked.

'I think so,' he said.

'That's good.'

As the temples and concrete shorelines of Bandra and Worli receded into invisibility, he folded his cigarette packet and matches and notebook into a polythene bag.

'Will you be staying in Bombay?' he asked, getting to his feet. 'Things are different in the wet.'

'I'll be staying,' I said.

The wind falls, and now the only remaining light in the sky is behind me, to the south. As I twist my watch inwards on my wrist, the grass is cold beneath my bare feet. There's not long to wait.